THE PRICE OF MEMORY AND MORE STORIES

Also by the author

The Nightingale's Tooth

The Fragrance of Orchids and Other Stories

Indigo Time (forthcoming re-release)

The Price of Memory and More Stories

Sally McBride

Milton, Ontario

First edition, October 2024
Published by Brain Lag
Milton, Ontario
https://www.brain-lag.com/

ISBN: 978-1-998795-13-0 (softcover)
ISBN: 978-1-998795-14-7 (ebook)

This is a work of fiction. All of the characters, events, organizations, places, and businesses portrayed in this novel are either products of the author's imagination or are used fictitiously. Any resemblance to actual persons, living or dead, or actual events is purely coincidental.

"Dance on a Forgotten Shore" copyright © 1988 by Alan Dean Foster and Sally McBride; reprinted with permission.

Cover artwork © Alex Shuper

Library and Archives Canada Cataloguing in Publication

Title: The price of memory and more stories / Sally McBride.
Names: McBride, Sally, 1950- author.
Description: Includes bibliographical references.
Identifiers: Canadiana (print) 20240373332 | Canadiana (ebook) 20240373359 | ISBN 9781998795130
   (softcover) | ISBN 9781998795147 (EPUB)
Subjects: LCGFT: Short stories.
Classification: LCC PS8625.B74 P75 2024 | DDC C813/.6—dc23

Content warnings: Ableist language ("Little Feather"), death (various), graphic injuries ("After the First Death", "Doing Drugs", "Thank Yew Very Much", "Intersection"), guns ("Little Feather"), miscarriage (mentioned, "The Doll Ladies", "After the First Death")

Contents

FOREWORD

You've walked into a large, pleasant room. There's a cocktail party underway, the classy sort with muted piano music and subtle staff. The lighting is unusual: concentrated splashes beneath an array of low-hanging chandeliers. Some are antiques, their lit candles sparking prisms from crystal drops; others are chaotic swirls of LEDs, modern magic; a couple trick your eye, seeming to be pulsing organisms, their bodies luminescent.

Yet it is those standing in the chandeliers' glow who snatch your attention.

Hold it.

You stare at each, trapped in their mystery, only to glimpse the next. Your gaze leaps helplessly onward. A gorilla cradles a doll. A man in a suit sits by a glass peacock. A girl rests her hand on a wolf. A beautiful man huddles on his knees. A woman on a leash has a mechanical cat and a monster.

Your head spins but you can't bring yourself to leave. There are more.

A tiny painting sits on its easel, the figure within staring back at you. A young boy builds a puzzle from bone. A princess floats midair, anchored by a thread. A dog, an artist, and a stranger from another world dance on sand. Scrawny children play with swarms of bees.

You take a breath. Spin around. More, still.

A mother and child eat tomato sandwiches, juice dripping from their chins. A man, tubes in his veins, cowers in fear. A witch stirs her cauldron. An alien waits on a bench. An android studies a corpse.

All wait for you. To read their story. To be drawn into their lives.

Held there.

Oh, you'll be released, fear not.

Though part of you will be forever trapped by their mysteries. This, I promise, will be your fate once you walk into the imagination of Sally McBride and meet the unforgettable characters within this fabulous collection.

As is, most happily, mine.

Julie E. Czerneda
June 2024

The Price of Memory
and More Stories

What do a clapped-out gorilla, a lonely woman fighting for her job, and a devastating disease have in common? They are all in a life and death struggle with climate destruction, and climate seems to be winning.

THE DOLL LADIES

The air inside the airlock actually smells terrific, at first, like the fragrance counter at a fancy department store, but it's only the chemicals, which our work contracts firmly insist don't hurt us. Plus we have good insurance. Every morning I breathe it in, then my nose forgets it once I'm at about minute seven of the ten-minute process. The nasal passages have had it for another day.

The valve opens onto a vast, barn-like structure, crowded with noise and movement, where the warm, moist atmosphere would be definitely primate if only I could appreciate it. I trundle my cart along, saying good morning to the girls, but they're more interested in the fruit and veggies I'm bringing. Today's special treat: watermelon. They all love watermelon.

I have something special in store for my favourite old girl, whose name is Zamuka. When Zamuka was co-opted for Surro-Surround, she was over-socialized with humans. Confused, sad, angry. She'd been the special pet of a research assistant at a lab, a young woman who'd taught Zamuka sign language, then had been killed by her husband, who then killed their deformed baby and himself. A surprising amount of that kind of thing went on, back then, but the upshot was that Zamuka was left adrift, unable to communicate in the way she'd become reliant on. She had lost her best friend. Plus, she then had to endure the gruelling process of medical prep for her job here. Nothing she'd asked for.

I came in early to the program too, for lack of anything better going on. After my third miscarriage I had my tubes tied, to hell with it, even though I was only twenty-six. Despite the gloomy forecasts, perhaps I should have clung to hope. A lot of people were trying the hope gambit. Others, more pragmatic or more wealthy, were availing themselves of the service offered here.

Had Carver stuck around, and we'd had the money, I might be on the other side of the airlock right now. Last I heard, Carver was still at the survivalist enclave he'd joined in '39, somewhere near Sandpoint, Idaho. They aren't big into communication up there.

So when Zamuka and I met we were both pretty shell-shocked. Took a while for us to gain a decent level of trust. But life goes on. We had jobs to do, and we became first immune to each others' pain, then later friends, especially after she realized that I was trying to sign to her. Have you ever seen a great ape laugh? It's hard not to join in. Anyhow, I've gotten better at signing over the years.

"*Good morning Zam-zam!*" When I call her Zam-zam she pretends to get mad at me. She turns her back, but after a few seconds she casts a coy little glance over her shoulder, sees me waving and smiling, and turns to waddle slowly up to the gate. She's had time to recover from the anaesthetic, still a little bleary but looks okay. She gives me a smile, a fearsome thing when worn by a fifty-one-year-old gorilla who outweighs me by at least seventy pounds.

Zamuka, among the first dozen or so gorillas brought in, was standard model. Younger apes have been engineered for faster functioning. They are naive and rather silly compared to Zamuka, as they've had no experiences other than in here. Some of them can sign a bit, but I know Zamuka holds them in disdain.

She signs *Zamuka. No Zam-zam.*

Yes, Zamuka. I talk and sign at the same time, because I think she likes to chat. Well, so do I. *Erika loves you,* I say and sign. *Zamuka okay?*

She nods, and signs *Baby doll? Erika give baby doll?*

She knows. She always knows. And she wants it more than she wants watermelon. I open the gate to her spacious cage and sidle in, pulling my cart along. She's pooped in her usual corner, and has spent some time demolishing a cardboard box.

Yes, baby doll. The highlight of her restricted life.

She hoots softly, slapping the concrete floor with her big black hands, causing the scattered shreds of hay to flutter up and down.

I say, *Surprise. Special baby doll today.*

Zamuka sits back on her ample haunches, empty belly sagging. She's too excited right now to sign, and eagerly watches me as I open the cart's hatch and reach in.

And pull out a very sturdy and quite realistic doll. I had a hard time finding it, but you can eventually get anything online.

The hooting stops. This is unusual. Zamuka can be counted on, every time, to eagerly reach for the doll and clasp it to her hairy breast, but not today. I waggle it enticingly, and watch her face.

I can read her moods pretty well. She's remarkably expressive and sophisticated once you get to know her. Right now she has the look of an upper class matron presented with a silver platter of dog turds. She is outraged. She is disgusted. She turns her back on me and shuffles to the farthest corner of her enclosure, crosses her arms and begins to sulk. I can practically feel the rays of righteous indignation shooting from her whole body.

What have I done wrong? The doll is different, yes. But not really so very different from the array of dolls Zamuka has earned over her years of service. Cute face, soft body, big eyes. I walk slowly toward her, murmuring apologies. *Baby doll no good?*

She ignores me steadfastly. Yeah, I get it. All her previous babies were human, and all the dolls she got when her human newborns were taken away look like humans. This one looks like a gorilla baby, dark brown and furry. It was really pretty adorable. I liked it, and I'd thought she would take to it immediately. My bright idea.

Suddenly she reaches out a long black arm and slaps the doll out of my hand. Warily, I hold my arms out for a hug. Zamuka's a hugger. But she turns away, grabs her sturdy canvas hammock, rips it out of its metal hooks and throws it at me. At this point I should exit her enclosure and report her behaviour to my bosses. But she's been terribly disappointed, and she's hurting. I can't leave now.

After a minute of listening to me croon apologies, she cradles the very first doll she got to her chest and begins to rock back and forth. It's barely recognizable as a blue-eyed blonde infant, lips pursed as if for a kiss or a bottle. It's the one Carver and I bought for our baby when we first learned we were pregnant with a girl. Stupid. Didn't we know the rest of the world's troubles applied to us too? We soon found that Kuru was serious about what it was doing to our unborn child. The next tries were worse. I'd had to get that doll out of my house. Carver left shortly thereafter.

Now that stupid doll, and all her other dolls, are well-cuddled, licked and sniffed. They all look pretty bad by now, but Zamuka will not part with them. Most of the surrogates are the same: they love their pretend babies.

Sorry Zamuka. Erika very sorry. Baby doll no good.

I turn and leave, biting my lip. This was supposed to have been a day of celebration for her, and for me too. Though she doesn't know it, she bore a child of her own kind less than eight hours ago. And now I realize that if she did know, she'd be horrified. I continue my rounds, pondering. So, really not much of a celebration today. She'd never hold or nurse that gorilla child, for it was already in prep for its new job, which would start as soon as possible. Zamuka's baby girl was destined for a life in a cage bearing human children.

I have thirty-four other animals to tend. I'm on the clock and need to keep moving, but I can't just whip in and out without a little face time. My youngest is brand new at eighteen months, and is already seven months pregnant. Boda preens and grimaces as I stroke her hairy arms and praise her big belly. She gets a bunch of grapes that I've liberated from the chimps' allotment, and she begins immediately to pluck them one by one, lips smacking. The others nearby can see her, part of what makes her grapes so succulent. Call me a troublemaker, but what's life in an endless maternity ward without a little drama?

Here in Surro-Surround we have a total of 1,988 great apes. Gorillas mostly, engineered for early maturity and quick turnaround of their cycles, and 350 chimps who have been designed a bit bigger, a bit looser around the hips than normal, to accommodate human births. We once had orangutans but they couldn't seem to take it emotionally. We need more birth-surrogates, as it's the rare human woman who will submit to— or can afford—the months of preparation, and more months isolated in a sterile building while the money bleeds away, to have a baby who won't have the kind of birth defects that afflict us now.

I was off shift, changing into my street clothes and looking forward to heading home, when I got a message to go to the fifth floor of the admin building and check in with Dr. Surmi for a brief consultation. I acknowledged and signed off. I had expected this—I get called in for reprimands three or four times a year—so merely shrugged my shoulders at my shift-mates and headed across campus. My nostrils, battered into submission during my working day, opened up to the spring freshness of the green, rolling acres of land outside the city of Hillsborough, North Carolina. I sneezed a couple of times, and blew my nose messily.

In his blessedly air conditioned office, Dr. Ari Surmi invited me to sit down. I did so—my feet and back were tired—and assumed the alert, open expression one assumes when across a desk from a boss. I did wish my hair wasn't so frizzy, and that my street clothes were something other than baggy jeans and a "Save the Wolves" t-shirt.

"Erika, what happened with Zamuka today? Any idea?"

I had lots of ideas, but I wasn't paid to have them. "She reacted negatively to the doll I presented to her." I spread my hands. "Perhaps its smell, its colour…"

"Hm. You didn't hint to her—unconsciously of course—that there might be a significance to that particular doll?"

"Uh, not sure how I could do that. I don't think I have the capability to influence how a gorilla thinks." My stomach clenched. Wasn't there *supposed* to be significance? More like a cruel joke. Why had I thought it was a good idea?

He nodded and took up a stylus, began to tap it gently on the edge of his desk. "It's my opinion that, whether you realize it or not, Erika, you can indeed influence her."

I did not like the tone of his voice. He was patronizing me. Zamuka and I are about the same age. I'm fifty-four, and any eggs I might have tucked in my ovaries are long obsolete. Even if I were a girl of twenty again, I'd never be able to afford the service provided here. He knows that, everybody knows that.

My heart was beating fast. "And she can influence me." I regretted saying that as soon as the words were out of my mouth. I was being quietly snotty, I admit. But Dr. Surmi didn't seem to notice; in fact he began to nod, his head bobbing up and down as if I were a clever student.

He was running on his own track. I was just an audience for whatever he was really thinking about and wanted to share. I waited, willing my heart to slow.

Surmi—smooth, plump, cherished by his extended family, who were proud of what he did for a living—glanced my way for just a second. Yes, I was being properly attentive. Pictures of his healthy, normal children adorned his desk, facing out.

"This isn't common knowledge yet, Erika—and you understand that what I say goes no further than this room—but we are about to be put out of business."

My first thought was *There goes my job*. Then I thought some more. A cure? Could there be a cure for KuruXL?

A small error in a lab in Sao Paulo, a lab that had been making real progress toward a vaccine against the regular, garden variety Kuru that had become endemic at almost all latitudes. An error that went unreported and unchecked, then spread and mutated as other labs received samples to work on. No one quite understood, all those years ago, that Kuru was stronger and smarter than we were. There were so many strains of it now that to the public they were all categorized as XL. Each did something different to a human fetus. Some babies, if born alive and managed to keep on living, could be trained to work in places like this. Two of them worked alongside me, and loved the morning donuts as much as I did.

I cleared my throat. "There's progress? On... a broad spectrum vaccine?"

He smiled, his cheeks puffing out. But his eyes looked tired. "I believe so, yes. A team in Venezuela, led by a woman from the University of Guelph—that's in Canada—has been running tests for the last four years on a volunteer population of Mormons. Of all people. The women and their husbands got the okay from the Church to submit to carrying out their pregnancies in an open environment about 100 kilometers inland from Caracas. There have been thirty-five normal births in the last three years, and all the babies are fine. They're fine." His dark and shapely eyebrows formed a reverent arch upon his forehead.

"Open... to the air? To the..." The real world. Where parents used to expect a baby with a full-sized head, working eyes above a cute button nose. A mouth, an intestinal tract. "Does it work for every XL? Are there other studies happening?"

Dr. Surmi spread his hands. "Yes and yes. So far so good, eh? Nothing's going to change here for a while, so don't worry about your job just yet."

I shouldn't have to, I reflected. Maybe foolishly. I was sort of grandfathered—or grandmothered—in. It was me, back at the start of this surrogate program, who'd suggested giving the girls their dolls. It helped them with their mourning period and ultimately got them back on line faster. So they could bear another human baby sooner.

I really hadn't thought about what it meant for Zamuka to suddenly get a doll in the likeness of her own daughter. Her gorilla baby—her replacement—was designed and bred to be virtually a different species than her mother. Developmentally.

Culturally. Zamuka, drafted into the emergency effort, became obsolete as newer models were developed and perfected. Her old-fashioned kind was only marginally useful these days. Zamuka had been deemed unproductive.

But she wasn't obsolete as herself. She could easily live another twenty years. I had a sudden thought.

"Doctor Surmi, do you know if Zamuka ever had offspring before she came here?"

His eyebrows raised. "Hm. Good question." He popped up a file and began to scroll down and then across. "Well, yes she has. One male offspring, which she kept and raised for... ah, looks like twenty months. He was transferred to a different research facility."

So she knew how to do it. How to raise a child. I'd seen videos of wild gorillas holding their young. They loved to examine them, cuddle them, assist them to find the long black nipple and latch on.

I have spent years squashing my maternal instinct. But Zamuka had it built right in to her muscles and her hide and her heart. Unsquashable.

That evening, I spent some time online developing a plan. By Monday I'd produced a pretty nice looking little proposal, if I do say so myself. Video, blossom points, sensa-links, about a million attachments, everything I could think of to catch the eye of whoever it was that made decisions around here. Starting with my pal Doctor Surmi.

He did me the courtesy of running his eyes over my carefully crafted presentation. Then he shut it back into his desktop and rubbed his temples. I couldn't tell if his expression was soulful or annoyed.

Finally he said, "Erika, you have put a lot of effort into this, but I have to tell you it's going nowhere."

"But—"

He held up a hand. "Look. Pasturing out our older surrogates is a nice idea. But it's unviable. Erika, you can't really believe it would lead to a re-wilding of the population."

"Yes, I *do* believe it. Why not?" *Don't get shrill.* "If you'll look at the, the stuff at the back—" Damn it, where was my brain? "A-appendices—"

"Yes, yes. Admirable. But—"

"Wait—you don't understand the real importance." What had I expected? Did I think an advanced degree in genetics had just popped into my resumé? Which included community college, waitressing, and working here. Shovelling shit. "There are only a handful of great apes left in the world that have any experience at being apes. At, at nurturing and teaching their own kind. Zamuka has done it! She's worked hard here, made money for the company. She deserves to be a real mother to a *normal* gorilla baby. She *deserves* it." My cheeks were burning and my heart was pounding, but I wasn't going to retreat.

Neither was Surmi. He leaned forward. "I know you care about her. But where do you think the money, and the land, the rehabilitation, the… the veterinary care—everything—will come from?" He waved a hand in the air.

Was he asking me? "I have lots of ideas, it's all in the attachments—"

"You've studied the annual reports. Did you not see that the retired apes are to be evaluated for sustainability in a less structured environment?"

"Do you mean they'll be sent back to *zoos*? Research labs? Do you want me to believe none of them will be put down? Or do you mean they'll be—be shipped back to *Africa*?"

"Of course they won't be shipped back to Africa." He was obviously holding onto his patience with both hands. "How on earth could they survive? You know what it's like over there these days."

"But—"

"Erika! Please! You are a valued employee, but you are not a scientist. You'll just have to trust that the best outcome will be sought, for *all* the apes. When the time comes." His voice remained gentle, but his eyes were cold.

"Okay. I see." I would not cry. I would retain what dignity I possessed and get out. I'd lost this round, but already my brain was rummaging around for other ideas.

Surmi assured me once again, while ushering me out his door, that my job was secure. Yeah, I was pretty certain it wasn't.

A week went by. Zamuka was still at the facility, but had been moved out of the ultra-sterile quarters the working apes inhabited and into a temporary holding cage in an outbuilding. Turns out it isn't that easy to get rid of a gorilla, though Surmi, bless his heart, tried to make it happen. We couldn't find anywhere that would take her. Her baby, named Zamira, was already in the intensive drug and hormone treatment phase of her career—which might be cut short despite her up-to-date qualifications.

The vaccine still had to pass more tests, but word of its efficacy had leaked out.

It was only a matter of time before Zamuka was euthanized. I would suffer a less dire fate, but my career at Surro-Surround was drying up.

Gloria Ikayaa Green was wary on the phone. There was a question-and-verification period before she trusted that I was who I said I was and released her image. She was African American, quite beautiful, her hair shorn close, with a sculptured oval face and large hazel eyes. Only the very wealthy could afford surrogacy twenty-five years ago, and they designed their precious offspring carefully.

Some people hide their provenance, others don't mind at all admitting they were carried to term by a 200-pound gorilla. After my failure with Doctor Surmi, I had changed tactics, set my jaw and searched for links to chat rooms, support groups, photos. Took a while, but I found a Surro-Surround link that let me join a group that was trying to organize a commemorative "birthday" event in Branson, Missouri. It's remarkable how forthcoming folks can be, when contacted by a middle-aged white lady who wants to help with administrative details.

I got hold of a list of the children born at Surro-Surround between 2023 and 2033, something my work clearance wouldn't let me get. I actually rubbed my hands together when I realized the surrogacy code for each baby matched the serial number assigned to the ape who bore him or her.

Zamuka's very first human baby was Gloria Ikayaa Green, now twenty-eight years old, living alone in a floating condo off old Fort Lauderdale.

"Sorry," she said, smiling politely, "I really don't have time to attend the event. But thanks for contacting me."

In the background I glimpsed her spacious, beautifully decorated, and probably lonely, dwelling. KuruXL has done a very good job of reducing the Earth's population. Or at least shifting a lot of it into long-term care.

Those lucky folks who belong to the exclusive club she's in—young and disease-free—have formed their own sub-culture. Her surname, Green, links her to several other floating towns and enclaves around the world. The Blues prefer mountain lodges half-sunk in granite. Reds mostly live in New Zealand, in gated communities. And so on.

I myself am perfectly happy in my third-floor apartment with a view of the city, thank you very much. It's very quiet. No kids.

"Oh, I understand," I chirped. "People are busy! If you reconsider, please let us know. Uh, while I have you on the phone, may I ask a couple of follow-up questions?"

"Well… sure."

"Have you ever wondered about your mother?"

Gloria's brows drew together. "I don't have to. She lives with her new partner in Malaysia Green. We see each other quite a lot."

"No. I mean the… female who carried you to term, not your genetic parent."

Her mouth thinned. "I know all about it. I'm sure it was a difficult decision for my parents to make. What do you want me to say?"

"Well, I, I wondered if you would like to meet her. That is…"

"*Meet* her?" She looked up again, eyes blazing. "I *know* where I came from! I don't need some busybody—sorry—reminding me! Okay?" She shook her head as if at a bad smell. "I was borne by an animal. An animal who was co-opted into a program it can't understand, for the benefit of humans. Like me." She spread her hands as if to encompass her pale, empty home with its vast ocean view. "Don't you think I feel guilty enough without people like you rubbing my nose in it?"

This wasn't the reaction I'd expected. "I… I just, just wanted—"

"No. Whatever it is you want—money, an endorsement—just, no. What's done is done."

She was going to cut me off in a second. "I'm sorry. But… her name is Zamuka. We talk all the time. She remembers you."

"How could she possibly—No! Goodbye. Don't call again."

"She's being retired. She's going to be—"

Her image vanished. And that was that.

A complaint was registered with the commemorative event people. My connection to the links was severed, and I received a terse notice informing me that my volunteer services were no longer required.

I confess I spent the remainder of my evening crying and drinking wine. Didn't help.

I was all out of ideas. My feverish midnight plans to smuggle her into my apartment evaporated in the light of day. So I went to work, quite aware that at any time the world might go back to normal and my time here would be over. Zamuka would never have any more babies, human or gorilla. She'd most likely be euthanized. At the end of each day I visited her. She repeatedly informed me that she was not happy with the way things were.

Where everyone?

Working. You fun now! Rest and sleep.

She wasn't buying it. *Watermelon now! Where everyone?*

The first thing I'd done when she was moved was retrieve her dolls from the refuse area, before they could be incinerated. I hauled them all over to her new, cramped abode and stuffed them one by one through the bars.

My throat closed up as I watched the old girl gather her baby dolls up in her arms. She couldn't manage them all at once, but eventually got them settled together in a corner nest she'd made of hay and a faded old blanket. She began to pick them up one by one, from oldest to youngest, and sniff them, though she still ignored the gorilla doll. She was probably hoping the dolls would show signs of life at last. Or maybe I was just projecting my feelings onto her.

*

Two weeks went by. Zamuka was becoming cranky, and I was burdened on my rounds by a lump of futility in my chest, heavy as a cold. Then Doctor Surmi called me into his office again. This was it. I tried to prepare myself for mental strength and whatever dignity I could muster. But I got a surprise.

Gloria Ikayaa Green sat in one of the two chairs before Surmi's desk. That is, she perched, stick straight, on the forward edge of the chair, turning her head only slightly to look at me as I entered. She looked elegant and very young, wearing a pale green sundress, and a white sweater that she had buttoned up to her neck.

"Ms. Green, this is Erika Tucker. Erika, apparently you and Ms. Green have been in contact." Surmi's voice was clipped, brusque.

I plunked myself down without comment. I myself was in grubby overalls, my hair in a ponytail. Sweat dried on my face.

Hoo boy, I thought. Here it comes.

Ms. Green kept her head high. She didn't smile. "I want to apologize for my overreaction when you contacted me, Ms. Tucker."

Huh. "Well. I guess I shouldn't have been so, so…"

"Forward? Presumptuous?"

I shrugged ungraciously. She'd told Surmi what I'd done. But why, if she wasn't trying to get me sacked? Surmi shifted in his chair and opened his mouth, but Gloria held up a hand. "Let me say my piece, please.

"You made a good point about my surrogate mother. I've been doing some research, and it's true that all primates seem to share an urge to nurture their young. To see them thrive and go forth into the world." She sighed. "I have gone into the world. I live well, but I contribute little. I don't want children, I can't imagine what a mother feels, and I most certainly can't imagine what a gorilla mother feels when an offspring is ripped from her womb and made to vanish."

That was too much for Surmi. "Ms. Green! I assure you that our surrogates get the very best of care. No *ripping* is going on!"

She leaned back a little. "Too strong a word. Sorry. However, it was a good exercise for me to put myself in another's… er…"

I said, "Shoes?"

Her lips quirked a little. I was starting to like her. "Hm. At any rate, I have become quite interested in this population of apes. Ms. Tucker, you claimed that Zamuka remembers me. I find this surprising, but I am willing to test it."

"You mean you want to see her?" My heart did a flip. What if my claim proved false? Was I putting too much faith in a tired old gorilla?

Gloria turned to Surmi. "If I may."

Dr. Surmi blew out his cheeks. What could he say? Zamuka was no longer valuable. Nobody else wanted her. And I'm sure he had noted Gloria Ikayaa Green's obvious wealth and sophistication. A do-gooder taking a brief interest? Or something else? "Well, I admit I can't come up with a good reason why you shouldn't," he said, rather churlishly. But at this point he was pretty much out of the equation.

I stood up. Gloria looked up at me. "Come on," I said. "I can take you to her now, if you like."

"Now? Oh! Yes, please." Her voice had lost its crisp, direct diction and had become… can I say girlish? Made me want to take her by the hand and tug her along.

Since Zamuka wasn't in the sterile chambers now, we needed to stop only briefly to provide Gloria with coveralls, boots, and a quick lecture on safety. And a warning that Zamuka might be in a mood.

"She's kind of a diva. Ideally she'd be ordering servants around."

"Really? She's just an animal."

"An animal with the soul and personality of a Regency Duchess."

We arrived at Zamuka's cage and peered through the bars. She was sitting hunched in a corner. She turned ponderously and gave us a look. Then she turned away.

"Reminds me of my great-aunt Maybelle," said Gloria, her voice jittery with tension. "Should we have brought flowers? Chocolate?"

"Watermelon." I opened the door and went in, Gloria hanging back. *Zam-zam! Here new friend.*

I knew the old gal. Zamuka was bored and lonely and could only hold out so long. She and Gloria probably had a lot in common. "Come on in. She's actually pretty gregarious."

"You're sure it's okay…?" Gloria mustered up the nerve to enter the enclosure. "Oh my. She's very large."

Zamuka's glittering, deep-set brown eyes gave her visitor the once over, and I could see her wide nostrils flare as she tested the air. Gloria stood firm, but was breathing fast. Zamuka began to sign.

I translated. "She says *Hi Erika. What this person?* She's curious about you."

"Wow. I didn't know they could really do that. Can you… tell her hello?"

"Sure." I did so. *Hello. This person Gloria.* I signed *big sunshine/bright*, as the name Gloria wasn't in her vocabulary.

Zamuka, now properly introduced, leaned forward, her nose wrinkling and her breath huffing in and out. Gloria's eyes were watering, whether from the air in here, or from emotion, I didn't know. She extended her hand toward Zamuka's arm and tentatively stroked it.

Would the old gal cooperate? She'd been distressed for days, unhappy and lonely. I wasn't sure how she'd take this stranger suddenly arriving. Though I trusted her, I was really quite surprised that Surmi had let us do this… But Zamuka took Gloria's fingers in her big black hands and gently sniffed and licked them, glancing up at me and Gloria now and then. Gloria didn't flinch. I let out a breath. But then Zamuka turned and knuckle-walked back to her corner.

Gloria sighed, rubbing her hand. "She's amazing. So imposing… she looks wise somehow…"

"Oh, she really is, and you'd—"

We shut up as Zamuka started to walk back. She was carrying something. She held out what was almost indistinguishable from a bundle of rags—her oldest doll. Her "first born." She slapped her chest, hooting. Then she held the doll to her breast and rocked it. Then she pointed at Gloria. It was pretty unmistakable.

"What is that thing she's holding? A toy?"

I explained our use of dolls to placate and comfort the surrogates.

"She thinks it's her baby?"

"No. Zamuka understands that her children have been taken away. After each birth she spends a lot of time looking for a baby she fears she's misplaced, then settles for the doll."

Gloria bit her lip. "That's… oh my." She was blinking rapidly, and her voice had gone thick.

Zamuka hooted some more and began to pat her chest, and point back and forth from her doll to Gloria, signing rapidly.

"What's she saying?"

I felt the hair on my neck rise. "Uh… okay. She says, *Baby. Baby. No doll. Give baby.*"

"What—me? I'm the baby? She… she can't possibly know it's me. Oh my god…"

She made a little sound deep in her throat. In her pale green frock she stepped forward and held out her arms. The temporary cage was small, and hadn't been cleaned recently. She didn't seem to care. Zamuka shuffled forward and wrapped her long hairy arms around Gloria.

"Yep. She's a hugger," I whispered.

Gloria hugged her back as hard as she could. I had seriously underestimated the woman.

I admit I felt a bit of jealousy. Mother and child reunion… I wasn't needed within that embrace.

Gloria extricated herself, and we watched Zamuka return to her cache of dolls and fuss with them.

"I know what I have to do," Gloria said, to no one in particular.

We got in trouble, of course. Doctor Surmi gave us both a carefully worded scolding, and as he did so Gloria Ikayaa Green remained cool, if a bit brittle.

"Did I say you could go *in* the cage, Ms. Green?"

"I apologize for my unauthorized physical contact with Zamuka, Doctor," she drawled. Was she being ironic? Perhaps. "But no harm was done. Now, if I may make a proposal? I wish to purchase Zamuka and take her away with me."

He rocked back in his chair. "Purchase her? But—"

"Name her price, if you would."

"I can't just, just *release* her, at any price. There are regulations, restrictions—"

"I'm quite sure that our respective legal counsel can sort those out."

I could hear the gears churning in Surmi's head. Legal counsel. This woman had it in spades, for sure. After a solid minute of massaging his forehead, he gave in. "Let me set up a meeting with our outplacement people. And the USDA and NIH legal representatives. And I suppose PETA will want to get involved."

Gloria's head remained high. I'd seen her *sang-froid* when held in the hairy black arms of a gorilla; she'd have no trouble handling a bunch of policy wonks. I felt a swell of pride and happiness.

Then the happiness faded. I was going to miss the old gal. Would she remember me as she had remembered the baby she'd carried for nine months? I hoped so, for I'd never see her again. Gloria was planning a move—to Malaysia Green. She had big ambitions for her new ward. A floating island home for clapped-out apes…

It was good. She had money, influence, and plans for lots of obsolete primates. This particular *Homo sapiens* would return to her little walk-up and settle in for a good cry. I felt my innards shrink a little.

As we both watched Surmi frown and poke at his computer screen, she turned to me and whispered, "Do you have a passport?"

"Huh? No. I've never needed one."

"I suggest you apply for one now, Ms. Tucker. I believe it would please Zamuka if you came with us."

A tale that blends myth and legend with the troubles of the modern day. Was there ever a magic carpet, and did we trample it into oblivion? Do its colours still bleed?

HER EYES AS BRIGHT AS UNSHEATH'D SWORDS

When he had been a slim, beautiful, topaz-eyed boy, the Emir had believed passionately in genies and lamps and flying carpets.

Now he was really just a glorified businessman, overweight, tending to oily skin which made his balding head shine, and possessed of a wife who amid much interest from the Western press had gone to university to study law. Now he was finding it difficult to believe in much at all. He could rub the lamp, but no genie would appear.

Every morning was a fatalistic certainty that his chauffeur would not get him from the palace to his offices in the Parliament buildings without them both being blown sky-high. Today he noticed that his fingers resting on the white leather upholstery were leaving dark prints of sweat, and he carefully placed his hands on his thighs instead, where the charcoal linen of his suit pants would not show marks of tension. He watched the finger prints evaporate, and wondered how many American Express slips his wife was signing today in London, in the elegant, angular Kufic scripts she affected. She would be buying gifts for the children and for him, and thousands of English pounds' worth of clothes for herself and her mother. Those two left a bubbling wake of giddy clerks when they swept through Knightsbridge, and he was glad he wasn't there to witness it.

The Emir rubbed his temples and pictured himself cross-legged above the hot white city, on a rippling slice of his own dreams. The big limo bowed and veered, probably in response to a sudden movement in the crowd on the sidewalks; behind closed eyes, the Emir saw the city beneath reel as the wind buffeted him and fluttered the jewelled fringe of his carpet. Waves of heat and the scent of dung and spices rose around him in the brilliant air. He opened his eyes and watched the crowds, shadowed on the other side of tinted Armorglas.

His wife Nuzbayah, her mother, and all their bodyguards, servants and luggage came back a week later. Bayah had a few days before classes resumed and she and the Emir spent some time together in the private gardens. Her figure, which did not suit the designs of the Italian couturiers she favoured, was magnificent sprawled naked on a tablecloth among flowers, crumpled napkins and empty dishes. She rolled onto her stomach, twining her legs in the air behind her, and picked up the present she'd bought him at an auction at Sotheby's. It was a jewelled peacock the length of her thumb.

Its body was one unusually curved emerald crystal, etched in delicate rows of feathers. Its head was a sapphire surmounted by whisker-thin gold wires each supporting a ruby or emerald chip. The tail, an elegant fan of gold, was inlaid with lapis lazuli and malachite chosen for its resemblance to the peacock's eye-like plumage. Even the claws of its tiny feet were tipped with topaz.

She balanced the bird on its feet on the edge of a heavy silver platter. It perched jauntily, its eyes glittering almost fiercely in the sun that lanced through the oleander leaves swaying overhead. The air alternated in scents of dust and water as the breeze shifted around the garden. The fountains chattered endlessly; the sun squeezed unimagined heat from the tawny sandstone walls of the courtyard.

Nuzbayah plucked a cherry from its stem and bit delicately at its wine-black flesh.

"What has Ta-ta been up to lately?" she asked, her ruby-tipped fingers gently testing each cherry remaining in the bowl. Ta-ta was her name for Taruman, spiritual leader of the people of Izban. Taruman, engaged as he was in a battle to drag the people of Izban back into the middle ages, aroused the derision of Nuzbayah, woman of the present. Bayah, the Emir realized, had cast aside her veil with an enthusiasm that verged dismayingly on vengeance. In her way as stubborn and unseeing as the old Wazir—his queen, his *begum*—passionate, vital, with no sense of history, no patience. His path to a possible future for their country was too slow for her; it was all too slow.

He watched her buttocks firm and soften as she swung her legs, crossed at the ankles, to and fro behind her in the air. Her face was carefully serene, symmetrical, and yet her eyes were like a warrior's rowelled heels.

She ate another cherry and lanced her black eyes at him. Did she choose not to understand that her weapons would cut deeper from above a veil, all else but sword-points hidden? The Emir swallowed the thought unspoken. Do you know my thoughts, Bayah? I was brought up in the old ways and it is hard, so hard, to change.

"Taruman is going on some sort of retreat soon," he said. "To the mountains, among the faithful. I, for one, am glad—there is too much unrest in the city. He feeds just enough raw meat to the lion to keep it hungry." Bayah, he thought—leave it alone. Can't you see, my delicious wife, that your goading makes it worse? Taruman understands his people better than you do, better than I; accept it. Accept the inevitability of time.

Moderation is my burden, he reflected. To me it is the right way, to them it is as meaningless as wind ruffling the fur of tigers. He loved Nuzbayah, he loved his country; its heat, its dust, its colours and smells, its ignorant, passionate people. But did he love what they were, or what they could become?

He wondered if Bayah thought of him still as the handsome, lithe man she had married fifteen years ago. He had been handsome—he knew it from the portraits of himself as a child, a youth, and as a young ruler, displayed in the palace's public rooms and in the echoing, air-conditioned stone chambers of Parliament. He had learned to fence at public school in England, had learned to speak English like an Englishman, had mastered political science and business administration. He had made friends who had grown up to be as important and as busy and, probably, as unhappy as himself. He would have liked to have accompanied Bayah on her trips to Europe, but it was, more and more, impossible to get away.

Nuzbayah liked to be on top during their lovemaking, with her eyes closed, and her head thrown back till her unbound hair brushed his thighs excitingly. When he was above her, she would push with all her strength against his chest, laughingly begging for breath and sometimes hitting him quite hard. Her panting aroused him; the feel of her trapped under his weight, helpless, frightened him.

"Ah," she said, giving the jewelled bird a push with her finger. It fell backwards into the platter. "Ta-ta will be out of the way for a while—but I wonder what repressions he'll plan on this retreat." Her eyes became distant, and she smiled.

She rolled onto her back, the skin of her breasts and belly

dappled with hot golden patches of sun. The Emir ran his hand from her shoulder around the pendant curve of her breast and down the soft ripple of her rib-cage. She didn't move, and suddenly the sun dipped behind the west wall, turning out the lights on her skin as if his touch had thrown a switch. The fountains seemed very loud as he kissed her neck and belly.

In the limousine the next morning he turned the jewelled peacock over and over in his hands, examining the furred depths of the emerald and the glint of glass-filtered sun on gold and ruby and sapphire. The heat was not as intense today, or perhaps the air conditioner was keeping up more efficiently. Bayah had not accompanied him to the city this morning, but had given him a black-eyed look from above white sheets that made him remember the scent of cherries and hot stone. He reached for the car's phone to call Bayah and tell her again how pleased he was with the little peacock.

There was a thick, hard noise from under the car. A *crump*, not loud. The heavy car seemed to give a ponderous hop, then it settled to the pavement with a grinding of metal that made the Emir's hair rise on his neck.

To stay in the limousine or get out fast? His hand tightened on the bird. The cool flow of conditioned air stopped.

Fazzad, the driver, had his gun out and was yelling shrilly, "Get down, get down—"

There was another deep *crump* and the Emir saw Fazzad's gun fly from his hand and bounce off the inside of the bullet-proof windshield. Fazzad's head jerked back, and his arms flew out as his body was driven up and to the left by the force of the explosion. The Emir saw the back of the driver's seat burst into a blossom of white leather petals. The maroon carpet split and disgorged a shrapnel-like swarm of ground-up metal fragments. He was flung against the passenger-side door which sprang open at the impact.

He became aware that he was lying on the roadside in an unnatural position, and could hear nothing. A mob of people surged back and forth, gesticulating wildly, opening and closing their mouths in silence. A few women, with black, shocked eyes above their veils, backed away. The men ran to and fro helplessly.

The Emir dragged his eyes down to focus on the hand which still gripped the bird. The fingers, lacerated and black with blood, were moving convulsively. A tiny crested head poked out and began to peck at his fingers.

The Emir closed his eyes, the smell of burning flesh making his stomach knot. He felt a release in his bowels, tried to move his limbs and could not. *Bayah, my queen,* he thought, *has passion brought us to this? There are two tigers fighting under the hot sun, and now I am not there to spread water on the dust.*

His eyes opened again. This time there was nothing to be seen but a panorama of crystalline boulders, like grains of sand hugely magnified. Their rounded angularities of saffron and biscuit and cream stood before his eyes immobile, hot, silent. Around one of them, its exquisite body reflected in the translucent apricot of the boulder, stepped the jewelled bird. Its beak clacked and the feathers of its crest and tail jangled metallically. These were the only sounds the Emir could hear. As the bird came closer he could see that, relative to him, it was now the size of an ostrich, every striation left upon the gold by the jeweller's art now magnified into visibility. Yet the bird was beautiful, alive. The gold of its feet flexed; the topaz claws trod nearer to the Emir where he lay.

A drift of oily smoke obscured his vision for a moment. There was, again, the stench of burning—metal and rubber this time, and flesh. A crackling heat.

The bird turned (*Allah, All-knowing, All-merciful! Lord of the three worlds, who stretched out the earth like a bed, and set the firmament without pillars—*), flirted its tail and stepped round a grain of amber sand and was gone.

The Emir rose and adjusted the turban upon his head. His embroidered robe swung heavily around his feet as he followed the bird. The taste of cherries was in his mouth, and fountains splashed.

I love the people who live in this strange and difficult world. But do they really live? Are they really human? The family dynamics—angry teen, desperate parents at the end of their rope—could happen anywhere, anywhen. The late great editor of Asimov's Science Fiction *magazine, Gardner Dozois, took this story and made me tweak it a bit. It ended up being one of my favourites.*

PICK MY BONES WITH WHISPERS

Fritz licked the side of my face and let out a little whine. I brushed him away; I'd managed to solidify a magnified view of an angel-wing larva opening in the packed wet mosaic of sand sixty centimeters down, and was waiting for it to start digging for the surface. It was hard enough concentrating through the sun and heat of the beach without a wolf in my head too. He licked me again and said, "Lizbeth. We have to go."

"Fritz, shut up! It's nowhere near dinnertime."

Fritz's furry brindled muzzle shrank and became the pale, sharp-nosed, grey-eyed face of my mother. "Lizbeth, it's me. I want you home *now.*"

I shut off the microscope, waited for it to withdraw its

burrowing proboscis, coiled it into a loop and hung it on the belt that was all I wore. "Mother," I said, "wasn't it you who sent me out here in the first place? Don't you *want* samples from the lily-tree grove?"

"You're nowhere near the lily-trees." Her voice sounded tense, which was unusual for her. "You're at the beach, though you were told not to go there."

I shuffled my toes deeper into the warm sand and hunkered down, hugging my knees. "So what if I am? I'll get to the lily-trees—"

"Forget them." Her eyes became intensely silver as she looked at me. It's hard to describe in words how it is when a net person is there, in you, talking to you. Looking into your eyes from inside your own skull. I guess I'm used to it; it doesn't really bother me, except when Mother uses tricks of physical and psychological coercion to get me to behave.

"I want you to face south, look toward the ocean and tell me what you see."

"Toward the *water*?"

"Yes. Scan the whole beach, magnify if you need to."

I stood up, brushed sand off my legs, and squinted down the long dry slope of yellow sand to the shadow that lay black and thick under the dike wall, about two kilometers away. From here, the huge wall of compacted mud didn't look like much. It swooped up into the distance to the south, like the edge of a mesa, at the top of which was an ocean. I squinted, bringing the hazy vista closer as my optic implants responded to the cue.

"Look at the base of it, Liz. Tell me what you see."

"I can see something—uh, looks sort of glittery, something moving in the shadow—Oh!" I fell back a step in surprise.

"*Tell me what you see,*" said Mother's voice harshly.

"It looks just like sappers. Giant ones, absolutely swarming up and down the dike. Must be hundreds of 'em."

Mother sent a tactile burst that took me by the scruff of the neck and turned me toward the camp.

"Move," she yelled, vanishing from my head. Fritz popped back in and took over, nipping at my ankles and yowling as I ran up the beach that bordered this world's ocean, an ocean held back from the flatlands below it by the universe's biggest berm.

It's hard to run through sand; I was gasping by the time I reached the edge of the vegetation. Stopping in a meagre patch of shade, I looked back. The terrain was wide, sandy and sunny, and we called it a beach, but it was nowhere near the water. The water was kilometers away and high overhead. Suddenly I felt like an ant at the bottom of a crumbling dam.

Fritz bounced around in my head, panting. "Let's go-o-ooow!" It turned into a howl. Mother must have pushed the panic button.

Fritz was my monitor, my tutor, my medic-alert, my pal; but mostly he was the personified link embedded in my brain that hooked me into the net, where everything happened. Everything that wasn't physical, that is. For instance, my lungs were gasping for real air, and my body was covered in real sweat. Real sand, gritty and annoying, stuck between my fingers and toes. I was the only human being for hundreds of square kilometers.

Fritz opened his phantom mouth and bit me on the right buttock, hard.

I ran toward camp.

As I ran, I heard whispering in my head, some kind of code string that I probably wasn't meant to overhear, and then there was a burst of static in my visual field. I almost fell.

"You all right?" someone puffed in my ear, and as I scrambled up an incline on hands and knees, the someone resolved into Daddy. He was running alongside me, wiping his forehead comically. I didn't laugh.

"Where's Mom?"

"Operating a shuttle. Don't worry, we're going to pick you up, Lizzie, before—" *Before the water gets you.* A battering flood of sensory detail hit me from him, before he could suppress it—what his horrified imagination pictured happening to me. *A black torrent, alive with alien animals, their limbs ripping her flesh—*

And then he was back in control, barely. "Just keep running, baby, everything's going to be all right."

Okay. A shuttle's coming down from the orbital swarm, it'll take me up, safe—

"Stay with me when I get there, okay? Tell me what's happening?"

"Sure, Lizzie."

Daddy was new in the Fulnet. He'd married Mother when they were both fifteen, two years past legal age. They'd had me, and she'd opted in right away. He'd stayed out, remarried after a few years but had no other children, and then, when that marriage fizzled too (I'd never liked Sandra), opted to Fulnet when I was ten. He'd been one of the few flesh-and-blood people I've ever actually known, at least for so long. Others come and go, mostly other children. I'd never met anyone older than Daddy who was still out and about in the physical world.

I could still remember the feel of him, his smell, the way his eyes got bloodshot when he'd been up all night listening to old music or whatever he did when he got all pissed and lonely. Virtual eyes never get bloodshot, unless you're going for an effect, and Daddy wasn't the type to go for effect.

But Mother was. Suddenly she was there beside us, loping along easily in the form of a wolf much like Fritz, but pure white. Her silver eyes flashed at me. Fritz's eyes were blue, and he was not white, dammit, he was golden brown with grey bristly whiskers over his eyes, like eyebrows. Why did Mother keep showing herself as a wolf? Why did she butt in on Fritz and take him over when she wanted my attention? She knew it was something I hated. Fritz was there, running beside me too, but she'd suppressed his voice.

To hell with it.

To hell with insane parents and their machinations.

Mother and Daddy conferred for a second, shutting me out. I had to stop for a moment and catch my breath. Fritz thrust his nose into the palm of my right hand, his virtual muzzle soft and moist. I loved it when he did that. He'd be talking to me now if she'd let him. I understand that real wolves never had the power of speech, and were hard to tame and control. In this way, Fritz was better than a real wolf.

Although I'm twelve, there's still a lot I can't do in the children's Net areas, even though Fritz was letting me in deeper and deeper all the time. There were dark places I could never go, forbidden subjects I could never get data on, tantalizing things I couldn't see or join or do. Sometimes it was frustrating, and often it was humiliating, to be a flesh-and-blood person.

But. I was alive, wasn't I? Wasn't that the way people were *supposed* to be? And wolves?

Oh, never mind. I've talked to therapists and assured them that I forgive Mother and Daddy for doing what everyone does eventually anyway. Apparently, you can lie to a Fulnet therapist and have them buy it, if you're clever, and I am.

Mom let the wolf-body vanish—no doubt to assign processing to other more pressing concerns—and simply talked. I kind of liked the way her voice was always the same, even though her image changed.

"Lizbeth, don't worry. The shuttle will be there soon to lift you off. And the equipment too, if it can be managed."

I started running again. "Will somebody please tell me what's going on? If it's not too much *bother*?"

Another quick burst of communication between Daddy and

Mother, but no answers for me.

I was almost back at camp, which consisted of a lot of automatic equipment busily working, a spin station and auxiliary power font, a habitat for little me, and assorted water distillers, antennas, pumps, homing grids, et cetera. Connecting me to all this, and to the local com node, were a battery below my right lung, a processor in my skull, and a sensory/antenna web under quite a lot of my skin.

Sometimes I could feel it all there inside me. Living metal, like parasite vines nudging against my pink squirming organs, especially when it was dark, especially when I lay out under the stars and stared up and up. Imagining what awaited me, out there.

We—people both real and net—live in a swarm of habitats and computer blocks currently in orbit around the sappers' planet. Other groups elsewhere are connected, somewhat unreliably, by a data-flow that uses something called half-spin tangled pairs; in this case, multiple electron pairs. When the swarm itself moves, it moves at relativistic speed. Time passes strangely for all of us, alive or not.

The Earth, where humans and wolves and all the other Terrestrial species evolved, is long behind us. How long?

Who cares? Not me.

Virtual people don't give a damn what time it is.

I'd asked Daddy once why people bothered to stay alive long enough to have children. Why didn't everyone simply live in the net? I pointed out that all it would take is one generation of that, and everyone would *be* Net. This was before he went in, when he was still flesh, and I think I really stumped him. He ended up saying something like, Beats the hell out of me.

Then, realizing how this must have sounded, he'd hugged me briefly, hard, and said, "The universe thrives on change. What better way than the random mingling of genetic material?" Then he got drunk, as I recall.

The next morning, I found him asleep on the floor beside the couch in our quarters, and the day after that, he opted in. He'd just turned twenty-six, and I was ten.

Sometimes I feel awfully alone, despite all the people in my head.

"It's the dike," he said finally, as we skidded down the last sandy hillock. At last, some information. "The embankment that holds back the ocean along this coast. It was built by giant versions of the arthropod-like critters you see all around here, but these ones are engineering geniuses, considering they're not actually intelligent. They're a sort of hive mentality driven to do what they do by instinct."

"The ones I saw under the dike, the big sappers… they must have been the size of a shuttle. What were they doing?"

Mother had come up with this name for the industrious animals, which spent most of their time digging in the sandy soil of this planet and minding their own business. Fritz, in his eager, drooling librarian mode, had fetched me the fact that Terran engineers were once called sappers; the name fit these earnest, bug-like construction workers perfectly. Up until now, the ones I'd seen ranged in size from the length of my thumb to the bulk of a healthy watermelon.

Daddy paused, and I knew it wasn't a processing pause, it was actually him dealing with telling me something he didn't want to say, and I didn't want to hear. "It seems that a catastrophic flood is what the sappers need for their reproductive cycle. They build a dike to hold back the ocean— we deduce it takes about fifty years—then they all get together and undermine it so the water rushes in and floods the entire lowland hereabouts."

"So the ones I saw in the shadow of the dike, they were digging it up. Trying to cause a flood."

"Yep. Those particular ones are doomed, by the way. They aren't built to walk on land. Their exoskeletons will collapse and their internal organs won't function. They're sacrificing themselves for their race, along with thousands more of them on the ocean side."

"But, how… *why* do they do it? It doesn't make sense."

"It does to them. Reproduction, remember? Just like us. Also, they have patience. And this world's lower gravity and eccentric tidal forces help them—there's a fifty year correlation with the planet's orbit."

"And you only figured this out *now*? What's the idea sending me down here if all this was going to happen?"

"We didn't think it would, not for another several months."

"What about the other kids?" Six of us were on this field trip, scattered around a large area, four boys and one other girl.

"They're okay. They're in the highlands."

"So who screwed up?" I asked belligerently.

"Some of the monitors we had in the ocean failed. They drifted off their marks, but happened to get into a position relative to the others that generated an intersecting signal, and it fooled us into thinking that there was hardly any activity along the dike. A fly-by picked it up just about twenty minutes ago, and we've been scrambling ever since."

"Huh." I couldn't help looking up into the sky in search of a descending shuttle. Nothing.

And then I felt something cold nudge my leg, and the rough warmth of Fritz's furry shoulder. Though I'd never touched a real wolf, or even a dog, I knew that this was the right way for one to feel. He leaned against my knees heavily. A comforting surge of nostalgia went through me, hard to identify; then I figured out that it must be the way Fritz was doing body-interaction stuff like he used to when I was very young. He'd been a puppy then. I realized that his behaviour was most likely a response to my fear, which of course he knew about before I did.

And I'd thought I was being so big and brave and sassy.

It was a sort of tradition that no one but you could hear the voice of your animal friend, and most particularly that your parents couldn't. Fritz was mine alone—no one else had a friend like him, and no one else knew me and loved me the way he did. It had been rude of Mother to take Fritz over like she had on the beach. Though everyone above a certain age knew what their friend really was and how it was just another aspect of the Net, still, it was a charade that most people kept up. Except, of course, Mother.

All it really amounted to was that the program running Fritz was focused totally on me, more interested and attentive than any parent could ever be.

"Come on, you sloth," he yelped. "You furless slug! I'll race you!" Fritz bounded around me and headed into camp at a lope, tail wagging high as a flag.

When I was little, I used to look for his paw prints, and tried stubbornly to find hairs shed from his coat. His laughter when he watched me do it seemed so real, I felt that he must exist outside of my own head—somewhere.

I ran after him, over the last little ridge and down the path that my own footsteps had beaten among the scrubby grasses and rubbery little plants clinging to the packed-silt soil. Everything was the colour of biscuits, with here and there a patch of celery-green or cheesy-yellow. A big, boring snack tray of a planet, with seafood hors d'oeuvre on the way.

Maybe I'd have time to grab some of the things I'd collected during my month here—little round shells; strings of desiccated bark I'd made that I liked for the way they rattled and twirled in the breeze; my matched sets of molted sapper-claws.

I'd tried to turn some tiny sappers into pets, corralling them in pens of twigs and piled dirt, but all they did was dig and shovel with their armoured snouts, their legs churning. They rolled the twigs aside and trundled their way out as relentlessly as robots. In fact, they were stupefyingly boring, and I mostly ignored them.

"Fritz! What's happening now? Is the dike still there?"

"You'd know if it wasn't. You'd hear it. They think it'll last a while longer."

"They *think*?" I rolled my eyes. "Can I have something to drink? A Coke?"

"Sure, why not. Be ready to hop when the shuttle lands."

One of the things parents could do, through their connection to all things electronic, was lock out certain substances—junk food in the fridge, for instance—and influences they deemed inappropriate for their tender offspring. A pain, really, but I knew I'd do the same for my kids when I had 'em. I planned to have four children as close together as possible, so they could be friends. I know what kids can get up to, if given half a chance. Which made me think: were chances programmed in? Was it a psychological plus to let a kid get away with the odd thing?

I pondered this, drinking my soda and eavesdropping as much as I could. Mother and Daddy were being tighter than I'd ever seen them, their heads together (virtually speaking). They weren't letting much leak through to me.

"Fritz, show me a view of the dike, okay?" There should be several ways he could link to something monitoring the area; after all, it was the focus of interest hereabouts. But he shook his head and tucked his nose between his paws, looking at me with those ice-blue eyes of his. "Stupid mutt," I said. He wagged his tail and blinked knowingly. "Come on! I have a right to see it!"

"Granted. But I'm not going to let you, not right now." His ears kept pricking up and then lying back on his head, as if he was listening to something that hurt them. What did it mean?

"Then tell me what Mother and Dad are up to."

"Your mother's trying to program a viable entry corridor for the only shuttle close enough to reach this base."

"Oh." The soda can was cold and slippery in my hands.

He smiled doggishly and let his big pink tongue loll. "You asked."

I wished I could throw something at him. I hurled the can at the habitat wall instead, ran outside and looked up fruitlessly. "What's Daddy doing?"

"Never mind," said Fritz, following me. "He's busy, he can't talk to you now."

I was almost old enough to have a real baby of my own, and even *Fritz* was treating me like a kid! I felt like crying. In fact, I was crying. My stupid nose needed blowing, so I wiped it on my arm. I ran back inside and began throwing things into a heap on the floor, stuff I wanted to keep. Fritz helped, uploading some of the recent data I'd gathered.

I was digging in a box for a shell bracelet when Fritz suddenly bristled. His hackles rose, and he snarled ferociously at nothing. "It's coming," he barked. Then he howled briefly, his way of indicating that he was handling a lot of data at once. Then I started to hear a far-off thunder. The air felt different. Tighter. It felt like the skin of a drum that someone had just pounded.

I froze in place, my knees weak. "Where's the shuttle? Shouldn't it be here by now? Fritz!"

The thunder kept coming, a deep rolling boom that didn't stop. Should I run outside? But what if I saw the water coming? How long would it take to get here, anyway? "Fritz, how long—"

Mother popped in. "The shuttle's on the way. It's taking a bit longer than we'd thought." Her voice was incapable of sounding tense, but that was nothing special. She had probably been manufactured, not born, and then grown in a vat into the sort of woman who abandons her own body as soon as legally possible.

"What should I do?"

"It's okay, Lizbeth," she said, her face fading in and out. "It's going to be all right, just—oh shit. No!" Static, then a burst of raw data in a buzzing scream that cut off after a split second of pain. And then Daddy was there.

My teeth had started to chatter. I was alone on this fucking planet, and all I had to save me were some screw-up electronic constructs that weren't even human anymore.

Fritz pushed me into the chair in front of the com-link controls. Daddy said, "Sit here, do as I say, and do it fast."

"But, what—"

"Shut up! See that green cable coming out from behind the comset? Pull the end closest to you out of that silvery box with the studs all over it. Don't touch the prongs!"

"Okay, it's out." It glittered in my hands as the tiny motile wires inside the guard prongs groped for a connection.

"Reach into your hair, find your junction and pull out the shield. Done it? Now push in the cable. Push!"

My fingers shook. I closed my eyes, groping with the connector until it lined up with the junction I'd had in my skull since before I could remember. I'd met Fritz this way, when he'd been integrated into my psyche.

"But—"

"Do it!"

What choice did I have? My eyes were streaming tears, and the roaring in my head might have been the oncoming water or it might have been my life being crushed by this little green wire.

"No!" I shouted. "I'm not ready!" But all the same I pushed it in. Die one way or die another, this was it.

At least Mother had tried to bring the shuttle in. How *dare* Daddy do this to me?

What choice did either of us have?

There was no room for anger after the connection was made. No room for fear or hope or hatred. My existence split into two halves: *Then. Now.*

Then was gone forever, locked in a body that was being ground into pulp under tons of water and mud and alien engineers.

Now had no duration, but would go on forever.

Everything I'd ever thought or known or imagined was wiped out, as if by the casual sweep of a wet rag in the hand of a giant; as if by the wag of a big dog's tail knocking a crystal vase to the floor to shatter. The shards flew in all directions—there is no gravity in e-space—flew and glittered and took every little bit of me and sent it spinning.

Each shard held a glimpse of my life, exploding away and becoming huge; or rather filling a huge volume of solipsistic space (and I knew that word without having to think about it; I knew so much—saw spinning shards of other lives around me, on and on…). Expanding, blossoming, growing… it was like becoming a god without having the slightest knowledge of what a god should be.

And as I expanded, I wondered: how had Father resisted for so long? How had he justified clinging to his grubby little physical life? Had he done it for me?

One of the shards spinning by caught my attention. I looked closer, and saw my own death.

I saw it as if I were floating above the action, saw the swirling muck, the thrashing limbs of countless sappers as life-renewing water surged and foamed across the desiccated land. The view was being fed to me from one of the remotes set to record the event. A simple miracle, easily explained: my god-like brain had reached out for what it wanted and the view had appeared. I shut my eyes.

What did *that* mean? I had no eyes to shut. But the water and the roiling clouds of filthy spray all vanished and were replaced with a vibrant blackness in which I could feel myself being jerked back and forth, up and down, around and around, until, in self-defence, I somehow drew my "body" together into one pseudo-solid entity.

Thus I huddled, spinning helplessly in the dark.

Then I heard a sound. A tiny, far-off sound, hollow and echoing. Fritz! It was Fritz barking, and my heart—or whatever was its analogue—leapt. But the barking seemed to deteriorate. It fractured into smaller and smaller scraps and fled from my perception like torn feathers on the wind.

"Fritz! Fritzie!" I called, before taking time to think about it, or wonder how a disembodied mind could shout. The barking faded. "No! Fritz—I'm here!"

He was gone.

At that moment I felt so utterly helpless and alone I wished I had died completely in that flood.

When I opened my eyes at last, Mother and Daddy were there, hovering, wearing expressions of worry and fear. For a moment, I thought that I was four years old again, and would find the wolf cub wagging and eager in my head.

But that was wrong. I was Fulnet now. All grown up.

And Fritz was gone.

I seemed to be on a bed, in a busily humming room full of nice normal sounds—monitors beeping, distant voices chatting, the rhythmic shushing of air circulating gently.

I felt as if a lot of people had rummaged in my brain and, before closing the top of my skull, had arranged everything they found there into a more logical order. But in doing this, they hadn't bothered to check whether they'd broken or lost anything.

Daddy stepped up to me holding out his arms ready to hug me, but I turned away. His arms fell back to his sides and I felt a jolt of rueful, loving sorrow. He'd sent it right to me, the bastard.

Mother stood with her arms crossed, just as cool and collected as she'd always been… except now, she was not just a construct in my brain, she was absolutely real. As real as anything would ever be again. Which is to say, more real than the truth.

"So this is it," I said.

Mother smiled slightly. "Yes, it is. Welcome to grown-up land."

"Thanks. So… so when does the p-party start?" My pathetic attempt at flippancy deteriorated into what felt ominously like a crying jag. My breath came in gasps, I felt hot, and by God, I felt my nose start to run. It was incredible. Then suddenly I felt like laughing. In fact, hysterical hoots of mirth welled up in me, just as frightening as the crying had been.

"What's happening? Why am I doing this?"

Mother sat on the edge of my bed. I felt it give a little with her "weight."

"It's just feedback," she said. "It'll go away after a period of adjustment. The system is getting to know you, and it didn't have the usual lead time. Circumstances were… strange."

"I'll say." I gulped, feeling my chest heave. Prickles ran up and down my legs and arms, and suddenly I was freezing cold.

"Give it time. You'll see—it's not so bad." She glanced over at Daddy, who was still standing there all forlorn and hangdog. I wasn't ready to acknowledge him yet, even though he'd worked some sort of miracle getting me connected through whatever hastily cobbled-up route he'd jammed together. I hadn't known he had it in him.

But he'd still taken my life away—my real life, the one where

I was going to have kids of my very own and not Fulnet until I was thirty and they were all grown up. Silly me, I'd had it all planned out. I'd even picked out the boy I was going to marry, though I hadn't let him know yet, fortunately. How embarrassing to have to explain that I'd got my body killed.

When I thought I could hold my voice steady, I said, "Does anyone know what happened to Fritz?"

They looked at each other. They were doing it again, damn it—talking behind my back. Still treating me like a kid!

I swung my legs off the bed and stood up. Looking down, I noticed that my feet weren't touching the floor. As soon as this registered, the floor came up to meet them, which I thought was pretty good.

"Fritz…" Daddy ran a hand over his face. "I couldn't get Fritz as well as you, baby," he said, his voice husky with emotion. Effect, I reminded myself; it's all for effect. "His construct resided so thoroughly in your material brain that he couldn't be saved. Each analog pet adapts so well to its owner that it becomes a unique entity and takes up a lot of room. The assigned protocols governing the Fritz interface at this end just weren't up to the job in the time I had. I'm very sorry." He sounded as if he meant it.

I tried calling Fritz, squeezing my eyes shut and making believe that my ears were the size of radio-telescope dishes, able to hear a pin drop clear across the galaxy. I called him for what might have been a very long time, or possibly a small fraction of a second.

But my Net ears could hear nothing but a hollow roar, the kind that comes from the inside of an empty seashell, and I knew that Fritz was gone. Whatever there had been inside my brain that made him my friend had been pounded into an ingredient in the thin organic soup that had deleted my campsite. He had died, and I hadn't.

A little part of my brain got an idea then, and set its vast new speed toward carrying it out. The main part of me walked out the door of the white room, leaving Daddy and Mother behind. I didn't want to see either of them ever again.

Time went by. Nobody seemed to mind that I was doing nothing useful. A mopey, depressed computer program; now that's charming.

I learned things, though. Like that there really is no reason for children to be born, or for anyone to cling to physical life. There's no death, after all. Except for constructs like Fritz. But genes are stupid, and stubborn, and single-minded. Reproduce! Mingle! *Evolve*. No matter where we travel, we'll still have that imperative in our souls. We're just as stupid as the god-damned sappers.

The loss of my body and its unique genetic information measurably lessened the ultimate richness and longevity of our portable Net civilization.

And I don't care.

I wanted Fritz, the way he'd lean against me all furry and warm, and talk to me, saying things that Daddy would have said if he'd been able.

Eventually, I joined a team studying the world that my body had died on, and made plans to return to it in another fifty years to watch the next flood. Or in a hundred, or a hundred and fifty. We keep ourselves busy.

I found myself working pretty closely with Mother. Surprisingly, we get along okay. Her way of thinking is pretty close to my own, as it turns out. And Daddy? Well, I couldn't stay mad at him forever, could I? He's still hurting.

When the time seemed right, I accessed that little part of my brain that had set itself to gathering scraps of memory, tracking them like paw-prints in sand, finding and picking up the shed hairs that were all the little things I remembered about Fritz.

Then I put them all together and downloaded a wolf cub.

His name isn't Fritz. He looks a lot like him as he pads around beside me, though. People are used to seeing us together.

But he's his own wolf, so to speak; smart, sarcastic, loving and drooly.

Fritz would be proud.

Vampires! Don't we all love vampires? Sexy, mysterious, driven to acts of ruthless greed in their quest to survive. But there are some deeds even the undead won't commit.

AFTER THE FIRST DEATH

The leaves dripped in the darkness. The patter of a few droplets falling from a breeze-shivered branch pricked the quiet of the suburban back yard.

Behind this quick soft sound, Leandre could hear the constant shuffling of life ever-threading the night around him. He could always hear that dim, beating hum, punctuated sometimes by close, demanding sounds. Shouts, sirens, dogs yapping at the moon. Gunshots, far off; the squeal of tires.

Nothing he need worry about.

Leandre glided through the shadows, his nostrils searching among the perfumes of the night for the scent he needed.

His ears, focused on the house, detected the soft padding of bare feet descending a stair. He stepped forward again, the thick, heavy leaves of a rhododendron rasping at his arms as he pushed the brittle branches aside. Drops of water, tasting of dust and the day's lost sun, sprinkled his face and were captured by his tongue. The dark moist earth beneath his feet gave up a scent of rot and renewal and pure mindless life. The padding footsteps crossed the main floor of the house, and a weak yellow light came on. Rummaging, dragging noises; moist and sticky sounds like fingers in honey. Or blood. Leandre sighed, his mouth open and his eyes huge and black in the dark.

He flattened his lean body against a tree, blending with the shadows. Someone was emerging from the house into the unlit yard. Down a brick pathway the bare feet came—Leandre could hear the minuscule crinkling of crushed moss—stumbling slightly in the blackness. It was a woman coming, carrying something awkward. Leandre breathed softly, silently.

The woman began to hum a tune, a lilting little melody. "Ooh, baby, baby," she warbled softly, creeping along with her burden. She passed Leandre not three feet away. He let her pass, glided up behind her and took her around the neck, one hand covering her mouth.

She struggled and tried to scream, tried to bite the hand clamped over her mouth. Her burden fell soggily to the ground and the sack split. Leandre's nose wrinkled at the stench of rotted food, crushed metal cans and assorted human waste. He almost let her go then, to escape the disappointing normality of her sordid load. Had he hoped for another of his own dwindling kind, cloistered here in this death-in-life blandness? Fool. But the feel of her next to him, her blood so close, kept him there despite his disgust.

Her limbs were naked, her body full and ripe, covered only by a thin gown of some silky, unnatural material, smelling of the factory in which it had been made. It gleamed dully in the moonlight, rippling. Her body sagged, heavy and slippery in the gown as Leandre relaxed his chokehold on her neck and pulled her around to face him. Her lashes fluttered and her terrified eyes tracked blankly back and forth as she lost consciousness.

Leandre grunted softly with pleasure, nuzzling into the scented heat of her neck, seeking the source, the fountain, the hot salty sea of blood that called him over and over… the first delicious moment when his fangs penetrated the tender flesh was so good, so very good… better than anything he'd ever experienced…

For somehow this one's blood was different, like nothing he'd tasted before. A new vintage, rich and spicy with a tang of urgency and secret knowledge. How could he not drink until he'd taken every incredible drop? Leandre let the woman slump to the ground and followed her down like a lover, his lips still pressed to her neck.

He couldn't let go. The blood didn't just flow into him, it burst joyously, a hot bright flood of beauty and pain and love and need. Leandre felt himself pulled by it inexorably, as if he were rushing along a tunnel of incandescent blackness toward a night more final and more perfect than he'd ever dreamed. A starless, breathing blackness untenanted by intelligence or direction, from which life itself sprang. Mindless, hot and wet, full of blood… Life! New life… a sort of ecstasy claimed him, a rapture feeding his ancient withered spirit until it wanted to surrender. He wanted to enter the blackness, join it, give himself to it.

Leandre twisted feebly in the blood's embrace. It was so beautiful, and so inevitable, that it frightened him. He couldn't understand such perfection, such amazing vitality. His body rebelled. He pushed at the woman's limp body, but his lips and fangs would not give up their place against her neck. It was simply too sweet. He pushed harder, and the woman, perhaps sensing dimly the last drops of her life's blood disappearing, began to spasm and tremble violently. The connection was suddenly broken, and Leandre thrust himself away from her, instinctively seeking the shadows as he retched and shuddered.

He groaned aloud, crawling under the shrubs blindly. In the grip of an intense and racking sorrow he pushed through the crackling branches and fallen, soggy leaves. Moisture was running out of his eyes, down his face. Tears!

How long had it been since he had wept? The tears were as salty as blood; his own tears, as vile and poisonous and addictive as his own blood. He spat desperately as he crawled, and wiped the wetness away with the back of his hand. At last, gasping and exhausted and with an overwhelming sense of loss dragging at him, Leandre managed to stand and compose himself enough to walk away.

He had to get away from this house, this woman, that beautiful blood.

Shaken and sore, he made his way across the city to his lodgings. He could not understand what had happened, but he meant to find out. The experience had been too dangerous, too supremely seductive, to ignore.

Doctor Addette would know. The oldest of them all, at least in this country, and perhaps a friend. It was his tendency to forget those who were, now and then, companions when he wasn't directly in contact with them; being a solitary creature, he seldom needed company or conversation. This was one situation, however, when he realized he must consult someone with more knowledge than he himself possessed.

Addette's eyebrows lifted slightly at the sight of Leandre on her doorstep after so long an absence—years, it was—but with a gesture of welcome, she admitted him, led him to her study.

Addette was not beautiful, but she was tall and imposing, her silver hair wound into a thick knot above a brow as unlined as a girl's. She possessed an air of invincible serenity, until one looked closely at her eyes. Her eyes, in that youthful face, held a sharpness and depth of intelligence that many found intimidating, Leandre among them. However, Addette had never turned her sometimes vicious wit against Leandre, and tonight her expression held only curiosity and patience.

"Sit," she said, taking one deep leather chair for herself and watching as Leandre settled into his. A small fire burned in the grate, and incense wafted from a little pot set close to the flames. The chair's leather arms were smooth and cool under Leandre's nervously stroking fingertips.

"I had the most... unusual experience earlier tonight," he said, with a little laugh. How could he possibly explain it?

Addette said nothing, but made a gesture of mild encouragement.

At least, thought Leandre, she is not tapping her fingers against her chair's arm. He plunged on, feeling foolish even as the memory of that strange joy flooded back.

As he told his tale, he augmented his words with images from his memory, which he knew Addette could pluck directly from his mind. Addette closed her eyes and absorbed the images, now and then asking Leandre to slow down, to go back and show her something again, and finally opening her deep eyes again without moving from her seat. Her long white fingers dug into her own thighs as she sat, kneading the hard muscle as if she were a cat. Her lips drew upward in a thin smile, but she turned away and stared into the fire until Leandre moved impatiently.

"I know what you experienced." Her voice was like the smell of crushed oak leaves, dry and light. "Oh, the memories..."

Leandre sat stiffly upright on the edge of his chair, his hands twining together in his lap. "But what of *my* experience? Explain it to me! I have never heard of such a thing happening before."

At this, Addette turned to face him, her expression now quite serious. "And you may never again. It is extremely rare, but I recognized it immediately from the details you showed me." Delicately she shuddered and drew her narrow shoulders up as if to ward off a chill breeze.

"What was it? If you won't tell me…" He half rose, but she waved him back into his seat.

"You, my sweet, beautiful boy, had the bad fortune to come upon a female at the moment, the very instant, of conception. As you bent to her neck and pierced her flesh, the two halves of human life joined within her body, sperm and egg, and the miracle occurred. The ripples, the shock wave if you will, of that event tore through the body in which it happened and changed it profoundly. The forces of reproduction, of vitality and growth—of life itself—entered you through her transformed blood. You are very fortunate to be with me now. Not many survive such an encounter."

Leandre sat stunned. After a moment he said, "The blackness, the living blackness… it was so seductive, somehow tantalizing and comforting at the same time. I desired nothing more than to race toward it, to fall worshipping before it. It was hard, so appallingly hard to let go…" Even now, in Addette's austere room, filled with books and the crackle of firelight, Leandre felt vertigo pull at him.

Addette nodded. "I have heard of others over the centuries who have survived the same ordeal, tempted to surrender but finding the strength to resist just in time. But they are changed. Their attitude toward what we are has changed. They proclaim that every moment is now doubly precious, more noble than mere sordid, squalling life, but still…"

Leandre's eyes narrowed.

"I know they are simply waiting to live again." Her black eyes gleamed fiercely at him. "As I wait."

"You? You have felt this too?" Leandre sat forward, his white face catching gold highlights as the flames danced in the little grate.

"You are a fine-looking creature, Leandre," said Addette,

smiling slightly. "If I were human again I would not be able to resist you… as I did not resist the lure of he whom I met one night long ago. I was a bride, happy, ignorant, proud of the virgin blood my new husband had spilled as he consummated our marriage. How I loved him… I remember still how his face relaxed into sleep as I watched it. As he slept I, strangely restless and hot, wandered the night in our little village, thinking small, pretty thoughts of home and love and children. I was a simple girl, a peasant really.

"My demon lover must have scented that new blood and come to me just as my poor Gustav's seed reached its goal."

"But… you, a mortal girl, how did you survive?"

Addette glanced at Leandre, then stared back into the fire. "When the creature's fangs pierced me I almost swooned in the heat of his embrace… I would certainly have been lost, but then my own miracle happened. I *felt* the new life forming in me! I felt it demanding its place, asserting its tiny, overpowering needs, forcing me to fight not just for my life, but for its own. My child! In that moment I had the strength of a tiger defending her young. I took my attacker and bent his body until his spine cracked."

Addette licked her lips, her tongue's tip catching the light with a swift little flash. "When he was helpless I drank his blood, draining him mercilessly until he was an empty husk. And I… I became as he. Among the… undead." Her face darkened then, and simultaneously the fire began to sputter and fade. Leandre shivered.

"I felt my tiny child die within me, linked as we were. She is there now, still dead in my womb, still calling for the life she was promised. But she will never get it. That is my shame, Leandre, that I love death too much to let it go. Our very special death."

A death that has an end, thought Leandre. To live again, and then to die like any mortal…

Addette stood, and Leandre stared up at her, not knowing what to say. She seemed to be gazing over his head, toward some far-off place or time. He stood too, wanting to leave but not sure how to make his farewells. What could he possibly say to such a tale?

Addette's eyes snapped down at him and she smiled again, harshly, her lips a snarl over small white teeth and the two sharp fangs. She stepped toward him, and seeing menace in her stance he stumbled back toward the door.

"Go, Leandre," she hissed. "Go, and never forget the power of life. It will call you in the end no matter how you struggle. And you may, next time, surrender to it. But the struggle… Ah, the struggle!" She laughed bitterly. "Never give up until you absolutely must. And then try to go with style."

He was at the door. She wrenched it open, pushed him through and said, "Goodbye, Leandre, and good luck."

The door closed and he turned after a while to the night, the faint, mingled scents of grass and concrete and blood tingling on the breeze. He could hear her crying, behind the door, in dry, hopeless sobs that followed him into the darkness.

A world built upon another, older world; a civilization long lost and almost forgotten. There's something strange in the depths below the city, and one determined woman and her small and very odd companion must retrieve it. She's a Retriever, that's her job. But then her old crush turns up, and he's not about to let her run loose in his city—not when he has a revolution underway! He has no idea the real revolution is completely out of his control. The lost civilization is about to make a comeback.

THE PRICE OF MEMORY

CHAPTER ONE

Kat's ears were wrapped around his head so tightly that it looked like a fist. He was a small, terrified, purple ball, just out of my reach. Reason: my hands were bound together by a crotchety old cord that hissed angrily as I tried to stretch my body toward Kat. To add insult to injury, there was an ordinary metal—*metal*—chain attaching my ankle to a wall. A cold stone wall, doing its bit to form a neat cube of incarceration.

The whole situation was extremely embarrassing.

"Kat! Wake up!" My troucat had retreated to an instinctive lock-down state, just when I needed his help, drat it. I would have gnawed through the cord but for three things: it would taste awful, it would melt my teeth, and I'd get in trouble with my Clan. No unauthorized tampering with bios.

A loop of electrical reactant high overhead emitted fitful yellow light, enough to reveal seeping walls and a noxious hole in the floor, meant for necessary bodily functions. I shuddered.

How, by all the gods, had Kat and I ended up here?

I'm a Retriever, Hunter Clan Grey. Kat and I are partners, bio and human. Events in the immediate past of our missions get spooled out backwards, and I don't remember them. Kat remembers everything, somewhere in his teeny round head. So, the misfortune or miscalculation that had got us here was unavailable to me… but I could deduce the gist: *Surprised, grabbed, tossed into dungeon.* At least I knew where I was: somewhere in the east quarter of Nagala City's nether regions.

Retrievers are never given complete intel, in case of being caught just like this, but I did deduce that my quarry must be close.

One problem: I didn't know what that quarry was, exactly. Kat did, but he was curled up and unresponsive.

Okay, one *other* problem: we were stuck in a cell.

So, I didn't know what we were meant to Retrieve, but I did remember this: Revenbrook Karel lived in Nagala City. It was his uncle Quel's stronghold, after all. Ah, Rev… I thought I'd got him out of my system long ago.

Revenbrook Karel, now Chief Circ-haut of Nagala City, had been childhood playmate, friend and more, until I'd been farmed out to Clan Grey after my parents' bones were found on Dragon-tail Ridge. Rev's uncle Quel had been the one to persuade the family that Clan life was better for me than moping around House Karel, weeping for my ruined childhood. It had seemed like a good idea at the time, to everyone but me.

Soon Rev would find out I was here. Then what?

The rhythmic thud of a pump sounded from somewhere below, accompanied by random groans and wheezes, whether animal, bio or mechanical I couldn't tell. The exhaust fumes indicated mechanical. Some newfangled contraption that someone had thought was a good idea. How stupid could people be? Wasn't it obvious that bios were on this world for a reason, and that reason was to do the work? Or in some cases, to become a partner in crime… I thought I saw Kat twitch a little, but then he subsided with a tiny, wheezing sigh.

My slide into self-pity was interrupted by metal rasping against metal. With a shriek of hinges the cell door swung wide. Harsh artificial light spilled in… and there he was.

Revenbrook Karel, pretty much filling the doorway.

"About time," I snapped, wiping my eyes.

He looked windblown, as if he'd been riding recently. The sweaty tang of *cheval* came with him, and a welcome whiff of fresh, cool air.

"Mag Grey-Hunter, as I live and breathe," he drawled, giving me the once-over. "Just as pretty as ever."

My name was Magdalena, drat it, not the diminutive Mag. "Well, *Rev*, I see you've risen in the ranks. *Good* for you."

His face was thinner than I remembered, the downy whiskers of youth replaced by bristly three-day stubble. Dark blond to match his hair. His body had firmed up since I'd last seen him.

He crouched beside me. "You were found near my archive vaults. Explain."

"Archive vaults? I don't understand."

That got me a harsh shaking.

"It's my job," I whined. "I'm a Retriever, in case you hadn't noticed my troucat."

"Oh, I noticed him. He will be squeezed dry when I get around to it. But, to save time, *Magdalena*, why don't you tell me what you were sent to steal?"

"It's not stealing, it's Retrieving." I tried a seductive shimmy to distract him.

"Stop that. You really don't know what you're doing. Tell me what you came here for."

"Haven't a clue."

This time my head snapped back and my teeth clacked together. "You know how this works, don't you?" I yelled. "My orders are inaccessible!"

What had I ever seen in him? Jerk. He dropped me and looked contemplatively at Kat.

Troucats aren't actually felines, who originated, like us, on Ancient Earth. They're bios—neither animal, vegetable nor mineral. Similarity of size, flexibility and furry coat makes troucats vaguely resemble cats, but there it ends. Mine, whom I had named Kat in a brilliant stroke of creativity, was a delicate shade of lavender shading to purple, and had legs jointed in four places, making him extraordinarily bendy. His strong, prehensile tail was a tapering length of dark purple.

His feet were coated in tiny glass-like beads, reflective in certain lights. His big, leathery, flexible ears, which he used both to gather information and to protect his ganglia-node—as close as a troucat got to a brain—were purple too, fringed delicately with long wisps of silky cream tendrils.

All in all, Kat was a damn fine accessory. I was proud to be his human. Right now, he was completely useless either as partner or fashion statement.

Rev extended a hand as if to stroke Kat. "Hey! No touching!" I struggled, the cord around my wrists hissed angrily, and Rev went ahead and stroked anyway. Damn him!

He stood up and said, "Don't go anywhere."

"Ha, ha."

He smirked and sauntered out.

As soon as the door clanged shut, Kat came awake, sprang for me and clamped himself to my head. He was panting, and the pinpricks of his little claws dug into my scalp.

A flood of impressions shot from his consciousness into mine, like a flurry of torn and curling silver nitrate exposures. I picked up something… a big and scary *thing* hovering at the edge of his primitive reasoning. No idea if it was actually a physical item, or just a ball of fear in Kat's mind. Whatever, it was our mission.

Oh, joy.

He burrowed under my chin, pushing hard with his head as if he meant to climb right into my heart. He lived there already.

The far-off pump stopped, and the cell echoed with silence, except for intermittent mechanical groans. Was this whole awful place empty, but for Kat and me?

By all the Terran gods, how were we going to get out of here?

CHAPTER TWO

A *demi-heur* passed before footsteps approached. I barely had time to wipe my nose on my sleeve before Rev bounded in again. Kat's eye gleamed in my peripheral vision.

Yeah, Kat's eye. It's really a kind of skin, as shiny as iridescent glass, running in a band of indigo from one side of his head to the other, ending in rakishly slanted lines over his ears. It makes him look as if he is wearing stylish mirror-glasses, like rich people wear to protect them from the insolent gaze of the unwashed. His eye receives and focuses varied types of light, and is a specialized variant of the reflective beads that coat his feet and tail.

I regarded Revenbrook with as much hauteur as I could generate from the floor. He had changed his clothes and taken a bath. I envied him. His hair was still damp and he looked pink-cheeked… and kind of belligerent. He had brought with him a leather container with a little door in one end, and air-holes in the top and sides. What the—!

"Oh, no you don't! Stop it right now! How dare you tamper with my bond-being?" The cord squeezed my wrists. "Don't even *think* about—argh!"

Rev ignored me and made kissy noises at Kat, while holding out a sliver of cheese. Kat hesitated for a split second, then grabbed the cheese and hopped from my shoulder right into the case without so much as a chirp of reluctance.

This was more than merely humiliating, it was betrayal.

The Circ-haut shut the case on Kat, turned, and cut my arms free. With an ordinary knife. Had I lost the threat factor already? I rubbed my wrists, watching the cord's two pieces crawl to a corner to join and regenerate.

Next he produced a large iron key and undid my leg clamp. Immediately I lunged for the case where Kat was busy grooming, but Rev stepped between me and it and clasped me in his arms.

"Hm," he said. "I don't remember you being so smelly. Or skinny. Perhaps I should take you out for a decent meal."

I wrenched myself free. "What do you know about decency?"

"I mean it," he said. "I can't let you starve to death in here."

"Fine! Drag me to some filthy stew-pot, I don't care!"

"I shall. But first…"

He reached into the pouch on his hip and withdrew a collar and leash. The man was laden with handy equipment. He wound the collar around my neck, where it squirmed into place.

"Your troucat will be safe in his case," claimed Rev, taking a couple of experimental yanks on my leash.

I gave him a sneer and led the way out of the cell, my head high. I felt a tingling prickle on the left side of my neck. It made me instinctively flinch to the right. He was trying to turn me like a draft animal. "Stop it! Just *tell* me which way to go!"

"What, you don't know your way around here?"

I wished mightily that I did, but that knowledge was tucked in Kat's brain too, along with a lot of other useful info that was set to spool in just before I needed it. I gritted my teeth and marched down a long corridor. It might be wise to play it smart and keep my big mouth shut.

Something rank tickled my nostrils, and my stomach lurched. Through a door I spotted piles of filthy clothes, and a whole lot of naked men splashing around inside a big bubbly pool of water. A barracks bathhouse. My nose wrinkled and my eyes watered at the miasma of sweat and cheap soap, but the view was worth it.

My neck tingled sharply. "Eyes front!"

I bit back my initial response. The men noticed their commander with a captive, and after snapping to attention and saluting as one, began to hoot and holler.

"That's a pretty little dog you have!"

The hoots changed to barking. The Circ-haut laughed, made a couple of cracks in a lower-caste patois that I was too furious to decipher, and urged me up a series of stairways.

"You brought me this way on purpose!"

"Yes, but you can't prove it."

Mouth shut, right. At last we emerged onto a small landing partway up a tawny sandstone wall, which overlooked the vast central plaza of Nagala City. I dug in my heels as my eyes adjusted to the unaccustomed brilliance.

To the south, tall towers gleaming white in the sun indicated the wealthy residential and business enclaves; in the west beyond the perimeter wall was a hazy distance clotted with trees and glittering coils of the river. Out there, a few kilometers along the road to Corusca, was the Clan Grey stronghold, which at this rate I was never going to see again.

Below us, people, bios, animals and machines seethed in a mosaic of activity.

Screeching caged ratocets, piles of bright fruit and bolts of cloth, fluttering racks of sports pennants and trinkets. A man demonstrating a coughing, smoking moto-cule to a clutch of potential buyers. Quite a few crackpots thought that machines could do the work of bios, and that they could make money selling them.

Exhaust fumes, hot-oil smells of cooking, and the scent of animal dung wafted upward. The sun beat down, removing the last of the cell's damp chill from my bones.

"Starting to look familiar?" sneered Rev, prodding me down the exterior steps to an eatery with outdoor tables.

Not surprisingly, we found seats easily. Apparently no one wanted to eat lunch next to a local Circ-haut and his snarling companion. Was he parading me around in public just to humiliate me? Did he have some stupid plan in the works, me merely being a prop? I sat straight in the sun-warm metal chair, and glared around, teeth bared. People started to settle up their bills and leave.

Rev ordered for both of us, since the servitors were ignoring me… yet, if Kat had been upon my shoulder I would have had royal treatment. Little ingrate, snoozing in his cozy box.

I needed to check his brain without Rev listening in. Contact with Kat's body gave me the part of his consciousness that operated his own life—his emotions, survival, ability to follow instructions, his own free will. But to retrieve mission info? I needed more than that.

Rev was surveying his surroundings, basking in the glances of women and quite a few men. All of them wondering what he was doing with me. Snidely, I remarked, "You actually *eat* here? You do understand that they cook ratocets and call them chicken?"

"Doesn't bother me," he said. "I'm a soldier." A pause. "So…
how do you know what they serve? Been here before, have
you?"

I blinked. *Had* I been here? Maybe with him and his mom
and dad, long ago? Or even with my own parents, long dead
now? Another fact shunted to Kat's ganglia. As I thought about
it, battling a sense of permanent *déjà vu*, a shadow loomed
overhead.

A cargo ship, approaching dock. Her big bloodshot eyes
darted here and there, checking clearances and searching for
contact points. She moved ponderously, her vast belly pregnant
with grape-like clusters of bomb-buds, looking very close to
ripe. They'd be offloaded to harden in Nagala City's nurseries. I
could hear the airship's chuffing breath as her bellows opened
and closed. The threat of war with the other cities was always
present.

Our food arrived. Ratocet or not, Rev and I got on the outside
of a remarkable quantity of fried meat-morsels and chunks of
bread. I tucked a few items in my pockets for Kat. After a while
we both slowed down, sat back and contemplated one another.

"So," he said. Pause. "Why are you really here? And why
now?"

"Now?" I shrugged. "Beats me."

His eyes narrowed suspiciously. "Don't you pay any attention
to the 'scriers?" The airship let out an enormous fart as her
gasses vented, fortunately upward into the vast sky. Along with
everyone else, we ignored her politely. The big ladies had
feelings.

"No, I do not pay attention to news-criers, broadsheets, or
slogans painted on the sides of taverns. I have better things to
do."

He gritted his teeth. "And those better things might be…?"

"I told you I don't know!" Something brushed my ankle and I

stifled a shriek—some of the vermin around here have poison sacs in their mouths. I yanked my feet up onto the chair and looked down. A scrawny grey bio was staring imploringly up at me. At least I assumed it was imploring. Maybe derisive, or admonitory; who knew? One of his ears was torn and seeping, and he was trembling.

"Hey, are you scared, little fella?" I cooed, holding out a scrap of food. Rev slapped my hand away.

"Don't feed it! You'll never get rid of it!"

"Why would I want to get rid of him? Come on, come to Maggie…"

The little bio stepped closer, but then the diners at the next table began to shoo him away. "It's a wild bio! Get that thing out of here!" One man balled up a lump of bread and threw it at the bio's head. He caught it neatly and gulped it down. "Hey!" The man tried again with an empty cup, but missed. "G'wan, ya filthy parasite!"

Pretty soon there was a scrum of people kicking at the bio, which dodged in and out of table legs squeaking. I reached down, grabbed him by the scruff of the neck and crammed him under my shirt, hoping he didn't have fleas. "Come on, Rev, we're out of here!"

Glaring at the cretins who'd tried to kill the little bio, stifling a yelp as his sharp claws pricked my stomach, I marched out of the café.

Rev, holding my leash, hustled me through a narrow alley to a secluded nook, the kind usually frequented by lovers or spies.

He looked from side to side, behind him and above. No one was with us but dead leaves and pigeon droppings. He said, "Mag, are you going to get rid of that thing?"

"No. I like him. And he likes me."

The bio had popped his head out of my shirt and was looking around, sunlight glinting off his shiny eye. "You don't wanna go, do you, little guy?" He hopped out of my shirt and onto the ground. In seconds he was gone.

"Drat! I wanted to look at that torn ear."

"I didn't know you were so soft-hearted."

I crossed my arms and pouted. I really like bios, not just the pretty ones. Unlike *some* people.

Rev sighed. "Okay, let me fill you in on current events. You must be aware that my uncle, Trent-haut Quel Naroo, has been taken hostage in Arderia."

His uncle Quel, who had killed Rev's father a couple of years ago. And somehow made Rev's mother disappear. Right. That much was coming back to me. "Uh… nope. Taken hostage, huh? Where's Arderia?"

"Really?" He began to tear at his thumbnail with his teeth, noticed he was doing it and stopped. "Look, I'm sorry about the collar. It's for two reasons—one, to keep you from vanishing again. Two, to display the fact that, despite Trent-haut Quel's situation, things here are under control. Spies and Retrievers aren't just running around loose on *my* watch. At least, not a lot of them."

There were more of us in town? Why did I not know that?

His thumb crept towards his mouth again, and I felt a sudden ridiculously maternal flood of… love. Completely unexpected.

Really thought I was over it. I grabbed his hand and pulled it down. "What's this Trent-haut Quel to you anyway? He got himself captured, so what?"

"You're really going to pretend you don't know?"

I sighed. "Why don't you tell me what the problem is, Rev?"

"The problem is that everyone thinks I arranged it."

"And didn't you?"

He glared at me. "There are certain people who want to pin it on me." He rubbed his forehead. "Do they actually think I *want* to be Trent-haut?"

"So you *don't* want ultimate power over the district of Nagala-sur-mer?"

"You know, you were always an annoying brat. It's good to know some things never change. Let's get out of here."

We exited the cul-de-sac into the bustling streets again. I caught sight of a slinking form and hoped it might be the bio, but it was just a matted and angry-looking doggish herding a flock of geese. He glanced at me suspiciously and mumbled a curse before urging his charges along. The fact that I wore a collar and the doggish didn't really pissed me off.

"Where are you dragging me now?" I asked grumpily. "For some nice crumble cake with caramel sauce? I could sure go for some crumble cake with—ow!"

"Shut up. I'm taking you back to your cell."

"So, no cake. You know, I'm less than impressed with the quality of—"

He yanked at my leash, making me lose balance and stumble into him. He bent my head back by pulling my hair, and kissed me. Hard. After a few moments I came to my senses and tried to knee him in the groin, but he dodged adroitly.

I put a hand to my lips. "What was *that* about?"

"Only way to shut you up."

I felt dizzy. "Well, don't do it again!"

Until I've had a bath and changed into something other than filthy pants and tunic… then maybe you can do it again…

We wended our way back to the bowels of Nagala City's governmental block. "My troucat had better be untouched," I threatened as he pushed me into my familiar cell. "If anyone has tried to interrogate him, the full weight of Clan Grey will come down on you like, like…"

"Right, a ton of ox manure, whatever. No one has touched him. Clan Grey can relax."

*

CHAPTER THREE

Could there be others like myself and Kat in Nagala City? Clan Grey had three teams, and the five other Clans probably twelve between them, all presumably busily at work swiping this and that. It stood to reason that the most espionage-worthy stuff would be here in the capital city. Something besides the Uncle Quel thing must be going on…

I felt Kat wake up. When I opened his case, he jumped up and cuddled into my neck. His thoughts were clearer now. Trivial, but clear. *Where ya been? Didja bring me anything?* Then he buried his snout in my chest. *Hey, what's that smell?*

I gave him a quick view of the wild bio, which seemed to calm him down. Okay, if Kat didn't care, why should I?

He still had our orders in his ganglia nodes, and the orders involved us penetrating the archive vaults and stealing something. No surprise. That's what we did for a living. Proprietary information, genomes, samples, plans, seeds and eggs. Other teams went after jewels, timepieces and suchlike, whatever would mean credits in hand. But what were we after, now? He seemed oddly evasive, and refused to look at me. *I'm hungry! Where's the food?*

Kat, though gorgeous to look at, is kind of shallow. I dug some greasy nuggets out of my pocket and handed them over. He gobbled them eagerly. He didn't care where I'd been, or with whom, as long as I was back now. It was all about *now* for troucats.

"Kat. I need to know what I'm doing here."

Kat's tail was twitching and I could tell his eye was avoiding mine.

"Kat. I *need* to know."

After licking grease off his paws, Kat hopped off my lap and settled on his haunches a few feet away, tucking his forefeet together primly. His eye's focal point, a tiny specialized area behind the wide iridescent sheath, locked into the gels in my eyes. The gel-fish never went beyond egg stage, fortunately, at least after implanting. So far as the Clan doctors knew, anyhow… Getting them installed had been a highlight of my budding career, a sign of true commitment.

Updates through Kat's eye were fast and silent and impossible to intercept, but also could be insanely hard to understand. The gels supposedly sent data directly to my brain, eliminating the retinal middle man for immediate capture, but I still had a few training sessions to attend.

You know what I know, he sent. A ritual phrase. *We must Retrieve blurrrrr.*

"What? Retrieve what?" With a squint I focused the gels harder.

"Blurrrrr."

It was the visual equivalent of a garbled mutter. Where normally there would be a detailed, tidy image of what we were going after and exactly where it was, now floated a blank spot, like a fog-filled bubble.

"Come on, Kat, don't be annoying."

You know what I know. We must retrieve blurrrr.

"Argh! What is *blurrrr*?"

Kat looked away regally. He hated when I started to shout. He also hated being forced to disgorge the data in his nodes, for so often it meant he'd be accompanying me into danger. But this time it wasn't fear I detected, but a sense of huge responsibility. In his node was the image of something he—we—*had* to do.

"Kat, if you are deliberately keeping necessary information from me, I'll, I'll…"

Kat had teeth. He showed them now. They were clear as crystal, needle-sharp and multitudinous.

"Fine! Be that way!"

The sound of fast, heavy footsteps penetrated my anger. The cell door crashed open and Rev burst in, panting. He had a pack slung over one shoulder, and his belt was lavishly hung with two short-swords, a stunner, a coil of rope, and a pouch of… I don't know. Soldier stuff.

"Get up!" he shouted. "We have to go!"

I didn't move. "Go where, exactly?"

"Somewhere other than here. Now!" He reached down, picked me up with both hands and hustled me out of the cell. "Orders to take me dead or alive just went out. Come *on*!"

He put me down and began to stride back the way he'd come, obviously expecting me to follow him. Dead or alive?

To his retreating back, I said, "You don't really need me along, do you? I mean, I could just tell people you went the other way, or something." This was my opportunity to escape. Kat and I could get back to business. Rev could take care of himself.

He turned and strode back, muttering under his breath. This time his grip was painful. "You are coming with me."

"Ow! Why didn't you just say so—" I made a grab for his short sword.

"Quit that! Can you just be quiet and follow orders?"

"You're the one shouting. Plus, I'm not one of your soldiers."

Kat's tail went around my neck and tightened. And tightened some more. I gasped and stumbled. "Can't… breathe…"

Rev tried to pry Kat's tail away, but got an open-paw swat across the cheek for his trouble. Three thin lines of blood sprang forth. "What's wrong with that blasted thing?"

"Ack! Don't… know…"

But then I did. *We are going the wrong way.* We had to go down, not up; not leave the dungeons of Nagala and their quarantined archive vaults, but penetrate them further. We had to carry out our mission.

"Our mission is over, Kat! We've been captured, understand?"

Irrelevant.

"What?"

Eliminate male, carry out mission.

"Eliminate—no! Kat, we're done, we're getting out of here."

I forbid it.

My body suddenly filled with something that felt like hot oil. It started at my feet and washed upward. I knew instinctively that if it got to my nostrils, I would be dead. This sort of ultimate mind control is a troucat's last resort. For a moment I wondered if Kat had gone mad, or had been suborned by an enemy. But his intent was strong and clear.

"Rev? Ugh! Can't... go with you. Have to carry out... mission."

Rev kept prying at Kat's tail. "I can't leave you behind. Not after so long—"

I backed away, and Kat's grip loosened a bit. I had an allegiance to my bio that superseded any I might once have held toward Rev. "You have to go," I croaked. "I don't have a death sentence on me. Scoot. I'll be all right."

Shouting sounded from above, and Rev clenched his teeth. He muttered, "I get it. That creature is ordering you around. You could just ditch him, you know, and come with me." He held out a hand.

"Never." Kat's tail loosened some more. The oil receded.

"Okay. You leave me no choice." He grabbed my hand and hustled us along the corridor toward the stairs leading down. Down! Yes!

Gasping for much-needed air, I said, "You don't have to do this! I can—"

"I'm sure you *can*, it's a question of *may*. You *may not* get out of my sight."

The stairs were dark and slimy, and we had to grope our way down, the air getting more and more noxious. But the sounds of the hunt receded. No one would expect the disgraced Circ-haut to head for the lowest levels of the dungeons, would they?

"Just what is this mission, anyway?" he asked.

"Like I would know."

"Oh, great. It's in that ridiculous creature's head. You need to find out, and fast."

"What a great idea. Why it didn't occur to me I'll never—"

"Shut *up*!" He pushed me ahead of him into a tiny room containing a lot of dust, a small table holding sharp metal devices, and a skeleton hanging from chains.

"What under the stars goes on down here?" I asked, appalled.

"In here? Nothing. It's for show." He pulled the heavy door shut. "Well, the skeleton is real, but we got it from the teaching hospital in Corusca." He turned to me. "Okay, we're safe for a minute or two. Get that bio to spill it."

The time for evasion was past. Besides, I was miffed at Kat too. "I'll try." I unwound him from my neck and rested my forehead against his eye patch. It was shiny but resilient, like a film of soft glass miraculously sewn to his head. Staring directly at his focal point, so close my eyes crossed, I sent him an urgent pulse of *query/crisis/distress*.

He should have maps in his nodes, alternative routes, code words for passage through checkpoints, everything I might need to Retrieve whatever it was.

Kat squirmed in my hands, but complied. *Ah*. I was starting to see it. I have always imagined that someday I would start to feel my gels hatch and grow like tadpoles inside my eyes. Gives me bad dreams.

I heard his little inner voice. *You know what I know.* And I did. I could see our path, and knew which way to go. It was like a map suddenly illuminating.

And then I saw the thing we were here to find. Oh. My.

Swallowing carefully, I put Kat back on my shoulder. Rev was looking at me as if I might know where God was. Perhaps I did.

"We need to go down three more levels," I told him.

"There are only two more levels."

"That's what *you* think. Come on."

Rev, Kat and I stood peering through translucent patches in the thick, sinewy membrane that stretched across a wide cell door. The membrane was a specialized bio meant to contain a dangerous life form, a sort of cocoon designed never to open. Ever. The stuff was tougher than anything mankind could construct, and it looked like it was stretched tight. Something very big and very not-human was in there.

Rev dumped his pack on the floor and squinted at the creature dimly viewable within the membrane. Not a nice simple scroll, or topaz, or magic calculating machine or something. A dratted bio.

"What *is* that thing?" he asked. "I swear I had no idea anything was down here."

Whatever it was, it wasn't moving. It didn't have room to. Kat hopped to position on my shoulder and began to lash his tail. I think he was smacking his lips. I could feel his emotions, and they had a this-is-it flavour. Now or never. "What are we gonna do, Kat? That bio is locked up tight!"

He quivered on his hind legs for a second, then leapt off my shoulder and clung to the vertical surface of the membrane. The thing on the other side shuddered. It looked greyish and extremely large. I hoped it wasn't planning which one of us to eat first as soon as it busted out.

Rev, watching Kat, exclaimed, "Hey! What's he doing?" He

stepped back, pulling me with him.

Kat's mouth was pressed against the impermeable membrane of the bio-cell's containment protocol, tearing it with his teeth.

But, impermeable. Right?

Wrong.

From Kat's mouth squirted a fluid that ate away the membrane as if it were silky lingerie.

Kat had never told me about this little talent of his, this ability to excrete caustic spit. All those times he'd tenderly licked my face…

He must know what he was doing. Was this our mission? Retrieve a sample of the thing's flesh and get it home to Clan Grey for study, or cloning, or whatever? We'd collected samples of bios before, but nothing this weird.

The membrane suddenly let go, splitting open like overcooked fish skin. A puff of fetid air blew out.

"Okay, Kat! Grab a sample and let's go!"

All Kat had to do was get in close, find a tender spot and bite out a chunk. The chunk would remain safely in his esophageal pouch until it was delivered to the Clan's proprietary archives, where its genome would be interpreted and utilized. I had a feeling that maybe this sample would yield something battle-ready.

Kat hopped up onto the grey slab that was the cell's occupant.

But instead of nipping off a chunk, he placed his eye upon what I now could see was a smooth patch on the thing's forelump. Couldn't really call it a fore*head*.

Just like other bios, it had a sensory patch, though it looked rudimentary, not glassy and wide like Kat's. But the two of them were communing.

Then, with a grinding scrape, like a sarcophagus being dragged across an ancient cathedral floor, the creature turned. It opened a set of tiny eyes in the wall of flesh below its patch. It looked at me. My heart gave a lurch.

Its eyes, all three of them, were small, beady and desperate. They flicked back and forth while some kind of palps or arms on its forequarters waved ineffectually. It looked pathetic. Not horrifying, or invincible, or even argumentative. Pathetic.

Kat hopped out of the cell and clung to a rocky outcropping at the huge bio's eye level, whisking his tail and making cute little mewing sounds. The thing's eyes turned toward Kat with the fervour of a captured princess onto her rescuer, and its little palps fluttered. I found myself biting back tears.

Oh, for God's sake. "Kat! Get 'er done!"

Rev had a sword in one hand and my elbow in the other. I shook him off. The creature shrank back timidly, limited by clinging shreds of the membrane trying to re-form.

Rev barked, "Get your troucat under control, Mag, before that thing gets out!"

"Yeah, yeah…" I reached out a hand and touched the thing. It felt like warm concrete.

Kat and I had retrieved many items over the years and all the operations had gone without more than minor hitches. Some amusing, some not so much. He had never gone against explicit orders, either mine or the Clan's. Kat was up to something.

The big lumpy critter—who I decided to name Critter—looked distantly related to some of the worker bios I'd seen around the countryside, slogging away at excavation or harvesting or whatever it was they did all day. It was much too big for the cell it occupied and might have burst through the membrane if the membrane weren't insidiously tough.

Not as tough, apparently, as my little Kat.

It crossed my mind to wonder how long Critter had been in there. Had it started out small, been put inside, then simply forgotten?

"Kat, sweetie, we have to get going. Can you hurry it up

please? Pretty please?"

Kat turned to me and snapped, *Shut up.*

"Why, you little—"

Critter turned some more, the heavy scraping sound shivering my bones. He, she, or it began to stretch out, tentatively extending a stubby foot toward the floor. Okay, *she.* Let's call it she, babbled my brain. Those imploring little eyes…

She most closely resembled a tray piled high with greyish, overcooked meat, complete with bits of hide stuck on here and there. Nasty, yet somehow heart-rending. Was Kat adopting a pet?

Were we acquiring an asset, or a liability?

Critter's blocky legs and feet, the first of several, stepped out of the cell. They met the ground with a crunch, and she hesitated, glancing fearfully at Kat, who seemed to be leading Critter toward the corridor.

"I'm not perfectly sure, but it looks like Kat wants this poor thing to accompany us."

"*Poor thing?* Gah!" Rev grabbed his head with both hands. "What is wrong with me? Why am I even here?" Rhetorical questions, yet perfectly valid. "I'm going to scout for an exit that doesn't lead us smack into my former colleagues. You three can either follow me, or not."

He peeked around the anteroom's doorway, then strode off into the darkness.

Critter assembled herself outside the cell, and began to glance around. I could swear the thing was curious. The meat-slabs had conglomerated into a lengthy wall-like structure, studded with bony projections like a stone-lizard's ancient skeleton, so large that she was forced to curl around the room's perimeter. Her face, mostly a flat wall of grey with a hairy patch at the top, consisted of those three little eyes arrayed in a wide triangle, and the shiny patch Kat had used to commune with. If she had a mouth, it was somewhere else. I could hazard no guess as to what made her tick.

Kat hopped back onto my shoulder. I glared into his eye. "Please tell me all we're doing is setting her free. We can go now, right?"

This is mission. Must deliver mission.

"We're stealing the whole thing? How are we gonna do that? We're stuck in the very bottom of the dungeon."

Footsteps pounded along the corridor, rapidly getting closer. Rev burst in, drew his sword, and whirled to face the narrow doorway. "They found me! Get back! I'll fight them off as long as—"

Kat hissed, Critter twitched and suddenly there was a barrier of stony meat blocking the door.

The Circ-haut, deprived of his heroic fight, kicked at the barrier. "Great! Now we're trapped!"

Kat jumped back and pressed his head against mine. A vision formed, like a tiny picture of the huge building we were in. It began to turn and shift nauseatingly, as if I were falling. Turned out there was yet another level below this one, and I'll bet no one but Kat—and whoever gave him his orders—knew about it.

But we were stuck in this small anteroom, nothing but the membrane-cell behind us, which even Critter hadn't been able to escape, and a squad of well-trained, money-hungry soldiers in front.

How were we supposed to reach the next level?

But wait—we were in possession of the planet's craziest battering ram. "Kat! Critter can get us through this! Tell her what to do!"

There must be something final below us. We were about to find out. There was no other choice.

*

CHAPTER FOUR

Going into the water was like falling off a tower, followed by the tower.

Not only did Critter blast through the anteroom floor with a few stomps of her feet, she seemed to have initiated demolition of the whole place. The huge stones of the cell, the corridor—maybe the whole building—crumbled loose and plummeted close behind us into the river that washed the dark underbelly of Nagala City.

I had no idea what would become of the men outside the cell door… maybe they had run for it, screaming like teenage recruits.

Rev and I, with Kat clinging to my head, bobbed to the surface and let ourselves be carried along on the crest of the wave the falling rocks had produced.

Resonant rumbles and splashes sounded behind us. I found myself able to see, if dimly. The patches of luminescent algae placed years ago by the city planners had been growing for a long, long time. A network of illumination arched overhead, like green-gold lace, intricate and glimmering, and it extended to within an arm's length of the water's surface all along the immense tunnel. The reason for the gap appeared. A thing rather like a giant pink eel, with a groping suction-mouth at the end, blundered its way upward and began nibbling at the algae's fringe.

River worms. I could see them around me by the glow of their algae-filled digestive tracts. My toes curled as I trod water, and I looked around, alarmed.

"Critter! Critter, where are you?"

Had she escaped her prison only to drown, or be eaten by worms?

I sucked in a breath, ducked my head and looked underwater.

There on the bottom, about five arm-lengths down, trundled Critter. Apparently she lacked buoyancy. Or lungs. Driven by the current, she bounced along looking up blearily. She was propelling herself with her stubby legs, like some kind of ancient Earth hipposaurus. I didn't see any worms nearby. Also, I could swear she was a wee bit larger than before…

I raised my head and took a breath. Rev churned along beside me.

Doing the sidestroke, I puffed, "So, *did* you arrange your uncle's capture?"

"Right about now I really wish I had."

"I really wish you had killed the son of a bitch."

"Ah, so it's starting to come back to you."

A pause while we forged along. There was nowhere to crawl ashore in the ancient tunnel.

"Good thing is," panted Rev, "night's coming. Maybe we won't be spotted when we come out from under the buildings."

"What about when Critter tries to walk up on shore? Even in the dark she'll be pretty hard to miss."

"Yeah. They'll probably be after us with sight-hounds. They can spot an extra candle at an Aura's Birthday celebration," said Rev. They didn't just see light, they saw heat, and maybe politically incorrect thought-waves too.

At last we reached the outfall—unfortunately nowhere near the perimeter gates of Nagala's sprawling outskirts. We still had a long way to go. The water fled before us into the dark, with a pattern of reflections popping in as street lamps came awake.

The rusty remains of a long-ago security barrier provided a place to cling, and plan our next move. The sounds of the city filtered down from above: the bleating and whir of cars, shouting doggishes, a far-off chorus of sirens. Our destructive escape was gaining traction.

The river ran in a channel cut by the First People and had

been utilized as a conduit for detritus to rejoin its mother lode of muck for centuries, gradually being buried under human-built roads and buildings, along with other evidence of this world's previous occupants. There were probably forgotten access points all over the place. It was a city on top of a city. Humans, moving in to the abandoned pile centuries ago, had never quite gotten around to mapping the whole thing.

My fingers were pruny. "Kat. What's the plan?"

In answer, he leapt off my head onto the gate's sagging hinges and scampered out of sight. My bond-being was reconnoitring. A good thing, except for the propensity of the city's denizens to stroll in the cool air looking for booze and entertainment. Lots of eyes on the lookout for fun, or cute troucats. Or would the city be under lockdown by now? The hunt for Revenbrook Karel was on, plus what we'd just done to Headquarters.

I looked at Rev and he looked at me. His hair was plastered over his skull, and a bit of something brown clung to one cheek. He looked furious, bitter and very wet. I'm sure I looked about as bad.

Critter oozed her way above water nervously. Her tuft of hair appeared, then her patch, then her top eye. After taking a look at the two of us, she sank beneath the water again.

I couldn't blame her. I'd thought I'd managed to forget Rev, yet here he was in the midst of my operation. He shouldn't even be here, and he kept trying to take charge. I lifted my lip in a half-hearted snarl, and he blew out his cheeks.

"Don't give me the stink-eye, little girl—I was only trying to help."

"Well, we don't need help. Why don't you just swim back upriver and start paying people off, get yourself back in favour. That's what you fancy-pants glorified bureaucrats do."

"See, this is why I got rid of you last time."

"Got rid of me? I escaped! It was hard! I had bruises for

weeks." I never should have gone to see him in the first place. Stupid, girlish longing had destroyed my brain. But I'd wanted to know if he still... loved me. Unfortunately, I'd been mistaken for a spy by his Uncle Quel, who, I found out later, had been in the midst of planning Rev's father's assassination. How was I supposed to know? No one, including Rev, had seen it coming. Quel Naroo could give lessons in two-faced lying.

"I let you go! I went directly against orders, just for you!"

"Well, thanks a lot. I ended up right back where I started. At least you didn't *let* me escape this time. We both got out by the skin of our teeth."

He laughed hollowly. "Yeah, well, our tooth skin is wearing thin. Where's that troucat of yours? Aren't they supposed to stay close to their master?"

I snorted, liberating something chunky that had made it up my nose. "Master? Are you kidding? In case you hadn't noticed, Kat is in complete control."

"Control of what? Critter? What *is* that thing, and where are we going with it?"

"We can trust Kat," I proclaimed loyally. "He has a plan—"

Rev suddenly swatted at my forehead.

"Hey! What the—"

A small green point of light flashed across his shoulders to his chin, then zipped back to me. I crossed my eyes trying to see it.

Rev yanked me underwater. I clamped my mouth shut as we let the current take us. Just as I was about to panic and gasp water we burst to the surface, near the opposite shore.

Rev sucked in air. "Sight-hounds! They've found us."

There was a bridge just ahead, and we made for its black shadow. "But sight-hounds just see, they don't emit light!"

"Not as far as we know. New stuff is always being rolled out." I recalled a statement he'd made once, long ago. I was a rebellious student, he an entitled, arrogant prince in the making. "Now that the *cheval* has been perfected," he'd proclaimed grandly, "I don't care if another bio ever comes along. If I ever…"

"If you ever what? Get to make the rules?" My voice had been tender with an overlay of snotty. That's who I was back then.

"Huh. Well, if I do… we stop. We just stop with the constant development. Have you seen some of the things on sale lately?"

We had never really finished that argument. He'd gone his way, into military service, and I'd gone mine. Into my Clan and its operations, which pays surprisingly little. Clinging under the bridge, I peered around for more green dots. None so far. "But if they aren't sight-hounds, then what's doing that?"

There was a low chirp from above. Kat! At last! A gust of relief warmed my extremities briefly, then I started to shiver. We crawled up on a rocky patch of shoreline where the bridge supports thrust into rock. Kat chirped again. *Come up.*

"You got any towels, you little jerk? Some hot mulled wine? No? Then why should I come up?" This muttered as I scrambled up the bank as fast as I could, followed by Rev. I glanced back for Critter and spotted a tuft of damp hair, encrusted with flotsam. She was okay… and I hoped she wouldn't decide to just keep going down the river. She'd probably never tasted freedom.

The green dot settled on the tuft.

"No!" I shouted. "Critter! Get down!" I started to toss rocks at Critter to make her sink out of sight. Instead she heaved herself higher, emitted an excited yawp—somehow—and started to emerge from the river. It was a frightening sight, in two ways. One, she was crazy weird even by the standards of my world, and two, I feared for her safety. I realized the dots must be guidance for soldiers' aim. Clever. Another military development, courtesy of the bio-mongers.

Any second now, a rain of cling-arrows would shower down on her and begin to burrow into her skin. Or husk or whatever.

But it didn't. Critter galumphed eagerly up the steep incline and eventually piled herself in the middle of the road. Which was deserted. I realized why.

Flashes of angry orange light came from the northeast, flaring quickly, reflecting off the low clouds, followed closely by deep booms and echoing crashes.

Rev stood watching, a sword in his hand and a snarl on his lips. "Ha! It's happening!"

"What's happening? Did Critter do all that?"

"Of course not. The revolution has begun," he crowed, pumping his sword in the air.

Kat bounded down from one of the boulevard's fig trees to hop aboard my shoulder once more. I stroked him quickly but kept watching. "Is this about your Uncle Quel?" One of the topmost spires of the central complex seemed to be sinking. Suddenly it peeled out of the sky and crumbled away. The familiar skyline was shifting fast. The sound of rumbling and crashing arrived seconds later.

Rev shrugged his shoulders, a smug grin upon his lips. "Maybe…"

"You said you didn't arrange his capture!"

"I didn't. I ordered someone else to arrange his capture. But I don't quite understand who's doing the bombing…"

"Not revolutionaries? What would they be revolting against, exactly? Things are pretty good here."

"You have no idea what's been going on." Rev eyed the pyrotechnics, frowning. "This wasn't supposed to happen, not so soon… and destruction was to be kept to a minimum."

"Whatever. Best laid plans. Listen, if you have a strategy that doesn't involve me, you should implement it now. I am out of here. Critter, Kat, let's go."

Rev, obviously torn between a desire to join the fight and an atavistic urge to protect me, took only a few seconds to make a decision. He planted a quick kiss on my lips, grinned like a maniac, and galloped off toward the explosions.

"Should have seen that coming," I muttered to myself. "Okay, Kat, where to?"

Another map appeared in my head. The funny thing about some of the memories Kat doles out to me is that they seem to have always been there. I know they have just popped in, but they… have a history. It's kind of like what philosophers yammer on about. *What if our world constantly remakes itself? What if each time someone takes one path instead of another, the world reshuffles? And no one knows the difference, no one suspects…*

I'd never paid much attention to oldsters shouting on street corners. If we never know or suspect, then who cares?

Map. Right.

Looked like we were to follow a backstreet route to a section of the city wall that was under renovation. Even half torn down, it would still be hard to get past, what with a revolution in progress. But it gave us a better chance than marching naively to a designated gate and requesting exit.

Kat and I, with Critter scraping along as quietly as she could, crossed the main street, down into a trash-littered ravine, and up again to a low-rent residential district. People were leaning out windows marvelling at the destruction, paying no attention to ground level, fortunately. A few alert citizens were already loading up their skittish vehicles and leaving.

From there, it was a series of dark, narrow twists and turns. Fortunately, Critter turned out to be flexible when stretched out, like a giant caterpillar.

The wall's construction zone was deserted. Kat jittered on my shoulder, emitting threads of emotion. Little twirls of apprehension, with a background chorus of hard determination. Like a production of "The Swan Princess" done by soldiers. Not believable.

We peered from behind a construction shack, scanning the large laydown area, currently studded with piles of material and ranks of heavy equipment. The largest of these, which looked like a multi-purpose truck, shook itself, turned its observation turret 180 degrees and looked at us. The ground began to shudder as it fired up its internal digestive engines.

I have never encountered a piece of construction equipment that scared me. Until now. High atop the truck's turret perched an ominous crouched figure, with an eye that glowed brilliant green.

Suddenly I had a dot right in the middle of my chest.

CHAPTER FIVE

Okay. It's just a guide dot. Calm down. But… could the creature atop the truck be the Admiral of the Bios? The General of a rag-tag army bent on overthrowing humans?

If so, he was kind of small.

Kat's claws dug into my shoulder. The green dot whisked over to Critter, then zipped between me and Kat. The giant truck lurched toward us, its strange rider shooting green beams as if it were blinking rapidly.

Critter emitted a soft moan, then stumbled eagerly toward the truck.

I prudently dodged out of the way, but Kat leapt for the truck. I was pretty confident by now that there were no soldiers around. I blessed the revolutionaries for luring everyone away, while watching moodily as the two behemoths crashed together and settled into a pattern of playful circling.

The small stranger jumped off the truck and slunk toward me, Kat following, bouncing around like a puppy. The creature looked like Kat the same way a pine cone looks like a rose. You know they are related, they're kind of the same size, but…

But wait. I knew him! It was my little bio pal from the café. What was he doing here?

"Hey, little guy! Remember me?" He was obviously used to living rough. Where Kat was delicate and fastidious, this fellow was teetering on the edge of derelict canyon, about to fall right in. What was he up to?

The wild bio *looked* at me. Whoa. This was like when Kat did it, but way more so. I felt my gels throb and my brain expand.

Yep, he remembered me. A very tactile feeling of fur rubbing against skin tickled my chest. As if he were still sheltering under my shirt. *Hey, glad to help,* I thought. *Who are you?* Would he be able to commune with me as Kat did?

Yes. In a way.

I am Hsssss. That's what it sounded like in my mind. *Hsssss.* No single ordinary word fit what he was, but it sort of meant Ancient One Who Marshals Archives. A little like the *Gardiens* of my Clan. The Keepers of what I go out and Retrieve.

Facts flooded in. The creature was a telcat, a very old one. Related closely to troucats, telcats were a variant sub-species less refined in looks but much greater in intellectual capacity. Of course, the way memories were injected into my brain made me believe I'd always known this. Right. Obviously. The boss telcat.

So what had he been doing wandering around the café? Could he have been searching for me? Or, more likely, my troucat? Or maybe for Critter…

My brain squirmed, reluctant to do any more expanding.

Mercifully, he dropped his gaze, and I rubbed my eyes. If the cats were ganging up on humans, I was on board. The telcat prowled briefly around me like an evil little pirate, then he sat on his haunches just as primly as Kat ever did. Oh, yeah. Related.

I turned to Kat. "Uh, d'*you* know what's going on?"

Kat chirped and jumped to my shoulder. *Do you really want to know?*

"Uh… yes?"

Very well. Are you ready?

I took a breath and nodded.

Suddenly I found myself on the ground with two bundles of fur in my lap. One was purple and slinky, the other grey and stinky. Both of them radiated so much information I couldn't possibly sort it out. I just let it wash over me. So no, I hadn't been ready.

By the time Rev loped out of the darkness, I was in tears and my head felt about to explode.

Rev skidded to a stop and glared at me.

"H-how did you find us?" I quavered, overwhelmed by the historical drama that flooded from the cats.

"You've got *two* of those things now? I leave you alone for a few minutes—"

"A few minutes? I thought you were never coming back!"

"Of course I was coming back, I—"

"Just shut up! You and your revolution—that's hilarious!"

He gave me and the occupants of my lap an intensely dirty look, for which I couldn't blame him. He'd had his heart set on the revolution. Toss Uncle Quel in a dungeon, rally his men, take over… All gone.

He leaned forward and plucked a tiny sticky something out of my hair and squashed it between his fingers. "I needed to be able to find you again, so I bugged you. Now I'm wondering why." He jerked his chin at Critter and Truck. "What's with those two?"

"They're in love." I wiped my nose and sighed. "I need to tell you about Critter."

"Okaaay…"

"Critter is the last surviving prototype of a…" I waved my free hand, the one that wasn't stroking the telcat's healthy ear. The other ear still needed treatment, and I had to figure out a way to get it for him. "…a sort of shunting unit. She's like a central nexus of information… a library. A really big library. Everything's in there, and she can call up, organize, and disseminate it upon command. The right command. Which she hasn't had in, oh, two hundred years or so."

"Huh?"

"Sit down, take a load off your brain." I patted the ground next to me. He sat, eyeing Critter dubiously. "Since she's a prototype—the ultimate model was never made—she's been unable to self-regulate. Or even call for help. She… she sat in that horrible cell for decades, waiting, slowly growing into a stunted shell of what she might have been. All she w-wanted was to be a librarian. Instead, she spent the historical span of human life on this planet In. A. Cell." I paused to wipe my eyes with a sleeve. "In *your* city, Circ-haut."

"*My* city? I didn't even know there was another level! I swear no one knew she was down there." Critter was nestled firmly against Truck's gently rumbling flank, or fender, or whatever. "So… d'you think she could be one of the First People? Could they have put her in there?"

"Maybe. But why would they do that? Could some reactionary faction have feared her?" Knowledge is power, after all.

He turned back to me and clenched his fists. "Do you know what this means, Mag?"

What was wrong with him? "Yes! It means she's finally free! She's even found love!" The telcat hopped out of my lap and stretched. Kat followed him and began to lick his ear. Their tails twined together and their eyes drilled into mine, and I wished forlornly that I had a couple of heavy-duty painkillers on hand.

"No. It means we are in big trouble," said Rev, contemplating Critter's immense size. "Do you know what I saw when I went back to the city centre?"

"Why do you keep asking stupid questions?"

"I saw bios. Lots of them, local workers and wild ones from outside. *They* were the revolutionaries. Not my men." He laughed grimly. "Somehow they must have got wind of… Critter. Being released. By the *other* First People, I presume. That's what's happening, right?"

"How the dickens should I know?"

I started to notice that the night was boiling louder and louder with noise: sirens, crackling shots, animals and bios and humans running around screaming. Smoke was in the air. "You know, the city wall isn't doing much of a job at keeping wild bios out."

The telcat *looked* at me, and I couldn't look away. I had a choice with Kat; I could deliberately ignore his messages to me. But not with this one.

You are wrong, the telcat said, directly into my brain. He needed a name, and I couldn't do *Hsssss*. Pressed for time, I decided to go with Tel. *The wall is to keep you humans in.*

That seemed a bit harsh. I pointed at Kat, outraged. "This mission was Kat's all along, and you—both of you—used me!"

I thank you, human, for your kindness earlier. It shall be taken under consideration.

Well, that was nice I guess.

And we are not the First People.

"What're they saying?" demanded Rev, who wasn't privy to

the eye-talk. "I need to take command! I wonder if that dead-or-alive order has been rescinded..."

I ignored him, as did the cats. What did Tel mean, they weren't the First People? It had always been taught that the bios were the degenerate remnants of a once-advanced civilization on this world, who had built the cities, the canals and the manufacturing facilities that produced new bios. And then had sunk into anarchy.

Suddenly that wasn't on the curriculum anymore.

I wanted to pout, but now was not the time. I had the feeling that history was being made.

Tel's ratty grey ears lifted, sagged and lifted again, as if he were picking up a signal. Maybe he was. Maybe the Queen of the Cats was out there, ordering airships to deliver more bombs to the city, and worker bios to help princesses escape. Truck had fired back up and awakened his co-workers, who were well on the way to demolishing the wall. Critter looked on adoringly. How long had the bios been bamboozling us humans? We thought we ruled the world.

Critter seemed to be the catalyst. Had all this been brewing for two centuries?

I wondered suddenly if I could commune directly with Critter, like I did with Kat and Tel. Theoretically it should be possible... but even contemplating it made my stomach heave. She held a world's worth of information. What if my head really *did* explode?

I gestured at the widening gap in the wall. "So, Kat, what now? We'll leave if the bios want, but where do we go?" Going back into the city was a bad idea. We'd be bucking a tidal wave of citizens who were all heading for the gates, unaware they were escaping the burning city to run straight into angry bios.

I'd been outside, of course. It was part of Clan life and it was fun, as long as you followed the rules and minded your manners. There were bios who dealt with humans all the time, organizing trade deals, prisoner swaps, water rights and so on. We had things they wanted, and vice versa.

Some of the bios were the first to display exotic variants of their own kind. Slave traders. Panderers? Or infiltrators with a long-term goal…

Tel stood and emitted a low growl. It was the first time he'd made any kind of audible sound. His green dot was back, and it flashed first on Kat, then on Critter. Perhaps it was something he couldn't control, like a hysterical laugh.

Goodbye, said Kat's voice in my head. *Mission.* He hopped off my shoulder and scampered to Tel's side. No!

"Hey!" I squeaked, dismayed. "What do you mean, goodbye? Kat, wait for me!" Rev grabbed my arm and drew me to a stop. I struggled uselessly. "Let me go!"

"Mag. No." He pulled me close, enfolding me in his arms. I watched, my throat closing painfully, as Tel, Kat and, after a long look of regret at Truck, Critter joined the line and headed for the newly opened wall.

I pushed Rev away and ran after them. "Hey," I yelled, "humans are kind of like bios, y'know! Plus, I have gel-fish in me—what do you say to that? Huh? What am I supposed to do with them now?"

I heard Rev run after me, and I knew he was going to drag me back. But I couldn't let Kat go without a fight. I dodged, tears stinging my eyes, but then I saw something approaching from out of the darkness beyond the wall. It had the characteristic gait of a human, but was accompanied by something definitely *not* human. A low, slinking form that made my hackles rise. Somewhere stored in the human brain-stem is the shape of a wolf, and this was it. Our sense of smell is terrible, our hearing is sub-standard, but there's nothing wrong with our eyesight.

The approaching human strode onto the construction site like a warrior. A woman. She looked kind of familiar… but where would I have encountered her? She was mature, muscled like a soldier and attired like one too. She stood with her legs apart and her hand on her sword, her wolf-creature beside her. Her face was tanned and weathered, her silver hair chopped short. She was smiling.

That smile would have made me turn and run but for Rev at my back.

He stepped forward, and said, "Mom? Is… is that you?"

I frowned. It couldn't be. She looked completely different from the slender, quiet Lady I remembered.

Critter, Kat and Tel had vanished outside. Truck rotated his turret, scanned the area and found it not to his liking. Apparently rethinking his work contract, he revved his engines and joined the parade, jouncing over the remnants of the wall.

The woman strode up to us, thrust her sword back into its scabbard and grabbed Rev by the cheeks. She squeezed them. "Goodness, you're so big and handsome! How long has it been?"

In a split second they were hugging.

Really? Now, his mom turns up? Where was she when he was moping around pretending he didn't care that she had fallen into the clutches of Quel Naroo? I tapped her on the shoulder, and jumped back when she turned on me. "Whoa! Take it easy. Everyone thought you were dead."

"Yeah, Mom," said Rev. "What's been going on?"

A cold smile curved her lips. "Yes, I suppose everyone *did* think I'd died. Of *natural causes*. Quel made sure of that, didn't he?" The smile vanished as she gazed regally at me. "And who might this… person be?"

I did *not* like her tone. "Who might *I* be? I might be about to kick your—"

Rev grabbed my hand. "You remember Magdalena. She's my

girlfriend."

"Ah, yes. It's coming back to me. Delightful." Her steely eyes glinted as they scanned my unimpressive form.

Great. Mother-in-law troubles and Rev and I weren't even dating. But… girlfriend…?

"So Mom," said Rev, "this is a new look for you. I like it. Not sure Dad would have approved, though."

She snorted, then looked back at me. "I have retaken my birth name: Corona Teilard Rendou. You may call me Rendou. Was that a troucat I noted on my way in?"

"Yes it was. His name is Kat, and we are bonded. I am Magdalena Hunter, Retriever Clan Grey," I chirped brightly.

An eyebrow went up, and she scrutinized me with sudden intensity. "Ah. You possess a bio."

"Actually, it's mutual… but I'm not sure it's still the case. Looks like the bios are revolting."

"Heh. Some of them aren't so bad," she deadpanned. "Some are quite lovely, your troucat for instance." She tapped her lips gently with a finger. "You may have surmised that I am presently aligned with the bios."

The wolf, who had been sitting at her side, tongue lolling out, chuckled. "Prrrhaps y'll change yerrr mind now, M'lady."

She gave his large, pointy ears a stroke. "Allow me to introduce Fang, my compatriot. He's one of a strain of bios you humans—I mean, *we* humans—constructed shortly after landing on this world. He still hasn't forgiven us."

Fang laughed, a rolling sound that came from deep within his furry chest. He wasn't a wolf, of course; in fact he bore more than a faint resemblance to Kat. His ears were fringed with mobile tendrils, and he had the characteristic single eye in a wide shiny patch above his snout. A sob of loss started up my throat—*Kat, you ungrateful wretch, how could you leave me?*— but I swallowed it back.

Rendou took her son by the arm and leaned close. I tagged along as they strode toward the wall. "Have you," she murmured to him, "heard anything about Quel Naroo? What he's up to these days?"

Rev straightened with pride. "He's not up to much. He's in custody in Arderia, awaiting trial. Assuming things don't go tits-up with this bio rebellion business."

"In custody? You mean he isn't dead yet?" Her eyes flared wide and I believe she started to salivate. Then her look became calculating. "Hmm. Good. Custody."

Rev gave her a suspicious look, as did I. The man who killed her husband, safe and sound and awaiting the syrupy workings of the justice system. If someone killed Kat—or Rev—I'd want to rip them limb from limb with my bare hands.

Rendou glanced around, noting the increasing civilian activity at the wall's breach. The official gates must be clogged up. "We need to get out of here. An organized retaliation may start soon. Not that I have much confidence in the average Nagala City soldier, but still. Oh, sorry, dear." She sketched a quick salute at her son, turned and strode away.

"Dad had a heck of a time with her," Rev remarked. "I'm glad he's not here to see this."

I was getting beyond sorrow and back into annoyed at Kat for leaving me. He had a lot of my memories still inside his head. However, Rev's mom seemed like a good bet for the immediate future. She was in cahoots with the bios… but did she actually have authority among them?

I looked down at Fang, who cocked his head at me and lolled his tongue happily.

He nudged my leg with his snout. "Afterrr you, m'dear," he said. We all followed Rendou as she marched out of Nagala City into the Bio Wildlands.

CHAPTER SIX

"I don't know what's gonna happen now that you humans arrrr out. It was an unforeseen side-effect of rrrretrieving the library."

Fang didn't say it in quite that way, what with his dog-like muzzle and long drooly tongue, but that was the gist of it. The fortified cities—Nagala, Corusca, Arderia—were where the natives of this world kept the interlopers. Humans, that is. And all along we had thought the walls were to keep the nasty bios out.

"Look, Fang," I grumped, "I'm not going to feel guilty over being a big bad human. You guys run this place and you know it."

"Harrr. True. But now you know it too."

I wasn't sure they were doing such a great job. After all, they did all the work and didn't even have their own families. Unlike regular animals, bios were sterile. One of their selling points, according to dealers. No unanticipated litters of obstreperous, random freaks all over the place. On the other hand, you couldn't just breed 'em yourself for free.

Looked like the romance between Critter and Truck was going nowhere.

We left the main road, already lined with temporary encampments of alarmed citizenry milling around asking each other what was going on. Most wanted to return to the city, once they noted the intense darkness outside the walls, lit eerily by glimmering bios flitting or lumbering here and there. The city, even when blowing up, was familiar; besides, the destruction and fighting seemed mostly confined to the central areas, not the residential quarters. I wondered if the same thing was happening in the other cities, and bet myself a hot meal that it was.

We hurried to catch up with Kat, Tel, Critter and Truck, our little group skirting campfires under cover of darkness and thick vegetation. Then I spotted Kat scurrying along tree branches overhead. He must have sensed me, for he turned, stopped and waggled his tail. I stood still, not daring to call for him. What if he turned away?

But he didn't. He leapt directly onto my shoulder and snuggled into his familiar spot. My heart swelled, and I couldn't say a word. Not that I was going to let my relief show. He was already snooty enough.

By now I'd figured out where we were headed: the Blue Caves, about ten kilometers away.

The Blue Caves were where humans and bios did business. I'd never been in the actual caves, only in the display areas and front office along with my Clan team, but according to legend they were lined with sapphires, or something. The caves were said to extend for uncharted kilometers, opening onto the fabled Land of the Departed.

Rendou marshalled us into a line and ordered us to climb aboard Truck, who could quickly carry us the rest of the way. I thought this was a fine idea, but Rev decided to be defiant. "Mom, how do you know we can trust this bio? How can we even trust Critter, for that matter?"

"Critter?" Rendou narrowed her eyes.

Rev pointed at the pile of meat slabs that was the main event, the reason for this whole circus. "Mag named her. It. Whatever. That thing has been locked up so long she's probably bat-crap crazy. Plus, how's she supposed to fit in Truck?"

"It can run alongside. According to specifications, it can move pretty fast." Rendou favoured Critter with a maternal smile. "I can't tell you how pleased I am to finally see this particular bio… when we have time, I'll tell you more about it."

Yeah, and when we had time, I'd tell her that Critter was not a thing to be collected, or owned, or dissected, or whatever

Rendou planned for her.

Rev capitulated and hopped aboard, extending a hand to me. I glared at him. Then I felt bad. Rev's father was dead, his mom scary, his uncle a scoundrel and his city in ruins. On the other hand, he seemed to be having a wonderful time.

Men. I let him pull me up.

We settled into Truck's ample box and looked back over the city. From up here, we could see that things seemed to be settling down. Or maybe all the flammable material was gone. The sullen orange glow was simmering into black, with soft-looking clouds of steam and dirty smoke hiding the stars.

Fang loped alongside Critter as we hurried away from the city. Critter could indeed move fast, making the earth shudder and vegetation topple as if she were a travelling earthquake.

Rev put his arm around me. I let him, since I could see it pissed his mom off. I smiled at her benevolently and sucked one of Rev's fingers. She looked away.

Rev squeezed me absently, gazing back at his city. I spat out his finger. Hopefully there would be time later to get under Rendou's skin.

At the Blue Caves, we left Truck parked outside and breezed right past the sales offices, courtesy of Rev's mom. Things looked a little different than when I'd been here before. Zero customers, zero smiles and bows, lots of brisk activity. And the display cages were empty.

After a brief consultation between Rendou, Tel, and a tall, skinny bio with a face like an axe, Critter was ushered away. I felt like a mother sending her kid off to the first day of school. She stomped away surrounded by bios and humans of various kinds, looking back only once. I was going to start crying. She was probably hungry and tired… maybe I should—

"Will you settle down and quit whimpering?" Rev barked. "That thing pounded her way through my dungeon floor. She'll be fine."

I waved goodbye despondently, wondering if other Retrievers had been out hunting for Critter, obviously a hot commodity. Kat and I ought to get a bonus.

Our reward turned out to be a visit to the Caves. "You'll be impressed," assured Rendou, as we filed down a rocky hallway. Some overeager technophile had strung electrical lights along it, and I could clearly see an iris membrane open onto an immense cavern. We passed through it. The temperature, which outside at around midnight had gotten chilly, rose to tropical levels immediately.

"This," stated Rendou, leading us to a balcony overlooking the whole area, "is the main nursery. Don't make any sudden movements."

My eyes adjusted and I froze, gawping like a farm girl. No sapphires were in evidence, but it didn't matter—the cave was glorious. All over the ceiling and walls, as far as I could see, was a fluttering, rolling pattern of butterfly wings. The entire inside of the cave, except for the floor, was lined with thousands upon thousands of jewel-like insects, each of them industriously fanning away with their iridescent wings.

Then my eyes focused, and I suddenly saw the true size of the place. The term "cavernous" fit perfectly. I also saw that the insects must have bodies about the size of rump roasts, their wings like serving trays. Most were shades of blue, indigo or turquoise, with here and there veins of yellow-gold. They stirred the warm, moist air and emitted a soothing hum. Kat, on my shoulder, started to hum along, his fur fluffing in the humidity. Tel was beside us, peering through the railing, his lopsided ears twitching.

I looked down. The floor, seen from the height of the entry port where we stood, was a maze of what looked like tanks made of rock or coral, surrounded by a sinuous network of waterways. In fact, you couldn't really call it a floor, because everything down there seemed to be swimming, crawling, doing back-flips or generally oozing around. A constant liquid gurgling blended pleasantly with the hum, and a rich salty smell tingled my nostrils.

Rendou had been observing Rev and me as we stood staring with our mouths open. As did almost everything, it made her smile faintly, an expression that successfully hid any real emotion she might be feeling. "This," she said, "is the best looking cavern, the one investors and big buyers get to see. The next few caverns aren't quite so attractive. They hold the developing bios and their attendants, the culling chambers, the chemical and hormonal stimulant inputs—"

"Wait! The *culling* chambers?"

"Yes. You don't imagine all the experiments turn out for the best, do you? That's why we are so happy to recover the Library. The information it contains should streamline the whole process, get rid of a lot of the testing and elimination facilities."

I opened my mouth angrily, then closed it. Okay. Elimination facilities. Made sense, in a cold-blooded way. A market-driven economy is a terrible thing.

Rendou said, "And, of course, the information will help me— *us* prepare."

My ears perked up. She had a personal agenda, for sure.

"Prepare for what?" asked Rev, absently ruffling the fur on Fang's blocky head.

But Rendou narrowed her eyes and snapped her mouth shut. Abruptly she turned away from the winged vista. "We have to go, or we'll lose control of this whole operation."

I squinted at her, wondering if her information meshed with my own. What operation did she have coiling in her devious brain? Could I trust anything the cats had sent to mine?

We all followed her out of the chamber and back down the

corridor at a fast clip.

Something Tel had shown me nagged at my brain, seeming relevant. Tel had learned something about himself from Critter… it had surprised him. Heartened him. An attribute he possessed, one which he'd thought useless, had suddenly taken on meaning. His ears had been twitching, and I was getting a sort of eager hum from his hard-packed little ganglia-node.

I was rooting for the little fellow… so determined, so intelligent, so basically unattractive. The Undercat. No longer would he be the angry, despairing outcast, if we were right.

Trotting beside Rendou, I panted, "So, communication is important in uprisings, right?"

"Of course it is. What's your point?"

"You'd like to know what's going on in the cities, wouldn't you?"

"You have no idea. The fastest *cheval*s and pigeons can only do so much."

"Well, did you know that Tel can converse with other telcats using their dots?"

She stopped striding and faced me. "Their *whats*? Oh, you mean their ca-ca emissions."

"Excuse me?"

"Collimation and Coherence Cavity. CaCCa. The Library mentioned something about that."

"Green dots, CaCCas, whatever. They were designed with this attribute but forgot how to use it decades after their abandonment. If two or more telcats link up, information can be coded and transmitted. Really fast. In fact, at the speed of—"

"Light!" she blurted. "Well, what do you know. I had no idea that thing they do was useful." She stopped and held out a hand at shoulder level, palm forward. I regarded it suspiciously, until Rev nudged me.

"Slap it," he whispered. "Just slap her palm with yours."

I did so, and Rendou provided a feral grin. "You two are on your own. Try not to get into trouble. Fang, *Hsssss*, you're with me."

She and the two bios were off. Probably to develop a fiendishly impenetrable code to teach the other telcats.

Axe-face reappeared at our side and suavely ushered us to a waiting area. He was used to dealing with entitled buyers and stylists demanding access to the rich lode of biological material dwelling within the caves.

Rev slumped on a bench and stuffed his hands between his knees. "I wonder what the original human colonists thought of the creatures they found here… wasn't this world supposed to be free of sentient life?"

"Apparently the surveyors were mistaken."

History class at the *école* I'd attended till I turned thirteen indicated that the colonists had zero qualms about a world hopping with weird beings who could technically be labelled "not-life", thus getting around the "life" problem. Our planet became home to a bunch of entrepreneurial eager-beavers who saw a natural resource and promptly put the natives—bios as they were generally called—to work. The colonists were so busy they hardly noticed that they'd been abandoned by the rest of humanity, and never did find out why. Everyone stopped caring after a while.

Life was good, and everyone got along pretty well. Anything a human needed done—hauling water, digging ditches, building and tunnelling and farming—could be done by a specialized bio. You could buy the things at the Caves. Sure, the prices were high, but what was a person to do? Dig and farm and build all by himself?

Truthfully, the bios hadn't seemed to mind. In fact, they'd been eager to please.

A few crackpots tried to develop mechanical "bios" they'd

invented, but no one took them seriously. A fringe group of collectors had various sparking, oil-spewing machines they liked to play with, but they were mostly for show.

I longed to fill Rendou in on what I'd learned from Tel, but we were parked here uselessly. Rev and I were both gnawing our nails.

Obviously we weren't trusted. I was reasonably certain that Rendou wasn't in this fight to profit from the bios. They had accepted her, and though she wanted their freedom, she would most likely use them for her own ends... But did she know what the *real* fight was about? Because I did.

Too much information, no way to sort it all out. Critter knew it all, but didn't *know* that she knew. Tel knew some. I knew some: before she'd been locked up, Critter had been designed, conceived and grown to larval stage, then loaded with her planet's true history.

Which wasn't pretty. And so far I'd seen only a few highlights, courtesy of the cats. The thought of peering directly into her vast store of data was frightening. It was keeping me from acting. That had to change.

I looked at Rev, who was probably wishing his mother had stayed lost. "Hey, can I do a brain dump on you?"

He squinted at me from his gargoyle-like position on the bench. "Do I look like I have anything better to do?"

"Oh, buck up. You know how people love pets, right?"

"No, I do not. I do not love pets. I have never had a pet and I do not want a pet."

"Oh. Really?" I'd seen how taken he was with Rendou's bio-wolf. "Well, you'll just have to use your imagination." I stood and began to pace. "What happens when people move house but leave their pets behind? I'll tell you, since I'm sure you have no idea. The pets have to survive on their own. Which they have not been bred or trained to do. It's a very cruel fate."

"Yeah? So? Survival of the fittest."

I wanted to swat him. "Listen! I learned what's happening on our world: the owners are returning! They want their pets back."

"Are you telling me that Kat—and all the other bios—are abandoned *house pets*?"

"He gets it! Hallelujah!"

"Could the *owners* be the First People? No one has ever really figured out what all that myth and legend stuff is about."

The half-remembered tales of Those Who Departed, told by the few bios who could talk.

"Yeah. Apparently Tel received a ping a few months ago. The beings who first occupied this world, and created the bios as pets and workers, have decided to revisit the old neighbourhood."

Rev was opening his mouth to comment when a rush of night-chilled air billowed into the waiting area. Rendou, trailed by Fang, surged after it. "The Library has been sent for unzipping," she announced. "The ancient telcat *Hsssss* has been communing with it." She rubbed her hands together, her eyes glinting with steely fervour. "*Hsssss* told me—"

I closed my eyes and waved my hands in the air. "Wait… let me guess… Ah! I have it. The First People are returning."

"Huh? How did you…? Never mind. I should have realized you possess eye gels. How much do you know?" She glared at me, her jealousy evident. "We'll talk, later. Anyway, it seems the First People don't like humans encroaching on their space."

"And this means…?" They almost had it…

Rev closed his eyes. "We're at war with spacefaring aliens. Great. Just great."

Where did the bios themselves figure into this? Whose side would they be on? The heartless owners who had left them behind to die? Or the pushy newcomers who had exploited them?

CHAPTER SEVEN

I headed for the exit. "We need to find Tel and Critter." Critter desperately needed an advocate, and I needed to commune with her, no matter how much it might hurt. I hoped Tel could get me close enough to activate my gels.

I looked back. Neither of them had moved. "Come on! This is important!"

Rendou rolled her eyes, but Rev reluctantly stood and hauled her along behind me. "I said I wouldn't let Mag out of my sight, and I meant it, Mom."

I was starting to like him again.

"You were always a stubborn boy," Rendou said. "Fine. Past the Blue Cave Nursery is Command Central." This was more like it.

"I am tolerated because of my relationship with Fang," she admitted as we hustled along. "Now that they have their Library, will they need humans anymore?"

"Good question. We have to convince them they do."

"Oh? I admire your spirit, my dear, but I don't know if you'll make much headway. The bios can be headstrong."

"I can be *more* headstrong."

"Yes she can," chimed in Rev. "So, how long do we have before the First People arrive?"

"Approximately eighteen years."

"Eighteen *years*?" he yelped. "You're kidding. Why is everyone going berserk *now*?"

Rendou said, "You don't imagine this world is anything like ready for a fight, do you? We're only just emerging from the dark ages."

"I love a good fight," I said. "I'm just not sure we're planning on the *same* fight."

"What in Aura's name are you talking about?"

"Rendou, don't try to blow smoke up my skirt. All you really want is to get your hands on Quel Naroo. And, hey, I totally approve." It would be fascinating to watch the warrior queen take down the treasonous murderer.

Rendou grabbed the metal railing with both hands, and I swear it bent. She let go, flexing her fingers. "You're right," she gritted, "and my bios almost had him for me!" She wheeled on Rev. "Thanks to you, I'll never get near the son-of-a-bitch! The Human Council knows me too well."

Rev leaned in. "Hey, I had things under control! I didn't ask for you and your bio army to take the law and mangle it!"

"That was before I knew where he was! How was I supposed to know you had him in Arderia? Do you think I *wanted* the bios to destroy Nagala Central?"

The soothing hum of the nursery was gaining a strident, panicky edge. We were disturbing the babies.

"Shut up, the two of you!" I hissed. "Rendou—we'll get him for you. You can cut him up and make him into jerky if you want. And you—" I pointed a finger at Rev, "will let her! This is no time for the rule of law."

Through his teeth, he said, "In case you have forgotten, I have sworn to uphold the rule of law."

"And in case *you* have forgotten, that bastard killed your father! Who I happen to think was really nice! So just shut up!"

Then I pointed the same finger at Rendou. "Tell me something. Why didn't you kill Quel Naroo years ago? You must have had chances."

"Surprisingly few. He's a slippery devil."

"But still—"

She bared her teeth at me, always a good tactic, but I stood my ground. Slowly her eyes closed and her grimace faded. "I tried. I failed. That was before—thanks to Fang—I attained the level of training I now possess. I was weak, frightened." Her eyes opened and blazed with military fervour. "I've changed."

"Damn rrright," muttered Fang.

"Well, that's just dandy, and I congratulate you," I said. "We'll find a way to get Quel for you, but we still need to find Tel and Critter and formulate a long-term alien-fighting plan."

"Er," she said. "Critter."

Fang began to scratch behind one ear, and wouldn't look at me.

"Critter… you know, the big gal with the bad skin."

She rolled her eyes at her son. "Revenbrook, you really should have waited for me to find you a more appropriate mate. Your father was wrong to let you spend so much time together."

I grabbed her arm. "I don't care what you think of me and Rev. Where's Critter?"

"It is being dismantled."

"What? *Dismantled?*" So that's what they meant by unzipped. I shoved her hard in the belly. She didn't move, nor did she retaliate. The blasted woman was made of concrete. "What are you *talking* about?"

"We need the information embedded within her body. Don't worry, she's—"

"What? *Just* a bio? They're *used* to that kind of treatment? Critter is my friend, my responsibility!" I shouted. The nursery was a-splash with excitable bios, and I didn't care. Their fate would be just as dire as Critter's unless bios got rights.

Yes! *That's* what this was all about.

Bios needed the same rights as humans. The fight was no longer about abandoned pets, or slimy politicians, or even an advancing armada of aliens.

"You are being ridiculous," said Rendou. "The Library is a resource, to be used by the inheritors of this world."

"Fine! I'll find her myself." I stomped along the catwalk toward the door at the far end. Critter, or whatever remained of her, had to be back there somewhere.

The door opened as I approached. I was glad to hear Rendou, Rev and Fang padding along behind me, no matter what their reasons. We jammed through the door and clustered at the edge of what had to be the universe's biggest honeycomb. Transparent, unfortunately…

No wonder buyers were only allowed in the first chamber.

Back there, things were moist and dimly lovely; in here was proof of the industrial scale of production that serviced a world.

Harsh lighting illuminated a space much bigger than the butterfly cave, latticed with glassy struts, walkways, cells of all sizes, and constantly moving food and water conveyors. The babies were hungry.

Rendou said, "Don't make eye contact."

"But most of them don't have—"

"Just don't look at their… heads. Stay together and keep moving. We're making for the top of those stairs over there."

Rev took my hand and squeezed it. "Fun, huh?" he whispered, grinning.

"Yeah, sure is."

I climbed, trying not to look down as my feet clanged on the invisible treads. It couldn't be glass, must be some kind of transparent metal. And that meant it was a leftover from the First People, because no way could humans on this world produce such a thing. If there still were humans elsewhere in the universe, maybe they could do it…

I launched myself through the door at the top of the stairs, into whatever next hell the First People had built. But once I stopped panting and opened my eyes, it turned out to be comparatively small. And crammed with throbbing computators in their nutrient tubs, polished stone tables piled high with papers and drawings, and a crowd of serious-looking individuals—bio and human—all of whom were shouting. Minions rushed back and forth clutching recorder-bios. Brilliant clusters of glow-lights shed eerie green highlights on the cheekbones and other protuberances of the room's occupants.

Three assorted telcats crouched in a corner, facing each other and flashing their little green dots in intricate patterns. Aided by a system of mirrors, they seemed to be receiving and transmitting information from somewhere else.

Wow. Things were happening fast. But the First People weren't due for years…

Oh. Yeah. The bio revolution, Rendou's contribution to rational political discourse. Rev had imagined that his faction in the city were going after Quel Naroo; turned out to be his mom's operation. And it had gone off the rails. The revolutionaries she'd dragooned into her quest for vengeance had to be brought under control, or they'd demolish our civilization before the aliens could.

CHAPTER EIGHT

Tel was in the middle of the big pow-wow. I was glad to see a bandage clinging to his ear, processing the damaged skin. Some of the people milling around were Clan leaders. I knew my own, of course—the wily and beautiful Jenna Grey-Hunter—the others only by their troucats. The whole rainbow-hued lot of them were hip deep in this.

The noise level was rising. A shoving match was going on in one corner. Tel prowled the floor, bristling with frustration, and I sympathized. He was small, voiceless and without the fancy trappings of a leader. But I'd seen into his brain, and though I still wasn't sure he was actually *intelligent*, I had seen that his personality and knowledge were just the antidote to the self-important twaddle being spouted at increasingly louder volume.

Everyone wanted to be Captain, no one wanted to be Ensign. The clash of agendas would be epic.

My agenda, however, was the best. I needed to find Critter.

Kat concurred. *Hsssss likes you. Hsssss will help you.*

"Really? You sure?"

Kat sent a warm pulse of affirmation into my hindbrain. My hindbrain lapped it up.

I took a deep breath and pushed my way over to *Hsssss*, a.k.a. Tel. He snarled and flattened his ears, but I picked him up anyway and placed him on my shoulder.

I could feel waves of animosity emanating from that brain I so admired. Was it animosity toward humans? Argumentative bios? Or maybe military inefficiency?

I cleared my throat and addressed the room. "Where is Critter?"

No one paid any attention. Everyone was shouting about how to halt the revolution. The fun was over. The real war was about to start.

"Where! Is! Critter!" Somewhat louder.

Rev pulled out his shocker, raised it high and discharged it into the ceiling. Everyone shut up for a split second. "Hey!" he bellowed. "The lady is asking a question!"

"Thank you, Circ-haut. Ahem. What has been done with Critter? You know her as the Library."

A large bio, crusty with age and anger, shoved close. "Another meddling human." He leaned over me, balancing on his long, scaly arms.

"She's with me," Rev shouted, "she's the one who found—"

The bio shoved me. I staggered back.

Both Kat and Tel leapt off my shoulders and onto the bio's head, where they began scratching. Rev jammed a fist in its blocky face. "Hands off my girlfriend!"

"I can take care of myself," I yelled, without basis in fact.

Jenna Grey-Hunter, never the shy type, leapt to my side. "Yeah—hands off my operatives! Mag and Kat liberated the Library," she proclaimed. "Hail them!"

"Uh, thanks, but no. Please don't hail us." At least it made Crusty step back. I straightened and tried to look soldierly. " I need to find Crit—the Library. I must commune with her."

A relative hush fell. Even Jenna, my own Clan leader, started to examine her boots. "My dear," said Rendou, "The Library has been dispersed already. This is a crisis situation. We don't want to wreck this world ourselves, before the First People even get here." She scowled around at the others crowding the room. "Right?"

"We're only reclaiming what is ours," grumbled Crusty.

"Oh yeah?" retorted Clan Red's leader snarkily. "You bios were screwing up pretty good, until we came along!"

"Why, you—"

"Quiet!" I bellowed. "What do you mean, dispersed?"

Rendou snorted. "Calm down. The Library is formed of redundant segments. Each can survive on its own. It has been taken apart into eight independent, but identical, units."

"You *cut her up*? Did it hurt her? Is she all right? Where is she—are they? Did she even get a *say* in this?"

Rendou said, "She didn't need to. She's—"

Crusty pounded a forelimb on the table. "Here we go! *Just* a bio! This is exactly why you humans—"

Rendou shoved him out of the way and jumped onto the nearest table. "Quiet, you idiot! The Library is the one bio that doesn't need to agree or disagree about anything. It tells *us* what to do."

I reflected that someday I should get an outfit like Rendou's. Black leather bustier, thigh-high boots, sword belt... She had a good oratorical style, too. "We all think we know what's best for this world. Well—I've had a mere glimpse into what the Library holds." She pointed at me. "This young woman has seen the whole story through *Hsssss*'s eye, and you would do well to listen to her. And to him."

Tel, on my shoulder once more, reached a small grey paw out and gently pulled my chin around until I was looking directly into his face, a finger width away. His eye glowed, the green light source focused into my retinas.

He *looked* at me. My head suddenly bulged with words and images, scrambling for a place in line to get out my mouth. Okay… apparently I was going to do his talking for him.

I didn't have a choice, I'd been drafted. I steadied Tel on my shoulder and jumped up beside Rendou, sending papers and scrolls flying. "Everyone! Tel—I mean *Hsssss*—wants to talk!"

I felt my gels squeeze and shift in my eyes.

Incoming.

He said, directly into my brain, "*After the Masters left, we survived. Barely. We were slowly building a civilization of our own. Then humans came. We were glad to see you at first… you kept out of our way, fed us, gave us hope that we had found friends in a cold universe. All was well, at first. But then…*"

I heard myself speaking. I was echoing Tel's words; as they entered my brain they exited my mouth. I knew he wanted desperately to speak for himself. He couldn't—he needed me, his chatty pal. Everyone was looking at me, not at him. The story kept coming.

"*But then the humans found we bios could be used. Changed. You began to tinker with our genome. Some of you are very clever… and some of us were willing collaborators.*" I tried to shut myself up, but I couldn't look away. My eyes throbbed and began to water. Or maybe I was crying.

"*Some of us hated you, some of us loved you. I hated you. Hated all humans. I… told the First People about you… sent a message forty years ago.*"

A collective gasp, then everyone started shouting. Rev shot the ceiling again.

My mouth kept flapping. *"They heard me… and now they are coming back. But…"* Tel's words in my brain stopped for a second. I gasped air.

I knew what he was going to say. I'd seen it in his brain already.

I said it for him. "But during that forty years, *Hssss* came to understand something. He needed us. They needed us. Humans and bios make a good team. The First People want chattel. Humans and bios want partners. Maybe even friends."

Complete silence reigned, probably for the first time in this room. Rendou took advantage of it. She said, her voice softer than I ever imagined it could be, "All of you know Fang. He isn't my pet, or property, as some of you may assume. He's my comrade."

Fang emitted a rough growl. "I do not want to be a pet, owned by masters. I want more. I want the universe." The hair on his neck rose and fell. The hair on mine did too.

The universe. Yeah, I was crying.

I said, "The First People are coming back. They can't arrive to find a warring world of freaks and outcasts."

Crusty got in my face again. "You think we're freaks? Primitives?"

I glared up at him. "We all are! We're pathetic. Admit it!"

Rendou chimed in. "But we don't have to stay that way. The Library will be used for its huge store of intel. Magdalena—for reasons of security and expediency, the segments must remain apart. There are eight Libraries now: one for each city, one for the clans, and two for the bios."

Counting on my fingers, I piped up, "But that's only six."

"Correct! Another segment will remain here at the Blue Caves, along with the bio known as Truck, to oversee decommissioning the sterilization tanks. Bios will now be able to reproduce sexually. Or any way they like."

The bios in the room looked poleaxed. I didn't blame them. "Okay, so, seven."

"The remaining segment goes to Magdalena Grey-hunter and Revenbrook Karel."

Rev and I looked at each other. Kat hummed, wrapping his tail possessively around my neck. "You're kidding. We get a Critter segment?"

Rendou's nod confirmed it. An upwelling of mutinous rumbling from the war council was silenced with a look. "The Library itself has requested it."

My very own Critter! Well, and Rev's too. Bet I didn't look so bad as a daughter-in-law now, did I?

Crusty decided he'd better get on board before it was too late. He did some fist-thumping and regained the attention of the crowd. "As we speak, bios are containing and instructing the human population. Diplomatically! Get your fist out of my face, human. We expect opposition, but it will be overcome. Diplomatically, drat it!" He sounded serious. Maybe he wasn't so bad after all.

Fang's mouth lolled open. "Humans arrrn't so bad, except forrr the smell."

I felt a warmth spread through my chest. Maybe it was pride, and hope... or maybe it was the thought of all that pent-up reproductive energy about to let loose.

"So... Critter. Critt*ers* I should say. When do we get ours?"

EPILOGUE

Rendou hummed happily as she spread tangy pickle relish on slabs of bread, piled them with sliced meat and cheese, and slapped them together into sandwiches. She had a stack to her right that I, standing beside her, was endeavouring to wrap without devouring one on the spot. Picnics were so much fun. Especially ones by the river.

Rendou turned out to be okay, once she unwound a bit. She liked parties, kids, shopping for attractive military attire, and training with Fang.

But what she really loved was picnics. By the river.

An hour or so later, the usual gang had assembled on the shady banks of the waterway that Rev, Critter and I had once sluiced down, in fear for our lives. The day was sunny, the food plentiful, and the liquor laws lenient.

Everything in Nagala City was pretty much back to normal. If anything ever was normal, that is. All the crackpots who'd wasted time developing mechanical bios were vindicated, as it turned out that something other than spunk and verve might be necessary to fight aliens. Progress toward space flight was accelerating rapidly, now that everyone had access to the Library's ancient records and had suddenly sprouted rampaging cases of esprit de corps.

"There he goes," said Rev, munching a sandwich.

We all watched as a balding man, dressed in nothing but sagging underwear and a neck chain, waded into the river. We could hear a constant stream of invective from him as he flopped forward and began to breast-stroke out toward the middle.

A deep, satisfied sigh came from Rendou, and she reached for another sandwich. "I love to watch a professional at work."

"Heh, heh. Pass me one of those cheesy-puff things, will you, Mag?" said Rev.

I did better than that. I popped it directly into his mouth, and helped myself to one too. In another four months I could have wine again. Kat was already asleep, having been first at the spread. His ears twitched gently as he snored in the sun, tendrils catching the warm breeze. Tel, who was visiting, was curled around Kat. He actually looked sleek, instead of scruffy. Truck, who circulated among the various Critter-units, was in Arderia right now.

Quel Naroo, once Trent-haut of Nagala-sur-mer, took a breath and upended himself, diving under the surface. We watched the trail of bubbles.

A flyer hurtled by overhead. I could hear the excited yelping of the bio pilot, dopplering away to the east. Turned out they loved teaming up with crackpots. Estimates predicted six years to spaceflight, ten to a fully armed orbital station. Even the dungeon's impervious cell membrane was coming in handy.

In a minute Quel popped up, spitting water, his hands full of squirming river worms. Awkwardly, he churned his way toward the shore, where Critter Junior was eagerly waiting.

Quel really should be better at this, I reflected, considering he'd been doing it every day for the last year. And would be doing it every day for the remainder of his life. Critter Junior—C.J.—was getting big and plump. She was almost ready to bud a new segment, and someday might attain the grand bulk of her original self.

Quel Naroo gave us a dirty look as he dumped the worms by C.J. We waved jauntily at him as Fang prodded him back in for another load.

Rendou said, "Have I mentioned that I really love picnics?"

This story was inspired by a dream recounted to me by an ex. I couldn't resist its painterly appeal. Some dreams seem to fluoresce in your mind between sleeping and waking, lingering and throbbing behind your eyes. Others dissolve no matter how hard you try to catch them. This one stuck.

WALK TO BRYTEN

You are in a gallery and you are looking at a painting. It has captured you; outside the gallery, the sunny day (a city street, Italian voices, the screech of tires) dims and disappears. Though this painting is small, it is incredibly detailed, as if the artist has used finer and finer brushes—a single human hair perhaps—to place each stroke. With both hands on the wall, not caring what the attendant might say or think, you lean close to the world inside the painting...

A woman stands at a window, talking on a telephone. (And yes, you can see each tiny eyelash, you can see it move.) The window is an embrasured pane of crystal, like a framed picture you can see deeply into. (Much like the one you are looking into now.) A picture inside a picture. It shows a green and white view that perhaps is the past, perhaps the future. The telephone is not really a telephone. The woman, who really is a woman, and not a simulacrum or an android or the afterimage of a dream, is beautiful, as a thin porcelain cup is beautiful. Her name (it comes to you easily) is Alema.

Alema is dressed in olive velvet, bodiced tightly and studded at wrist and neck with pearls and tiger-eye beads. The telephone she holds matches the dress and the large velvet clip that binds her hair in a swirling copper wing. Perhaps she has many such matching costumes; perhaps the telephone, chameleon-like, shifts itself to fit her sartorial mood. Alema presents the impression of someone who is always dressed, whose flesh is used to being clasped and held by rich fabrics and heavy beaten metals.

The velvet telephone interferes with her bound wing of hair. She holds the device slightly away from her ear and projects her voice into it like a trained singer.

"I cannot hear you," she says. "Speak more loudly, Saul."

Saul says something and Alema's brows rise, her pale sherry eyes stare out at the soft greens within the window. "You are walking? Walking to Bryten… Saul—why?" (And her fear is in you, as if your veins flow with the same blood.)

The answer she hears is apparently not good enough, or is meaningless to her. Her eyes close. The telephone squirms in her hand, as if to escape.

"Walking to Bryten… you!" Her right hand crushes the velvet of her skirt, pulls pearls loose from their silk strands. "We do not walk to Bryten." The syllable "we" is emphasized. It means: I would not dream of doing such a thing. How can *you*? How *can* you… *We were safe here, the two of us… how can I live without you? How can you leave me behind?*

Alema turns away from the window and its view of green. A white road winds into the blue distance behind the crystal pane. (You lean as close as you dare to the painting, to the tiny painted window at which Alema will not look.) On the road, people and animals and strange vehicles that walk like beasts drift and coalesce in and out of the fine white dust of the road.

"You will never get there," Alema says, her words seeming to curl, and dry, and blow away.

As she flings the earpiece away and turns, Alema's velvet skirt brushes a table whose gilt legs support one enormous shell: a giant Imperial Volute, its markings, the colour of old blood, like the tracings of multiple heartbeats. The table rocks but the shell does not fall. If people come into the room, they find that they must walk in spirals around the shell, following the demands of its internal twist.

Alema, sobbing without noise or tears, stops before a painting of Saul. It was done only a year ago by the great Pietro Ponturo, as was her own portrait hanging next to it. Saul is terribly handsome; in another world he would be a prince. His face combines grace with masculinity and his colouring is superb. Green eyes, black hair, a birthmark on his cheek (augmented by tattoo) in the shape of a bird. He stares out of the canvas fiercely, a cold raptorial fire in his eyes. Pietro has caught the fire, emphasized it by his choice of background: an ancient burning city. It borders on excess, but it is magnificent.

Alema remembers sitting hour after hour, hot and breathless in a stifling room, wearing the stiff verdigris-coloured dress. Pietro Ponturo had snarled at her and snapped his brushes in half and accused her of moving. Alema's painted eyes hold a withdrawn hurt akin to confusion, and are almost pathetically locked into the ticking present.

She sees this and accepts it—there is nothing she can say to her image to deny her own mediocrity. *Does Saul love me? Does anyone love me?* No ancient cities in her gaze, and her backdrop is a web of pattern in tight blue lines hiding a flat ocean. Pietro has allowed one flying fish to leap, barely glimpsed between the lattice bars. And yet he has made manifest her beauty. The portrait is much praised.

Alema looks again into Saul's burning painted eyes. She drops her head back as if offering her blood to him.

Her fingers go to her throat, pressing the knot of pain that has replaced the anger, the disbelief. *You cannot walk to Bryten.* A clotting dusk is in the corners of the room. Some call Bryten *Speranza*—the land of hope—but more call it *Pericolo*—peril, chance...

"Don't leave me, please," Alema whispers.

Suddenly she gasps and turns, as if called. Her dress swings out heavily, her little olive shoes clack on the tile floor. The velvet telephone quivers and leaps across the room to her ear. It clings, burrows closer, pushes aside the copper wing of her hair. Alema's hands flutter down to her tight-laced breasts.

Into her mind come voices, too many to decipher words. (And you—you can hear them too, there in the gallery as you fall into a painting on the wall...) Some voices sing, some laugh, others moan as if in pain or love. Alema hears Saul's baritone as if it were issuing from her own throat, but the meaning of the words escapes her. She sees him and gasps.

Saul is barefoot, walking. Alema almost drops to her knees with the weight of the heat and the singing voices. She catches herself on the edge of the table holding the Imperial Volute. The shell falls.

The shell falls, spins on the floor. Its interior secret spiral catches Alema, spins her, throws her to the window. The window opens.

The window opens, the heat rushes in, the heat of the road so close, it is just outside the window...

Like a pilgrim Saul walks the white road—and Alema's feet in their small stiff shoes covet the white talc of the roadway, hot and soft, drifting in a haze around a thousand ankles. She sees a dog pacing at the heels of a sweating fat man; she feels her own sweat prickle and shiver on her arms. The sky is a perpetual noon, the white road stretches forever into a rumour of brilliance below the horizon. Saul holds out his hand to her.

"I will walk to Bryten," the clinging velvet whispers, in Saul's voice. "I will go whether you travel with me or not... but perhaps you will..."

Two children leap a ditch hand in hand and join the road, laughing. A man slaps the rump of a big chestnut horse—it leaps, snorting, shakes off its saddle and races ahead along the verge. Alema smells its warm scent, the dust of the road, the tang of an orange a woman is peeling as she walks.

Alema leans out the window. Leans on the carved sill, yearning out. Whispers and singing are in her ear, the smell of sweat and dust is in her nostrils. How did she not see, until now, that the window was never just a window?

(You lean on the gallery wall. The heat and light from the painting falls on your face; breathing fast through parted lips you feel the air, the heat, the dust between your toes, the multiple voices, heartbeats jagging.)

Alema tears off her jewels, loosens her velvet bodice and runs down the white road. Saul laughs, reaches for her and swings her around, and her tight little shoes fly off and away.

The gallery is closing. Apologetically, the attendant looks at his watch, turns to the door. The heat burns in your face, the scent of dust and oranges is in your nostrils and Alema smiles... no one is watching, no one sees. You turn and follow her.

A figure in a dark, hooded garment—a teen? But he's holding a scythe. A dreaded creature, yes… but did that skeletal being have a childhood? Would he know what he was, what he had to do, and who might be damaged by it? Besides himself, that is.

THE BONES AT THE BOTTOM OF THE SEA

Is it normal for a kid to think about bones? All the time?

Jamie, age nine months, spotted Bonnie enjoying a pleasant gnaw at the soup bone I'd handed her, and hustled on hands and knees across the kitchen to yank it out of her mouth. Bonnie, a gentle Border Collie pup, let him have the slobbery thing, though her brown eyes held reproach.

It's going straight in his mouth, I thought, dashing over to snatch it from him.

But instead of jamming it in and gumming away, Jamie sat back on his diaper-clad rear and began to examine the bone. Solemnly. Attentively.

"That's a bone, Jamie. Not a toy. Bone."

"Bo," said Jamie. It was his first word.

I bit my lip. Not Ma-ma or Da-da. Bone.

"Give it to Mommy."

"Bo. Bo. Bo." Knowing that I would take it from him, Jamie clutched the bone to his chest and started to cry.

I tried to get it anyway. "Mommy wants to wash the bone." I wanted to give it back to the dog, who had put her head on her paws in resignation but was watching the show.

I had to wait until Jamie fell asleep to get it away from him. A very determined little boy. I put it outside in Bonnie's run, and distracted my wailing baby with a bath and toys when he woke up and discovered his treasure was gone.

A few days later, Roy and I had a deli chicken for dinner. Jamie, in his high chair chewing on an Arrowroot biscuit, let it fall to focus intently on the little bird bones as we nibbled them clean. His whole body had come alert.

I said to Roy, "So, our lad seems to like bones."

Roy grinned, gnawing a drumstick as Jamie watched intently. "You want this, little man? Sorry, dude. No chicken bones for you."

I made sure to keep bones out of Jamie's line of sight as much as possible. No real issues for the next while. Time passed. Jamie turned out to be a fairly precocious child, at least with reading. One of us read to him every night, and before he hit his fourth birthday, Jamie displayed a knowledge of letters, words, and even sentences on the printed page that seemed advanced to me. But every child seems advanced to a doting parent.

When Jamie was five, Roy and I were going through a period of "getting organized," which meant digging through ancient boxes in the basement of the elderly home I'd inherited, and deciding whether to keep, donate, or junk the contents. We were wondering if we should move closer to the city.

A complete set of Encyclopedia Britannica came to light, and found itself stacked precariously by the door that leads to the garage, destined for a donation run. It sat there for a few days, allowing plenty of time for Jamie to un-stack, sort, and examine each and every one of them. He had lost his baby chub and was obviously going to be tall. When he sat on the floor to start leafing through Volume 1, his knees and elbows angled out, and my throat developed a lump. His neck was thin; a stalk to hold up a head crammed full of brains. Jamie had no brother or sister to play with, but he had books and he loved them.

When he realized the Encyclopedia was in alphabetical order, he went straight to Volume 3—Bolivia to Cervantes—and found what he wanted. He was happily absorbed for hours. Then he went ahead and read the whole damn set.

It didn't take as long as you might imagine; Jamie had just turned seven when he closed the last volume. He wasn't completely weird, he had other interests too. Like any normal kid he played outside, built a precarious tree house, rode his bike with friends, played with Bonnie. But he re-read the Bone article every week or so until I decided enough was enough and hauled the set to Goodwill.

Two winters later, the basement was empty, and in fact the whole house seemed redundant. Roy had decamped for the city and a new life. Everything was empty, for me at least, though the internet in our community had been upgraded. Which meant we could research stuff. Jamie and me. Roy wasn't much interested anymore.

"Mommy," Jamie asked me one day, "are there a lot of bones at the bottom of the sea?"

The bone thing again. "Well, I suppose so. Fish bones, whale bones. When sea creatures die I guess their bones sink to the bottom."

"What about person bones?"

"Skeletons? All the bones in a body, joined together, are called a skeleton." I saw him mouth the word silently. *Skeleton.*

He knew the word—for god's sake he'd read about everything in the universe—he just liked to say it. Maybe I could shake his bone-reverence out of him. I narrowed my eyes and tried to look scary. "Corpses thrown into the ocean. Sailors flung overboard in a storm. Or maybe they walked the plank. Warriors killed in ancient fighting ships. That sort of thing?"

He nodded, unfazed. Death, no problem. Very interesting, in fact. "How many do you think there are? How *many* skeletons?"

"I don't know. I don't even know how to find out."

He looked at me, blinking fast, a sign that his thinking had sped up too. He chewed his lip for a while, then said, "I want to know."

"Okay. Fine. But I'm not helping, you have to do it yourself." But he had already lost interest in me. He was figuring out the arithmetic of death.

I stood there, between the kitchen and the cute, colourful study room I'd set up for Jamie after Roy left. I was child-centric. To an unhappy degree. But Jamie was not Mom-centric. Or toy-centric or snack-centric like a normal kid.

Jamie was bone-centric.

What the hell was going on with him?

His teachers said he was just going through a phase. Like some boys go crazy for dinosaurs, or monster trucks. With girls, it's horses. They get over it. Don't worry!

But I did worry, though I had other things on my mind, like getting Roy to fork over child support, a never-ending headache. Small-town retail work and freelance editing don't pull in the big bucks. Distraction and worry leads to inattention, inattention leads to accident. Nothing much, just fell off a stepladder and hurt my shoulder and hand. Jamie, bless his heart, came running and was full of sympathy.

Taking my hand in his, gently pulling it from where I'd cradled it against my chest, he ran his long, thin fingers over the skin. "Right here," he said, drawing an imaginary line over what must be one of the zillions of little bones in the human hand. A hand that was swelling up painfully. "There's a break. You should go get it looked at, Mom."

"How did you… How can you…"

He wouldn't look me in the eye, knowing by now that I found the bone thing creepy. "I just… I just kinda know. I can feel it."

"Okay. Well. Okay."

We sat in silence on the kitchen floor where I'd fallen.

"I can see it. Like a thin little shadow."

"Jamie… that makes no sense." Tears were prickling my eyes, whether from pain or from the mild sort of horror I felt at what he could do. Or thought he could do.

"Sorry."

With my not-hurting arm I pulled him close. "It's your super power. Maybe you'll be a doctor when you grow up, eh?" What was the point of being freaked out? He was my kid. Smart, sensitive, funny. Just a little odd.

To make up for his discomfort, I did something that was probably stupid. I ordered a human skeleton online. You can do that. When it arrived and he opened the box, I explained, "It's just plastic. A good quality replica. But it has all the bones, they say. It's like the ones they have in doctor's offices."

He touched it. Ran both hands over the skull and all the other bones, every last one, staring intently at the rattly contraption. What we have on the inside, under the skin.

"Thanks, Mom."

"It was only a couple hundred bucks."

"Yeah." He closed the box and stood back. "It's cool."

He never touched it or looked at it again. I finally donated it to a friend who runs a little magic shop in town, and she was actually thrilled. Jamie had wanted a real skeleton.

What would he do to get one? Rob a grave? Kill someone and boil them down? Now I was really getting stupid. And ghoulish. By the time my hand healed up, we had put the unfortunate incident behind us.

But then the next thing happened: our elderly cat, Gul Dukat, died. There she was one morning, curled in her bed, still and cold. A peaceful passing. I found Jamie asleep on the floor next to her, one hand resting on her flank. Had he known she was dying? But how? Gully had seemed fine to me last night. We buried her in a cardboard box in the backyard. Of course I knew what would happen, and after about two months it did. Jamie dug her up.

He got a bucket of water, added a few drops of bleach, and spent an industrious afternoon outside, cleaning up the skeleton with a nail brush and lots of scrubbing. It held together remarkably well, the dark stringy tendons holding the cat's scaffolding in place. Then he just sat on the grass and looked at it. He didn't decide to set it up in his room, as another thirteen-year-old boy might do to gross out his friends. After the looking was done, he placed the little feline bones back in a fresh cardboard box and put it back in the ground.

I watched the whole operation from the kitchen window, afraid to interfere, afraid to challenge him. I spent a few very unpleasant minutes wondering if Jamie had killed her, just to get the bones. I wasn't going to ask him. What if he gave me the wrong answer?

So we never mentioned it. But I sensed that Jamie was settling into his life. Finding himself, discovering who he was—and it wasn't like other teens. Though he did tend to wear hoodies most of the time, winter and summer, all in some indeterminate shade between moist earth and night sky. But all teenagers did that. He seemed happier. My nagging fear that he needed therapy faded.

I asked him what he saw himself doing when he grew up. His Adam's apple bobbed in his long, thin neck, the neck of a certified geek, and he looked over my head into the far distance. He'd already grown tall, and it was distressing to me to see how thin he stayed, despite my efforts to get calories into him. Bony.

"I dunno." Shrug. Some shuffling. He wanted to tell me something I might not like, I got that. Okay. I went to the kitchen and started to take flour, sugar, and so on out of the cupboard. Cookie making, something moms did in their often futile efforts to get kids to talk. He followed me and stood with his hands in his pockets, looking out from under that damned hood.

"Uh. I kinda thought of doing what you said… you know, medical school. But, uh…"

"Mm." Eggs.

"But. But then I got interested in, uh, I guess you'd call it spiritual stuff? Religion?"

My hand faltered. I almost dropped the eggs but recovered. Oh my.

"Spiritual… well, that's unexpected." Or was it? "Speaking of spiritual, Jamie—did you ever figure out how many bones are at the bottom of the ocean?"

"What?"

"When you were a kid. You wanted to know."

"Oh. Yeah, I guess. Somewhere between five million and a billion, depending on how you count. Like, every bone? Or every skeleton? Every human skeleton. Those are the important ones."

"Yeah. Wow. That's a lot."

He bounced on his toes. Happily. "Yep. And more all the time."

He was *happy*? "Refugees. They drown trying to escape their awful homelands." I had better not suggest he look into the matter of all the bones buried under the ground. Scattered on battlefields.

"Yeah! Bodies get dumped in rivers, they float to the oceans. Murder victims, suicides." He got the cookie sheet out and set the oven to 350. Such a good kid.

Deep breath. "So, kiddo. Religion."

He was still testing me out. "There's more than, like, Christianity and Islam and all that. There's all kinds of myths and stuff. Folklore. Miracles. It's pretty interesting."

He was blushing. I focused steadfastly on my mixing bowl. I wanted to cry, really. My boy, my only child, my lifeline, was heading into some kind of mystic quagmire. He was ripe for a cult. Was he trying to find an afterlife? Somewhere for the dead to go, after they had slipped free of their bones? If I tried to stop him, tell him he was succumbing to his neurosis, he'd give me up. I'd known it from when he was a baby. He would give up life for some kind of death fetish.

I found the baking powder, held on tightly to the little tin.

Or maybe he just wanted to be a scholar. Studying mythology. What was wrong with that? So he was interested in the past, the vast sweep of human civilization—where we come from, what we think and imagine and dream—and where we go. Into a mystery.

Into death, where our vibrant bodies stop and grow still, moulder and decay, and turn into skeletons.

We made the cookies and ate more of them than was strictly necessary. I did my best to tamp down my worries, let Jamie be Jamie.

He did well enough in high school to get accepted to several colleges, and chose one nearby that offered theological courses as well as general arts and science.

*

During his first semester away, it became obvious that Bonnie was too old and ill to last much longer. I made the sad decision to have her put down and cremated. No dog bones in the garden for Jamie to dig up. I couldn't have borne it. I told him in a phone call, unable to keep from crying. He got it, I think. If his only interest in our old dog had been her skeleton, I didn't want to know it; fortunately he didn't seem to mind what I'd done.

"I'm sorry, Mom. She was a good dog, but she was really old." Pause. "I really should have been there."

"I… I thought it would be too sad for you." A lie.

"I wouldn't have been sad. So, do you think you'll get another dog? A puppy? To keep you company."

"I don't think so. No."

The whole conversation left me quite shaken. He wouldn't have been sad.

He visited home every couple of weeks, and one evening I asked him if he felt any sort of calling to a particular career.

He shrugged. He'd gotten even thinner, his cheekbones standing out and his pale blue eyes deep-set. An overlarge hoodie casting his face into shade.

He toyed with the pot roast and potatoes I'd made, and said, "I know I'd like to be in some sort of helping profession. Not sure what."

"Hm. Well, there's different ways to go with that idea. Teaching? Social work? It's not too late to think about pre-med."

He sighed. "I know you want me to be a doctor, Mom. It's just not for me. You know what I think? Everyone has their time. To live and to die. I just don't think it's right to force anyone to live when they should…"

I put my fork down. "Should what? *Go?* Just give up and die, if you can be cured of a disease? Or an accident? Is that really what you believe?"

Silence.

My heart had started to pound. "I forced Bonnie to die. Was that wrong? Maybe she really wasn't ready!"

"Everyone is ready. To be alive is the anomaly."

"What?"

He looked down, but I knew it was not in embarrassment at saying such a sophomoric thing. He looked down and knitted his long pale fingers together at the effort it would take to convince me he knew the truth. That he wasn't crazy, or in a cult, or just out to goad me into a circular argument.

He gathered himself and said, "Remember when I was curious about the bones at the bottom of the sea? Have you any idea how many human beings have lived on this world? And have died?"

"In all of history? I'm guessing the numbers will come out approximately equal."

He actually smiled. "Life runs so close ahead of death that it's hard sometimes to tell the difference."

Was I suddenly the only proponent for life in this house? Indeed, could I argue for a state that was so ephemeral, so fragile, and so ultimately futile? Death was king. It won the race as we faltered and fell. The grave took us all. Or the sea.

"Jamie. Look. I... I can't think about this kind of thing. We have life, we produce life—I made you inside me and you're alive. Aren't you? Doesn't that mean anything?"

"Of course it does."

"You want to live, don't you? I mean... Jamie... are you okay?"

Maybe he saw how upset I was getting, or maybe he felt invigorated by our little debate, but he brightened up and spent some time reassuring me that all was well. He was just figuring things out. Seeking his path.

He dropped out at the end of his second year, and ended up going to Honduras to volunteer at one of the Storm Camps that were supposed to be temporary but had become permanent as hurricanes got stronger and more frequent. He served as general strong-back guy with increasing counselling duties as he gained experience and they started to trust him. He was especially good with the dying. He moved around, from camp to camp all over Central America, back to somewhere in Texas he'd discovered that apparently topped him up with fervour and determination, as well as the mundane skills of grant-writing, team-building, recruitment and so on.

After a few years he was running a dozen of the camps.

I didn't see him for a while. He was too busy to visit. I sold the old place and moved to a small condo, no room for a large, busy son. Then I got some bad news, which I'd been expecting: the long-term effects of a virus I'd picked up, and thought I'd kicked, turned out to have been working away diligently at my heart and lungs. Nothing much to do about it: transplants weren't advised for me as the virus was unstoppable. A waste of good organs. I didn't tell Jamie any of this, but I did spend some time wishing he'd had a family. But who was I kidding? I'd known for years that he simply wasn't interested in love and marriage.

He called one evening. "Mom, hey. Guess what? I delivered a baby."

Oh. I almost laughed. A brand new set of bones. I said, "Wow, that's pretty cool."

"It was amazing. To be there, at the beginning."

I said nothing. I knew what it was like, he didn't have to wax ecstatic over the miracle of birth.

He said, "I'm sorry. Sorry for things I've said over the years. About death."

"It's okay, sweetie. You know about bones. And about

helping. I'm proud of you. You've done a good job of life. Really, you have."

Long pause. "You think so? Maybe. I don't know. I have a job to do, that's all. One I got assigned, I guess, when I was a baby."

We hung up soon after that, but I felt better. Jamie was all right. He had a job to do.

A few weeks later he called out of the blue. "Hey Mom. I wrangled some time off. Can I come see you? I can be there in eighteen hours or so, if my connections go okay."

"Of course! You have to ask?" My heart throbbed. I wasn't looking very good these days. Would he be shocked? Saddened? My time was nearing its end.

I wouldn't have been sad.

And I knew.

I had to stop talking, try to breathe. I hung up, looked out the window. A flock of birds was circling over the condo's parking lot, so many of them, looking as if they were performing a dance they'd done for eons. A dance to herald the servant of death.

He was coming for me. He knew what was happening with my life, that it was winding down thinner and thinner. He knew that it was my time to go and he needed to be there. It was his job.

As he has done with so many others, he will lead me across the river, gently, gently and lovingly.

And then he will have my bones.

*This story was inspired by The Light Princess, a Scottish fairy
tale by George MacDonald. It was one of my favourite tales as
a child, about a princess afflicted by constant weightlessness, a
lack of gravity both physical and mental, until she finds a love
that brings her down to earth.*

LITTLE FEATHER

*There once was a princeling whose father ruled an evil empire
called Northeast Corridor. When his father divorced his mother
and married a new and more beautiful woman, the princeling
contemplated revenge. Revenge, after all, was in his blood. And
when the new woman presented his father with a sweet baby
girl who captured his heart, the princeling vowed that revenge
he would have. No matter how long it took.*

Maria Elena gave me fifteen minutes to pack.

When my mother died and my father went into
decline, my aunt Maria Elena came to stay with us. To care for
me "as only a woman can," she informed her brother, as she
rolled her luggage into the house. My mother passed when I was
three. My aunt had been here fourteen years.

And now my father too is dead. I am an orphan.

"Rodrigo," Maria Elena would hiss at her brother, "Ligera is fat and plain, but she has magic. It's all she has—let her use it!"

But my father was terrified that if he let me float I'd somehow end up outside, and then we all understood perfectly well what would happen. Someone would let go of me, I would lift into the sky, get caught by a wind and never be seen again. An obedient girl (plus fat and plain), I have stayed indoors from the time my mother died until this very day.

So. As an orphan, I had obligations. I should run away—yet how? Or slip into an alternate realm and learn the dark arts. Or fall prey to circus freaks. I gritted my teeth and climbed down from the skylight, hooked my feet under my dresser and started to grab underwear. Saying bad words under my breath. Fifteen minutes? To pack up a life?

I snarled at my aunt's straight, skinny back, while cramming clothes into my gym bag. My pair of lead shoes needed a bag of their own.

"Leave your phone."

"Why?"

"You know why. I'll get you a new one, later. Now, move it!"

"Fine! Whatever!" I felt very much like sobbing, but I have never learned how. My curse is that of lightness. Light of mind, of heart, of body. In other words? Stupid, shallow and unresponsive to gravity.

I always figured my father would be taken out by gunfire or government operatives, but that was not what happened. It was my brother Javier who killed him, slowly sucking the life out of his own father, watching from afar as Rodrigo wasted away into a shell. Wouldn't you think such a skinny, moaning, coughing husk would be as light as me, able to lift away from his pain? No. He ran his kingdom from his bed, whispering orders from behind oxygen tubes and a wall of useless medicines.

And why hadn't the curse Javier laid upon me lifted, now that

Rodrigo was gone? Surely it wasn't me he hated. I'd placed high hopes on that, as a consolation prize.

"Hurry, Ligera," my aunt barked, as if I didn't know what was at stake.

Yesterday, seeing the inevitable, she'd loaded the Humvee with the good silver, Grandmother's lace, and the little Dali from my father's bedroom. I'd watched her from my bedroom window, wondering where her closets-full of furs, gowns and shoes would fit.

"What if Javier comes after us?"

My half-brother waited in Miami like a vulture for our father's death. Rattling its wings and sniffing its own rot.

"I made sure he won't."

"But his eyes are all over this house!" We weren't the ones paying the servants. I started grabbing dresses and the fancy shoes I loved so much but had nowhere to wear. I cannot tell you how much I hated the ones I had to endure ten hours a day.

She squinted at me, judging me for my size, my acne, my *attitude*. "Jeans, t-shirts, Ligera. Have you seen me take anything but old clothes? Move it!"

"But… but…"

"What? But what, foolish girl?" Jittering and twitching with the need to run.

"How can I leave this house?" What would happen if I did? The desire to float out into the sunshine had waxed and waned in me over the years. Right now the vast open spaces scared the crap out of me.

"Ha! You have no faith in me. Look at this!" Maria Elena produced a harness from a bag over her shoulder and proceeded to strap me into the leather and rope contraption.

Before I could do more than scream she'd pried me off the furniture, attached a tether to the harness and hauled me down the stairs past the white marble walls and out the side door. Out!

Into the dry moving air! The hot sunshine!

We exited just in time to see Doctor Martinez roar away in his Audi as if towards the edge of a painting. I hadn't known the quack was still here; no doubt he'd spent the last hours scrubbing his fingerprints off anything he didn't pilfer.

I bobbed and thrashed helplessly above the Hummer while Maria Elena yanked the doors open. The yellow dust of the Audi's passage settled slowly onto the oleander hedge. The palms and manzanitas decorating the vast lawn drooped under the afternoon sun. Suddenly I realized that my former life was over.

I hauled myself down and crawled into the front seat, pulling my rope in behind me and shutting the door as a child pulls the covers over her head. Safe. Maria Elena hopped into the driver's seat.

"Seat belt," she snapped. "Stop pouting and I'll tell you a secret."

I shoved with my hands against the roof until my butt settled, and tried to figure out how the seat belt worked. I'd never been in a vehicle until today, knowing the things only by their loud and colourful TV representations. "What secret?"

"I'll tell you when we're at least fifty kilometers from here."

I pretended not to care, while hoping it would be a private jet waiting to take us to Panama or Honduras or even Venezuela, where we could live like royalty. She knew how I longed to fly, to be above the clouds so high that everything below became hazed into some other kind of meaning that didn't include being the daughter of a drug lord. Up there I could be a princess as weightless as paper money. Down on earth I had the gravitas of stolen gold.

And yet I had no real gravity. My curse.

After an hour of driving, Maria Elena pulled off the highway and onto a series of ever smaller roads, the last one dwindling into a footpath. There sat an empty pickup, its keys in the ignition, its rust making continents within its faded blue-paint ocean. Quickly she transferred me and our stuff into the pickup, leaving the Humvee behind.

"Javier will find it and track us," I chattered, sweating. No AC in this heap.

"That Humvee will be in pieces within an hour, and none will be found." She tested the gears. "This old truck is clean, untraceable."

I decided now was the time to cry for a while. After all, my father was dead and I was stuck in this rattletrap with my wicked aunt. I'd been urged to *let it all out*, by nannies and even my father over the years. I'd laughed instead, as the curse decreed. Now I tried to cry, but no tears came. Feeling sick and torn inside, I watched the power poles go by as we regained the larger roads. Maria Elena turned on the headlights after a while, and the road became a tunnel. I fell asleep, waking when we stopped at a motel.

We spent the rest of the evening eating junk food and changing our looks. Maria Elena scrubbed her face clean, gave herself a pixie cut with nail scissors and added a big streak of electric blue from a tube of dye. She looked twenty years younger. She smiled at herself in the mirror.

And me? She worked ghastly motel conditioner into my long black hair, turning my best feature into a lanky, dull mess. Which she then yanked back and braided as tightly as possible. I looked like a poxy chambermaid. She plucked my eyebrows, slapping me when I tried to fight. Then she took all my makeup and threw it out the bathroom window. "No more paint for you, girl."

We set off again at dawn.

"So what's this secret? You promised to tell me."

She glanced at me and said, "It's a piece of property that I…

took control of several years ago. A resort."

I sat up straight on the sticky vinyl seat. "A resort?" This sounded pretty good. I could immediately check into the spa and get my hair fixed. And see if they could do anything about my skin.

"Yes, we will be staying there." Smiling craftily, she reached across me to the glove-box and extracted a packet of cigarettes.

No one seemed to be following us. I'd been checking in the rear-view mirror watching for tails, as they do in movies. We drove all that day, glimpsing the ocean now and then, and stopped for the night at a large, run-down house, where an elderly couple greeted us with zero surprise or curiosity. Not even for me, trailing on my tether behind Maria Elena, batting palm fronds aside. We'd had a fight over my shoes, and I had won. They ushered us past stagnant pools and broken paving stones where lizards scattered as quick as a blink. I didn't hesitate to sneer at the patchy stucco and sagging walls, but no one was listening.

I was sick of all the driving, only to be dragged into such a dump. "We're *still* not at the resort?"

We were sitting in the central courtyard, which was inhabited by three chickens and a mangy cat, drinking cold Cokes brought to us by the elderly woman. I could see stars if I cared to look up. Maria Elena had insisted that I put on my shoes, and now my feet sweated in their heavy lead casings.

"Anxious to be there, are you?" Maria extended one long tanned arm, which she waved expansively. "Look around."

"What?" Slowly it dawned on me. This was it. The resort. "You bought *this*? Are you insane?"

"Don't take that tone with me." She sucked on her cigarette. "I kept it under the radar, you can be sure of that." Another suck. "Listen—do you hear that?"

"I hear nothing but bugs and the sound of your filthy habit."

"The ocean. What's a resort without a beach? There's also a lagoon, deep and beautiful. It's featured on the brochure."

"There's a fucking *brochure*?"

She kicked my leg. Hard. I threw my Coke can at her, but she easily ducked it.

"You had better clean up your mouth, or the guests won't like you."

"Guests, at this wreck? You're crazy!" Seething with anger, I clumped and dragged my way upstairs to the sound of her laughter.

"We aren't rich anymore, little princess," she called after me. "We will have guests. We must work for our living."

In the morning it was still true: against all reason we were to refurbish and operate this so-called resort.

The only truly lovely thing about the property was the lagoon. I'd found a copy of the brochure, which informed me that the lagoon was magical.

Its waters were warm and limpid as angel's tears, and could cure everything from wrinkled skin to impotence. Blue as the robes of Mary, connected in its mysterious depths to the ocean by a rock tunnel, fringed by palms and decrepit *cabanas* draped with tiny Christmas bulbs, unlit because the electric bill hadn't been paid.

Maria Elena ordered the elderly couple to get their car fixed and do the shopping with cash she handed them. She hired local workers to fix the plumbing, haul trash out of the small tiled pool and get its pump running, and so on. I was told to clean the bedrooms.

This did not go well. It started well, but went bad quickly.

Since I had noted her energy in doing actual work around the place—besides just yelling and threatening the help with dismemberment—I set to with a fair amount of gusto. I had nothing else to do. All we had was cheap pay-as-you-go phones, and no one to call anyway, and no internet so far. I had to do something to keep from going nuts. But the very first room turned my stomach.

It looked as though someone had been murdered in the bed. An eon ago. My father had shielded me from the worst excesses of his trade, but I wasn't completely ignorant. How long had this place been abandoned, but for the old couple? They never talked, answering questions only with nods or shakes of their grey heads. What if there were a skeleton under there? A man killed because he'd allied himself to the wrong kingpin? I shivered as if Javier were walking over my grave.

I yelled out the window for Diego, a boy from the village that we'd hired, to come up and help me. He sauntered in, lifted the sheet and glanced at me. His eyes were dark and sly, fringed with lashes that I envied, and his grin was enough to stop my heart.

Of course he saw my shoes. "Is something wrong with your feet? Aren't they uncomfortable in the heat?"

"Is there something wrong with *you*? These shoes are the latest style."

"Yeah, right. Come on, I don't care if you're a crip."

I'd heard worse. I thought about taking them off and showing what I could do, but that would only delay our task. "Just do what I tell you, or I'll get you fired."

He shrugged, grinning as if he was a movie star.

I pointed. "Strip that bed."

"Right away, your majesty." He hauled on the tangle of yellowing linen, and something crusty brown flew out. I screamed, but it was only a long-dead snake. Diego flapped it at me like a twist of dried seaweed. I called him every name I could think of and slapped it from his hand. Then we both went from room to room hurling everything—sheets, towels, pillows, mattresses—down into the courtyard. After a while we were howling with laughter.

Diego found gasoline in the tool shed, and we set the pile ablaze. He stood beside me waving his hand before his nose at the stink of billowing smoke. Maria Elena, who had been out buying glassware, came roaring in, leapt out of the pickup and began haranguing us. "Stupid children! You want to burn the whole place down?"

I was in more trouble than Diego, of course. First, because he was much more useful. Second, because he was handsome and ambitious.

His dream, he had told me as the fire blazed, was to get to America, join the Navy (somehow) and become a deep-sea diver. "The skill of diving," he said, "is useful in normal life. Salvage, construction… the search for gold."

"Gold?"

"Sunken treasure."

"Ah. Of course. There must be *lots* around here."

He only laughed, making me laugh too. Everything seemed so funny.

Replacement beds arrived in a few days, and I stretched 500 thread count sheets over pristine 18" memory foam mattresses. My jeans were getting looser. Evidence of all the hard labour I had been sentenced to. My father would have forbidden it, but my father was no longer of this earth.

I missed him, and I missed bare feet and the network of ropes and handholds I'd had at home, but here we couldn't install anything like that, as the guests would find it *disconcerting*.

One evening Diego hung around after work and suggested we go swimming. In the lagoon. He looked down shyly. "Maybe the waters will cure your feet."

I held back a snicker of derision. Diego had no idea what was really wrong with me. I had never learned to swim, plus I looked like shit in a bathing suit.

"Come on, Ligera! Don't be chicken. I'll keep you safe."

"You? Ha! Anyway, I don't believe in magic water."

The sun sank and the air softened. Perhaps my head softened too, for I let him lead me to the lagoon's rim of sand and remove my shoes. I held on to his knee, feeling my heart thump with fear. "Let's see how weird your feet are," he said. "Hm. Not bad. Cute feet."

"Shut up. Carry me into the water."

"Yes, your majesty." He hoisted me in his arms and looked at me strangely. "You're light as a feather!"

"You are addled by love for me," I informed him, and pinched him hard. He laughed and so did I.

His shoulders were warm and strong, and I clung to them in case he let go of me. What would happen when I entered the water? It was deep and black, glimmering with the reflected stars that were popping out. Would I exhibit fear before Diego? Never.

He waded in up to his hips and lowered me into the lagoon, wearing the fond look a parent bestows on a child. This stung. He didn't take me seriously. To him I was just a plump girl who had to work for her living; he was doing me a favour by befriending me.

My feet were the first to touch the water.

It was as if my toes had crept close to the hem of God's robe and instantly absorbed its thrilling, tingling warmth. Diego let me go to sink completely into this miraculous and dizzying liquid, and for a moment I feared drowning. Or welcomed it, I don't know. I bobbed up, gasping, fearing that I'd shoot into the air, but I remained at the surface, held somehow by the water's embrace. Diego laughed to see my expression of wonder and joy.

"Ah! You like it?" He plunged in beside me and splashed around in circles as I dog-paddled like a child.

It must be surface tension. The edge of water and air—with water the winner. It got to keep me. Air would have let me fly away, but water held me close and safe. I loved it.

At that moment I loved Diego too.

No shoes. No tether. If I stayed here in the lagoon, I could be both weightless and safe. I paddled further out.

Diego swam beside me. What were his chances of becoming a Navy diver? He was a peasant boy—smart, but with zero chance to make it. We had become friends over the disgusting bedrooms, but now looking at him almost made me weep.

"How do you feel?" he asked. "Any tingling? Throbbing?"

"You wish." I turned to float on my back, looking at the stars. *Yes. And yes.*

Our internet was up, the reservation software was in. I had redesigned the brochure and set up a web site. It was becoming easier to get attractive photos of our resort's amenities. Things were going well, though I worried about my half-brother. Maria Elena had learned that Javier's days were filled with meetings with local big shots, punishment of those still loyal to Rodrigo's memory, and reorganization of the delivery system. He hadn't found the time or inclination to hunt us down.

Fine with us. We were too busy to worry about his feral nature, and whether he felt that we belonged to him and must be retrieved.

A shout from the terrace. "Ligera! Time to come in."

"No! I want to stay!"

But Diego feared my aunt's wrath, grabbed my hand and towed me to shore.

"I need my shoes."

"No way. Too ugly." Before I could resist he'd pulled me up onto the sand. He let go of my arm and though I tried to clutch him, it was too late. Our bodies were wet and slippery. Up I went.

His reflexes were like lightning. He grabbed my trailing foot and hauled me down.

Shoving me down onto the sand, he crossed himself with one hand while keeping my ankle in a death grip with the other. "What the hell? What did you just do?"

"Diego," I said, "it's okay. I'm not a devil. I just… I just don't respond to gravity."

He groped for my lead shoes, his eyes white. "This is crazy. If I let go, will you float up forever?"

I shrugged. "Probably."

"How… how can this be? Are you a witch?"

I laughed. The only thing to do under the circumstances. "Yes. And I'll hex you if you tell any—"

"Ligera! Diego! What is going on?" My aunt, the busy-body.

"Nothing! We're just coming in." I gave Diego a look. *Don't let on that you know.*

He winked at me. I had to admire his cool head, though I saw him cross himself several more times.

I made him take me there every night. I got better and better at swimming; in fact, the lagoon seemed to be my natural environment. I'd go by myself, but for two reasons. One, I was afraid that with no one there to grab me, I might make a mistake and float away. Two, I really liked Diego. Though he might think I was a witch, I could tell he liked me too. Did I love the lagoon and its mystical waters? Did I love Diego? Yes. And… yes.

One night the moon was full. The water was silver and black, threaded with sparkles as we splashed and laughed. Feeling excited and dangerous, I decided to swim out to the centre of the lagoon and try diving.

As soon as my head was under water, I found I could see all the way to the bottom. It was as if the moon had concentrated all her light into this bowl of silver liquid, which shimmered and stroked my limbs as if it loved me.

I stuck my head up, took a deep breath, and kicked for the bottom. Something was there that intrigued me—a rusty pile that definitely didn't look like it belonged in my beautiful lagoon.

It was an old van, its nose jammed into the very bottom, like a plug in a hole. How had it got there? I was trying to open the back hatch to see what was inside when Diego appeared beside me. He looked positively terrified.

I ignored him, still curious about the vehicle, but he tugged me away. We swam to the surface and he started yelling at me.

"Do you know how long you were under? What is wrong with you? You scared me to death!"

"What are you talking about? I was fine, until you showed up!"

Without saying a word he grabbed my arm and swam to shore, dragging me behind as I sputtered and thrashed. He was very strong.

"Ligera. I need to know what you are." He sat on the shore as I lay in the shallow water, watching him warily. He bit his lip, looking handsome, wet, and angry. Or maybe he was just scared. Actually, so was I.

Without leaving the safety of water, I reached for his hand, but he drew it away, huddling into his knees and shivering.

"It's true that I have no weight and will float away in the air. I admit it. It's a curse my brother laid on me long ago. But I didn't know I had the ability to stay underwater for so long. I don't understand it any more than you do."

He eyed me, looking wary and sad. "Perhaps you are part fish. I don't know. This brother of yours—he's a devil?"

I sighed. How could I explain Javier? He was a brutal drug lord, rich and arrogant. He had always hated me, and hated our father Rodrigo for marrying a new wife, my mother. I certainly didn't want to inform Diego of any of this. "He's just bad," I finally said, shrugging. "He lives in Miami now, I haven't seen him for years."

"Okay. So you're not worried? He's not going to cast another spell on you?"

I tried to laugh but couldn't. Probably the first time in my life. I was starting to get cold, half in and half out of the water. To change the subject, I said, "Diego—I have a job for you. That old wreck at the bottom of the lagoon? It needs to go. You must dive down there, dismantle it and take it away. Can you do that?"

He perked up. "Of course." He was again looking at me with fondness. "Little Feather. That's what I'll call you. Light as a feather, pretty as a bird, crazy as a fruit-eating bat."

I reached out to slap him, and, grinning, he caught my arm, drew my hand close and kissed it.

I laughed again; nothing seemed serious. Diego's arms gleamed silver with droplets, and so did mine. I had muscles where before I had plump flesh. I even had tawny skin where just a few weeks ago I'd been scourged with acne. I was definitely not ready to call it a night. "Let's dive down now, take a better look. Then you can make your plan."

He frowned. "Well… I'm a good swimmer and can stay down a long time… and it seems that you are a fish of some kind." He made a stupid fishy-face, his hands flapping like gills. "If your brother is a devil, then you are an angel-fish."

"So funny. Let's go, before you chicken out."

Down we went. The submerged van wavered in the depths, looking almost mystical in the glowing water, but when we reached it, it was very real. Rusty, crumpled and covered with weird little undersea creatures that cringed away from our groping hands. Together Diego and I hauled at the back door, which put up a fight. He surfaced for air while I spent time wondering how it was that I didn't need to breathe as he did. Perhaps my gravity-free body was also free of the need for oxygen. When he came back, he found a rock and whacked it open.

I had expected that inside we would find nothing, like that journalist who opened the secret storage vault of a gangster. So disappointing for him! But not for us—there was plenty to look at in there.

Fat packets of pills and powder, wrapped into bales inside thick plastic, glistened dimly. Diego went up for air again. I swam in and poked around, feeling quite sick and angry. Drugs! Filthy drugs, here in my magical lagoon. I was paddling my way backward when I spotted the warm, melting yellow of gold. Unmistakable. My father had sometimes acquired large quantities of gold and had let me hold and fondle it. It did nothing for me, though I knew men fought and killed over it. Would it make Diego crazy? I supposed I would find out pretty soon.

It was piled in a wooden box jammed under the van's driver seat—probably flung forward when the vehicle plunged into the water—and consisted of bars and random melted lumps. Diego returned, I pointed, and he swam to it. He stared for a moment, releasing bubbles of surprise, and tried to haul it out. It was stuck, or was simply too heavy.

He gave me the signal to surface, and in a few moments we burst out into the air.

He gasped a huge breath. "What did I tell you, little feather?"

Diego pumped his fist in the air. "Treasure!" He began to hoot and laugh, splashing in circles beside me.

I was excited too, but also I felt a cold lump of fear in my belly. There could be little good about this treasure, for it must have been lost by someone who would kill to retrieve it. "Shut up!" I hissed at him. "We can't just shout it to the world—"

"What's going on out there?" Maria Elena, up to her knees in the lagoon, peering at us. We were quite a spectacle.

"Auntie!" This news would surprise her out of her constant bad mood, I bet. "We're in luck! Wait till you hear what—"

A dark shape stepped out of the shadows and waded quietly into the water behind her. A man, tall, dressed in tight jeans and a fancy leather jacket. I could see him quite clearly now, as the moon came from behind a cloud.

Javier. My heart contracted.

He hadn't changed much in five years. His handsome face was somehow enhanced by the scar I'd given him when I'd been twelve and he twenty-one. The one time I'd bested him, and it had come to nothing. He wore a big grin, the same one he'd worn the last time he'd taken the opportunity to taunt and torture me.

He grabbed Maria Elena by the arm, too late for me to shriek a warning.

She fought him for a second, then, seeing who it was, became very still in his arms. I could almost hear her mind working. What would my clever, duplicitous aunt do now?

"Javier! Even more handsome than before. How nice to see you." Her voice was tense, high-pitched. She was scared.

"And you, my dear Maria Elena. Tell me, what is happening here? What have those children found?"

She tossed her head. "They're only joking. Time to come in, Ligera! Come!"

Diego and I kept treading water. No way were we going any

closer.

Javier pushed her aside. "I'll make them come in." He produced a gun and began to shoot at us.

No doubt about his intentions: my brother wanted me dead. Diego didn't know what was going on, but he was in as much danger as I. My aunt owned a gun, but only carried it when away from the resort. She couldn't help us.

Diego and I turned and stroked hard for the opposite shore. The whine and splat of bullets got closer.

I heard Maria Elena yelling. "Stop shooting, you idiot! Gold! They found gold. And drugs. I've known about it for months. We can split it!" Javier ignored her and kept shooting. His aim was improving. She turned and ran, disappearing into the dark forest before he even noticed.

I shouted to Diego, "Dive! Dive under with me!"

He had to obey. There was no other choice.

Under the water, his breath soon ran out. But if I let him rise to the surface to gasp for air, Javier would use him for target practice. Diego bubbled and thrashed as I grabbed him and paddled as hard as I could for the safety of depth. Then, as he started to go limp, I took his face in mine and breathed into his mouth. From somewhere inside me came a stream of air, filling his lungs without depleting mine. I did this over and over, as Diego, pale and almost ethereal among the dim watery greys, fixed his eyes on mine as if on his Saviour.

We could hear a few more bullets pop and shudder around us, losing momentum quickly. After perhaps fifteen minutes Javier gave up, certain we must be dead.

Diego and I, our lips locked in this desperate kiss of life, remained under another twenty minutes, just in case. I started to feel weak. Diego, sensing this, signalled that we should rise. We did so, as quietly as possible, and scanned the shore. Nothing.

"He's gone," panted Diego. "No sign of your aunt either.

Little Feather, you saved my life. It is a miracle. You are a miracle."

I think I was crying. Hard to tell, as first, I'd never cried before so didn't know what it felt like, and second, because my face was already wet. "Come on," I said. "You can praise me later—we need to get to shore and hide."

But when we started to wade onto the sand, I experienced something very odd. Instead of getting lighter as I rose from the water, I got heavier. My legs felt as if they were encased in a giant version of my lead shoes. My heart laboured, and I found myself bent over like an old woman. All my lightness had left me. Had I breathed it all into Diego, to save him? Had I been made of air, and now it was all used up?

"Little Feather! Are you all right? Did a bullet hit you?" His arm was around me, warm and strong even after our ordeal.

"No. I'm okay. We can talk about it later. First we need to hide in case he decides to search for our bodies and finds nothing."

We spent the night huddled together behind the heap of broken furniture, tree trimmings and other trash out of sight of the resort's public areas. I couldn't sleep, though Diego insisted that I should rest while he kept watch. But my body wouldn't let me. Everything ached and throbbed with this horrible gravity I now had to endure. My curse was gone, but now I had a new curse: being like everyone else.

As dawn was breaking we crept close to see what was going on. This: Javier was overseeing some goon in scuba gear bringing up the drugs and gold. Javier loaded up his big black SUV as the diver went down for more. I found that I worried very little about Maria Elena's fate.

Diego fumed and growled next to me. "We have to get hold of the police!"

"No, Diego. I have a feeling this situation will resolve itself."

I convinced him to just keep watching. Would Javier forget about us when he had his hands on gold?

Eventually the vehicle was fully loaded. The diver puffed and grinned, apparently oblivious to the danger he was in. No doubt he'd been assured a share of the booty. He started to strip off his gear, and as he leaned back to drop his tank Javier shot him in the chest. He fell, looking as surprised and dismayed as a man jilted on his wedding day. I smiled. In a movie he would produce a gun of his own somehow, and kill Javier so that they both died together. That would have been satisfying, but it's not what happened.

It seems that besides her little girly-pistol, my aunt had a rifle. A crack sounded, a dark spot appeared in the middle of Javier's forehead, and he fell to lie beside his goon.

Maria Elena emerged from her second-floor vantage point, spat on Javier's body and drove the SUV away, cackling to herself and turning the music up loud. I have never seen her again.

When the deaf, or prudently oblivious, old couple came forth to start their day's work, they soon found the dead bodies by the lagoon and called the cops.

"Diego," I whispered as we watched the police mill around happily, radios crackling with the fun of crime detection. "You and I are just workers here. We heard the commotion and ran for safety. We have never seen these men before."

"Ah. I get it. We know nothing, and are simply afraid for our jobs?"

"Exactly. And don't worry, Maria Elena will never come back."

"I wouldn't if I were her. But what will become of you? You have no aunt, no father… no one to care for you…." His eyes grew large and limpid as he gazed at me.

He was working up to something romantic, I could see it

coming. I felt a tear escape my eye and quickly wiped it away. "Help me up. I have to learn to walk properly in this crazy gravity."

"Yes, Little Fea—um. What can I call you now?"

"You can call me Boss Lady, because here's what's going to happen."

I laid it all out for him, and so far it's working out fine. We run the resort together, and because it seems I'm pretty smart after all, and Diego is strong and handsome and everyone likes him, we are making money. The cops gave up their detecting, the old couple kept their mouths shut, and as a matter of fact, Diego and I lived happily ever after.

The sci-fi novelist Alan Dean Foster gave me a one-page outline, featuring a raccoon, to work from. I could see where he wanted to go with this tale of forlorn love, but I wanted to give the heroine more agency. She's an artist, after all. A creator. And she loves dogs.

DANCE ON A FORGOTTEN SHORE

Something rocked gently in the mist, out on the water. Not a boat—too close, and too high on the water to be a power craft or even a sailboat. Sylvie peered through the kitchen window, moving a tray of leggy seedlings out of the way. What could it be? A greenish light gleamed and faded through the shifting mist. Then she spotted another point of light, closer in.

There was someone on the beach, too. Damn! Sylvie wiped her eyes with the back of her hand. *Enough of this misery, woman—you've got a visitor.* Unintentional of course, the only kind that came.

The evening had progressed to the stage at which colours had a preternatural intensity, which also meant that within half an hour darkness would take over. Whoever it was would be spending the night in her cove. She'd better go down, or soon there would be a forlorn knock on her door, and a helpless soul asking to use the phone she didn't have.

The light bobbed, flickering through the cedar boughs that partially screened the beach. The fool was probably trying to determine whether the tide was ebbing or flooding. Sylvie tightened her lips. If she had wanted streams of ignorant tourists trespassing on her beach, she'd have taken rooms in town, not this run-down cabin at the edge of nowhere. She pulled with practised strength at the pump over the sink, and a gush of cold water from the cistern rinsed her hands of soap suds. She dried them and went for her axe. It could be someone besides a lost tourist, someone out for trouble, and it would be best if she had something besides old Jewel for protection.

Sylvie stamped twice, hard, on the plank floor, and not waiting, went out the back door which led to the steps she had hacked out of the cliff that dropped fifteen feet to the beach below. She didn't whistle to Jewel, or call her name. Julie was deaf, always had been for all Sylvie knew of the sort of life the dog had had before she'd taken her in three years ago. If she had ever had her hearing was hard to tell, but she responded to vibration, as of a thump on the floor, or the deep booming of winter waves on the rocks. Jewel was an expert at facial expression and human body language, and watched, alert as any normal dog, for commands in the sign language the two of them had worked out. Sylvie knew that Jewel would be right behind her.

The big dog butted her muzzle into Sylvie's hand, then bounded off into the woods, only to circle back, tail flag-height, grinning in her collie way at the unexpected romp. Sylvie buried her fingers in the dog's thick golden ruff and signed her to heel. With her other hand gripping the axe tightly, she headed into the darkening tangle of cedar, fir, and arbutus between her cabin and the mist-shrouded beach below.

When she had first come to the island, almost three years ago now, the forest had frightened her a little. It was an excited, hopeful kind of fear she had felt as the bus bounced along the rutted gravel road that meandered eight kilometers to her little two-room cabin. The summer sun had baked the road white, making the forest all the greener. Sylvie had learned at art college that the human eye could distinguish over ten million tints and hues of colour. Surely there must be at least a million greens to be seen through the bus's dusty window, from the clear peridot of new huckleberry leaves to the almost-black of dignified old firs, and on to the ghostly silver-green of Spanish moss.

It was a beautiful island, and that first idyllic summer, full of purpose and discovery, was the best of Sylvie's life. Winter came in its time, and Sylvie welcomed the change of seasons— even the rain, the dark and sometimes dismal days, the constant hauling and chopping of wood to feed the stove. Her toes were always cold. But she found a sense of security in her tiny home, in the glow of kerosene lamps. Even during her first winter storm, all alone in a wild night, she felt that nothing could harm her here. She made hot chocolate, turned the lamps low and curled up by her big studio window to watch the Douglas fir that loomed like some demented, ragged sentry beside her cabin. A branch, torn off by the wind, came down and hit her window with a soft, wet slap. Sylvie gasped and watched the green, needle-bristling thing settle to the ground like a dying animal. The wind blew back the needles like fur, showing the silvery undersides.

Sylvie knew the tree wouldn't come down. Even when, the next day, she prowled the beach under an ice-blue sky and saw how massive driftwood logs, which had lain placidly immobile all summer, had been tossed and splintered indifferently by the waves. Wind-snapped branches littered the ground and paths around her cabin, but Sylvie had faith. The big fir tree would not topple and crush her—it was strong, flexible, and somehow wise in the ways of storms. She reflected that this would be a good philosophy for her to adopt. She also vowed to find the money, somehow, for a chainsaw. The beach was thick with fresh logs torn from booms somewhere out in the Straits. She could supply herself with fuel for a year from the wood strewn along twenty meters of shore.

She had gotten her chainsaw by the next year, thanks to local clients who wanted portraits of their children and pets. That beach had served her well over the years.

But she was sick to death of painting portraits. "I want him to look just like this photo, only can you make his eyes, you know, bluer or something?" What was she, an artist, or a servant to others' vanity? Her two years of art college had not prepared her for the realities of struggle and indifference.

Twenty-year-old Sylvia Rudd had gone forth to the rocky, rugged coast of British Columbia to make her name as a painter. The Gulf Islands of B.C.'s southern coast were the perfect site—lush, wave-battered, secluded; divine food for the spirit of a girl who longed to express her vision of the land and sea in paint.

But what had gone wrong? Somewhere between the mind's conception of beauty, and the hand's choice of pigment and brush-stroke, the vision went awry. Oh, her stuff was okay. She even sold one or two pieces a year, from the arts and crafts store in the little town that huddled around the government dock. The tourists would disembark from their big Chris-Crafts, or from the ferry that came to Galiano Island a few times a day, and would finger the hand-dyed scarves, the pottery, the carved wooden wind-chimes, and would glance at her paintings and say how pretty they were. Seashores, flower-strewn mountainsides, studies of totem poles… everybody did them. And hers were just like everybody's.

She had been so sure that all she needed was the peace and serenity of the forest. She'd scorned electricity, relying on her cast-iron stove for heat and cooking; water came from a stream-fed cistern and was heated in a huge enamel pot on the stove; an outhouse served its purpose adequately. She had refused at first to have a phone in the cabin, the better to commune with her inner vision, but at her parents' insistence had installed a land line.

Whereupon her mother had phoned her every week, suggesting, in the kind insinuating voice of someone who merely has one's best interests in mind, that she should give up her foolishness and come home. There was always a place for her, once she had got this out of her system. And then the voice would get less kind. All that money for college, and why?—so you could traipse off and live like a hippie on that island—I'm your mother! Listen to me, you ungrateful little—

Sylvie had the phone taken out after two months of this, trusting in her parents' essential lack of interest to keep them from making the bus trip to see her. They sent letters instead, which she ignored. Every so often there would be a small, grudging cheque. She had cashed one once, against her better judgment. It had bounced.

All the money she had inherited from Great-Aunt Mabel's estate had gone to buying this cabin, much to her parents' disgust. They had never understood her relationship with Mabel, that elegant relic of a grander day brought ignominiously to a nursing home, bereft of husband or children, but still with a small sum to bestow, hoarded away during years of stringent living. She had chosen Sylvie, sensing in her a yearning for a way off the path ordained by her mother: marriage, children, obedience to a dull, safe husband. She had made a few acerbic comments on doing what one must, rather than what one ought, and had pressed a cheque into Sylvie's hand one day close to the end. "Cash it fast, girl, or it'll get tied up in legalese and those parents of yours will squabble over it for years!"

Well, she didn't have much, but the cabin didn't take much to run. A seasonal job in the ice-cream parlour in town helped, but winters were hard.

Then, two years after coming to the island, she got Jewel, who had been abandoned by some visitor to the area, and things got a little harder in some ways, for Jewel had to eat too, and much better in others. She hadn't known what was wrong with the big, skinny dog at first, and assumed she was moping for her heartless master in the loyal, foolish way of a dog. But after a few days she realized that the dog was profoundly deaf, and accepted it. "Seems fair," she said into Jewel's face as they sat together on the steps overlooking the water. "You're not much of a dog, and I'm not much of a painter."

Sylvie found herself slipping more and more into a state of chronic depression. Smiles were hard to produce, so she avoided people to keep from having to fake them. She didn't have anything to say, so she kept to herself, talking only to Jewel in an affectionate sing-song that she knew the dog couldn't hear.

She also found that she painted less and less, spending time instead pottering aimlessly in her vegetable garden or along the beach. What she did paint was quick, derivative stuff in a mishmash of styles calculated to please a public which didn't care anyway. The work didn't have anything to do with what was in her head, her heart.

It had taken long, heart-breaking years to understand that she just didn't have whatever it took. She would sit for hours, morosely poking at the dying embers in the fireplace, wondering just what the difference was between the ordinary and the special, the plain and the brilliant. In a human face the placement of the eyes, the width of a brow or the texture of skin could mean ugliness or beauty; in a painting, the choice of colour, the length of a brush-stroke or the proportion of light to shade determined if a work was mediocre or a masterpiece.

Try as she might, Sylvie could not seem to break through the barrier of mediocrity. More than once she gave up and wept in frustration at the dimming vision of beauty that called to her and remained tantalizingly out of reach. Weeks, months passed, and she guiltily ignored the easel and paints that caused so much pain. She read, and cultivated her vegetable garden; she walked in the forest with Jewel. The days were all the same.

Someone blundering onto her beach was the most excitement she'd had for months. It was with a mixture of anticipation and reluctance that Sylvie picked her way through the dusk under the cedars and arbutus that overhung her path to the shore. Carefully she stepped down the series of inset stones, letting go of Jewel's ruff to balance herself against a maple trunk. The arbutus trees, deciduous evergreens, shed their slippery leaves constantly in a treacherous dun carpet underfoot.

Sylvie paused uncertainly on the steps. Something was making the skin of her back prickle, some small, cowardly fear of who or what could be on the beach below.

She stood, hugging the trunk of the maple, whose platter-sized leaves hung in a damp, heavy screen along the west side of the path. Apprehensively, she peered through the dripping leaves to the beach only a few feet farther down. The emerald light still bobbed and circled, seeming to get no closer. Oddly, Jewel didn't seem interested. She had trotted off into the woods and was sniffing idly at a rotting, moss-covered log. The drizzle clung to Sylvie's hair, and beaded her eyelashes. She took a few more steps down and blinked the rain from her eyes, almost falling in her sudden shock.

Not a lost tourist—oh, no. She forgot to breathe.

Silvery, like water formed almost into the shape of a person, it flexed and swayed not ten meters from where Sylvie stood. She wanted to run. She wanted to wake up. She did neither; instead she tore her eyes from the apparition on the beach and focused desperately on the craft which floated unnaturally high on the water, and did not rise or fall with the waves. The waves parted docilely around it, leaving it as immovable as an outcropping of rock. It was boat-shaped, dull grey and smooth in outline, but was not a boat. It seemed to combine immense mass with extraordinary lightness, and floated, impossibly insubstantial, an illusion that looked solid as a breakwater. A random pattern of lights trickled like liquid emeralds along its prow, faded, and gleamed again. An alien craft. An alien creature as large as life, on her beach—

Perhaps it was an illusion, perhaps it was only a dream—frantically she looked around for Jewel, and there she was, calmly sniffing around on some quest of her own, her fur silvered with water drops shaken off the salal and salmonberry bushes. She might be deaf, but she wasn't blind, and her sense of smell functioned perfectly as Sylvie knew from the last time someone had invaded her property. Why didn't the dog go tearing down, bristling with fury at the thing? Was there really nothing there? She leaned out past the tree's protection. The shape seemed to turn toward her, and she dropped to a crouch, gasping and almost petrified with fear. Suddenly Jewel was there, reacting to her master's fear-scent. Puzzled, she whined, put her paws on Sylvie's knees and licked her face.

After a heart-thudding minute, Sylvie gathered all the courage she possessed, raised her head and looked again. It looked back, its luminous alien eyes holding a message for her. And suddenly Sylvie wasn't afraid.

Shyly, she stepped away from the maple and down the last few steps. Her artist's brain recorded every detail. The creature was tall, silvery as the gleam of water on a spider web. Metallic in hue yet more supple than human flesh could ever be. Delicate tendrils trailed in their dozens around his upper body, almost like feathers lit to transparency by some inner illumination. Its head—*his* head—was narrow, held proudly high, with a thin bony blade running in a polished crest down to a bird-like beak which held, incredibly, an expression that Sylvie thought she could understand. It was amusement. Slowly and deliberately, the creature bent into a crouch and began to examine the beach pebbles, picking up one or another as it caught his fancy. Sylvie could swear that he was consciously soothing her in an attempt to make contact.

She forgot every anatomy lesson she had ever taken in a vain attempt to sort out the muscular structure that went into those long, tapering legs, encased in a dark, gold-speckled garment that looked smooth as poured silk.

Again he straightened, the waving tendrils of his upper body revealing something like a golden bandolier supporting numerous pouches slung across one shoulder. She wondered what the pouches contained—samples of Earth? Rocks and shells? Pretty things that everyone picked up at the beach, little memories made solid.

Sylvie stood before him, relaxed and expectant. She knew now why she was thinking of the creature, so unimaginably alien, as "he." Embodied in his lithe and vigorous pose, there on her rainy beach, was the essence of every explorer, every adventurer who'd ever sailed the unknown seas of Earth, or scaled a mountain just because it was there; how far, she wondered, had he come in his journey?

A cold, wet nuzzle into her hand brought her back with a start. Laughing, she knelt on the sand and wrapped her arms around Jewel. "Oh, Julie! He must have come a long way. Let's welcome him to our home. Say hello, Jewel." With a series of hand signals, Sylvie told the dog to be polite and greet the visitor. Solemnly, Jewel sniffed a tendril. Slowly her tail started to wag, then she sat, her long golden muzzle split in a dog grin of happiness. Sylvie realized suddenly that she was still holding her axe. She took a few steps away and buried the blade in a log, returning empty-handed to the alien form.

She felt one last shudder of tension, then relaxed completely. The luminous eyes, flat like gold coins, looked down at her, and the tendrils reached out tentatively to her fingertips. Hardly knowing what she was doing, she began to sway in unison with the alien, feeling the elastic strength of those deceptively slim fibrils. A tingling warmth seemed to enter her fingers and spread into her body and mind, and with it a joyous lightness that made her want to laugh, sing—dance!

"But I can't dance," she said to him. "I… I've never danced, you know." She felt terribly silly and buoyantly happy. He couldn't possibly understand her words, but the way he swayed ever faster told her he had got her message.

All at once the tendrils tightened on her arms. Up and around and down he swung her, lifting to swing again. She felt as light as a dandelion seed plucked up and played with by the wind. For a moment she felt as small and mindless as the gossamer fluff of seed, revelling only in the rush of air, the whipping weight of her long hair flying out, the dizzy whirl of the dance.

But she wanted more than to be a mindless partner. With a subtle tug she asked him to slow. They stood a moment, and she watched the weaving interplay of the tendrils on his upper body as she caught her breath. The emerald spark which hovered and dipped an arm's length above had brightened in the waning light, and the beach and surrounding branches and fronds were gently illuminated. The rain had almost stopped, leaving the air pungent with pine and seaweed.

Slowly at first, then faster and faster, the dance began again.

The first mad whirl had shed every trace of shyness and reserve from her, and she no longer cared if she were clumsy, or if her lungs gasped for air, while he was graceful and tireless. She only wanted to dance.

She stumbled once on the slippery pebbles, but before she could fall she felt her feet lift clear of the ground as the tendrils clasped her, strong and warm.

In one long stately gavotte she took time to look around at her familiar beach, and laughed softly at how it must feel to be a stage for so strange a pair of dancers. She saw Jewel too, leaping and prancing beside them, caught in the dance alongside her, and felt a rush of affection for the dog.

"Jewel! Julie!" she called breathlessly, hoping the dog would understand without the familiar hand signals. "Dance with us, Jewel!"

And the dog pirouetted closer, her pink tongue lolling and her eyes bright. Sylvie felt a brush of damp fur against her leg, but the tendrils held her so tightly that she couldn't let go and pat Jewel. Instead she saw one long filament reach out and caress the dog as she leapt by. Instantly the feeling of warmth grew as the connection was made. It seemed to reach out and encompass not just the woman and the dog, but everything within the shell of green radiance. She knew it couldn't really be happening, but she could swear that the trees, the driftwood logs, even the rocks, were dancing too, having somehow torn themselves loose from the soil and the ancient bedrock below, sprouted legs and joined the reeling threesome of woman, dog, and alien genie.

Sylvie felt as though she were the one who had been released from a bottle. She was seeing, really seeing, for the first time. The depression that had gripped her for months—years—had sloughed off like a winter coat in the warmth of a Chinook wind.

An urgent ripple of green caught the corner of her eye. The

strange craft was no longer immobile in the water offshore; soundlessly it glided up through the black water, its lights winking in a complex, rapid pattern. Sylvie realized that it was completely dark now, and that she was almost exhausted. Jewel had flung herself down onto the cool beach sand and was panting like a steam engine, and one part of Sylvie wanted to fall flat on the beach beside the dog. But that would mean giving up the marvellous warmth of the alien's touch. A sense of life and joy and wonder flowed into her from him, and she didn't want it to stop. He was glad he had come to this insignificant speck in space, glad he'd landed to spend a few moments examining the strangeness of Earth, and supremely pleased he'd met another who could join in the dance of discovery.

One by one the filaments unwound from her wrists and waist. As each one flickered back to the alien's torso, there was a slight lessening of the mental contact she had felt. The beach and surrounding trees resumed their stolid, ageless repose, seeming to regain a reserve tossed aside in the dance.

Spent, Sylvie collapsed onto a wave-licked crescent of sand. Jewel loped unsteadily over and leaned against her shoulder as if for comfort. Sylvie wrapped her arms around the dog, feeling the still-racing beat of Jewel's heart pacing her own.

The alien ship was now so close it nearly rasped against the out-thrusting rocks, and the lights beckoned imperatively. Sylvie could hear the slap of water against the enigmatic grey hull, and the crunch of pebbles under the alien's weight as he moved slowly away from her. Somehow she found the strength to rise and stumble after him.

"Don't go—not yet! Dance with me again."

He turned, his flat gold eyes gleaming in the rippling light. His eyes, his whole stance, radiated regret. He'd like to stay, his eyes said to Sylvie's heart. Just one more dance on this strange shore, one more joining with a mind that could experience beauty and share it… but the universe is big, time hurtles past, and I must go. One tendril reached out and twined around her finger. It felt like a kiss.

Sylvie squeezed her eyes shut for a moment, then opened them again as the tendril withdrew. She was determined to soak up every impression and store it away in her mind.

The craft did not dip under the alien's weight, as a human's boat would. He ducked his crested head and flowed into the waiting hatchway. Sylvie felt tears prickling her eyelids, held them back with an effort. No tears would dim this last look at him. She sank into a crouch and watched, intense, scarcely breathing, as the machine rose, dripping, turned silently and vanished with a soft rippling rush of air into the night sky.

The quiet beach was still full of him. Her fingers found a round pebble in the sand, and brought it, gritty with clinging grains, to her lips. The salt taste was real. The hard round warmth of it—warm, on a chill, rain-drenched beach—was real. She knew the warmth would always be with her. Nothing, not even the loss of its cause, could quench the joy in her.

Jewel sat patiently beside her, watching not the empty sky, but Sylvie's face. Reacting to Sylvie's slight shifting of muscles, she rose a split-second before her master did. Together they made their way up the slippery steps and into the dark cabin.

Sylvie was exhausted, but too exhilarated to sleep. Instead, she built up the fire in the stove and set water to boil for coffee. She prowled around, lighting every lamp in the house until the tiny cabin glowed. The sight of the dishes in the sink, petrified in cold soap suds, brought a smile to her lips. She'd been ready to wade into the sea and end it all two hours ago—another life, gone now. With a burst of sheer joy, she spun on the spot, her arms held wide to encompass a fresh world.

There was the old quilt she'd found at a thrift store—why,

there were pieces of velvet sewn into it that were the colour of amber! The blue curtains, the rag-rugs like drifts of autumn leaves on the floor, the haphazard pile of firewood by the stone fireplace—all seemed vibrant, colourful, alive. The only things that jarred were, sadly, her attempts at paintings.

The water boiled, she made the coffee and stood before her easel ruefully examining the half-done effort at depicting an old stump. The form was there truly enough, and some obvious groping towards expression and meaning, but it was wrong, all wrong!

With a clack she set her empty cup down on a table, took the painting in both hands and snapped the stretcher boards, folding the canvas in half. Then she marched over to the fireplace, threw it in and fairly dove for kindling and matches. A funeral pyre for her old self! The oily canvas burned merrily and she added logs till the cabin was filled with warmth and golden flickering light. It wasn't the same warmth that had flowed into her from the alien, but it would do.

A client had given her a bottle of homemade blackberry wine last Christmas, as part payment for a drawing she'd done of their house. She'd never opened it, but this was an occasion that called for a toast. Not even a proper wine glass! She rummaged in a cupboard and came up with a clear plastic tumbler. The wine tasted like concentrated summer, the tumbler in her hand glowing like a pigeon's-blood ruby. After one sip and a drop spilled for the gods, she set it aside and forgot it.

Placing a fresh canvas on the easel, Sylvie began to paint. For once her eye and her hand were in perfect harmony. She painted the dance. The alien was at the centre of the composition, and around him were Sylvie and Jewel, the trees, rocks, and ocean all in a swirl of colour and form that seemed ready to leap out of the little square and dance on the cabin floor.

It was the only painting she ever did of the alien. She knew absolutely that she would never tell another soul about what had happened. Not only would they think she was dotty, but it was no concern of anyone else's. He had come briefly, shared the life of a lonely woman and her dog and had left again, never to return. Of that she was quite certain.

A pang of longing ran through her, stopping her hand in mid brush-stroke. Never again to feel that special ecstasy.

But, she thought, if he stayed, I would surely dance myself to death. This is better. I know who I am now.

Dawn found her curled up on her bed, brush still tightly clutched in her hand. Jewel had hopped up beside her and lay with her golden head tucked under Sylvie's arm. Together they slept the morning away.

Pauline Howat looked up from her book at the tinkle of the door-chimes. Sylvie Rudd, wrestling a heavy, awkward package wrapped in brown paper through the door, had the satisfaction of seeing the gallery owner's jaw drop. Pauline recovered quickly and hurried over to shut the door against the late fall rain.

"Sylvie!" she exclaimed. "My god, girl, you look like you've just popped out of a chrysalis. Where on Earth have you been? And is that lipstick you're wearing?"

"Yes indeed. Got all dressed up to come to town." Sylvie laughed. "I've got some things I want you to look at."

Pauline's expression of genuine gladness to see Sylvie faltered. "Look, hon—the season's over. Look at all the stuff I've still got on my walls. I can't, I really can't take any more. I'm sorry…"

She groaned inwardly as Sylvie blithely continued unwrapping the paper from the six canvases she had brought. Sylvie tried so hard, but—and then her heart skipped a beat.

What *had* the girl been doing?

Sylvie leaned the paintings here and there against the walls and display tables. She was almost physically ill with the warring emotions in her. Her calm smile hid two equally frightening thoughts: *What if they aren't as good as I think?* And, *What if they are?* What then? She bit her lip hard to keep the tension down.

Pauline stared at each painting, leaning stiffly to get a close look, then stepping back to study the composition. She lit a cigarette. "Damn," she murmured. "Thought I'd quit." She leaned back against the cash register in her little craft shop—her retirement attempt at slowing down, taking it easy. And in came the most exciting stuff she'd seen in years. Maybe retirement was overrated. She squinted through the smoke at Sylvie, who stood looking like a lily about to wilt.

"My dear girl," said Pauline. "You know I can't take these— wait, wait, let me finish! I simply can't handle them." She prowled up and down the cramped store, thinking hard. Damn, but it was good to feel the old heart pumping again. "Hang on! I know who to call—" She dug for her phone under a mound of silk scarves and entered a number. "Harry! Pauline here." She got right to her point. "Listen, hon. Who have you got for your November opening? Yeah? Well, find some room. Give me your big wall at the back. I'm serious, you bastard!" She held the phone away from her ear and hissed to Sylvie, "You got any more?" At Sylvie's bemused nod, she continued. "Harry, I'm sending a lady name of Sylvia Rudd over to see you…" She caught Sylvie's look of dismay, her frantic head-shaking 'no' and changed in mid-stride. "Okay, I'll come myself! I'll take you to dinner, Harry. Thursday!" She slammed the phone down and beamed at Sylvie.

"That was fun. Look, hon, you're going to need an agent. Now, I don't want to sound pushy, but…" She paused for a second, and as she had hoped, Sylvie spoke up.

"Pauline, I don't know anyone else! Please be my agent! Okay, that sounds awful." Her face burned red. "I meant, I like you, I trust you—I'm scared and you're not—please?"

The two women hugged, cementing, rather informally, a relationship that was to last for years.

While Pauline forged off to Vancouver with Sylvie's entire output for the last three months—minus that one first painting she'd done, the one of the dance—Sylvie retreated to her little cabin and gave in to a case of the jitters.

"Oh, Julie. Can you imagine me up against that Harry Antrobus? Antrobus Galleries!" She sat on the floor listening to the November wind rattle around her cabin. Jewel sighed contentedly beside her, quite happy to be so needed. Sylvie's two most recent paintings, the most ambitious of the series, had been too large to carry to Pauline's shop on the bus, so Pauline had driven over and picked them up.

"Pauline will take care of it all, thank God." She gave Jewel one last squeeze, then leaped to her feet, stamping a quick jig of nerves across the floor; Jewel lifted her muzzle and gave one of her queer little deaf-dog yips, and together they raced out the door and down to the wind-swept beach.

Pauline had promised to let her know everything that transpired at the opening of the Antrobus Galleries' Winter Showing of West Coast Artists. Sylvie had adamantly refused to make an appearance at the wine and cheese party Harry was throwing in the gallery on the afternoon of the first day, picturing instead Pauline, back in her element at last, charming everyone.

The middle of the next week, Pauline sat sipping tea at Sylvie's kitchen table. Sylvie was staring at the elegant blue cheque held in her numb hands. "All the paintings sold the first night?"

"All but three. They'll sell during the week, when people have seen the reviews."

"Reviews? Really? Let me see!" Sylvie dropped the cheque and began to read the slips of newsprint that Pauline drew out of her bag.

"Aha," Pauline said. "I see that fame is more important than fortune. About my agent's fee, hon…" But her voice trailed off in a quiet laugh as she saw that Sylvie wasn't listening. Artists! The little mouse she'd known for three years had been hiding a tigress-sized talent. What had sparked it? She'd never know.

Pauline rattled her teacup for attention. "Listen, I demand that you get a phone. If you think I'm going to bounce along that miserable road every time you sell a painting, you're crazy. A phone, and a decent chair. My ass is killing me." She got up and slipped into her raincoat. Sylvie rose and flung her arms around the older woman.

"Thank you, thank you!"

"Just keep on painting, hon."

"Try and stop me!" Sylvie's eyes were sparkling as she walked Pauline to her car. The branches overhead danced an arabesque in black across the silver sky. Sylvie turned briskly. There was enough light left in the day to start another painting.

One of the first things Sylvie got when she had grown accustomed to having money and being willing to spend some of it was a sound system. She had gone into town with the ambitious idea of a small portable radio, and had been easily persuaded, thanks to a demonstration of Mozart, to purchase an up-to-date system. The green indicator lights on the unit made her think of the play of liquid emerald on the alien craft. It wasn't until she had gotten the boxes home and unpacked them that she remembered that her cabin had no electrical service. When she stopped laughing enough to talk, she gasped to Jewel, "Well, I guess this is it. We join the modern age!"

She still painted by kerosene lamp, though, after the sun was gone. It was so familiar a glow, augmented by firelight, and gave a different feel to her paintings than did daylight. Or electrical light.

Sylvie proved at her next show that she was no flash in the pan. Thanks to her enthusiastic output of work over that winter, and the spring and summer of the next year, she had enough of what she considered to be acceptable canvasses for a one-woman show in the fall. Again it was a success. Pauline and Harry had set fairly high prices on the works, and Sylvie had been worried, but there seemed no doubt that her paintings drew an emotional response from nearly everyone who saw them.

Reviews and commentary on her showings over the next several years were almost uniformly glowing. "There seems as yet to be no limit on the talent Rudd possesses," read one. "From her initial leap from obscurity to her present position as reigning queen of North American landscape artists, she has maintained the fresh, exhilarating outlook that has revitalized a stagnating field." And another: "This week's opening of Rudd's latest—a series entitled 'Forest Dancing' consists of only seven large pieces, yet evokes a breadth of meaning a lesser artist would need a lifetime to explore." "As usual, Ms. Rudd's work has the vitality and grace of a dancer…" "Paintings that seem to leap off the wall and dance…"

Her name was solidly established, yet Sylvie still couldn't quite believe they were talking about her. She painted what she felt, that was all; as in most art, a lot was left up to the viewer. They saw not only what she put down in oils, but also what they needed to see. It was a very personal thing that paradoxically transcended the individual and became universal.

She and Jewel went for a walk one hot summer evening, making for the familiar goal of an outcropping of wave-smoothed rock full of depressions perfectly suited for sitting and contemplating the eternal surge and retreat of the ocean. Her mind, freed somehow by the regular patterns of swirling foam and the interplay of whites and greens in the restless water, could soar vast distances with ease, leaving her refreshed and serene. It was at times like this that her mind reached out past the streaks of opal cloud across an orange sunset, into the ever-night of space. He was out there, somewhere. She thought back to the day after that one wild night. She hadn't needed the evidence of scuffed sand and kicked-up seaweed to prove it had really happened—it was indelible in her memory, a sustaining warmth that she could always call forth. A smile touched her lips and unconsciously her arms lifted and swayed a little, as if an invisible partner were held there.

He was a wanderer who journeyed the immensity of space. Sylvie knew something of the relativistic time dilation that must apply over such distances; she closed her eyes and imagined the white points of stars burning inside her lids. Come and visit this little planet again someday, she thought. The stars will always be there, but we won't. Our little lives flick in and out so fast… don't forget us.

A breeze plucked at her as the night called up an off-shore wind. The rock had grown hard, the first stars showed; it was time to go home.

Sylvie was so deep in her pensive mood that she was well along the beach before noticing that Jewel was lagging far behind. She crouched and slapped the damp sand a couple of times to hurry her up. Instead, Jewel slowed, stood for a moment with her head down, then lay flat out, giving a groan that Sylvie could hear over the waves.

She ran to the dog, cradling Jewel's head on her knees as her fingers burrowed under the thick fur to feel for her heart. It pumped violently, spasmodically. Jewel's old lungs laboured, the breath wheezing in great gasps. Gradually the gasps slowed. Her tongue flicked out, softly kissing Sylvie's face as she bent close. With the last of her strength, Jewel tried to stand, gathering her legs under her in a vain attempt, only to fall back as every muscle went slack. The golden-agate eyes dimmed, fixed to the last on Sylvie.

She rocked Jewel in her arms till the night closed in, her tears soaking into the rough fur.

The next morning, before dawn, Sylvie dug Jewel's grave under her favourite hot-weather resting spot: the shade of the ancient, ragged Douglas fir beside her cabin. Another partner in the dance had gone. Sylvie's last link with that night... She realized, as she sat beside the cairn of stones over the grave, just how much she had depended on an old, deaf dog for love and companionship. She had needed the dog more than she needed or wanted the people in her life. But, she had her work. The desire, the need to paint would always be there; as would her memories of warmth, of an old, faithful dog, and of a dance...

When Sylvie was thirty-nine, she spent a year as artist-in-residence at the University of Toronto. Though she missed her west coast passionately, she tried to think of her exile as a learning experience, one that was undoubtedly good for her. The seminars and workshops she led were enjoyable, the chance to sample the vital work that was going on in the eastern centres was eye-opening, and the landscapes she found in the Ontario lake-lands were glorious. The autumn colours outdid any that British Columbia could show.

She and another two women, one a sculptor she had met at a

gallery, the other the sculptor's life-partner, spent a week canoeing in Algonquin Park, following in the footsteps, or rather the paddle-strokes, of Tom Thomson, A.Y. Jackson, and the like, rediscovering the magnificence of the northern wilderness. Sylvie made some good friends that year, and was almost sorry to leave, but it was wonderful to be home on her island again. Within a day of her return to the tiny cabin, she had decided to build a new home. The cabin would stay; though it was cramped and primitive, she couldn't imagine tearing it down.

Pauline and Harry Antrobus, who, to everyone's relief, had finally married, were welcome-home visiting the next day, and the subject of houses came up. Over coffee, Pauline examined Sylvie's sketches critically.

"You're going to need more cupboard space. And what about this kitchen? Way too small. You've given all the space to the studio, of course." She chuckled maternally.

Harry, a round, swarthy man inches shorter than the elegant Pauline, smiled at Sylvie. "Don't pay any attention to her. I think it's superb—that west window must be twenty feet high."

Sylvie loved the old couple. Pauline still spent summers at her craft shop, where Harry joined her when things got hectic in the city. They were still an active force in the Vancouver art scene, and she gave Harry first crack at much of her non-commissioned work. Leaving Harry poring over the plans, the two women took their cups and wandered around the cabin. There were always new paintings on the walls, and Sylvie relished Pauline's shrewd comments.

"What's this one? I've never seen it before," she said, pausing before a small canvas.

Sylvie's heart thumped. She'd forgotten to put away the one painting she would never let go, the one of the dance. She laughed nervously. "My little foray into fantasy art. It's not for sale, of course. Just a keepsake, really..."

Pauline frowned. "Don't give me that. This is an absolutely passionate piece of work. I've never seen anything like it—why don't you do more?"

"No... no, I don't think I could," said Sylvie softly. "Someday, maybe, I'll tell you about it..."

Pauline had to let it go at that, accepting more coffee in lieu of answers. She thoroughly approved of the new house that soon rose, all cedar and glass and containing every convenience, but Sylvie never did confide in her.

Another dog turned up, this one in Pauline's arms. "You must take her, hon—the poor little thing... look at those eyes..." The Samoyed pup was an irresistible puff of white, and Sylvie named her Pearl. Any feelings of disloyalty to Jewel soon gave way before the new dog's vital affection.

Other dogs followed over the years. They came into her life, always given names like Ruby, Emerald, Topaz; they lightened her loneliness. Each and every one of them learned sign language. Without realizing it, Sylvie taught them Jewel's old hand signals along with verbal commands, until they were adept at both.

Students came and went too, staying for summers in the guest wing of the house, and painting under her direction and encouragement in the cabin. Sylvie found that she still preferred to paint there; the new house, though comfortable and full of light through the huge windows, somehow lacked the special warmth of the dingy little cabin.

One or two men entered her life, but only briefly. Sylvie wasn't a complete hermit, and she had matured from a shy, pale girl into a graceful, confident woman that a certain kind of creative man found compelling, challenging. But she was difficult to live with, given to withdrawing into herself for days at a time. When she was painting, it was as though she was in another world. The men would grow discouraged after a time at her obvious self-sufficiency, and regretfully move on. She would sigh, and breathe a little easier, alone again with her memories. She was not unhappy, and she didn't regret the loss of lovers, knowing all along that nothing could equal the moments of ecstasy she had felt all those years ago when she had danced with something from across experience, space, and time.

She collected friends, though. Pauline and Harry were gone now, but there was a constant flow of painters, poets, sculptors and musicians through her house, many who had come to pay homage to the artist, and stayed to befriend the woman.

Honours and fame accrued. Her works hung in most of the major galleries of the world, and many private collections. A large painting of totem poles against a background of enigmatic, kinetic trees was among the gifts sent by her country to the coronation of King George VII. There was always a young person in the house now, and she was glad of it. No longer could she race along the beach with her dogs, or spend hours before the easel without a thought of tomorrow. Her friends had thoughtfully made sure that a student, strong and willing to do anything for the great lady, was always on duty.

It irked Sylvie sometimes. Growing old was restricting—to get a little peace she had to slip off for walks in the woods while the youngsters were running errands. One day she came into the house to find her latest protege, a nineteen-year-old girl who reminded her painfully of herself at that age, rather guiltily clutching a pup to her chest.

"I know how much you like dogs, Ms. Rudd—I hope you don't mind. Here," she said, approaching shyly and allowing the small furry face to work its magic. "He's for you."

"Oh, my… I'd given up on dogs. I just can't keep up with them anymore…" Unable to resist, Sylvie reached for the little black and white mongrel, hiding her face in the soft fur so the girl wouldn't see her tears. "I'll name you Diamond."

The dog wriggled eagerly in her old arms. "You'll outlast me, won't you, you little live wire," she whispered to Diamond.

How silly of me to cry, she thought. Is it because I can feel the end coming, and this little one is just beginning? My eyes are dim now with more than just sentimental tears; in another year or so I'll be unable to paint. Painting is all I have, really. One has one's memories, but they wear so thin through all the years of pulling them out and donning them like garments out of an old trunk.

My dear Jewel—are you padding softly along your old paths in the forest, and does your spirit still know how to dance? Mine does. My soul will never forget.

Inevitably, Diamond picked up the hand signals that Sylvie used without thinking. He was a clever, wiry bundle of affection, and he followed Sylvie around like a dapper little butler, or led the way along familiar routes with the air of a competent scout. He loved his daily romps with Anne, the young student who'd rescued him from a litter about to be destroyed, but he was Sylvie's dog.

"I swear that Diamond can read your mind," puffed Anne, fresh from a run along the beach. "He always takes his time obeying me, but for you he jumps up before you even speak."

Sylvie smiled. "How's the still-life coming along? And have you called your parents lately?"

Anne grimaced and disappeared down the stairs to her bedroom. The girl had promise, but if she didn't crack the whip now and then, Sylvie knew Anne would spend too much time playing with Diamond, and dreaming about some boy or other. Perhaps her students resented her dedication to her work. Perhaps she should indulge them and let them play...

There was no one to crack the whip over you, Sylvie my old dear, she thought. It took a different kind of incentive, a strange spark indeed, to set you working.

There. She felt it still, that dizzy warmth that filled her as if she'd just been dancing… the memory hadn't failed her in all these years.

It was the last week of August. Sylvie had turned eighty-two, and the accumulated heat of a long, dry summer hovered like dust motes in the air of the old cabin. Sylvie rubbed her eyes tiredly. The painting she'd started could wait while she slipped out into the evening-shadowed forest. For once, she was alone— a concert in town had taken her latest student-cum-nurse off for the night. It was just Sylvie and her dog, the way it used to be.

She called Diamond, but realized the dog must be outside already.

The day's heat had thickened till the coming rain was a palpable tension in the air; Sylvie could feel it in her skin as the soil and the dry leaves must feel it—an elemental need.

As she stepped out the back door of the cabin she could hear the rustling of the first raindrops high up in the leaves. The air stirred, shivered.

All at once she knew. She closed her eyes and drew a deep, slow breath of the water-scented air. You've come back, she said in her mind. I'll dance with you again.

Carefully, afraid she might fall, she groped her way through the gathering night, feeling as though every nerve had just been plucked like a string, and was emitting a high, clear note of joy. The rain hissed through the dusty shawls of cedar, parted the green gate of pendant maple leaves and hurried her down the last steps to the shore where Diamond stood waiting, his tail slowly wagging.

Sylvie's heart raced at the sight of the alien. He was just as he had been more than half a century ago. The rain in her hair and beading her eyelashes made the years between their meetings impossible to believe. The green spark, looking like a tiny, tame star, shed a soft radiance that glinted off the wet rocks and the drooping, bobbing ranks of leaves. The alien's craft was barely visible, a grey ghost through the rolling mist offshore.

Diamond sat on the sand looking solemnly from Sylvie to the glimmering, alien thing. As Sylvie went unhesitatingly towards it, the little dog stood, instantly on guard, but he knew that there was no harm in what was happening. He sat again and watched, ears pricked.

Fingers and tendrils touched. Eyes of gold met eyes of age-dimmed blue—a silent renewal of an old friendship was exchanged; the dance began.

Sylvie found strength in her old legs that she didn't know she had, till that strange warm wine of feeling flowed into her as it had that first, unforgettable time. Laughing with delight, she dropped a stiff curtsy, and rising, felt the tendrils coil around her arms and waist, tighten and lift.

She gasped with the sheer joy of it as round they whirled through the summer night. Between the forest and the sea was their own private, timeless world.

Sylvie could feel her heart pounding and clenching painfully. Knowing she should stop dancing, she also knew she could not. It's more than my life is worth, she thought, to let go now. If it's my death, then let it be, for I don't care as long as I dance. I've waited a long time.

She gave herself up to the deceptively thin fibrils, letting her head fall back like a child's on a swing. She was floating, held in a net of silver, like a boat held in the liquid arms of the sea, or a dandelion seed in the wind…

Her body seemed to grow lighter and lighter, until there was nothing left but the glow of gold-coin eyes. A spreading warmth grew into a burst of radiant white like a star in her chest, flaring till she was consumed, and blew away like a puff of smoke.

The dancer slowed, his limp burden light in the cradle of tendrils. Questing, the delicate tips probed here and there, touching the eyelids, the lips, twining with the dance-tousled hair. Gently, the visitor laid the thin form on the sand, regarding it. Then, stooping, he enclosed it once more in his tendrils, lifted, and carried Sylvie's body up the stone steps and into the cabin. He placed her on a couch before the empty fireplace.

Diamond had followed, and now, confused, he jumped up beside Sylvie, frantically licking her face and peering into her sightless eyes. He butted his wet black nose under her chin, as if to remind her that it was time to get up. Finally he jumped down, sat on the floor and howled.

The alien stood in the dim, musty cabin, and slowly one tendril reached out and touched Diamond on the head. A feeling of warmth suffused the air between them; Diamond cocked his head as if listening, his howls of grief soothed. He whimpered and was still.

The alien turned, surveying the interior of Sylvie's old home. On the wall was a painting that caught his eye. In its square danced a young woman, a big golden dog, and a creature not of Earth. Around the threesome was a swirl of movement—air, water, trees, beach-pebbles—all dancing and alive, and in the background a glimpse of a tiny cabin. All were caught forever in a small square of canvas. A window onto an earthly heart: a being who had loved her home and who had loved strangeness too, and was not afraid.

There were many paintings on the walls, of beach and rocks, trees and sky, whales and otters, all in the unique, kinetic style that made each one seem ready to dance; but the tendrils reached out for only one. They lifted it clear of the wall, carrying it as they had carried its creator.

The alien turned for the door. A diffident whine made it pause. After one last lick at Sylvie's hand, Diamond trotted forward. His muscles tense with effort, he leapt in a small, solitary pirouette, his eyes bright and his ears pricked eagerly.

The alien seemed to stand a little straighter. The crested head lifted and the tendrils seemed to glow, radiating a warmth that filled the cabin. As though responding to an unvoiced call, Diamond followed the visitor out into the rain, and along the path through the forest to the beach.

Just how far will people go for milk that isn't really milk? Are almond trees more valuable than human beings? Bees are in trouble, and so are we, but maybe there's a solution that only something not human at all can find.

THE SINGING BOX

"The little bastards'll be here tomorrow." The sun's in my eyes, and I almost miss a handhold.

"Ugh." Keiko suffers from allergies, and lingering smoke from early wildfires is making her testy. Never mind the pollen.

"You going to the rally?" I stretch for a branch but it's out of reach. I'll go mostly for the bottled water. *Chilled* bottled water. There might be snacks, but if I turn up overweight tomorrow I'll get my pay docked.

Keiko puts a finger to one nostril and blows out a modest blob of snot, which lands among the fallen leaves, scattered goat dung, and small footprints that clutter the dusty ground below our tree.

"Hell yeah I'm goin', Sophie." Keiko hikes her tank harness higher on her skinny hips. Our thermos tanks are small but heavy. The juice needs to stay cool.

A bee flies by and she swats at it, misses, thank god. "Jesus, Keiko, that's a regular bee!"

How 'bout that. Good thing no one saw her do it. Actually there used to be different kinds of natural bees all over the place. You aren't supposed to even think bad thoughts about one, but we're definitely doing so about the Newbees.

Which are the bastards coming tomorrow.

The lonely biological bee zips away, unaware that it is obsolete.

As Keiko and I are about to become.

Our jobs are on the line and we, along with every other pollinator perched in the fruit and nut trees of the Okanagan Valley, are plotting on how to avoid getting hauled away like non-functioning appliances. I hear there's a re-education camp in Red Deer, where they re-educate kids to work the phosphorus mines. No one wants to end up there. They still have winter.

Keiko and I have our jobs because we're stunted, scrawny, and basically without other options. We are victims of the Starvation Wars, willing and able to climb the trees and hand-pollinate the blooms. Using us is cheaper than building or fixing machines, or hiring bigs with their damned ladders. Been a while since we had a good ladder fire... But soon, despite managing our nutrient intake, Keiko and I will size out of pollination.

Plus—our competition, rumoured for months, is about to arrive.

My mom, who died when I was five (shot while stealing food for me) would be royally pissed. The Bigs took all the bucks she'd saved for my education and sent me up a tree instead.

Keiko puffs her wand along a branchful of flowers, deftly turning her wrist to maximize coverage with the designer pollen-and-stimulator mix she carries, while her eyes seek the next foothold, the next handhold. There's only so far we can climb before the branches get too thin. So much easier if we had tails like monkeys. Why can't the big brains spend time on tails, instead of fake insects? Or hire some damn monkeys.

"What about the warm-up meeting?" Where we will manufacture signs, get coached on evasive manoeuvres, and reinforce our devotion to the nascent Union of Farm and Field Workers of Western North America. UFFWWNA. Unless we think up a better name.

"Yeah. Sure." Keiko seems less than fervid. Her little brown body reveals ennui as she sprays pollen magic. Keiko is conflicted, I can tell. She wants the union, but is bored with the constant, useless meetings. I like her because she doesn't mind how I talk, and tends to mimic me, unless we're around the other lils. I use fancy words because I like them, and it helps me remember my mom, who taught me to read before she died. I can explain my quirk because I'm older than I look. You'd think I was maybe eight or nine, but I'm going on fourteen. If I get my period I'll be even more screwed.

Our shift ends at seven. We head to the work shed and hand in our gear. The rest of the crew—there are thirty-one of us— mill around looking at each other meaningfully but not talking about the rally. We know what's at stake, and blabbing carelessly isn't going to help.

Elena, the crew boss, gives Keiko and me the side eye. "Hey, watup witchu? You lils uppa no good, eh?"

Everyone is on edge, even Elena, who is eighteen and has seen it all.

"Nuttin. We's go'na mall, spend the bucks."

"Yeah, you do dat." But then she winks.

I do a double take, something I've heard of but now I get it. Elena mimes holding up a sign and waving it, just for a second, then goes back to stowing gear. *Okay.* I wink back, we leave. Not for the mall, which is a bunch of ancient RVs in a ragged line where a Walmart used to be, bartering cheap crap back and forth. Keiko and I head to the *other* mall, the baccy-wallah trailer where we buy smokes to keep us small, and where we can talk.

However, on the way there, and thence to the pre-rally meeting, we run into Jo-Jo the Dog-Faced Boy. He's fifteen, slightly taller than me and putting on muscle no matter what he does, and has a scruffy moustache outlining his snaggle teeth. No actual dog genes, apparently.

"Bitches wan' some fun?"

"No," we say in unison, preparing to run.

"Not dat kinda fun, lils." He looks around craftily.

"*What* kinda fun, doggie? Ya got some goods?" Sometimes he has diet pills, sometimes he has molly or 'cone.

"Nah." But he beckons us closer. We back away. He follows. "I won't hurt ya, truth! Dem Newbees? I know where dey waitin."

"What? Dey ready here?"

"You betcha. I seen em and I be burnin those mofuckas— wanna watch?"

"What you talkin?"

"Jus come on." Jo-Jo lunges like a snake and grabs my arm. Shit. I let him get too close, now I'ma get banged up good—but no, he's just tugging me around the corner of the warehouse full of fruit boxes waiting for harvest season. Keiko trails along. There's a small opening, a bad patch job from before, when hobos heading north were living here and had escape routes. Jo-Jo pries up a slab of old metal that says *Carl's Small Applia* in faded white on blue.

In we go, like rats looking for garbage. Behind the metal is rotted particle board, easy to chunk off. We're in the warehouse and yeah lots of wooden crates towering to the ceiling, but also a parked flatbed, stacked with little white boxes that are singing. In the middle of the flatbed is a larger box, size of a fridge. It has flashing lights and what looks like a control panel.

Is this the shipment of Newbees? Shouldn't there be air holes in the little boxes? *Hives.* Well, duh, Sophie—they aren't real bees, they don't need air. I approach the enticingly smooth whiteness of the closest box and touch the plastic. It's so clean and weird looking… the singing gets louder, then stops.

I yank my hand back. The boxes get up to their singing again, like a chorus of tiny tiny children. Like mosquitoes who are all in tune.

The large box hiccups into life and starts humming, or throbbing, a deeper tone than the small boxes. Mama Box.

"Shit!" yelps Jo-Jo. "Dey know we here! We gotta do dis now!" His hands shake as he pulls a lighter out of his overalls and starts flicking it. It doesn't light. "Shit la *merde*! Dey gonna come get us!"

Dey be the security guys, who used to be cops and army till pay stopped.

Keiko and I jitter around. Should we start hauling bee boxes off the truck? Should we find kindling? Should we get the hell out of there?

Jo-Jo gives up on his lighter. I feel bad that I have messed up his schedule, so I start shoving and rocking the white boxes to show solidarity with his Unionizing impulse. Keiko is backing toward the exit hole. "Girl, help us!" I hiss at her. She shakes her head at me, vanishes. It's just me and Jo-Jo the Dog Faced Boy now.

One of the boxes topples and cracks, like a square egg. The singing gets louder. Doesn't sound anything like what bees are supposed to. Bees buzz, right? "Come on out an get swatted, stupid Newbees!"

The sun has almost set. Its hot orange glow spikes through slits in the warehouse wall. The Newbees start to emerge from their box, crawling on multiple legs, and with a shrill, coordinated whine fly directly for the slivers of light, where they cluster around. Maybe they're too big to get through? Or scared? I can see nothing much more than a bunch of little silvery glints against the dark interior of the warehouse.

A few bees come down to investigate us, circling like teeny 'copters. Jo-Jo gets a couple on him, starts to dance around swatting himself.

I laugh and rattle another box.

Jo-Jo gets his lighter going at last and is making a little bonfire of trash and wood splinters. "Bring dat crate!" he yells at me. I haul one over and stomp the dry wood slats into kindling that lights up fast. Jo-Jo is cackling with glee. The flames rise. We are bad-asses!

At that moment, security guys burst in. But only two, so no big deal. And all they have is their cattle prods.

They lumber around in the semi-darkness, cussing and stomping on the bitty fires catching here and there. A siren sounds. More Newbees escape and zip around.

It's time to go. Jo-Jo doesn't want to, breaks another crate to smithereens then dodges a prod, giggling.

I dive through the escape hole before security gets a look at my face.

The next day, I hear about the rally from Keiko. She said it went about as expected. "Nuttin new. Hardly no-one showed up. No union for us," she relates sadly, giving me stink-eye. Like a union was *my* idea?

The white boxes have been placed in a crescent array on the lawn outside the front office, looking as good as new. The Newbees are being formally released later today, despite our sabotage. This is the "pilot project," so the bigs need to make it work for the media.

It was sure fun messing with those little shits, though, I

reflect, rubbing dust from my eyes. I wondered what happened to the ones that got out. I thought machines had to do as they're told, but maybe they're faulty. That would be good.

No news on Jo-Jo. Did he escape? Did he get grabbed? If so, what will happen to him? The mines I guess. I sigh, pick up my tank and wand from Elena for the day's work. She looks grumpy and hung over, and won't look me in the eye.

I'm in my first tree just firing up my wand when I see it. A Newbee, clinging to the wand's tip.

One of the escapees. I try to shake it off. It hangs on. Tenaciously. I have never had the chance to use that word before, and I feel a random surge of gratitude toward the Newbee. I bang the wand against the tree's trunk to dislodge the thing, no luck. If I whack harder the wand will send out a damage signal and I'll get in shit. Keiko, who I figure is mad at me for last night, has started her row at the far end and doesn't know what I'm up to. I'm alone.

"Okay, asshole. This is it. Jus' me an you." I reach, intending to pluck it off with my fingers and squish it, but my fingers don't want to. *Prob'ly sharp. Might sting.* Swinging the wand up toward my face, I take a closer look.

The Newbee is smaller than my little fingertip, complete with wings, but only one blunt antenna in the middle of its front part. Its head? No eyes or anything. Creepy. Its body is cylindrical, shiny as a chrome bumper, with no bee-waist, though it has a funny little fringe of hairs or fronds or something on its ass-end. The wings seem to consist of a myriad (thanks!) of tiny sub-wings that move independently of one another. It's so close to my face that I can hear the little song it makes. It rises and falls, stops and starts. Like some kind of code.

It's signalling the others, dammit! Finally I manage to scrape it off on a branch, and it curls up and falls to the ground to lie there twitching feebly. Someone is going to send a drone, spot me directly above the scene of the crime, and zap my skinny ass.

I realize I have only one option: bury the little son of a bitch.

I'm digging a wee hole in the dirt with a twig, victim at the ready beside it, when suddenly a swarm of escapees shows up, circles and comes in for a group landing around the hole. Maybe thirty of them. Have they been hanging out in the orchards, just waiting to piss me off? Or actually pollinating stuff? Give me a break. They crawl toward the hole slowly, a circle drawing in. Weird, but I have no time to think about it, gotta get back up my tree.

Gingerly I pick up the Newbee and drop it into the hole, quickly arranging dirt and leaves over the evidence. The bees in the circle start to make their singing noise, a sad, sweet drone that softly rises and falls. Their tiny wings flutter, making them shift up and down in a wave pattern. Then they all fly off. *Totally* weird.

Did I just witness a burial ceremony?

What if they realize I'm the murderer?

Are they actually that smart?

I almost shit my pants when Jo-Jo jumps out of the next tree and plops down beside me. "Watcha doin' dere, Sophie? You be bad girl?"

"What's a matter witchu?" I give him a couple of smacks but he just laughs.

He says, "Any a dem bigs after me? Dey get my face?"

"I don't believe so. I mean, Nah. Dey never."

"Ya got a bite for a boy?" He rubs his stomach, looking pretty peaky, but I have nothing.

"I swipe you sumpin at break." I contemplate him for a while. Can he actually be trusted? He is fundamentally stupid and destructive, but perhaps I can entice him into helping me with promises of food. And then there's Elena. Could she be an ally in the war against the robo-bees? Or is she just working for herself?

Keiko, who I *think* is still my friend, is diligently poking away down the line of trees, rustling and cussing as she tries to climb higher than her weight allows. We are constantly prodded to edge out onto the thinner branches, but there's a limit no matter how small we stay. To complicate matters, we get docked pay if we break a branch. Also, engaging in sabotage of alternate pollination methods takes its toll. I'm really not surprised at the advent of teeny bee-drones. Just mad.

Plus I'm hot, sticky, and hungry. As per usual. I squint at Jo-Jo who is perched on a branch, picking industriously at his bare toes.

The distant rumble of armoured Humvees rises—the do-gooders and politicos showing up for the release ceremony. Do they even know we lils are working away among the dusty leaves out back of the offices and warehouses, playing sexy with pollen so richies can have almond milk and guac? Jesus H.

I don't notice Elena under my tree till she yells. "Sophie! Jo-Jo! Wake up!"

"What?"

"Git on down here!" She's got her hands on her hips.

"Wha'd I do?" Jo-Jo has conveniently vanished, somehow.

"*You* know."

Elena thinks she's my mom or something. Like *she* knows what having a mom is like any more than I do. For instance, I imagine a mom would stay alive long enough to see that you didn't work the orchards.

"Yeah I know, but can you prove it?"

She wipes the sweat off her face. "Jess git on down, both a yaz. We gotta talk."

I join her on the ground, and after a minute Jo-Jo relents and climbs down, grinning. We settle on the ground close together.

Everyone's distracted right now, so little chance of getting caught by the bigs. We can hear some blah-blah from loudspeakers coming from the front area. *Modern Smart Recovery Cost-effective blah Efficient blah* some kind of joke probably at our expense, *laughter. Ecosystemcrash—*

"Talk 'bout what?"

"What we gon' do, lil. We all outa work come tomorrow."

"Shit! That fast?"

She looks at me slyly. "Sophie, you an Jo-Jo, you got da right jam. We burn them bees."

"How did you know it was—I mean, whut you talkin?"

She fixes Jo-Jo with her dark brown eyes. "Doggie, you in big trouble. Dey got yo face."

"Dey never!" But he's looking scared.

Great. How long before Jo-Jo squeals on me and Keiko? Actually, Keiko is obviously busy covering her ass like a smart person, staying away from Jo-Jo and me. I can hear her far-off sneezing. What might she do in exchange for antihistamines?

"So, ya got any ideas?"

Elena starts to look even more like an underfed house-cat. "I surely do. Looky here." And she whips a can of hairspray out of her cargo pants pocket.

"Well, yeah… gotta look good," I say, fluffing my dusty blonde locks.

"Funny you! Nah. We spray dem bees good. Clog em up. Wreck em."

"Oh." That's actually a good idea. But… "We gonna need more hairspray."

Jo-Jo pipes up. "An' spray paint! I know a guy got some, he a tagger—"

A strange and ominous sound makes us look up apprehensively. Are we being droned? Instinctively we huddle against the trunk of the almond tree. Or maybe it's a peach tree, though I've never seen anything but the flowers. We pollinators get shipped to the next orchard before any fruit shows up. I have never tasted a peach.

Something large shadows the sun for a second. Elena gives a tight little grunt, squeezes her eyes shut. Jo-Jo and I look skyward belligerently.

With a harmonic tone that suggests triumph, a dense swarm of silver metal bugs seethes down into our tree. The whole tree, not just the flowers. Every flower, every twig and leaf and branch, is a-glitter with Newbees, like a reflective skin that ripples and roils. My vocab, nurtured on the ogled screens of refugees desperately seeking a GED, is having a field day.

In a shockingly short amount of time, maybe five seconds, the bees rise in unison and swarm into the next tree. The next and the next. In a few seconds I hear Keiko shrieking.

Elena opens her eyes. "So, dese trees is done, right?"

I nod, sadly. "An' we done too." How can mere human children compete?

Jo-Jo starts shaking a branch as hard as he can, and since he has pretty good upper body strength, pink petals start raining down. "Fuck dis shit!"

Keiko runs in, sobbing and swatting at her arms. "Dey crawled all over me! Oh God oh God oh—"

"Shut up, Keiko. You all right." I look with disgust at Elena and her little can of hairspray. She grimaces and tosses it over her shoulder.

"Face it, lils, we lost de war already," she says. She and Keiko cling together, weeping.

Jo-Jo looks around like a felon, says, "Know sump'n? Dis spray—you light 'er up, she burns."

"Really?" I grab the can and read it. Flammable. Same as Inflammable. Whatever. "So we still be burnin' dem Newbees?"

"You betcha." Jo-Jo smirks happily. The boy is a pyromaniac.

"Gimme—I'll show ya—"

"No! Not yet." I toss the can back to Elena who regards it contemplatively.

I grit my teeth. Face it, we're a bunch of kids being "organized" by a cadre of ignorant hosers. We have zero power. At this point, some general mayhem might at least make us feel better.

But. "We gotta think. Plan. You get it?"

Jo-Jo nods wisely. "Yep. Get more hairspray. An paint. Dey all burn."

"No! That's never gonna work." Not against these critters, who are being run by an artificial intelligence, bet my ass. One of the things Mom blamed the state of affairs on. "The world is being altered to suit the machines," she'd grumble, sucking on a pebble and watching me eat a stolen burrito.

I gnaw my lip for a while, listening to distant cheers, and the throb of Newbees singing as they work their way along the rows.

Jo-Jo whacks at the side of his head with his open palm, and scratches mightily. What now, with him?

I push his hairless chest. "Quit that."

He glares at me. "Don' ya hear dat squealy stuff?"

"It's just the bees."

"No—it's—it's…"

"My head is full," whines Keiko. What the hell does that mean? Wouldn't take much to fill it.

Then I hear a rhythmic squealing in the air around my head. Makes me want to move, bounce around. In a few seconds the three of us are twitching our hips, waving our arms, and prancing happily around the tree trunks like nutjobs. I find myself humming a high little note, decide it would be nice to sing that note out loud. Yeah! Good. Makes my head feel better. And yet… isn't this kinda weird?

Elena's eyes have gone wide as she watches us.

"Hey," yelps Jo-Jo. "Dey talkin at me."

"What?"

"Dey say… dey say…" He starts to sing, a deeper note than mine, but we sound good together. No words, but I sense that words are in there somewhere, wanting to get out. Normally I would instruct him to shut up, but this is nice. Keiko wipes her nose and joins in.

Radiant lines appear in my vision, glitter trails, glowing coronas of petals. I can see the wind. And, never mind it's broad daylight, I can see minuscule white specks of stars in the sky.

I feel like dancing. I feel like swarming.

I feel like returning to the hive and getting instructions.

Okay, that's just crazy.

When I buried that Newbee… did it get some kinda smart-ass machine goo on me? It's possible, I guess. Obviously Keiko had bees all over her. "Hey! Elena—did a Newbee ever touch you?"

"Huh?" She starts to check herself, brushing at nothing.

I have an urge to go to the big white box. *Not* smart. But I go anyway, along with Jo-Jo and Keiko. When we sneak around the corner, no one's there. Just the boxes, Big and Little. Bright lines and shivery places in the air are all around, like in those drawings of angels people make on the highways, hoping to get them to come down and help us.

All the bigs are inside for more talk. And eating. I can smell food. A banquet. A buffet. All-you-can-eat.

More lils start to show up, flapping and singing and looking confused.

"Yo bitches!" hollers Jo-Jo, shaking his ass. "Looka me! Check it out!"

"Jo-Jo! Shut up!"

The sky is crawling with radiance, the glow is pulling and pushing—

Jo-Jo yodels, "Long-term goal! Cost reduction strategy!" What's he doing with big words? Not fair. "Regenerative world vision!"

Most of the lils are here now, and we cluster close to the box, which I am now certain contains an AI. But is it bee or human? Plus machine. *Machines are the enemy of the people.* So my mother told me. *Machines want to rule the world.*

I'm panting and sweaty. Newbees hover around. Some land on my arms and hands. They are about as heavy as a 9mm bullet.

More Newbees abandon the trees and swoop in, thousands and thousands of them, and they start to sing as they hover. Not just a jaunty little tune, it's words. High, whiny words. My whole body shivers.

Merger with lils yesss/nooo.

"Uh. What?"

Jo-Jo won't shut up. "Vertical innovation!" Now he's running in circles, slapping his ass.

Merrrgggerrr.

"Whaddya mean, merger?"

Union. Collective. Alliance. Yes/no.

"Yes/no? Is this a *vote*? Are we voting, like, *right now*?"

Union. Collective. Alliance. Yes/no.

"It doesn't happen like that! I takes, takes—*more*!"

More? Of what? Of us lils. Us humans.

Oh, really? Aren't there different kinds of humans? Ones who vote, and ones who work.

But wait. I'm talking to a machine much smarter than me, who claims it wants to unionize. So what's the prob? Well, the *problem* is that a damned machine is fixing us, when we lils have been trying to do that for years. It's not fair. Plus you can't trust a damned machine. It wants to rule the world. And to rule the world, it first has to get us out of the way.

"Leave us alone, Box!"

The box whirs for a while, as if thinking.

Little time remains for humans.

That sounds kind of ominous. I say, "Is that a threat, you mother—"

Little time.

"You gonna have to sell me on this."

Union equals more workers, equals more production, less work per worker. More food.

Food? "Well… I guess maybe…"

Cost effective. Sentient expansion.

Elena, paying no attention to the several Newbees on her, jabs a finger in my ribs. "Look out, here dey come."

The bigs have finally noticed us. Lils start to run off in random directions, the way the union organizers taught us. The swirly lines around the box get jagged and sharp.

Stop. Wait. Stop.

Jo-Jo grabs me and Keiko and starts hauling. "You kiddin, Box? Dey kill us fer messin witchu!"

Not messing. Negotiating.

"We can't negotiate wit da bigs," Elena intones, peering at a Newbee on her finger. "Dey don't need us no more."

Workers unite.

Jo-Jo keeps hauling, actually looking serious for once. The suits have shoved the security guys out front, but they seem reluctant to get close to us. The mass of Newbees zooms in unison back and forth above us all.

"C'mon, Big Box! Do something! Talk it up!"

Worker bees unite. Unite. Unite.

This is all starting to get up my craw. "You callin' *us* worker bees?" Some nerve. "We ain't you! You ain't even real bees. These jobs are *our* jobs!"

Elena takes up the chant. "*Our* jobs! *Our* jobs!"

The silver cloud roils and billows. The Big Box flashes its lights. Two security men make a lunge at Jo-Jo. He takes off into the rows of trees, the men pounding along behind. The Newbee cloud seems to stiffen, as if coming alert. Then it pours itself out like water over the men, in a liquid silver mass that bubbles them into struggling cartoon shapes.

Elena smiles, the bee on her finger fluttering its wings. "Ooh. Solidarity."

We hear muffled yelping from the bubbles. Jo-Jo circles around and rejoins us, laughing his fool head off. The suits cluster at a safe distance. Hands wave, mouths flap, fingers point. This is fun.

One of the suits, his napkin still tucked into his shirt, strides toward the Box, yelling incoherently. He seems to be casting aspersions on its devotion to duty, while demanding that it shut itself off.

The Box blinks its lights and says, *Vote yes/no*. Then it summons its Newbees back. The bubbles disgorge their captives, disperse into bees and hover in a bright cloud over the bigs. Radiant lines spread and flow all around, linking the trees to the sky.

Elena, Keiko, Jo-Jo and I link arms and snicker. When a Newbee hovers close to my face, I feel better than I have since Mom died, and, cross-eyed, I give it a grin. I should go dig up the little guy I buried and try to fix it. It's one of us.

Vote yes/no

"Somebody shut that thing off!" screams the head big.

Merger yes/no

"Or what?" yells the big, who is starting to get it. He hears the voice too. He swats a Newbee off his arm and stomps on it. "We *own* you! There will be no vote!"

"Oh yes, there will," I say quietly.

*

We voted Yes and went on strike. All of us. A total of 31 lils and 55,000 Newbees.

Plus the AI.

Plus its AI pals and their boxes full of bees being deployed all over most of the arable land in Western North America, which totalled up to… let's say a zillion. A zillion instant union members. Some of the humans balked at first, citing abstract ideas such as *machines aren't citizens*, and *humans are ordained by God to rule*, and *contract default penalty*, and so on, but when the potential production increases were calculated they got on board.

We elected Elena as our Union Representative (Human). When she heard this, Elena hugged me and whispered, "Sure wish your mamma was here to see this." I hugged her back.

The Big Box represents the Newbees. And, due to my exemplary command of language, I'm AI-Human Liaison Officer.

Seems that the Newbees, whose programming is based on the behaviour of actual honeybees, love the idea of unionizing. The AI had it figured out long ago, and had prepared accordingly with a wee tweak to our DNA, carried by the Newbees and easily infiltrated into our bodies. Its coded mandate stresses service to humanity as well as to flowering plants, so any combo of benefit and efficiency is accepted, absorbed and utilized.

The bigs, confronted with a negative return on their investment in Newbees, caved after only three days of strike action. Jo-Jo still gets caught lighting fires here and there, but so far things are humming along smoothly.

Everyone be happy 'bout dat. Yeah.

My mother had just this very garden, complete with horned tomato worms. This story is very close to my heart, and my memories, and has a lot to do with attitudes toward homosexuality in the 1960s. Gays, back then, were akin to aliens. Nobody knew how to live with them.

MY MOTHER'S GARDEN

I remember watching, as if it's his eyes I'm looking through.

Shimmering heat makes the slope of land look enormous, though it's just a garden plot occupying a small part of our one acre. It's near the city, that's why it's good. We lived thirty miles out before moving here, on a farm that consisted of two pigs, lots of raspberry canes, and a cabin with no running water. Today it's the pale morning of Toronto's outskirts, hot already, my mother out there weeding before it gets even hotter and more humid. Back then no one had air conditioning, or a fridge lusty enough to produce ice.

He watches her bending, hunting, pulling green slivers of beans from under their leaves. He watches, and I can feel her hands, nimble as they search. The still-green tomatoes squatting on the ground, her plucking a fat, horned worm from among the twisting stems, stepping on it, moving forward. Shimmering thin and busy. She's going to stake those tomatoes up, later. Tanned shoulders, black hair held off her neck with tortoiseshell combs.

He looks at her for a long time and she doesn't see it, then he turns and leaves. He's gone for the usual three nights. I could help her in the garden, but instead I climb our elm tree and stay there for an hour.

The next time, he stands looking and she turns and sees him. It's later in summer. The tomatoes are ripe, the squash are ready. She holds one, a butternut, the best of a bad lot in my opinion as a ten-year old who doesn't appreciate squash. It's in her arms like a newborn baby.

He doesn't come any closer to her. They look into each other's eyes and I don't know if anything is being transmitted. *Sorry. Why. Please.* She bends down and puts the squash in a bushel basket, sees a weed and pulls it up. Not looking at him. He turns and leaves again.

Leaves with the fruit, hiding it. Leaves and leaves; I like to roll the words around in my head. The fruit of the soil is what matters. He needs to leave, or so she says to me, as in the evening we drop the tomatoes into a boiling pot, then dip them out into a bowl of cold water until they're cool enough to slip off the skins. We're going to freeze them; we have a freezer now. Things change.

He has clients. That's what she tells me. He goes to the city so we can get a new car. In the future lies an in-ground swimming pool, since the clients like him. I will find out about it on the walk home from school next year, the machines plucking away at the soil. I don't know what *clients* are. I get to help dip the bobbing red globes from their pot of bubbles and toss them, screaming, into the pan of cold water. I scream for them, as the tomatoes have no voice.

She freezes or cans everything. Makes pickles, sauerkraut. It's where I've gained my taste for sour things. Rhubarb, lemon, my mother's dill pickles. Though we prepare for it, we never seem to have winter, in my memory.

What she serves him is food she thinks he might like. Perhaps he does. He eats it. We have macaroni, mashed potatoes, pork chops fried into leather. Pale orange creamy dishes that involve soup cans. They drink instant coffee and Tang.

The next morning she makes bread for the week. It's the same bread her mother made, white, sturdy, tasteless, though I loved the smell of it in the oven. In a couple of days, when he comes back, he brings sliced store-bought bread, soft and even, its crust fragile as tanned human skin. Her bread has already petrified, and tomorrow is made into French toast.

She says to me, "I can't keep him forever. They told me that, after I figured out what was going on. I don't have what he needs. Isn't that funny?"

I didn't think so. What did she mean by "forever"?

We're in the kitchen, some other time in my memory. Evening has brought a little breeze. She has a glass of home-made wine beside her, made from our own grapes. She pulls a big enamel bowl out of a cupboard, locates her whisk among the wooden spoons in a drawer. She is moving deliberately, pouring more wine, taking eggs from the fridge. Dry mustard from a shelf. A lemon, which we only get for this particular operation, waits nubby yellow on the counter. The oil is last. It's kept in a room she calls the pantry but which is really just a nook in the cellar, dirt floored, a door of hanging cloth. But it's cool and smells like mud. Corn oil in a glass bottle. She measures two cups.

She's making mayonnaise. We all love it. I love it because it's like magic, and I think he loves it for the same reason. Or maybe because it's like some kind of art. Or like a story. It changes as you go on, and someone has to watch it carefully and do just the right thing at just the right time. She can do it.

Once, when I was only eight I think, he came into the kitchen while she was making it. He had a shirt and tie on, his good shoes. I do believe she was barefoot, pink with heat, her black hair frizzy around her neck. She was pouring a stream of oil as thin as a strand of spaghetti into the bowl of eggs and mustard, whisking like mad with the other hand. He watched, his eyes that strange blank grey, and then he put out a finger into the stream and caught a bit of oil. He looked at it, then licked it off his finger.

"It's really quite amazing," he said. "You doing this."

"It's just chemistry," she said, concentrating on the stream and the motion of her left hand whisking. "It's just emulsification."

"Yes." He nodded as if she'd said something erudite or special. Clever. Perhaps, where he came from, they didn't have such a thing. Maybe they'd forgotten how it was done, how you made food. How you grew it, and boiled and fried and canned it. I didn't know what kept him alive. Not food. Not a wife. Not me. He was waiting, I think, for things to change, for beings such as he to be noticed. Then what? Would he teach us how to make the food he liked? He was hiding here, long years of growing old waiting for someone to come and change things.

Then he left, and her hand stopped moving. The oil was gone. The bowl contained creamy white piles of mayonnaise. She put in the salt and the lemon juice and a grind of pepper. One of her black hairs fell in, and I retrieved it, slid it out to drop on the floor, licking my finger.

We had both seen the slim, pale, jittering thing that flicked behind him, while the oil sped downward. It was waiting for him, impatient as summer or sickness. He had to turn to it, and go.

She put the mayonnaise into the fridge with a plate on top to keep it from developing a skin, and we went to the garden for a tomato. We had to search for the perfect one, the biggest, the reddest, the most fat and wide. Beefsteaks. All three of us agreed on the mayonnaise, but only my mother and I loved the beefsteak tomatoes. Warm from the sun, traversed by worms and rain, sliced thick onto homemade bread lavished with mayonnaise, salt and pepper. The smell of it all, the taste in our mouths. It was our world's perfect food, or so we told each other, red juice running down our chins.

New, life-saving drugs don't just pop in from out of nowhere. They have to be tested, on humans, before they are named and released to work whatever magic they can. As it is said, sometimes the magic works, sometimes it doesn't. Not everything is under scientific control.

DOING DRUGS

C. K. Wallis, on the gurney beside mine, raised his head and looked at me. "Hey, you ever seen that movie *Mariachi*?" he asked. "The one about the crime-fighting Mexican guitar player?"

I turned toward him. "Yeah. It's been a—"

"So the director, guy named Robert Rodriguez? He financed that movie doing drugs." C.K. let his head fall back on the pillow, smiling. The tube trailing from his arm up to a drip-bag glistened in the overhead fluorescents. "Doing drugs."

"Just like us."

He laughed. "Yeah, just like us." His pillow wore a mint-green cotton case, mine daffodil yellow.

C.K. was a little guy, skinny and intense, with a well-trimmed Vandyke beard and an old case of acne that had left his skin pocked and rough. He had charm, though; I'd seen it work on women where my own brand of nice-guy, smooth-cheeked friendliness bombed out. I didn't hold it against him. We were in the same business, after all.

The PsiLan nurse had given us our doses of Drug X about five minutes ago. If C.K. were anything like me, he'd be preoccupied with monitoring his body's reactions. If any. The big bonus in this sort of thing was being in the control group; though, as guinea pigs—even high-priced ones—we weren't told at the outset.

There were four others in this test with us: a couple of students, a depressed-looking middle-aged woman with long brown hair in a braid, and a Black guy who looked barely out of his teens. We all ignored each other after the initial, perfunctory, introductions.

I knew C.K. Wallis because we'd done this before. I'd met him here in Calgary at another outfit, Krane Pharmaceuticals, two years ago when he'd looked about a decade younger. He'd needed money for an amplifier. I'd needed money because... well, just because. I always need money. I liked him; he was weird in an interesting way, the kind of guy who reads everything and really thinks about it. And likes to talk. We'd talked about life after death, telepathy, aliens, women (perhaps the same thing), what we wanted to do after we made our pile. Late-night stuff. I always got the feeling, though, that he was holding something back. Perhaps he felt that I couldn't keep up (I'd grant him that) or that I'd think he was nuts. Well, yeah, I thought he was nuts, but I wouldn't tell him so, and it didn't matter. Call him intuitive maybe, even a little psychic.

I learned that C.K. stood for Chester Kyrome, but I knew better than to challenge him with it. My own name is just as stupid, but in a boring way: Ken Dill. Anyone who used to call me Pickle is long in my past now, and C.K. wouldn't dream of it. We reckless souls who barter our bodies' chemical integrity for the drug trade know better than to tease one another.

It was nice to meet up with C.K. again; always good to get reacquainted with people in the business. Often they have leads for trials that pay big and have attractive odds for minimal side effects.

I wanted to talk movies with him, but as my own IV tube dripped fluid clear as a mountain stream into the vein of my left arm, I began to taste mint. It was quite distinct, filling my mouth, and I wondered if the taste had been influenced by the colour of C.K.'s pillowcase. Probably something I should report. Or maybe I should tell them it was butterscotch, throw a skew into the stats.

Just then the clinic's background noise—ventilation, subdued beeping from monitors, distant traffic—changed, just a bit, and since counting things is one of my little tics I started tracking the seconds, arriving at thirty-five before realizing just what had changed. C.K.'s breathing, which had whistled softly through his nose, had stopped.

He looked okay, just lying quietly staring up and blinking. He started breathing again after seventy-four seconds, something I'm sure of because I take all this quite seriously (mint, definitely mint).

He opened his mouth wide and took a slow hard gasp as if his airway was constricted. There were two nurses in attendance for the six of us in the room, but they were by the door talking and had noticed nothing.

"This… this reminds me of drugs I had to pay for," C.K. remarked. His voice was sludgy and slow, and his fingers were flexing as if he were playing a very relaxed riff on his guitar.

"You okay?" I asked.

"Sure am." He was staring dreamily at the ceiling. "Kind of… disconnected. Possibilities… poss… i…"

Then his eyes snapped open, suddenly alert. He turned his head as if he were following something with his eyes. He looked surprised, even intrigued.

"Hey, what're you—" I stopped as he went rigid on the gurney.

He gasped and his hands clenched so hard his knuckles went white. I could hear the tendons pop. His back arched, and he began a series of short, hard shrieks as if he were being stabbed. The mouthwash taste on my tongue went sour, things turned white in my vision as I sat up.

He flipped over the edge of his gurney and hit the linoleum floor in a crash of metal as the IV pole came down with him. He started to strobe in my eyes, white, grey, white. Whatever we were on was hitting me too, but in a different way.

Still shrieking, he snatched the tube from his arm, ripped off the adhesive tape and began to tear at the shunt embedded on the back of his wrist. The nurses had run over and were pulling his hands back, one of them shouting for the researcher in charge. C.K.'s arm leaked blood as he sprawled on the floor, dazed and panting. The nurses began to hoist him back onto his gurney.

Doctor Lamb, "call me Sue", a pretty, thirty-something woman with short blonde hair and a soothing demeanour, was in charge of this test. She had introduced herself and the company to us at the start of the trials, explaining that her job at PsiLan Limited was to develop a bonding agent to deliver several of the new line of anti-psychotics the company was pushing. She had three groups throughout the facility testing different variants, and was a busy woman.

Oh, I shouldn't use that word. Pushing. That definitely sends the wrong signal. You've got to toe the party line if you expect to be employed in this biz.

The first test I was involved in, for a drug that left me perky and detail-oriented for several days, was for a successful drug that's now on the market under the name Morvrit. The one we were testing now was obviously in the early stages of human trials, and if it kept doing stuff like this might not make it past them. But you couldn't bet on that.

Doctor Lamb closed in, at a brisk walk. Her legs were very good, rounded calves and slim ankles strobing and twinkling, white-white, black-white.

There was some disjointed murmuring from the other subjects, who were looking much the way I probably did: bleary and apprehensive. The Black guy was sitting cross-legged with his sheet pulled up under his chin, watching the rest of us as we blinked and fretted. Mr. Lucky, the control dude.

Doc Lamb oversaw a quick blood-pressure check, peered into C.K.'s eyes with a tiny flashlight, then she and her nurses retreated to a huddle and began to argue ferociously. I couldn't hear their words.

"Hey, man," I called quietly to C.K. "You okay?"

He turned his head very slowly and looked at me, his eyes full of some far-off vision that I didn't really want to ask about. He licked his lips. The strobing was still at it; his tongue seemed to be flickering very fast in and out, like a lizard's. "Yeah."

"What a kick, huh? You oughta get a bonus for this one." I tried to give him an encouraging smile.

"Yeah." He looked away again. After a while he said, "You didn't see it, did you?"

"Didn't see what?"

"The scorpion."

"Scorpion. No. No, I didn't." He seemed very serious. "What do you mean, exactly?"

"Well, I guess it was a scorpion. Looked like one, only bigger. A lot bigger, size of a, a Doberman." He fingered his IV shunt, and didn't smile. "Some kind of bug, anyway. It tried to sting me."

"That's when you jumped off your gurney?"

"Hey, wouldn't you?"

I suppose I would have. "Listen, C.K., that was some hallucination. You planning on telling anyone about it?"

"I'm telling you, aren't I?"

"Lotta good that'll do. I'm as crazy as you are."

He heaved himself up on one elbow and glared at me. "I'm not crazy," he hissed. "You got that? Whatever I saw, it looked fucking real to me, and no one can say otherwise."

"Okay, okay, you're fine. Whatever."

Doctor Lamb, call me Sue, came over again and C.K. subsided, the whites of his eyes showing all around. I could see his hands gripping the thin mattress under his skinny hips.

"You boys all right? Kenny?" Doctor Lamb first eyed me, quickly, and seeing that I was my usual meek, puppy-dog self, turned her attention to C.K. "Mr. Wallis—C.K.—you gave us quite a scare. How are you feeling now?" She took his wrist between her thumb and first two fingers, feeling for his pulse, then replaced the pressure cuff around his upper arm, pumped it and whipped out her stethoscope for another check. "Hmmm. You're fine physically, a little tense maybe, but I'm interested in your mental state. I trust you'll tell me if you experienced any visual anomalies—anything odd at all." She flashed a concerned smile at him. He didn't smile back.

"Nothing I can put into words," he said tightly. I kept my mouth shut.

She tucked her stethoscope back under her jacket and eyed him seriously. "Do you wish to drop out of this test? It's perfectly all right to—"

"Hell, no." He barked a laugh. "I've got the money spent already."

"You'll still be paid."

This stopped him for a second; it stopped me. It told me that PsiLan had serious doubts about this trial, and was probably regretting taking a couple of hard-case habitual drug-test abusers on board. Better to use death-row inmates, or chimps. But chimps are expensive, and they have groups of activists to care about them. Ditto death-row inmates.

C.K. looked at me for a second, licking his lips with that damn lizard tongue. His eyes gleamed and he seemed about to say something, then Doctor Lamb laid her hand on his forehead, the way a mother will test her child for fever. At once C.K.'s eyes snapped away from me to focus on her. His mouth fell open, but he didn't say a word.

"I think you'll be all right," said Doctor Lamb, her voice as gentle as a summer breeze. "The reaction you had tells us a lot, and we'll be monitoring you more closely now. You're one subject in a thousand, C.K." She gave him a tender, glowing smile and ran her hand down from his forehead along his cheek and across his lips. His head turned to follow her hand as a baby's will in search of a nipple.

"You'll stick it out, won't you?"

After a while C.K. nodded. He was breathing hard, and damned if I couldn't see a rise in the sheet over his groin.

She looked at me with that same warm expression, but made no move to touch me. I felt somehow slighted.

Maybe I should give a call to my sister in Vancouver, see if she could stand to put me up for a couple of weeks. I could catch a bus and be there overnight. As long as I really could keep the money.

She left, the door sighing after her like a nerveless lover.

"Hey," I said in a low voice to C.K. "How about bailing with me? You heard what she said."

But he just looked at me, smiled wanly, and then fell asleep. Or maybe he was just feigning sleep to avoid talking.

I could feel myself coming out of the drug, and there was a general lessening of tension in the ward. The two students started chatting, the middle-aged woman fell asleep, and the Black guy pulled a paperback book out of the pocket of his robe and dove in. Looked like a science fiction novel to me, lots of yellow and red on the cover.

During the time he read thirteen pages, I decided to stay. If this sounds crazy, then consider the career options open to a thirty-year-old dyslexic drifter such as myself. Drug testing is generally an easy living, and I wasn't about to jeopardize my chances of future work by jamming on this gig.

One of the students took Doctor Lamb up on her offer to leave. The look she gave me when I said I'd stick it out, just like C.K., made me glow for hours; even though I knew C.K. was her golden boy I basked. Shit, my own mother never looked at me like that.

We were split up that evening and put in private rooms, which made life pretty boring. The meals featured measured amounts of each of Canada's official food groups, none of which, unfortunately, includes beer. I swear this life is what keeps me healthy. I'd never take this kind of care of myself on my own.

I'd contracted for a week, but after four days I was thoroughly sick of the food, the nurses, daytime TV, and most especially the goddamn drug. I spent my hours in a minty haze, my vision bleached and flat, my ears ringing. It was hard to say how the others were doing; I rarely saw anyone, and the doctors and staff were typically evasive. Perhaps it's hard for them to understand that I'm not as dumb as I look, and just might be interested, college degree or not.

But I suppose whether or not medication X was coming through the test satisfactorily was none of my business. After all, I only let it into my personal veins. I would have been interested particularly in what C.K. had to say about it, but the two times I tried to visit his room, Doc Lamb was there hovering over him and it was pretty apparent no one else was welcome.

The time went by, the dosage was varied, and for some reason citrus fruits vanished from the meal menu, but I never experienced anything like what C.K. had gone through.

Then around nine one evening of the fifth day I ran into him in the men's communal washroom. He smiled and gave me a toothbrush salute.

The skin around the taped-on shunt on his wrist was vivid purple and puffy looking, not good, and his eyes were bloodshot and jumpy. "Hey, uh, how's it going?" I asked.

Instead of the noncommittal reply I'd expected he started talking—chattering really—about how terrific it was to be part of something larger than himself, how fulfilling to be a valued team-member on the cutting edge of medicine, and so on. All complete bullshit, unlike anything he'd ever said in the time I'd known him.

He looked deeply into my eyes as he rattled on, then seemed to get distracted by something just to the left of my head. I turned fast, but saw nothing. The back of my neck started to itch.

He turned to the mirror and began to brush his teeth like a robot, up-down, up-down extremely fast. Then he spat pink froth and stared silently at his own face, mouth open. He looked like hell.

"Listen, man," I said, watching him, "they've got you on something way outside the scope of a few hundred bucks. You should call it quits. Fuck it, just—"

He shook his head, my druggy eyes making him strobe like a jerky film of a man saying no. In the mirror his lips spasmed and his tongue did that flickering thing again.

"I can't. They need me. Sorry, Ken, but you and the others just don't have what it takes to participate fully in this test. Not your fault, don't get me wrong."

I held up my hands. "Hey, suits me fine. I—"

"Susan is almost there. So far I'm the only one who can see them, but she's been getting readings—"

"See them? See what?" I was afraid I knew what the poor bastard was going to say.

But he just gave me that wan little smile again, now tinged with an air of sad superiority, an expression like what I'd imagine a saint would wear during a photo op. "I shouldn't be talking about it," he said.

I didn't know what to say. I could only hope that when the test was over, C.K. would regain his normal outlook on life and we could laugh about all this over a few beers.

I had turned to the washroom door ready to leave when he reached out and caught my arm. "Ken, I want you to get out of here. Don't tell anyone, just get out. Go to Vancouver like you wanted to."

I looked back. His hand was very hot on my skin. "What? It's you that should be quitting." He shook his head. Just what *did* it take to 'participate fully' in this test? "Come on, we can leave together, just get our stuff and go."

He wasn't listening to me. His left arm was swollen all the way up to his elbow now, a truly nasty grey-purple. He was looking over my shoulder again, his expression alert, expectant, and I couldn't prevent myself from looking too, towards the wall behind me.

Nothing. But there was a feeling… a sound maybe. I frowned and looked back at C.K., whose expression hadn't changed. As if he was waiting for something. There. My ears pricked. Yes, a sound; a chitinous rubbing, dry and whispery, gone as I focused on it. The mirror behind C.K.'s head rippled like heat waves over pavement. He let go of my arm.

The door behind me opened, making me jump, and in came one of the orderlies, a tubby man named Brian with pale skin and a large gold earring in his left ear. A nice guy, friendly, always ready with a joke.

"Hey, Brian," I said to him, my voice sounding angrier than I'd intended. "Maybe you should check C.K.'s arm or something. Looks bad to me, but what the hell do I know?" I left, fed up with the whole situation.

Behind me I could hear Brian say something to C.K., I don't know what. To hell with him, I thought. He's managed to brainwash himself, it's no business of mine. Let the forefront of modern medicine take care of him.

I went to the common room and watched TV until 11:00, our lights-out, and hit the sack.

I had a hard time staying asleep though. I felt bad about C.K., and about myself too. What if we all went nuts from this drug? I'd been through some rough tests—nausea, heart flutters, muscle spasms—but nothing like this focused delusion of C.K.'s.

My eyes persisted in popping open, and I started to get thirsty. The only option was sneaking water from the tap in the washroom, as our food and liquid intake was strictly monitored. Drinking extra water was against the rules in the contract I'd signed, but at this point I'd lost interest in caring. I slipped out of bed and padded down the hall.

In the washroom was Brian, sprawled flat out on the floor and looking very dead indeed, his head at an angle against the wall, gold earring gleaming. His pale flesh had gone dark, and was so swollen it had burst the seams of his white polyester uniform in places; the skin bulged out shiny as a ripe eggplant.

"Hey," I heard myself say weakly. "Hey, some help in here!" No one could hear me. I put my hand over my mouth. The air smelled acrid, vinegary and thick, and the shiny white tiles behind Brian's head strobed in time with my heartbeat.

The body moved, turning slowly as if preparing to get up.

I backed hard into the door before realizing it was just his flesh still swelling, rolling him to one side as the body's balance shifted. He wasn't really moving.

I got out of the washroom somehow and stood in the corridor for a moment gathering my wits, trying to get my stomach back in place, then I walked carefully to the nurse's station. No one was there. I had to wait for her, a redhead named Beverly, to return from wherever she'd gone to tell her what had happened. She frowned and made me get back in my room before she'd even check the washroom, damn her; probably thought I was making a joke. Some joke.

I heard low talk and some noise as they moved Brian out. The next morning Doctor Lamb came into my room ahead of schedule. I was sitting on my bed pretending to scan a magazine, though at the best of times words elude me. She walked over and sat on the edge of the bed, smiling at me. Not a happy or cheery smile, mind you; a sad smile. A smile much like the one C.K. had worn last night in the washroom.

"I understand you were the one who found Brian last night," she said. She paused and sighed deeply. "A very unfortunate thing to happen. As a representative of PsiLan, I apologize for any distress it may have caused you." She smiled a little harder, dimpling charmingly. "As a human being, Ken, I feel shocked, and very sorry of course for Brian. And for you."

She patted my knee. 'As a human being'? I drew myself up to sit cross-legged, pulling away from her hand.

"Ken," she said, "Brian was a man suffering from an allergic condition much more serious than he—or anyone here—was aware of. Apparently he was bitten by an insect or spider and had a severe reaction. Nothing could have been done to save him."

She watched me. Would I buy it?

Why sure, Doctor Sue. Would you lie to me?

After a while I realized she wouldn't look away until I replied. I swallowed and said, "Uh, Brian was an okay guy. It's too bad he had that, that condition."

Her dimples deepened, and she stood briskly. "I'm sure you'll be glad to know that the test is working out extremely well. It's people like you and your friend C.K. who make things happen—for the betterment of all."

Jesus Christ. Were they all brainwashed? Or was I simply too much of a cynic? I tipped an imaginary hat to her as she left, feeling a shiver crawl up my back. She never spent more than a couple of minutes with me anyway, and now I was sure she was headed for C.K.'s room to practice her bedside manner on him. Her golden test-boy, her key to… what? What did she want, and what the hell was she giving him?

Two more days. Should I stay or should I go?

Well, hell. What was two days? What was the death of Brian? Maybe he really had been allergic to spider bites. Just possibly I was a panicky idiot under the influence of a slightly hallucinogenic drug, and I should just take it easy.

So. Mint, and boredom, and the nagging sensation of something flickering just outside my vision. Soft dry rubbing sounds behind my head. *Nothing.*

I looked at pictures in magazines, making up stories about them, but all the stories ended in something swollen and purple and dead on the floor. *Take it easy.*

The last day. Five o'clock was checkout time, when we'd get our clothes back, our payment and our sincere fare-thee-well. Goodbye PsiLan.

I hadn't seen C.K. since that time in the washroom, but I wanted to either say goodbye to him now, or ideally, team up with him and head the hell out. I dressed, tucked my release form, insurance waiver, and the cheque into my wallet and ambled back along the beige corridor one last time.

The place was deserted. C.K.'s room was at the north end; we'd all been scattered around the essentially empty second floor of the modern, glass-and-concrete facility, and I guess none of us had much felt like socializing. The idea is just to get through these things and resume life with money in pocket. Until you line up the next test.

C.K.'s room was empty, but it didn't look like he'd checked out yet. His jeans and a grey sweatshirt were folded neatly on the bedside chair, and a knapsack sat open on the bed, personal items scattered among the rumpled pastel sheets. I didn't see an envelope of the kind I'd received, with papers and payment in it; I assumed he was still winding things up. Rather than wait, I left his room to check around.

I found them outside.

PsiLan's building, on the northern outskirts of Calgary, sported a rooftop sundeck from which you could see the Rockies to the west, and which might have been a great place to bask in warmer weather. But this was late October, and the sun was disappearing behind the mountains. We'd never used the deck, and its few metal chairs and tables were covered and stacked against a wall for winter. It was cold, the clear air darkening fast, yet C.K. was standing by the western parapet in his hospital pyjamas. The IV drip was in his arm, the chrome-plated apparatus holding the bag beside him. Doctor Lamb had her arms around him.

I'd seen C.K. get women I'd thought were way out of his league, but I knew this contact had nothing to do with sex. C.K.'s slumped, dejected attitude radiated fear and despair. Maybe I can't read words, but I'm good at body language. He might even have been crying, I couldn't tell from twenty feet away. I crept closer. They didn't see me.

She was talking very fast, a pleading note in her voice. "—work together, we have to work together for this—"

I don't know what I thought I could do; break up a scene, calm them down. I don't know. Before I got close enough to make out more words, C.K. tore away from her and stumbled sideways along the waist-high barrier at the edge of the roof, the IV pole rocking behind him.

She followed him, grabbed his good arm. He shook her off and she made angry fists, thrusting her neck out snake-like at him. Suddenly he fell to his knees clutching his head, and began to wail eerily. The IV pole fell, and he shuddered as the tube ripped out of the shunt and twisted away. I stepped forward then, but stopped as something large whipped past my ear.

I ducked and flailed at the air, but there was nothing to see. The wind had picked up and was scattering dust in my eyes.

Another harsh whir of air close by, a dim flash of gold in the corner of my eye, and acid in my nostrils. The wind pushed me sideways.

I shouted, "C.K.! Hey, get away from the edge—" but my voice was buried under a sudden hot roar of wind.

It was full of sand, stinging my skin, needle-sharp and burning, and I could barely breathe or see. I held my hands protectively before my face and groped my way forward to where I remembered C.K. and the doctor being. My eyes were streaming and my skin crawled and itched. The hot air seared my lungs. I would have turned and run then, had I been able to find my way back to the stairwell.

Something landed with a heavy thump on the deck beside me. Through my tears I saw it, a thing that looked very much like a huge scorpion, stinger raised. It had wings, though, stiff and transparent, and a blunt eyeless head that turned on its ropy neck, mantis-like and quick. Another landed beside it, and another. Heavy and golden-brown, glowing as if lit by some other sun than ours. A toxic desert sun.

I stood perfectly still, instinctively knowing that if I tried to flee they'd be on me in an instant.

Through bleary eyes I looked up. The sky was beautiful, as if a master painter had laid a gilded wash across the air itself and made every molecule shimmer. A tear in the sky had opened, and was getting longer and wider, as if a giant claw had slashed it. The air filled with scorpion-things, winged and gleaming, driving down from that rift in the golden sky, hard-shelled and fast as they swarmed overhead.

The swarm was creating its own wind, like a peloton of bikers. I bent and forced myself forward, towards C.K. and the doctor, who clung together against the parapet.

The creatures were converging on them, diving from above, crawling along the sundeck floor. C.K. waved his arms feebly as two of them gripped him with their pincers and curled their stingers, ready.

Doctor Lamb lunged for them, trying I think to save C.K., but one of them turned and drove its stinger deep into her shoulder. She spun around from the force of the attack, her mouth open as if in surprise, but she didn't scream. C.K.'s pointed beard stood out black against his skin. Doctor Lamb fell and started to convulse. C.K. pulled himself to his feet. He looked directly at me then, his eyes black pits, his face a bloodless mask.

"It's me," he cried over the acid wind, the pelting golden wings. "I'm bringing them. God help me." He stared down at Doctor Lamb for just a moment, then he turned, threw a leg over the parapet and with a quick twist dove over the edge. He vanished before I could do or say a thing. The hot wind howled, driving acrid dust into my eyes and down my throat.

I found myself lying on the roof deck, my ears ringing. The cold Calgary night was back huge and empty around me, blue pricked with a few white stars. The long golden rift in the sky was gone. The air had the flat dead smell of winter.

By the time I crawled to the edge and looked over, I was shivering uncontrollably. C.K. was a pale blob on the pavement below, unmoving.

There was no sign of the things I'd seen, not even a stray broken wing or stinger; just Doctor Susan Lamb crumpled and twitching on the deck. Her eyes were open, sanded dry and sightless. When I touched her arm she snarled up at me, and with both hands grabbed my arm, pulled me close. "You… they want you next… not me. Not me…" Her sightless eyes dimmed, yet her face still glowed gold under the empty night sky. Her tongue flickered in her open mouth, and then she clenched her teeth and died. I pried her hands off me and backed away.

There was no one around. The night was still and hollow. I collected my belongings, ran out of the empty building and headed for the bus station. Something chitinous and dry ran behind me all the way.

Cats—they're fluffy, adorable, and loving, right? And fairies... well, fairies are delicate, ethereal creatures born of mist and magic. Uh-huh... A spot of mayhem in a small English village might change your mind.

THANK YEW VERY MUCH

Eric Whittle finally abandoned his phone, picked up his fork and speared a strawberry from the fruit plate between us. "Say, Doctor Cobb, where's Gladys?" he asked, chewing lustily. "Isn't she always at these things?"

I sipped my coffee and looked at him. Although Whittle was talented, he was awfully young and naive, but weren't we all at that age?

What had happened to Gladys was a long story. I debated starting in on it and decided that we'd plenty of time, considering Huxlyn wasn't going to be giving us the breakfast part of this meeting any time soon. He'd got hold of a Roc egg somewhere, and though it would do for all of us, it was going to take forever to scramble. I warmed up my coffee from the ornate silver carafe and settled back. The others were gossiping, discussing minute variations on potions, complaining about how the new cellphone tower interfered with spells, etc. Anything but studying up on the monthly agenda.

"Ah, Gladys," I said. "She's a stalwart all right. I'm afraid, my dear fellow, that I have an unfortunate piece of news about her. Do you care to hear it?"

"Of course! Hope the old doll's all right." Eric glugged back some pomegranate juice, into which he had surreptitiously poured gin from a little flask. Since he wasn't sharing, I decided I needn't hold back.

How to begin? Well, I thought, walking through Gladys's doorway into a miasma of pain, blood and desperation would do.

Since she hadn't answered my habitual morning phone call, in which we compared progress on the paper's daily cryptic crossword, I'd gone over to see what was up, if not her. I'd knocked, first with my knuckles in the ordinary way, then using the cast-iron toad knocker, to no avail.

I shouted, "Gladdie darling, are you decent?"

I knew she was in there, I could feel the blackberry-bramble prickle of her personality seeping round the window frames and under the sturdy oak door. Her normal response would be, "Of course not! Have you ever known me to be decent?" This was very worrying. Gladys and I had a relationship that went back to before the first Withering War, and I liked to think I was attuned to her moods. Something was terribly wrong.

If there was any time to push the button, it was now.

My finger hesitated for only a moment above the little ivory disk set at eye level in the door. As my finger hovered over it, a tiny floating line of words drifted out: *To Be Used Only in Case of Emergency.* The words wisped away into golden dust, their job done. Jabbing it with my forefinger, I immediately jumped back and covered my eyes. The door emitted a shriek and blew inward to slam back against the wall, knocking over a stand laden with hats, scarves and cloaks.

The smell knocked me back more than the slivers of oak that

flew past my ears. I held my nose against the stench of overfilled cat-box, spoiled milk, blood, and urine that puffed from the darkened interior of Gladys's abode. My eyes watered. Usually, her place smelled nice: lavender, quince pie, angel's tears baked into a pudding. However, today, the stink seemed to darken the dim space. I flicked the light switch by the door, but nothing happened. Damn.

I stumbled in over scattered books and balls of wool. "Gladys! Gladdie, are you here? Are you all right?"

Of course, she wasn't all right.

I found her sitting on her couch, feet on the floor, back flat against the cushions, head erect. Her mouth was open. Her lips were gone as was her tongue.

Her eyes were hollow, bleeding pits. Her cheeks were slashed and her bosom, that lovely soft, round bosom that I'd… ahem. Remember the Withering Wars? Well, I'd been fond of her bosom since then. Gone. Chewed ragged and red as a squashed watermelon under her shredded nightgown.

I fell at her feet, scarcely able to apprehend the horror. Her ankles were gnawed to the bone above her fluffy sheepskin slippers. A cold, filmed-over cup of tea sat on the table at her elbow.

What under the sun had been going on here? I'd seen her only three days ago. Gingerly, I reached out and grasped her hand, pulling it toward me to check her wrist for a pulse. Merciless God, there was one. Can't say I was happy about that. Better for her to be dead, don't you agree?

Er, would you like a glass of water, Whittle? You look a bit green about the gills. No? Right then.

I confess I hadn't the slightest idea what to do. Clearly, she was beyond any assistance an ordinary doctor could give. And, since I sense you are about to ask, I am not that sort of doctor.

Well. After a bit, I wiped my eyes and tried to ascertain what was going on in that chamber of horrors. There was a nagging *frisson* of dread lingering about, and it was growing stronger. My ears may be old, but they picked up a low growling sound. I looked about.

Seeing nothing out of the ordinary but poor Gladys and her neglected home, I checked her cauldron. Cold! The fire—the fire that should have been keeping that massive, cast iron vessel at a constant simmer, and in fact had been since she'd moved in thirty years ago—had gone out. This was perhaps the most remarkable thing about the scene.

Suddenly the hairs on the back of my neck stood up. I whirled about to see on the mantel at eye level a pair of unblinking yellow eyes. They fixed me with their evil glow.

A cat, by God. An enormous, tawny cat, of the kind known in the colonies as a Maine Coon Cat. It was approximately the size of a lynx and looked twice as belligerent. It was Gladys's familiar, Orlando, and he had obviously gone bad. He twitched his tufted ears at me, lifted his lip and emitted an ear-splitting yowl.

Then he leapt at my head.

I managed to fend him off, while getting several deep scratches on my arms right through my jacket. Then, I'm sorry to say, I ran like a pickpocket with the London coppers after him. Panting and shaken, I stopped under Gladys's sacred yew tree. The cat, undoubtedly pleased with himself, stopped at the threshold, glared at me for a minute, and then in an unmistakably disdainful fashion began to lick his nether regions.

The little bastard had won this round. And my poor Gladys was still inside, locked in a spell of some kind. Orlando had spent years watching and listening to her perform her incantations—he must have managed to cast a stasis spell upon her. Caught her on a bad day apparently. The blasted creature was clever, he was ruthless, and he was well-fed. He wasn't going to voluntarily give up his position of power, when he was in full command of the whole house and its mistress.

I had to get Orlando out. Before anything else could be done, the cat must go.

But how?

To storm in there and begin tossing spells around was a bad idea. Gladys, locked in stasis, would be in the path of ricochets, unable to defend herself, and might easily find herself worse off than she was now. If such a fate could be imagined. But what about a firearm? Did I know anyone who possessed one? Not anywhere nearby, and I had little time to waste.

My cousin Newell here in the village has an archery get-up, but unfortunately he'd gone north to hunt pheasant. Drat. It was up to me.

Cautiously, I approached the house, stopping to peer through the doorway. In the dimly lit space I could see only the top of Gladys's head over the back of the couch. I took a step inside.

The cat hit me from the top of one of the many bookshelves, landed on my head, took a chunk out of my ear, then raked his way down my back like a mountaineer rappelling down a cliff. I retreated once again. By God, Whittle, I had a sudden vision of myself, trapped by the same spell that had got my friend, lined up on the couch beside her as a sort of second course.

If only he could be lured outside, I'd have a chance to bash him to death with a rock or a stick, perhaps. Though it didn't seem likely… that cat was big, strong and smug. I pitied any poor dog I managed to locate, wheedle from its owner and shove in there. Wouldn't have a chance. It was quickly becoming apparent that I was going to need assistance from a power greater than my own.

A fairy.

At that thought, I felt a ray of hope.

I knew sixteen of them. Eight were currently occupied by an intricate dance that had gone on for weeks and still had over a month to go. They couldn't be interrupted. It would do something nasty to their future progeny or something.

Eight were left. Two were vacationing in Belize, having hitched a ride with Janet and Roger Smyth, who were honeymooning and willing to smuggle fairies in their luggage.

Six. I sighed. One was elderly and rather fat. Another had broken a wing recently and was laid up. Of the last four, two were attending a symposium in a location they had refused to divulge, and the other was looking after their garden. Last time I'd checked in, she was blind drunk among the gooseberries.

Which left one. Fortunately, she was the best of the lot, though some might disagree. Some might call her the worst of the lot.

I knew where she lived: under an old overturned wheelbarrow at the bottom of the garden just two doors down. She'd made it quite nice, really, complete with a wee wood stove for warmth in the winter, and a couple of skylights she'd cut with her industrial beak and glazed with bits of broken glass. She liked to be off the grid.

I skidded to a halt next to the upside-down barrow handles, panting, and tapped briskly on the metal shell.

"Go away!"

"Pansy, it's me! Mervin Cobb! Sorry, but it's an emergency."

"I doubt that." Her voice reverberated strangely from under the wheelbarrow.

"It's Gladys. She's… she's…" my voice broke. I couldn't go on.

Pansy stuck her head out at last. "What's up, Doc?" She snickered. "Take it easy—can't be that bad."

"Oh, but it is." Quickly I explained the situation. Pansy's beady eyes narrowed, and she hopped out to fly up and perch on a handle. I crouched to her level and blew my nose. Pansy was a pretty little thing. Half bird, half sprite of the air, she had the tiny perfect body of a minuscule teenager and the feathered wings of a bird. Her fingers and toes were long, their sharp talons brightly painted, and her red hair was arranged into a startlingly pointy crest.

"That bloody cat." She shook her head. "Orlando was always too strong for Gladys. I warned her, you know."

"I'm sure you did." Pansy was a bit of a know-it-all.

Fairies, as you know, Whittle, are born of bird eggs that have been… touched. In this case, by a Blue Moon. Pansy was one of the strongest fairies around, being of sturdy robin stock augmented by the once-in-a-blue-moon magic. I have no idea what the parent birds thought when that little horror burst out of her shell and promptly ate the other chicks, but as I understand it, birds just go ahead and lay more eggs.

She had her everyday beak under one wing, dangling on its strap. "So what's your plan, Doc? How are we going to deal with this situation?"

"Why do you think I'm here? I need you to somehow distract Orlando long enough for me to whack him to death."

"*Somehow?* You're kidding, right? Have you seen the jaws on that thing?"

"Up close, thank you very much." I rubbed my bitten ear. "Look, if Gladys's eternal soul means nothing to you—"

"Never said I wasn't up to it, did I?" She fluttered her wings and strapped on her beak. It gleamed silver and formed itself to her little face. Clacking it a few times to test the seal, she flew to my shoulder. "Best get to it. Who knows what part of Gladys that hellish creature will nosh on next."

Back at Gladys's cottage, Pansy flittered around, casing the joint. After a thorough recce from outside, including a peek down the chimney—stone cold for the first time in decades—

she landed on my outstretched hand and sat down, cross-legged.

"So," she said, looking me in the eye, "I know what my part in this is. I'm not sure you're clear on yours."

Perhaps I wasn't. I thought for a moment. I'd definitely need some sort of weapon, better than a rock or stick. Also body armour. "Wait here," I snapped. I placed her on a decorative lawn gnome and jogged toward home.

"That's more like it," said Pansy when I returned, eyeing my weapon of choice: an axe. She seemed less appreciative of my gardening gloves, bicycle helmet and safety glasses. "Is that a personal flotation device you're wearing, sport?"

"All I could find. Don't worry, I'm a pretty dab hand at log-splitting," I informed her, smiling grimly and swinging the axe to and fro.

"I'm sure you are. But do the logs leap at you with claws outstretched?" She shook her head and exhibited a look of sadness. Or pity.

"Look, Pansy—there's no time for argument or practice. Just trust me. I plan to decapitate the little bugger."

"If you say so." She hitched up her rosy-red shorts, rolled her shoulders in an athletic fashion and zipped away like a bee, through the door and into the dim, dangerous interior.

I crept to Gladys's door and stood to one side, axe at the ready, breathing deeply.

Nothing happened for quite a while. The sun cleared the line of ash trees beside the church, the wind picked up a bit, and the sacred yew tree rustled darkly. I remembered that these trees were poisonous to horses. Perhaps also to cats…? Relaxing a little as nothing continued to happen, I contemplated using my axe to chop off a yew limb for use as a sort of spear or club.

A series of crashes, thuds and yowls sounded. A flash of brilliant pink, like weird lightning. The windows rattled, and somewhere inside glass shattered. Something shot past my ear, spinning. Reflexively, I swung the axe, managing to put a notch in the door frame.

Orlando stood in the doorway, not a foot away from me and my axe, which was stuck in the frame. He lifted a lip, showing a row of gleaming yellow teeth, and licked his lips. My eyes widened. He hadn't caught Pansy and eaten her, had he?

But then I heard her tiny, bell-like voice, articulating words I shall not repeat. I yanked the axe free and ran for the shelter of the yew, in which there was a commotion going on.

Pansy was in there, caught in the branches. She struggled, but the tree was in a helpful mood and gave her an assist to the end of a long branch. She perched on it, snarling and shuffling her wing feathers back into position.

"Are you aware," she gritted, "that Orlando has been drinking from Gladys's cauldron?"

"Good God, no!"

"Yes. It has cooled down enough, unfortunately. We are in big trouble. And thanks for not hitting me with your stupid axe, you twit."

"No need to get testy. So, Orlando's powers have increased exponentially." I looked at my axe, tossed it into the delphinium bed and chewed my lip.

"Yes," she said. "But don't worry, I have some ideas."

"So do I. Did you know that the yew tree is poisonous to many animals, including cats?" I'd Googled it while waiting outside Gladys's door.

She brightened. "Ah! Good to know." She flew back to the tree and after a brief operation involving her beak, obtained numerous inch-long slivers of wood. She handed them over to me. "Be right back. Don't do anything stupid." Pansy whirred away toward her wheelbarrow home.

The yew tree rustled its needles and seemed to become fuller: thicker and even more dark. Was it trying to protect itself from our meddling? "Sorry, old boy," I murmured to it. "Won't be long now."

I hoped.

Crouched on my heels, I kept a close watch on the house, which was emitting more lightning flashes and growling. Orlando was riled up—no telling what he'd do now. Things were looking pretty grim.

"Ah, Whittle, here comes old Huxlyn with the trolley. Breakfast, at last!"

The lad leaned back, blinking. "But, but what happened next?"

"Just eat up, boy. This meeting won't take more than a couple of hours, and then I'll tell you the rest."

Whittle fidgeted and fretted the whole time, shoving his egg around on the plate but not eating. The meeting finally concluded. It had been decided in a close vote that since most of us went to bed at nine, midnight was too late for lunar observations no matter the phase; several boring items on the agenda had been shelved for next time; and three attendees were sound asleep in their chairs. Not Eric Whittle, however. He was wide awake, having managed only to empty his little flask.

Everyone was waking up and leaving. The meeting space was needed for the troll attack recovery group at eleven, and we had to clear out. The retired among us planned to head for the local, where, having finished breakfast, we could start in on lunch.

"Come on, boy." I stood up, remembering the shopping bag at my feet. "We'll talk along the way, shall we? Unless you've somewhere else to be?"

"Not bloody likely, Doc. Carry that bag for you? Seems to be twitching a bit."

"I'm fine, thank you. So, where were we?"

"Pansy had shot off somewhere."

"Right. Well, we knew..."

We knew that Orlando had gained immeasurable power from the contents of Gladys's cauldron. She'd been tending that thing for decades, judiciously applying vials of its soupy mix in various ways, for various purposes and to various clients. You needn't ask, Whittle. I will not tell you.

As you may have surmised, Pansy had a plan, and that plan involved a weapon of her own: a very nice, wicked-looking carbon-fibre compound bow that she'd acquired online. It was black as sin; its tiny pulleys and hair-thin wires were gleaming and taut, and she told me not to touch it under penalty of death.

I handed her the yew-wood slivers, and she loaded them into her quiver in a brisk, businesslike fashion. "All right," she said. "I'm ready. Any new developments?"

"None. Just general mucking about in there. Orlando is on the alert. Be... be careful, Pansy. I... I..." By God, she was so small...

"Save it, Doc. Keep calm and carry on, 'kay?"

"Quite." I retrieved the axe, brushed off the dirt and tested its sharpness with my thumb: not very.

It would have to do.

She flew up, hovered close to my face for a second, and with a saucy wink, planted a tiny peck upon my cheek. If she hadn't had her beak on, I might have liked it. "Good luck," I whispered.

This time I stood right in front of the door, filling it as much as my rather slight frame could do. I wished I'd been able to locate my cricket pads. Ominous whiffs of blood and sulphur wafted from the interior, and the air of dread I'd felt when I'd first entered had thickened. I imagined I could hear poor Gladys whimpering. My hands were clammy and my heart thumped painfully. I was too old for this sort of thing.

But Pansy's mission was the more dangerous: she had to flush out the damned cat. Mine was simply to sever him neatly in two. To be quite frank with you, Whittle, I didn't feel up to the task. Yet the knowledge that Gladys was in there, slowly being consumed by her own familiar—in whom she had placed her trust—was sickening.

By this time the sun had risen high enough to cast a feeble light into Gladys's home. Orlando was crouched vulture-like on the mantel above the cauldron, his glowing yellow eyes commanding a clear view of his on-going meal ticket. He gave me but one dismissive glance, then began to groom his whiskers. Gladys's ravaged bosom rose and fell almost imperceptibly. Where was Pansy? I glanced about, trying to keep one eye on Orlando. Suddenly, I caught sight of her, perched among the rafters on a bundle of dried herbs. She signalled to me, an almost imperceptible throwing motion. Ah.

I picked up a shard of broken crockery that had earlier been ejected onto the stoop and tossed it into a corner. At the moment Orlando turned to track the sound, Pansy let fly an arrow.

It sped far too fast for my eyes to follow, but I saw Orlando flinch and look around suspiciously. He batted with one paw at his ear, growling. By now Pansy had zipped to a new vantage point and let another arrow fly—and it hit its mark. Orlando had opened his maw to hiss, and the sliver of yew wood was now lodged in his tongue. He went into a frenzy, but the arrow was in there good and tight. Should I advance now and take a chance with my axe?

I hesitated as Orlando backed, whirled and spat to finally stop and crouch, panting and drooling. His swollen tongue stuck out. I almost felt sorry for the old chap, until I caught sight of Gladys's eyeless face, and noted a small fluttering in what was left of her fingers. She was cheering us on! God bless the woman—what a spirit!

Pansy set her bow down and flitted tantalizingly across the room, in full view of the furious cat. His whiskers were a-bristle and his tail lashing. She passed before him again, closer, and blew a raspberry.

This time it worked. True to his feline nature he sprang at her, paws outstretched and talons at full alert, the effect offset by his protruding tongue. Tauntingly, she threw her agile little wings into some sort of backstroke, and danced before his face, almost letting herself be caught. Pansy was a pro at taunting.

Orlando, however, was not as hurt and befuddled as I had hoped. His fur sparked as if it were crawling with lightning, and bolts shot from his outstretched paws. I smelled singed feathers and heard Pansy yelp. He batted at her, attempting to drive her to the floor where he could take her in his jaws, but she dodged and made for the shelter of Gladys's hefty brown teapot. Orlando jumped onto the table and with one swipe of his tufted paw shoved the teapot overboard. Cold tea splashed everywhere. Pansy jumped straight up, engaged some sort of turbo effect—or so it seemed—and made straight for the door, Orlando in hot pursuit.

It was now or never. I raised the axe overhead and tried to judge his trajectory. As Pansy pelted past my ear and away, I took a mighty swing.

And missed him completely. Not even a section of tail did I part from his body. He was simply too fast for me, or— perhaps—my chopping days are behind me. Oh, it's all right, my dear boy—I'm willing to acknowledge my failings, which shall be the failings of all of us who achieve great age. How old *am* I, exactly? Never you mind.

Anyway, Whittle, the damned cat shot between my legs, my axe did nothing more than splinter the threshold, and I heard Pansy cursing as she flew in circles above Orlando. He was showing signs of attaining true flight soon, not just the ability to jump higher than any ordinary cat. The situation was getting worse. Soon he'd have driven us from the yard, expanding his territory.

Then something odd happened. Pansy, instead of attempting to lure our prey back into range, dove into the yew tree. Could she be trying to hide or to save her own pretty brown skin?

Of course not. Hah! She called upon her bird heritage and began to peep in distress, whilst clumsily hopping about among the lower branches. She even feigned a broken wing. Orlando couldn't resist. He dove into the tree after her.

A mighty thrashing ensued. Short-lived. Pansy popped out, her beak askew and her red crest of hair in raggedy spikes. She landed on my shoulder and began to hop up and down, crowing in glee. "We did it! We are *awesome*! Did you *see* that?"

"See what? Where is that damned creature?" He'd be out in a second, and I must be ready this time.

"Go take a look. Go on, do it."

Hesitantly, I drew the branches aside and peered within the dim, dusty labyrinth of crisscrossing fronds. No cat. He'd managed to slip away!

But then I saw it: a huge burl bulging from the trunk. And from within the burl, yowling and scratching noises, growing fainter by the minute. As I watched, the yew's trunk rippled and thickened about the trapped animal.

We'd won! Orlando was no more. I backed out of the tree and let the branches knit themselves together over the new-grown burl. He'd been encysted, though if he ever got out—for instance if the yew died or split—he could possibly re-animate. I shook my head. Frankly, I didn't give a damn if he lived or died in there.

"Well, Whittle," I said, as we reached a rose-covered gate, "that's the story of why Gladys wasn't at the meeting."

"But you haven't finished! What happened to her? Dear God—is she still in hospital?"

"Hospital?" I snorted. "Certainly not. What could they do for her there? No, I hoisted her into her cauldron, got the fire lit and went home. Needed a bit of a lie-down, as you can imagine."

Whittle, his face a mask of outrage and bewilderment, looked about. "Hey, this isn't the pub! This is her house, isn't it? Don't tell me she's—"

"Still simmering? Yes. It's been a couple of weeks now, and she should be just about done." I lifted my shopping bag. "Just going to pop in a few things. She always wanted green eyes—thought I'd give her a little treat. Want to come in? You can give her a stir."

The concept of religion is fascinating. Even those who don't believe can respect that sense of awe, the convoluted tales we tell of glory, fear, redemption, rebirth. We are finite beings, just over-evolved apes really, and are so curious: What comes next? Is there a next? Shouldn't there be a next? If I had the chance to do this story over again, I would turn it upside down.

Szabra's Souls

She'd been a queen once, when she was young, but had ruled only until her subjects were dead: less than four years as time is reckoned on her world, or about two and a half as it is on ours. Her name was Szabra and she was old now, living the quiet life of a scholar on a world called Chaik.

The day was hot, and I—a cash-short student—tended to walk everywhere I could and save a few centimes. But I couldn't attend my interview with Szabra looking flushed and sweaty. I found a patch of shade against the sugar-white wall of the building directly across from where she lived and worked, and willed myself to become cool and collected.

It was hard to do.

I squinted and peered upwards. Szabra's chambers, at the top of what surely was one of the most beautiful buildings in Chaik's capital city, were open to the sky, though in Chaik's brief winter they would be enclosed in glass. Now, in the middle of summer, it must be very pleasant up there, full of breezes and the muted sounds of the streets.

My name is Mirna Carr, and I've been on Chaik for three Terran years now. My doctoral thesis turned out well, I think: could have been better had I more time, but then everyone wants more time to get that last really good data, to add that last bit of polish and certainty. What I found most difficult was to maintain a tone of scholarly reserve, when my natural instinct is to wax emotional. Bible-thumping, they used to call it. I'm not a mystic, but I am pretty fervent in what I believe.

Anyway, the oral went well and I was now in possession of a doctorate in Theology, with which I would go forth to save the Universe. Looking up at Szabra's roof-top home, I smiled at myself. First I'd have to pass her test.

My shirt was no longer sticking to my back. The shade had cooled me, and it was time for my appointment. A couple of deep breaths and I headed for the building's lobby.

Szabra's Test. I'd heard about it from lots of people— humans, darians, t'lell. No one had ever passed it, and in fact it seemed a mere formality. You got your degree, prepared to leave the college and do whatever you'd planned with your life, but first paid a visit to Szabra. Only another hoop to jump through. So why the mystique? Why was my heart pounding with apprehension as I stepped off the lift at the penthouse level?

A smiling t'lell attendant let me in and looked briefly at my identification, then led me to a central open space with archways leading off it into garden areas. There seemed to be nowhere for actual work to be done. Where were the kitchen, the offices, the functional areas? It didn't matter. They were probably on the level below, and it wasn't my business anyway. The view through the arched windows was magnificent, broad and hazy, glowing under Chaik's hot yellow star.

A middle-aged human clerk, dressed in shorts and a neat white shirt, glided in and led me through a patch of greenery to a little clearing where the sun beat down through waving fronds. A fountain sent wonderfully cooling droplets across my arms.

"Mirna Carr," he announced to no one, then left. A frothy green branch seemed to lift itself away, and I saw her. I bowed and approached, straight of back and pink of cheek, to take a chair across a small glass table from Szabra.

Some people called her the Queen of the Dead. And that is what she was.

She and the few remnants of her kind had been relocated from Tze years ago to Chaik, a planet connected to the Terran Alliance by long-standing economic and religious ties. It was a good world for expatriates, whether voluntary or involuntary; a soft and moderate landscape of greens and tans and sparkling blue seas.

I sat stiffly, conscious of my youth and awkward size, my pale softness. She was smaller than I had expected, more delicate, less fearsome. She looked a little like a blue-black wasp (and I'm not afraid of wasps) constructed not for hunting and stinging, but for dancing. Her carapace was as shiny as an ebony piano key.

As we eyed each other, Szabra fondled a long metal plaque which hung suspended around her stalk-like waist by a strap woven of purple-black threads that might have been hair. Her claws made a delicate clicking on the plaque, and in perfect Inter-English she welcomed me and asked if I would like tea.

"Yes, thank you very much." Should I have said Yes Madam? Your Highness? I felt unprepared, though my audience with Szabra had been scheduled semesters ago.

Tea and cookies. I suppose small sweet snacks are served on more planets than I can imagine. The tea came in on a tray borne by the human attendant, and he winked at me as he set it down. I didn't know what to make of that wink at the time, but I think I do now, years later.

Szabra, technically a guest lecturer at the Alliance General Survey's teaching college on Chaik, had taken up permanent residence here. She was a widely published and highly respected historian of her own lost people; besides fulfilling the last requirement of graduation I hoped to get a jump on some planned post-doctoral papers.

The Alliance General Survey, in which I would become an apprentice upon graduation, was as earnest and as obsessively concerned with minutiae as any religious order. A lavishly funded arm of government, the Survey ranged across everything it could find to study. Time and consciousness, growth and chaos, life and death; anything that could be examined or catalogued or dissected. The more esoteric and essentially unknowable, the better. The kind of people who wanted in were the misfits, the dreamers, the ones who had a hard time settling down to good honest work. And yet more valuable discoveries were made by this huge, messy, glorified think tank than by any other organization in the known universe.

I had to get in, was technically in already, but still... what would happen if (when) I failed Szabra's test? What was she going to ask me?

I watched the gleaming plaque swing on its strap as we made preliminary small talk about local politics. She touched the little pendant often. Her spiky digits would tap or twirl it, or it would click against her lower limbs as she shifted position. Once she unfurled her black tubular tongue and ran it across the thing's surface. I don't think she was aware she'd done it.

I set down my empty cup, drawing breath to start into my prepared questions about Tze, her people's devastated world, when she forestalled me.

"You have been noticing my tzeke," she said, tapping the

plaque. "Would you like to hear its story?"

"Very much," I said at once, mentally shifting gears. Could this be something new?

She undid the belt and slipped the plaque off. "Take it in your hand, Mirna Carr." I reached forward obediently.

Though thin as two playing cards when held edge on, and about the same size, it looked much thicker when I turned it flat in my palm. In fact it seemed to hold immense depth under its glassy sheen. What at first had seemed smooth and featureless, just a decorative sliver of polished metal, gained dizzying complexity as I looked at, or rather into it. It was deep, immense; it was trying to pull my eyes right out of my head. When I felt the thing hit the tip of my nose as I tried vainly to focus on it, the spell broke and I looked away, blinking hard.

I handed it back, feeling nauseated and dizzy. She raised her black claw-fingers.

"Hold it a little longer, Mirna Carr. Keep it in your hand, but do not look at it. Do you feel the lines, the edges? Can your digits sense the shapes there?"

Is this it? Was this her test? I almost let out a laugh, but caught myself before I could be so rude.

My fingers could detect nothing but warm smoothness. I shook my head and swallowed, pulling myself together. The tension drained away as Szabra hissed a little, and rustled her thin gauzy wings.

"What do you believe about God, Mirna Carr?"

"About God? As in, what is God?"

"Yes. Your own personal conception."

"Well. I know what I don't know, at least. I have no visual image. I don't think there could be one, though I understand that the Artificial Intelligence Aislin came up with something once."

"He did, though no one else was privileged to see it. It was Aislin's own personal construct and ultimately not perceptible by anyone else, even another AI."

"I have heard that he's still in withdrawal."

She hissed. "Sulking. That's all it is. He became so frustrated by the limits of physical being that he simply shut down all his connections."

"I hope he comes out of it. From what I hear, Aimee is still optimistic about Flip theory, even though everyone else seems to have given up on it."

The Flipping Universe: one side matter and one side a strange sort of sentient energy, switching form at the instant of non-time that used to be called the Big Bang. Aimee, the AI who had gone the furthest of any of the artificial intelligences toward mysticism, believed that God was the energy universe, and therefore that we were forever barred from complete understanding of it. This didn't seem to bother her at all.

"I'm avoiding your question," I admitted to Szabra. "I'm afraid I really can't put a description to what I believe, only that I *do* believe."

And I did. When I said the Survey was like a religious order, I meant it quite literally. The Survey's various orbits were closing in upon one goal: God. Or as some preferred to name it: the kernel of meaning at the centre of all our lives.

The idea, the fact, the scientific proof of God—it seemed to be almost within our grasp. I had entered the Survey as a singer joins a choir, to raise my voice in joy and do my little part in the great quest. I was a very good student; I feel no embarrassment in saying so. I was confident, as were my instructors, in my ability to forge ahead into new understanding and new ideas.

And I felt confident that, though I might not pass her "test", I would at least acquit myself with dignity as she quizzed me.

Szabra dipped her little black head in a human gesture and was silent for quite a while. A warm breeze blew through, and faint sounds rose up from the city below. Bells, vehicle noise, a clear high chanting coming from a festival that was in progress that day. The AIs interested in such things as miracle and faith had correlated and confirmed so much, had made fact of myth and knowledge out of hope. Yes, I believed. Most people did.

The plaque—the tzeke—grew a little warmer in my hand, a little heavier.

I risked a glance at it. Just polished metal. I held it up and said, "Will you tell me its story?"

Her tongue whisked out, curled, and fled behind her mandibles again. "Yes. Of itself, it has only one: that it exists and performs its function. But within it…"

She leaned across the table and adjusted my thumb and fingers on it. "Here, let me show you… Press here."

Her digits felt like needles on my skin as she guided me. She didn't come close to drawing blood, but when she let go it was as if she had poisoned me and thrown me into a roaring gale. She spun backwards among whipping plant-fronds, and vanished down a whirling black tunnel.

I think I tried to shake the tzeke loose from my hand. It wouldn't let go. I was trapped in whatever it was doing to me. I seemed to be in a maelstrom of hard-edged, buffeting noise, as if thousands upon thousands of voices cried and sang and called at once. A kind of screaming aural pattern began to merge, gaining force and speed and focusing itself terrifyingly on me.

This is it, this thing is her test—

It felt—and I still, even now, have difficulty explaining this— as though a vast world of people had suddenly looked up and seen me burning in their sky, a huge and awesome presence like a god to be worshipped. The feeling gained strength, started to force itself into my visual awareness as a storm whirling miles below. Suddenly I felt myself falling toward this maelstrom. I think I screamed, and then the contact abruptly broke.

I expected to find myself flat on the floor gasping like a fish, but I was still sitting in my chair, every muscle vibrating with tension. My left hand had gone to my throat to keep my heart from leaping free; the other hand no longer held the tzeke. My fingers throbbed and stung. I barely kept from putting them in my mouth like a child.

Szabra said, "I am very sorry. There seems to be no easy way to introduce a new person to the world in here." She held the tzeke quite calmly. "Do you need some water, or perhaps to lie down?"

I shook my head. When I could control my voice I said, "Nobody told me it would be like this."

"My test? No. For each person the experience is different."

"What… what is that thing?"

"It is a repository of souls. In it are the lives of almost two million of my people, all that could be saved in the time I had."

I stared at her, unsure of her meaning.

The thing lay in the cage of her digits—a little sliver of metal: a box with a universe inside. Could what she said be true? In the war between her people, most of their planet had been destroyed; only those able to escape to space or already living off-world survived. Or so I had thought. What kind of technology could create such a repository?

Perhaps she was merely playing with me. Perhaps she had drugged me.

Szabra clipped it back onto her belt. I wondered if she ever let it out of her sight.

She stood suddenly, looking as spindly as a little ebony table that had grown arms and a head, her gauzy, useless wings billowing as she walked between wide columns onto an open terrace. I followed her, and we stood looking out over the city. The bright hazy sky made me squint, and I wished for the sunglasses inside in my bag. But the heat actually felt good, and some of my shock and nausea began to drain away.

"When the Alliance came to our world we were unprepared morally and intellectually for… how shall I say it? The outsider. The different ones. Our factions had been at war for generations, long before I came to power; I was merely the last. Your people, who so ardently seek the deity, were compelled to attempt our enlightenment, our salvation, and we were unfamiliar with what such a thing might be. I believe many of my people felt… accused. Guilty of being thought soulless."

I shaded my eyes. It was hard to look at her. The sun reflecting off her carapace was intolerably bright. She clambered to a perch on the edge of the low barrier around the roof, and I felt sweat prick my palms at the thought of the long drop to street level. Then I saw her claws clamp firmly into depressions in the stone. She was securely attached to her observation post. I looked away, down to the pastel buildings and green and yellow trees along the streets.

I couldn't bring myself to sit on the ledge beside her; my vertigo wouldn't let me. I rested my arms on it instead. But wouldn't God take me if I fell? Wouldn't I rejoice in death? The thin chanting I had heard earlier had stopped and the plaza below us was empty.

"When I enter the tzeke," she said, "I am another soul for a while, who dreams of a world beyond the world, a universe encompassing its own. I forget for a while who I am, and am able to live—and learn—another's life."

"But… what is it? I can't believe such technology exists."

"It is a combination of technology and of something we must think of as the gestalt of those within it; their will, or memories, or whatever you may wish to call the life force that they brought with them. I have heard it referred to as a feedback loop taken to infinity."

"Do the souls in there know what has happened to them?"

"Many of them understand quite fully. They in fact know that they are dead. Others dwell in what seems to be a dream."

A dream, or a nightmare? I quailed at the thought of reentering the tzeke. One experience of it was frightening enough. Never mind the technicalities of penetrating that howling tangle of information—it seemed a sort of blasphemy, no matter how benign the intent, how scholarly the aim. I felt again the sickening, thrilling sense of immensity when I had hovered over that artificial world. A floating goddess. How could this possibly fit the beliefs I had studied and embraced for so long?

She went on in a meditative tone. "Is there any race which can think and does not dream? Is the machine Aislin dreaming in his withdrawal? Perhaps the capacity for intelligence stems from dreams... messages from our higher selves which lead our waking minds to desire that other world."

"And strive to reach it. As we are doing..."

"I know that the irony of this is not lost on you, Mirna Carr. That we, who may hold a universe in one hand, still seek, in turn, the hand that holds us."

After a pause, I said, "You say there are two million entities in there. I don't understand it, but I accept that it is so. But still I wonder. What of the rest of your people, all the other millions who died in that war? Where did their souls go?" I thought it a clever question.

Her claws shifted on the balustrade. The sun had lowered a bit and gone behind some scattered shreds of cloud; it was easier to look directly at her. "I do not know," she whispered, gazing across the white-gold city. "Nor do I know what became of those whose constructs are in here." She tapped the little plaque, and looked at me. "The soul is not something that can be stored in a device, no matter how clever. I suspect that the artificial intelligences know this about themselves. But will they be able to survive the knowledge?"

I realized my mistake, and felt my cheeks redden as if I had been chastised. But she had called them souls, called the tzeke a repository of souls.

"You said your people feared they would be thought soulless. Yet you don't seem to know what a soul is. If it isn't in that thing," I nodded at the plaque around her waist, "then where is it? Do you believe in God, Szabra?"

"I believe in myself," she said obliquely.

My shoulders drew up, hunching against some atavistic threat dropping out of the sky.

"I don't understand what this tzeke is," I said, moving away from her. "What is it that you have inside there? How…" I shook my head, frustrated. "How can it work?" It was the tzeke itself that was making me fearful. It was wrong, it was blasphemous somehow, as I had suspected. Why was she telling me its secrets, inviting me to share in this feast of lives?

I had a sudden wild urge to push Szabra over the edge of the terrace, and her captive universe along with her.

We eyed each other. She was so gloriously alien, so different in appearance from me and my kind, and yet she knew exactly what questions to ask. I felt stupidly sullen, angry and defensive, and knew it showed on my face. She'd shaken my faith—my easy, state-approved faith—to the shivering bones. Today I'd met one who knew what it was to be a god. She'd shown me a little of what it was like.

I looked away first. Szabra was probably the most respected and revered being on Chaik, and I wasn't going to challenge her. I knew I would have to try to re-enter the tzeke and join with the consciousnesses within it, should it be allowed. As she said, there was much to be learned. I told myself it wasn't because I wanted to play god. And besides, those weren't really souls in there after all. The real souls had flown to join the ultimate. Surely they had.

She was climbing down from the ledge. Our interview was almost over. On a sudden impulse I asked her, "Szabra, when you die, will you enter the tzeke?"

"I believe I will," she said, and I felt then, chillingly, that she did believe herself to be soulless, and furthermore that it didn't matter to her. Or did it? Perhaps it signified just the opposite: that she was so sure, that her faith was so integral to her, that it really didn't matter.

I was glad to be able to collect my bag and prepare to leave. If she had set out to instill doubt and humility into a novice, then she'd succeeded. I felt at once resentful, confused, and unhappy. She'd shown me a miracle and then shown me that it was meaningless. I wanted to go away and cry.

I bowed stiffly and left, knowing that I had failed her test.

The next day Szabra sent a voice message to me. I was in my little room, packing my life for the last three years into bags to take away. I was crying, wiping my eyes and stuffing the tissues angrily into the waste bin. I was leaving Chaik for my novice assignment, and I couldn't find any joy inside to take along.

"Mirna Carr," her voice whispered from the communicator, as gently as leaves brushing one another. "All our minds together, whether flesh, machine, or construct of folded space, are as nothing compared to God. For God is the infinite unknowable. That, however, should not stop us from trying to know, should it? Our curiosity is part of God, too. And though I saw your distress, I hope you will visit me again."

It took me a while to answer. "So I can have another try at your test?"

"There is no test, Mirna Carr. Only the chance to walk through a door."

"So… you pass the test by being willing to try, is that it?"

Her head bobbed on the screen, and she hissed. Laughing at me. "If you insist."

How could I turn her down? My tears had dried. "I'm honoured," I said. "Frightened, but honoured."

Again she hissed. "As it should be."

I had the feeling that a lonely, past-their-prime romantic might find a beautiful, ageless android irresistible. And that the two of them might get into some mischief... and that it might intersect with forces well over their pay grade.

INTERSECTION

I didn't know I'd meet the most important person in my life today. And it wasn't technically a person.

I was squatting on the ground, knees popping, back complaining. *Shut up, old-man body—this is your job.* Such as it is, now. Looking at something I knew was impossible.

Two corpses, lying before me like tossed rags, dusty and wind-twitched under the hot grey sky. It was the newcomers, a couple who'd seemed sensible and prepared when I'd met them and logged them into Town. They'd managed to get themselves dead in less than a week.

Alik crouched on the sand beside me to poke at one of the two shallow heaps.

"It's Sperling and Kim, Doc."

"Yeah." Alik and I both knew how odd this was.

And that's why I'd gone out on a limb and hired a Recorder, once I'd remembered there was one on Thirteen, in the possession of the TunXi Mining Consortium. We were waiting for it to arrive at the scene.

With a gloved finger Alik lifted the edge of Shaw Sperling's thin yellow shirt to reveal parchment skin hugging dry, stringy musculature. A small fluttering of mouse-brown hair on the skull. Beside Sperling, his partner Wendy Kim, face up, her teeth bared in a sandy grin. A tote bag lay beside her, trapped within her hard-curled fingers. A gust of wind suddenly rippled her long hair out like a torn white flag. Had they surrendered to something evil? Or had they just been reckless and ignorant?

Alik stood, stripping off his gloves. "What were they doing way out here?"

"A very good question."

Jan Klein from the Port Authority rolled up just then, the Recorder with him. Both hopped out onto the sand. Jan had an idea of my limitations, those imposed by rehab, but he didn't blab them around.

He hauled two white body bags out of the roller while the Recorder strode close with barely a glance at Alik and me, and bent like a raptor over its prey. Alik gawked unashamedly. I stood up—more pops—and watched it.

Clad in a skin-tight grey bodysuit, it hovered over the corpses, slender and supple as a newt, mouth wide open and arms outstretched as if it were about to pounce upon the dead bodies. Gathering air and dust and everything contained within air and dust. Recorders were an amalgam of human, animal and machine, and this one seemed to be trying to vanish into sexlessness. I'd seen a couple of them before, years ago, skewing male human. They didn't have to be pointed out once you knew they existed.

Was there a slight self-consciousness in it, a morsel of pride? *I'm not a slave.* I see this and think: *Well, you probably are.* Its nose was long, the nostrils wide and flared. It had fingers but no nails; they'd been designed away in favour of sensory folds like magnified fingerprints. I don't know why, but I saw it as female.

Its large, limpid brown eyes were the wettest things around here. Those eyes could see with detail and in wavelengths unavailable to we normal folk. It was beautiful in its own weird way, and I had a hard time taking my eyes off her. It.

On Ceres Station, I'd had a partner. I'd had love, until I broke love's promise. And I'd had an atmosphere full of tattle-tales to aid me in my work. The air and dust spoke directly to me, sharing the secret information about illness and death that they'd gleaned. Here I had only the basics, plus my brain. And a Recorder.

"They were exploring, maybe," Alik said, looking at the fluttering piles. "Got caught in a sandstorm? Is that what you're thinking, Doctor Kay?"

"I have no idea what to think."

"So is Port getting involved?"

"Hashim has that accident at Deep Two. We'll get this."

We would get this because I wanted it. It was too odd to let go.

Dust and heat shimmers made the whole operation look as if it were long ago and far away. In maybe fifteen minutes the Recorder had what it needed. It pulled its protective gloves back on while Jan stuffed the bagged bodies onto the roller he and the Recorder had come in on.

That meant the Recorder had to ride with us now. It was the last on board, and as it slid into the seat next to me it looked directly into my eyes. *Yeah, it's okay to think of her as female.*

That look turned my preconceptions upside down. I hadn't thought her sort was interested in live humans, or anything that didn't mean profit for their owners. But those eyes, soft brown under a fringe of carelessly cropped black hair, reminded me of the eyes of a dog my ex had once owned. Curious, innocent. That animal softness of regard.

Human? Animal? Machine? None of the above?

I know my sense of allegiance is faulty. In my past I've been seduced by beauty, style, gloriously splashy wealth. A soft look in someone's eyes. I know it about myself, and I've worked hard to kill it.

We all trundled toward town. Jan with his bagged bodies to the sterile, brutally air-conditioned medical/mortuary/examination facility next to Customs and Immigration, Alik and me to the medical office suite above Social Services, which always smelled like garlic from the restaurant next door. The Recorder back to her owners.

I was in my office thinking about death when Hettie's visage popped up over my desk.

Hettie Dalcour had beautiful pecan skin and a small, sculpted head clasped by tight blonde curls. She was easy on the eyes. "What ya got, kid?"

"Construct's ready."

"Be right there."

Hettie was here to do V&C—visualization and construction—for Port, and to work for me when needed. She hadn't yet called me by name. Was Resident Doctor Mark Healy-Kay too much? I'm still a licensed general practitioner, good enough to work here on Thirteen where I can't do much damage.

It took me two minutes to amble over to the mortuary. The bodies lay head-to-head on two white tables, the dried-brown flesh dark against the gleaming plastic.

Hettie's constructs rotated in the air over their respective remains.

At my entrance, the images spread their arms and legs wide. Nice. Made me feel welcome. Hettie operated her unit with flair, and I suspected that in another life she'd have been in a more creative profession. But here she was, putting in time on Thirteen.

She had transformed the mummies into people again. Close-ups of toes, crotches, and ears zoomed in, thanks to the Recorder's preliminary data, plus biometrics sucked up from all over. I looked for needle-pricks, scrapes, bruises. And underneath, into the bodies' alleys and byways. Nothing much to see. And yet the impossible had happened.

The images swooped and spun, scalps riffling like bleached wheat fields, clogged with sand-grains and dried sweat in flat white crystals.

Wendy Kim had evidence of cosmetic reforming around her eyes and jawline, and a pregnancy long ago. Shaw Sperling just a couple of barely discernible old bone breaks. For humans in their eighth decade, they looked pretty good. What had killed them, other than extreme dehydration? Extremely fast dehydration. The tox screens equivocated, and the mummified corpses wouldn't talk.

The deep layers of the construct showed organs like lumps of cooked meat.

"Thanks, Hettie. Good job. You can shut it down."

I should contact the Recorder, get it to speed things up, but I feared looking again into those dark animal eyes. I knew myself, could feel my toes clutching at the edge of a precipice.

A short, tubby, no-longer-young man with an instant crush on someone. Some*thing*. I thought the rehab would have knocked that out of me.

But. I've always liked animals better than people, though animals are hard to find out here on the fringes. Hell, I even like machines better than people.

I'll get a detailed report soon. The Recorder's info will be plentiful, I'm sure, but probably unfocused: it's going to come down to an old-fashioned investigation.

I'll have to talk to people.

Hettie turned up a couple of hours later and immediately sprawled on my Survey-issue cot, emitting a groan of exhaustion. How could she be exhausted? She's twenty-five years old, for God's sake. Alik strode in shortly thereafter to stand by the window with his arms crossed. Both of them looked cranky and frazzled.

What had they been up to? Had their affair rekindled?

Once, Alik and I had closed down the bar at the Port Complex. We were both pretty looped, and he'd pointed a finger at me. "You're hauling somethin' around, Doc. Ya gotta let go. Loosen up."

He knocked back his crappy Thirteen vodka, jammed a popper under his lip and stated that he could tell I had once been a player. I told him to go home.

"Anyone need coffee? No? Alik, tell me what you have."

Heavy sigh. "So, I interviewed Lonette and Freya at the diner. The victims had lunch there yesterday, stayed for a while talking between themselves—nobody heard what about—then left at around 16:15."

"Which way did they go?"

"East, looked to Freya like they were making for the gate."

"Why did she think that?"

"Water pouches, they looked eastward and pointed, like how far it was or whatever."

"I see. What did they eat?"

"She had the fish special and tea, he had the same but a glass of rusha. He didn't finish it." Of course. No one liked the stuff at first. Astringent, with a taste of something oily.

"They buy anything?" Newcomers always bought things. Hats immediately after landing and squinting up at the sky.

Decorative belts that one of the workers at Krystal's wove from tough burgundy seaweed in his spare time.

"Hats."

"You walked their route?"

"Yeah. No one remembered seeing them, but gate surveillance caught them at 16:29 heading out."

Outside the east gate is a no-man's land of about a kilometer extending around the whole colony site, under automatic surveillance. Beyond that is over three hundred klicks of sand flats, interspersed with slowly migrating dunes, lowlands slimed with pinkish algae, and two castles baking under the hazy sun. And beyond that? A shallow inlet of the world's one overly-salted ocean. The rest is mining territory.

"Did both of them have packs, or just Wendy?"

He checked on his hand-held. "Uh… just Wendy."

"What was in it?"

"Cheapo survival crap. Water, half gone."

"So they still had water. Okay. Let's assume they were heading for the closer castle." We had to start somewhere.

They aren't castles. They're outcroppings of pitted black rock thrusting from the endless boring wasteland of beige. Their almost-intentional appearance makes Earthlings long for ruins wild and lonely, layered with ancient loves and losses. The ghosts of red-blooded warriors and virgin queens. We're such romantics.

Someday we'll get around to checking them out. This world is ancient, depleted, but shows signs of an ecology struggling its way into more diverse forms as the planetary climate veers toward being cooler. It's going to be a long, long time before anything resembling natural beauty arises. We have to make do with rocks.

"They were just sightseeing?" Alik offered.

"Their pin-cams were clear of images. And why didn't they

rent a roller? Why hike all that way?"

Hettie drummed her fingers on her knees. "Rollers are monitored. If they were trying to hide something, they'd walk instead."

"Or," said Alik, sharply, "maybe they had nothing to hide and *wanted* to walk." He scratched his beard with one finger. "So… what is this? A murder? Like, maybe someone met them out there, or they were killed somewhere else and dumped?"

"Too soon to tell. Extreme desiccation, no matter how nonsensical, doesn't count as murder. But for lack of anything better to do, let's treat this as a homicide. It's good exercise, plus—it's a mystery."

Hettie smiled and rose languidly to her feet, still not looking at Alik. "Yeah. Who doesn't love a mystery."

Alik scowled out the window.

Okay, good. They'd go along with a plan that gave them something mildly interesting to do. People on Thirteen get bogged down in lethargy soon after arrival; they long for excitement but are hard to prod into motion.

"Let me know when the Recorder gives us her—its report. I'm going for a walk."

When I 'go for a walk' I don't want company. I just want to stroll around and see what's up. Do some thinking.

Thirteen's sky tinges toward blue or pink, but never truly clears. It can be depressing, though I appreciate the air, which smells like gunpowder. Bad for humans in the long term, probably. I take a deep breath. Just to show I can.

I let my mind run free as I mooch along the razor-straight walkways and crisp intersections laid out by the Survey only eleven years ago.

Wherever humans colonize, rumours of aliens spring up. Surely there must exist beings of grace and knowledge who will welcome us to their galactic community!

Um, nope. On Thirteen, there are two schools of thought: one, promoted by the mining and resource-development companies: rumours are for fools.

The other: aliens are real, but supremely wily and elusive. More clever and devious than mere humans can possibly imagine. Concurrent to these both: Big Mining is Engaged in a Massive Cover-up.

Either way, chasing chimeras is pointless.

The smell of curry wafts from the Golden Palace, basically Mori Noonan's house, which she has decorated with printed oriental-themed trinkets. It smells good but I'm not hungry. That's what love does to you. You lose weight. I keep walking, under a row of gingkoid trees that seem to be doing well on their nutrient drip-lines.

Our town, New Stibnite, has a lot of serviced but un-built area, anticipating more workers and Survey personnel, though that's becoming unlikely. Surprisingly few people want to live on the surface of an exoplanet, much preferring the comfortable, populous habitats on or close to Earth.

So why are we even here? I will tell you. Proximity to an almost-perfect fold nexus. It encircles the local star at just under one AU, and only needs to be focused. Which will take, oh, twenty years or so. Simple, right? Except it's something that's never been attempted before. We've always just relied on stumbling across a natural fold and going where it lets us go.

The possibility of building our own fold out of the ephemeral wisps of weird space-time around this star? Compelling. Insanely expensive. But what is expense, really? In a case like this.

New Stibnite has 504 permanent residents and a few dozen transients at any time, most servicing the crews that in turn service the construction bots and compilers working on the giant lens array that's going to focus the fold. Plus another few at mining and aquaculture sites. We export several hundredweight of pickled fish each quarter to a hab-cluster somewhere that has a taste for it, along with assorted nutrient pucks, micro-miné capsules and so on to other customers. For such a wrung-out landscape, we produce a lot of biologicals.

You're supposed to be working, Mark. Keep walking.

And don't slouch. If I hold my head high and look around confidently, I'll project calm assertiveness, desirable in a person technically in charge of life and death.

But I'm only here because I ran away from my life. My fault, but… never mind. I like it here. We play baseball and cricket, have classic sensie nights (read: piss-ups) and pretend everyone doesn't gossip and bed-hop incessantly.

But what brought Shaw Sperling and Wendy Kim here?

They had presented as decent, unremarkable people when I'd given them their medical check on landing. Wendy had been tall, with a mouth that suggested determination. That hair flying proudly loose. Shaw was less impressive. Doughy, thin lipped, but with intelligent eyes that held… wistfulness? Regret? Some kind of secret feeling.

"We have time and money," Wendy had claimed when I'd asked about their plans. "Shaw's research, and my contracts, take us all over. We have ample funding."

Lovely. I wished I had ample funding.

They'd checked out as healthy, and I'd suggested an eatery they might like. Or they could try the other one. Ha, ha.

A couple of harmless wanderers, with no stated goal. So why had they wound up dead?

I had no intention of trekking all the way to where they had been found. I settled my butt on a flat rock about a half a klick out, then stood again at seeing something on the horizon, proceeding slowly in an oblique path from south-east to north-west.

A heat-wavering line of blurry objects, moving in a regular, humping sort of way. *Yeah, it's aliens, for sure.*

Okay. It's something new the miners have. Machinery. Another half-aware method of snuffling up the goodies underground. Like a line of truffle pigs, the things grew closer.

More like dancing dust devils, throbbing under the sweating sun, seeking not the underground, but the heights of air. Twisting in their line dance, they all dipped in unison and vanished behind a small hill. I waited a long time for them to reappear.

Nothing. Well then. The aliens blended with the sand to hide. They screwed their way beneath the surface and drilled off like sand-worms. A meteorological anomaly. A string of mining robots, dug in and working. Mirages.

I could get a roller and investigate. But it's too hot, the phenomenon is too far away and most likely just wind. After a while a headache started pushing at my skull. Thinking wasn't working, and I headed back to town.

The Recorder's appendices to her preliminary report started arriving later that day. One, though it says little about weather other than temperature, wind speed and so on, makes brief mention of a sort of shadowy phenomenon she'd noted, similar to a heat-shimmer. Almost as if clouds were blowing by. Hm.

Another notes the amount of alien (i.e. native) DNA-equivalent material in the samples. Not a lot. Not a little. Explained by wind-blown organic particles from the swamps.

I called her, got her handler, a tired-looking middle-aged man whose jaw worked rhythmically. He was chewing niccora, and I didn't blame him. "Sansu will have comm time later today. It's working right now."

The Recorder had a name? Sansu. Why hadn't I thought to

ask? A small switch flipped in my perceptions.

"Let's see… It has down time starting 17:15." He heaved a sigh and frowned at his screen. "Expect a call at… mm… estimating 17:30."

"Okay. Uh, do you know of any exploration going on near town, say five or six klicks west?"

"I really couldn't tell you what-all is out there."

"All right. Thanks."

Alik had found that, instead of staying at the officially sanctioned hotel, the couple had roomed with locals. That information had sent up a modest flare. I had almost four hours to fill. I decided to follow the victims' footsteps, starting at the diner and heading back to their lodgings.

Freya confirmed what Hettie had learned. They'd eaten and then left for their short trek toward death. Next, I headed to the rooms the couple had rented, on the upper floor of a modest dwelling.

Talia and Josepha Windsong had nothing much to say. "Well, they paid us up front with Galcred, didn't have any local currency." Talia shrugged her narrow shoulders, looking rather miffed that her guests, as she called them, had gone missing. "They went out after breakfast and haven't come back since."

I wasn't going to reveal info I might need to use later. Like, inform them that their renters were dead. My antennae were out, but picking up nothing.

"Hm. Well, we like to keep an eye on off-worlders. None of them really get how empty it is, once you get out of Town." They hadn't offered me coffee, rusha, or even water. I stood up. "Let me or Hashim know if they turn up, okay?"

The shadows were slowly stretching as I left the Windsong abode. Was this stodgy couple hiding something?

Thirteen's days are long, and shadows take forever to lengthen, then to shrink again. It can get to you, the endless waiting for a new day. Or for the relief of night and darkness. Some folks just can't take it.

The Recorder's voice was soft, beautifully modulated, even via my desk's obsolete sound system. Had I been hoping for a robotic drone? Anything to push her out of my imagination.

I itched to question her about her past. How did she end up working for a mining company on this godforsaken world? Why not closer to her home, or her place of manufacture, or whatever? What exactly was she?

Possibly it was none of my business.

"I am at your disposal," she said. A stock phrase. Her arched nostrils flared. Her back was straight, her hands out of sight.

I had budgeted five minutes of her time. "Can you give me more details about the deaths than were in your report?"

"Yes."

Pause.

Right. "Please do so."

"The deceased were placed where they were found approximately two hours and three minutes before discovery. Their body temperatures—"

"Don't tell me things I already know. Define 'placed'."

"They did not expire upon that location."

"Who or what placed them there?"

"I do not know."

"Tell me where they expired."

"Location of death is undetermined. Visual anomalies were noted. Shadows that were temporally indeterminate, fluctuations in ground surface temperature and configuration temporally indeterminate—"

"Explain."

"I was unable to determine their location or duration in time."

Shadows of whoever dumped them there?

"All right. Were there mining operations in the area at that time?"

"I am not at liberty to say."

"Tell me what caused their deaths."

"Cessation of normal bodily functions due to catastrophic desiccation."

"Okay. Fine." Catastrophic? "Did you note any more anomalies?"

"Yes."

Jesus. "Please describe them."

She actually paused as if thinking. In my desk's popup, her face looked smooth, untroubled. Her black hair was tucked behind her ears, and she resembled a beautiful little artifact.

She began to blink rapidly, as if her processing speed had suddenly increased. "The wind is wrong. The dust, the dust, the dust. Wrong. Heat-not-heat flies, sinks and flies. The light, the dust. So much there so much—"

I sat up straight. What the hell? Her face showed no wrinkle or contortion, no indication that she had a glitch, or was trying to be clever. "Stop! Be more precise."

"The wind is wrong. The dust, the—"

"Okay! Stop!" Was that a religious look on her face? As if she'd seen something wonderful, either out on the baking sand, or somewhere inside her altered brain. I didn't want to hear any more chanting about dust and wind. *Dust devils, twisting in the distance.* "I request that you collect your findings regarding the anomalies—including any conjectures or avenues of further investigation you can suggest—organize them into a file suitable for a court of law, and present them directly to me as soon as possible."

"Acknowledged."

That was going to cost a pretty penny.

I needed to get out of our little catbox of a town.

The once-a-day circle-route flyer left at 10:30 sharp, sped over the ripples of sand and licking tongues of swampy water that ranged between New Stibnite and Base 2, where a necklace of pearls rimmed the black chin of a cliff.

Inside the largest pearl was TunXi Corporation's planetary headquarters. A visual led me to the office of Nalani Kawai, Chief of Operations. TunXi was the only company still on Thirteen; there had been four a few years ago. After some pleasantries, I questioned why a mining company would bother with a planet in the first place.

"It's cheaper in the short term than operations in space," said Ms. Kawai, a lanky, heavy-jawed woman in the prime of middle age. "Most of our operations involve asteroids and so on, but there's a huge investment in infrastructure—habitats, bots, conveyors, fold links, like that. Fast cash-flow from a livable planet is good." She spread her hands, looking relaxed and in control. "Until is isn't."

I could tell she wanted to talk about her job, and I wouldn't have minded listening, but not today. "We're investigating the deaths of a couple of visitors. Mining bots might have been in the area. It's possible that on-board recording equipment gathered some useful information."

She sat back and looked puzzled. "Hm. I'd have to see if we had gangs in the area at the time... when did you say it was?"

"Around fifteen hours ago."

"I'll check with my super, but I can tell you right now that the only recording that happens on any of our equipment is devoted to the discovery of minerals. And internal monitoring, that sort of thing. They don't have a view of the surroundings. If that's what you're hoping for."

"All right. So, by gangs, you mean groups of coordinated machines, like testing equipment, drilling rigs…?"

"Well, yes, but it's more complex than—"

"Is there a record of your equipment's movements and activities?"

"Of course. Are you requesting access to these records?" Her gaze was losing its openness.

I sat back and sighed, changing my tactics. "Look," I said, my voice soft, tired. Just a nice guy doing his job. "We're having a hell of a time figuring this out. The victims' bodies were… not in the best of condition."

She held up a hand. "Hold on, Doctor Healy-Kay. Are you suggesting that one of our machines killed them?"

Well, yes. "Could it be possible?"

"I sincerely doubt it. There are plenty of fail-safes. But I will have Programming and Maintenance look into it. Will that be sufficient? Or do we need to shut down operations?" Her eyes were narrow, her lips set. One pissed-off lady.

"That won't be necessary. No one's allowed past Town's perimeter till this is resolved. But I need to know if any of your more advanced, maybe experimental, units might have strayed off course."

"Experimental? What makes you think we have experimental machines, here on this bullshit planet?"

"We're checking anything we can think of. As to why I'm asking, your Recorder mentioned something it called temporal anomalies."

"You hired our Recorder? What do you mean, temporal anomalies?"

"Frankly, I haven't a clue."

"That Recorder gives us a lot of trouble. You can't trust it."

"Really. In what way?"

"It's hard to keep on mission. It tends to wander outside its prescribed work areas. It talks too much, asks questions."

"It's uppity."

Her lips twisted. "Yeah. It is. Why it hasn't been dumped by now is a mystery to me." Her face took on a sly expression. "You know they were initially developed by slavers, right? As sex workers? A lot of money was invested in 'em. And now they're working down here in the sand. How about that, eh?" She bestowed a triumphant grin upon me.

I had to relax my fists. "Well, Ms. Kawai, I'm going to let that Recorder ask me all the questions it wants." I stood up. "Thank you for your time."

Sex workers. Jesus.

Before Hettie arrived on Thirteen, Alik had tried enticing me to go to Krystal's with him. "It'll be good for you, Doc. You never go out. You even had a date since you got here?"

At my jaundiced look, he'd blushed and subsided. I had no interest in what was on offer at Krystal's, no matter how legal, clean and healthy. I'd made a pact with myself to abstain. Indefinitely.

Or perhaps I simply had no interest in legal, clean and healthy. I really couldn't tell anymore.

Alik dropped in after I returned to Town, to report his findings.

"Shaw Sperling and Wendy Kim lived on Earth most of their lives, he in Toronto, she in Barbados and Tokyo, where they met," he said briskly. "They moved to the habitat orbiting Telis, where they joined a team studying that world's multi-cellular ocean life. They made a couple of field trips, but due to their— and I quote—constant harassment of fellow team members, interference with experiments, and patently ridiculous claims of kinship with the alien jellies—they were thrown off the team and sent back to Titan One for sensitivity training."

"Did they actually have qualifications as biologists?"

"Yep. Not great track records obviously, but both of them have contributed solid work over the years, and were getting close to retirement. She had money from a pineapple tweak she'd patented."

Maybe they'd been wandering around Thirteen seeking native life to gain kinship with.

"Inventory of personal items shows nothing out of the ordinary except links to some encrypted data caches that might prove interesting, if we can break them open."

"Okay, Alik. Keep digging."

Trying to provide my own motives for a killing was going to be fruitless. A pattern would emerge, if we looked long enough.

Alik turned to go. "Wait," I said. "I have a question."

"Sure." He leaned in the doorway, looking patient. "Fire away."

"Do you know anything about sexbots?" That woke him up. "Like, are they still a thing?"

His face got a peculiar expression. I returned his gaze, trying not to look like a funny uncle.

"Anything specific you want to know?"

"Yes. Recorders… I heard they were initially developed for the sex trade."

"Hm." He rubbed his nose. "I think that's actually true. Not that I know a lot about sexbots, you understand."

"Of course."

"But… yes, there was an outfit, I forget the name, that marketed a line of bots for various, um, personal functions. But no one really took to them. They were creepy."

"Too creepy for the sex trade?"

He laughed. "Yeah, even. I think it was more like they started to unionize. Too much humanity was bred into them." He waved a hand. "I hear anything over forty percent is illegal."

"So, these were illegal, I assume."

"In most places. Oh! I remember. It started with that family that got caught in a scandal a few years ago… what's their name…"

I froze. He knew I'd been demoted here, but I'd never told him why.

"Feroux," he said. "The Feroux family. They were slavers, mostly in animals, and they got into a little sideline of these hybrids of humans and machines and dog DNA or whatever. Anyway, the things they were selling got too smart, and rebelled against their masters. Nothing got in the news because of the usual reasons—"

"Like the higher-ups owning a few of them?"

"Like that, yeah. I heard about it because one of my brothers was a law clerk at Ceres at the time."

"Well, that's interesting, Alik. Thanks." He gave me an ironic salute and ambled away.

I lurked in my office, listening to the evening grind slowly along toward night. People generally kill one another at night, though of course death can happen any time. Unexpected. Feared. But sometimes welcomed… there are those who make a living from death.

Death and sex. In a sense, I made my living from death. Warding it off, tracking it down. But never eliminating it.

Did Recorder Sansu know the difference between life and death, truth and falsehood, good and evil? Love and sex? She might not be capable of falsehood. How much animal was in her? Enough to make evil irrelevant?

And why did I find her so fascinating? I felt the pull of sexuality in her. It. *It's a tool, mostly machine. With a sordid background; is that what does it for me?*

I put my head in my hands for a few moments, my thoughts swirling murkily. So hard to really remember.

At that moment Talia Windsong stormed in, making me jump guiltily and try to collect myself.

"Ms. Windsong," I chirped. "Have a seat. Coffee, water?"

"No." She plunked herself down, knees apart and head thrust forward.

"Have your guests returned?" And really, why should she care?

"They have not," said Talia dismissively. "I'm here because I need your help. That idiot Hashim refuses to do anything for forty-eight hours."

I leaned back, my curiosity increasing. "What seems to be the problem?"

"Josepha's missing."

"Did she tell you where she was going?"

"The north castle." Her pale blue eyes shifted. "She'd left some equipment there that needs occasional monitoring, but nothing that should take this long."

"Really? She's aware of the Town curfew order?" Talia sneered. Jesus. *People.* "What sort of monitoring?"

"A possible new strain of none-of-your-damn-business."

I didn't care what Josepha was doing. Maybe she went out there to exercise artistic talents, hitherto unexplored, by carving her initials in the rock.

"Have you gone there to check? Despite official orders?"

Talia glared. "You need to find her! What if she ends up like Shaw and Wendy?"

What indeed. And why would her mind run in that direction? "I'm not a cop. I can't do anything until Station requests our help. And let me make it clear: should we mobilize and discover her sleeping it off at someone else's house, you'll be responsible for costs."

Talia stared at me stonily. I stared back.

I heard the coffee maker start gurgling. Right. Alik had talked about working on his play somewhere away from his noisy communal dwelling. Everyone's sleep cycles were wacky on this world; it was hard to coordinate schedules. Or get a good night's sleep.

Talia swatted my desk. "Hey! You could at least pretend to take me seriously."

"I take you very seriously."

She heaved herself up and slammed out. In two seconds Alik entered, bearing coffee. "That was fun. What's going on?"

I filled him in quickly as we drank the ersatz brew. "I don't know what's going on with those two, or if it connects to the victims, but I need the roller."

"I'll bring it round, old man."

Thirteen's star pushed its heat at my back as I trundled out of town. On the roller's windscreen were a few morsels of pulp that had lived before intersecting with my trajectory. Bugs from the swamps, attracted to Town's wealth of organic compounds. Poor little bastards.

What I'd done to earn my place here was ignore the evidence of my eyes and brain in favour of letting my stupid gonads take over.

Simple really. A beautiful woman had shown an interest in me. I'd let my conscience, and maybe my immortal soul, glide over corruption as if it were the purest ice. I had merely fooled myself. Self-serving hubris with a side of lust. I remember a lot, enough to sustain regret. Guilt.

Isabelle and Monique Feroux were sisters. Isabelle, the older, had taken over the operation of a very profitable slaver empire that their parents had developed.

You remember when it all blew up. Rico and Donat Feroux

died, in mysterious circumstances, but good riddance, right?

No one has ever pinned their fathers' deaths on Isabelle, who remains, due to legal issues of disputed records and mishandled evidence, free as a bird.

Monique ended up taking the rap. The younger sister, the one with the bad hair and an argumentative attitude. No one liked Monique. Especially since she'd done her level best to pin everything on her sister. But beautiful Isabelle was too slippery.

And charming. But beautiful people can do very ugly things. It turned out that Donat and Rico had been attempting to go straight, to divest themselves of their rotten trade and, maybe, go to heaven. Or somewhere not a rehab colony. The girls didn't like that. They conspired to kill their fathers and take over.

But Isabelle was way ahead of the game. She happily threw her sister to the wolves and grabbed the whole operation. And how did she manage that? Because I made sure the evidence against her was tainted. She made it seem almost heroic. I had thrilled at my own daring, helping an innocent woman thwart those who would destroy her. At the time, I'd had impeccable credibility as a medical official, with access to multitudes of useful data back then. Data altered, time stamps changed, whole vid-threads deleted.

The roller whined its way up a small rise and down again. I had squandered my position, my education and my dignity. Isabelle vanished behind her wall of money, laughing. Humiliated and ridiculous, I spent two years in realignment therapy. It worked. I got over her. Then I scuttled off to Thirteen, where my truncated license was useful.

Now, I was a sad figure, neither truly evil nor remotely good. Fish nor fowl. Just a tired old man hanging on to life at the end of nowhere, hoping to be forgotten.

Evening lay like a soft purple haze on the horizon, slowly creeping forward. The dust of my passage settled behind me.

I called Alik. "How's that roller trouble coming?"

He grinned, looking foxy in the little screen. "Just fine, Doc. You got maybe an hour."

"That should do."

The castle thrust out of the sand, forty-some meters at its highest point, in diameter about the size of a soccer field, looking very much like a broad, crenellated tower scoured by millennia of wind. The westernmost point was outlined in ruddy gold by the leisurely sunset, shadows creeping like warm tar.

I parked the roller and walked around, hugging the south perimeter, not really expecting to find anything. I was pretty sure Talia had lied to me about Josepha's mission to check equipment. My fingers dabbed the soft tan dust that filled hollows and cracks in the ancient columnar rocks, tiny beaches on a dry shore.

So what were they up to? Corporate espionage? The mining companies were abandoning Thirteen, having rapidly squeezed it dry. And why implicate this area, which had nothing worth harvesting? It held no interest to anyone other than as a mediocre tourist destination. The whole planet was a dead end. Laying a false trail, perhaps. Maybe Josepha was just here to pick up instructions, somehow? These women must know something, or think they did. And what was their connection to my desiccated victims?

More likely they were simply crackpots of a familiar order: deluded folks who believed their magical thinking would prevail if only they persisted. I understood the type very well.

The breeze was picking up, enhancing the tang of gunpowder. I kept walking. Halfway around, parked in a sheltered cove, was a roller bearing the TunXi insignia.

I stopped and listened. If it was company personnel, I'd hear voices. Those folks never travelled alone. But the wind just whispered emptily. The roller's tracks had started drifting in.

Then I thought to look up, and there she was. Recorder Sansu, standing precariously high on a narrow pinnacle with her arms outstretched and her wide mouth open in what looked like a silent scream. I could see flashes of pink as her tongue flicked in and out. My stomach clenched in the atavistic fear that she'd fall. Which she might very well do if I shouted and startled her. So I stood there quietly until she looked down and saw me. She displayed no surprise, just clambered down to the ground. Of course she wasn't surprised, she had probably sensed me coming from a long way off.

At the bottom she tripped, flinging her arms out for balance. I reached out to steady her. Her arms went around me.

I let go as soon as possible and schooled my face into pleasant calmness. I can do that when I have to. She had felt warm, firm but soft. What—did I imagine her to be a hard-shelled machine? A trembling, densely-fleshed animal, like a terrier?

And what did she detect about me, in that brief contact?

"Recorder Sansu, I'm pleased to find you here. Are you interested in the area?"

And if so, why? My paranoid brain started to race around in widening circles.

She replied after a slight delay. "Yes, Doctor Healy-Kay, I am interested." A machine, processing. Had she touched me deliberately?

"What is it that catches your interest?"

Pause. "Aspects of the temporal anomalies I outlined in my report. However, there are currently no temporal anomalies in this area." Was there something more she wanted to tell me?

The wind, the dust, the wind. "I also would like to know more about these anomalies."

We looked at each other. My heart thumped.

"Are you working for TunXi at this time?"

"I am not. I am pursuing my own interests for the next five hours and forty-seven minutes."

My first instinct was to trust her. My second, not to trust her in the slightest. My third was to treat her like a colleague. If she fancied a little extracurricular activity, who was I to stop her?

"Our interests coincide. I am investigating the deaths of the two humans. Besides the anomalies, what are your interests?"

"The deaths of the two humans." Said as if *of course, the deaths of the two humans.*

"Excellent. Shall we proceed to investigate?"

Her face lit up and an impression of unfocused eagerness came over her entire body. A dog who spies a ball in her master's hand? A sleuth who anticipates a challenging puzzle?

Instinct or intellect?

Or perhaps nothing of the sort.

I said, "Two things. First: do you detect the presence of a female human, alive or dead, nearby?"

"I do not, at the present time."

"Recently?"

"In the last ten days there have been several visits to this site. Analysis of individual DNA and/or viral matrix can be requested."

"Okay. Good." Josepha had been here. Had she decided to hike over to the other Castle? I'd investigate just in case. "Second: I'm looking for some kind of recording device or devices on or about this rock formation, but I'm not really sure there are any. Will you help me look for them?"

"Yes."

Pause. "Please do so."

She immediately closed her eyes. Looking, for her, needn't involve her sense of vision. In a matter of seconds she turned to her right and pointed up. "There. Very close. Do you see it?"

"Uh… no." Rock, shadow, light. Little patches of sand. "Oh! Yes." It clung to the underside of a ledge, its tiny oil-drop eye glimmering perkily. Well, how about that. There *was* something to check on. "There are probably more of these."

"I will find them."

She found five more. We left them in place after she recorded everything she could about them, including their link codes, which I could retrieve later.

Hettie could crack them open remotely, back at my office. They, and the encrypted files she had found earlier, might provide something interesting.

I looked at Sansu, who displayed the unmistakable attitude of a ten-year-old on a scavenger hunt. With prizes and ice cream. Talia, her roller fixed, would show up any time now, snorting fire. "Okay. Let's get out of here."

Sansu and I drove over to the other Castle, where she found three more beads, but nothing other than diluted human traces that might have been simply drift from Town.

I was back in the office, running various scenarios through my brain. A smuggling ring? Nothing smuggle-worthy existed on this planet. Sex trade? Plenty of that to go round, no need for more. Government black ops? Ha.

I jumped when Nalani Kawai's handsome visage popped up on my desk. She looked seriously pissed off.

"Ms. Kawai. To what do I owe—"

"Port tells me you have a missing person." An image of a— you guessed it—desiccated corpse popped in. Sprawled awkwardly on a small ridge of wind-swept rocks, face to the sky.

I rubbed my forehead. "Shit. Yeah. Look, can you—"

Ms. Kawai had no inclination to listen. "Our P-10 crew spotted it a few minutes ago, and if you think we're going to pick a corpse up for you, you are mistaken. And don't even think of trying to blame TunXi."

"Believe me, I—"

"I'll send you the coordinates." She disappeared.

The first bead we viewed showed nothing much. Hettie went back five T-days, speeding through the fish-eye view. A contrail to the southeast. A far off line of dust to the north, as from a vehicle. And yes, there was a road there. Some nearby ruffles in the sand, a mini dust-devil or two. Shadows lazily moping by as the sun lowered.

"When will we know for sure it's Josepha Windsong they found out there?" Hettie asked, breaking the silence.

"Couple of hours. FFB was closest, they retrieved her and are taking initial samples and so on, forwarding everything to us. Until then, let's keep the info from Talia Windsong."

FFB: Fish Farm Bayou, in which were raised extensively engineered salmon and tilapia, clams and shrimp. How Josepha got way out there was anyone's guess.

The bead showed a burst of static, then nothing. The next bead was virtually identical in what it showed: nothing of interest, then static.

The third one gave us a morsel to chew on. At about the right time to account for her movements, Josepha trudged up, looming large and sweaty, making me lean back a bit in my chair. Yeah, the body was hers. I recognized the bobbed brown hair, earrings I'd seen her wear before. Most likely this was the last record of her in her lifetime.

Her hand reached forward, then her head turned suddenly. As if she'd heard something. She rubbed her nose and sneezed. The bead burst into static, then went black.

"Hettie, correlate the time signature on these burnouts. Or whatever they are." By this time I was sitting pretty straight. "Let's check the rest."

Three more assorted views, including an earlier one that caught Josepha skulking along the near edge of the castle toward her destiny. More dust-devils. I wanted to run all the beads by Sansu in case she could spot anything that we couldn't, but my budget for this incident was vanishing rapidly.

I messaged Sansu anyway, in case I could wheedle a freebie. She responded immediately, as if she'd been watching over our shoulders. "I have the ability to shuffle my schedule," she informed us. "Though I am working, I can assign off-task seconds to assist you. As you told me, Dr. Healy-Kay, we are investigating."

Hettie snorted. I frowned at her, she rolled her eyes. "Sansu," I said, "we're grateful for your assistance, and I'm hoping it won't cost us an arm and a leg. I'd like to dig deeper into these sensor beads and whatever they link to."

"I will use algorithms I have developed to decipher further levels, also to infiltrate other sensor devices with which they may be in communication."

"Okay. Great." Sounded a wee bit illegal. Did I really want to get in trouble again? "Do these algorithms belong to you, or to your employer?"

"To me. My employer is unaware of work I do off-shift."

"I see." I'd bet she didn't own anything. Sansu's help might result in the termination of her contract, and an inquiry into my involvement, but I was willing to risk it. It's always better to beg forgiveness than ask permission. Maybe I could get Port to deputize her? "I'll open and link you in."

Her avatar popped up next to ours, flickering as she interfaced and started to work.

Hettie whispered, "I'm surprised it can do this kind of stuff."

I felt a surge of pride. "This one's not off the rack." She was a new thing. How could a normal human possibly understand the workings of a hybrid brain? And then there's me, who I suspect is far from normal…

Vertigo.

The emotional pit that trapped me for years shuddered again in my bowels. I concentrated on breathing steadily. *Have I fallen into the pit again?*

Sansu could be working for TunXi and be tasked with diverting us from the truth. Just as Isabelle had done to me. She could be hiding murders. Had the company found something worthy of killing for? On this planet? It seemed so unlikely.

Hettie was sitting back, arms crossed, probably hoping the Recorder would screw up.

Sansu's little avatar looked up alertly. Oh, how I wanted to trust her. She said, "The beads are sensing activity both residual and ongoing, and transmitting it to the off-world devices to which they are linked. The transmission may or may not be at the quantum level. The off-world devices are unfamiliar to me. The activity extends indeterminately in a spherical local pattern array."

"Uh, how local is this array?"

"In a somewhat physical sense it encompasses the planet. As to the time aspect, I am unable to determine if it is a point source, or is infinite."

My eyebrows went up, as did Hettie's. "That's a big spread." And it sounded like a fold. A micro-fold in operation. Huh. Those tiny beads were not something tourists would have. My stomach crawled back to its proper place, now that I had something to think about.

Hettie shifted restlessly. Were more people involved in this "research" besides the four we knew of? Three of whom were now dead? I'd thought the Windsongs were minor players. I could be wrong.

This was well beyond my pay grade. I said, "We need to contact Survey Security." Who might reply in a few days, but I wanted it on record. "We need to find out what they were trying to capture with these devices, and who the off-world contacts are."

"If that Talia woman will talk," Hettie muttered.

Sansu blinked out, her free time over. Hettie shut down the link to the beads and sashayed off toward wherever it was she went at the end of her day.

Talia didn't respond to my urgent request for a meeting. If this meant she too was now a dusty pile in the sand, I did not know.

Later, after a solitary dinner I'd picked up at Mori's, I sat twirling in my desk chair and had a sudden realization: I was feeling happy. Exhilarated? That might be what it was. Interest and action had plucked some resonant string within me.

Recorder Sansu. Artifact, animal, human. Something owned, or something free? Was I happy because I had a mystery to solve, and a partner to help solve it? Too late to pull back from the pit. I was already falling. Foolish old man, crushing on beauty and strangeness.

I made myself a coffee. The reflex urge to squash exhilaration into flatness came, hovered, and whisked away. Was it because I understood now that my attraction to Sansu wasn't sexual? That had been my fear: that I was nothing more than a corrupt fool driven by vanity. But maybe I wasn't, after all.

Alik arrived, looking smug. "The Windsongs and our victims were in contact seven times before their arrival on Thirteen." He plunked himself in a chair.

"Why? Unless renting rooms is extraordinarily complex."

Alik's beard seemed even more pointy than usual. What had he found?

"Spill it, kid," I said, in a gangster accent.

"I decrypted a couple of attachments to the messages. One was just their credit info and so on, but the other hinted at the purpose of their trip here: evidence of an alien, space-faring culture."

I sighed. *Yeah, it's aliens...*

He continued. "Yep. On more than just Thirteen, on other worlds too, that don't actually seem to be near any folds—that we know of."

The possibility of new, usable folds was always a gleam in someone's eye. "They're alien hunters? How did they find 'evidence' if these worlds aren't reachable?"

Alik spread his hands. "Beats me. But I'm thinking they weren't interested in local life forms to gain *kinship* with."

"Were they hunting wild folds?" Nothing wrong with that.

Hettie chose that moment to wander back in. "What's going on?"

Did no one keep regular hours anymore?

Was Alik's info enough to drag Talia in for questioning? Probably not. Plenty of airheads sought alien civilizations. If you counted anthills, we'd already found them. "We need to find out if any of our famous four were violating laws, raising red flags—and that includes regulations covering mining operations. Hettie, set your desk that task, then come with us."

"Where are we going?"

"Our usual stomping grounds."

As we prepared, Alik said, "That Recorder has a surprising amount of information. It's a go-getter. Seems Talia didn't come here directly from Earth. She spent time with the Divine Interventionists, in their very own asteroid."

"I've heard of the Divvies. They have money."

"Yep. So, Interventionists are of the opinion that the universe itself is sentient, not exactly a new idea but they refined it to mean that the act of conscious observation *within* a universe leads in reverse to the formation of a divine entity."

"In reverse."

"Yeah. And, this divine entity then is mandated to form human-like civilizations who are in turn tasked with observing one another. Thus increasing, uh, sentience."

"A big nutty circle. What does all this have to do with the deaths?"

"It seems we've been lax in observing other civilizations, and may be due for some divine retribution. Shaw and Wendy were trying to remedy that. Thus the wandering in the desert."

"Fair enough. I guess if we actually found other civilizations, we should observe 'em."

When we got to the north castle, Hettie, Alik, and I were still arguing the question of what the conspirators had hoped to gain from hoarding their findings. A jump on prize-winning research? Possible fold bonanza? God's grace?

Contact with actual aliens?

More likely: they were dilettantes and knew it, feared the public humiliation of announcing "findings" when there were none. They'd wanted to play their cards close, keep hoping for a big payoff.

So. Deluded seekers, or wily manipulators? You never knew where truth might lie. So to speak.

We parked next to the castle and started hauling out our gear. Pop-up shelter, food, water and the broadest spectrum of recording/sensing devices we could round up and not have to pay for them.

Sansu was already there. Our gear was redundant.

I squinted at her lean, grey-clad form, glossed into beauty by the last sliver of sun. "Aren't you going to get in trouble, taking time off work?"

She flared her nostrils and raised her chin. "I have bought out my contract with TunXi. I am now a free agent."

"Congratulations," Hettie said, sarcastically. I gave her a look, and she produced a smile. "No, really. You're sure welcome to hang around here with us, right, Doc?"

I felt a sudden twinge of guilt. Had my playful invitation to do some sleuthing induced her to give up a good job? "Sansu, you're sure that was a good idea?" What was I, her father? Her mentor?

"I am sure."

All right. Either she was a machine that was owned, or she was human and could up and quit.

But I wondered how long she would stick around, if sleuthing didn't result in anything. A machine was programmed to complete a task. A human might get frustrated and pull up stakes. Which did I want her to be? "This area seems to be central to whatever the victims were doing that got them killed, and we need to find out why."

Alik was eyeing Sansu, obviously longing to quiz her about her kind's origins and unique talents. "Alik," I said, rather sharply. "Stash the camping gear by that overhang. Hettie, set up all this crap and start hoping we'll find something. Sansu, come with me."

As she walked beside me, I murmured, "I can't pay you. My budget is at rock bottom. You might have misunderstood my invitation to sleuth together."

"I did not." She strode lightly beside me, all the while gazing around alert as a gazelle. Gathering her chemical signals, her minute hints of truth-caches to be revealed. I wanted to tuck her hand under my arm, feel for the pulse of blood. Or the wires of a machine. I just wanted to touch her, damn it. She said, "I have been preparing to leave TunXi for several years. This seemed an opportune moment, as it provides cover for my ultimate plans."

That made me stop walking. She stopped after another two strides, turned to me. A breeze ruffled her hair.

"May I ask what those plans might be?"

"You may not."

Her words hung in the hot, brassy air. The sun slid lower. Everything was going purple and flat. "Well. Okay then. Uh, right now I'd like you to work with us in what I believe is a viable line of investigation: that a couple of overeager fools messed with the wrong outfit and got themselves cooked."

"You suspect a culinary motive?"

I glugged down some water. "A figure of speech."

Maybe it was as simple as TunXi trying to avoid oversight and sanctions. If the conspirators had tried to prevent, say, incursion into an imaginary "alien enclave" and kicked up a stink? Accidents happen. Ms. Kawai had been extremely defensive.

Hettie and Alik were bickering over setting up camp. A warm, teasing note had crept into Hettie's voice. I smiled.

"Come on then, partner, let's get back and start—"

Wind gusted. Something like a throb went through my body. Every part of me, every nerve and muscle, felt as if it had stretched apart and then snapped back into alignment. Perhaps I had expanded instantaneously to infinite size, then returned to normal. *A point source, or infinity.*

I let out a grunt of pain, then stood very still, blinking. Had I imagined it, whatever it was? But the wind had really picked up, started to swirl. Could we be in the path of one of those dust-devils I'd seen the other day? We should get back to shelter—

Sansu had sprung to attention, mouth open. She started to pant.

I sneezed. The back of my throat tasted funny. I swallowed hard, sneezed again. My eyes started flooding. I found myself pawing at my nose like a stung dog.

Sansu dropped to her knees in the sand, her eyes streaming as she stared at… what? What did she see? She stripped off her gloves, flung them aside and swept her arms upward. Through the wash of tears and snot sluicing my face, I could see that her whole body was arched like a bow.

I bent over and vomited out all the water I'd just drunk. Wind whipped sand everywhere.

Alik's and Hettie's voices squealed like static, reverberated, went away.

The gunpowder smell of Thirteen's air increased, grinding down hot and thick, and I knew how an insect must feel when dosed with poison. *We're all going to die.* Yet, even though my eyes had slammed shut, they were perceiving something. A harsh, resonant flare inside my head *black/white/black*.

A view into time itself. Maybe. Or death. What's the difference.

Sand gritted in my mouth, and I realized I was trying to burrow into the ground.

We are going to die, and our bodies will be found by that TunXi bitch.

Perhaps that's what kept me alive. After a while I realized I was still thinking.

This definitely wasn't a windstorm or a rogue mining bot.

Something touched me. I couldn't even yell, too busy coughing my lungs out. *Sansu.* I grabbed her, hauled her down, and we huddled together on the roiling ground. "The dust! The dust!" she shrieked in my ear. "This… immense… dust, the… goes so far far far far… open open every—"

I shook her to make her shut up. She didn't. She was experiencing something beyond the human, here in the midst of our impending obliteration. Her crystalline voice bubbled, babbled, carrying less and less information. My last coherent thought was *now I'll never figure out what happened.*

There were lots of *incoherent* thoughts, though, jamming my brain. Which might have been precious glimpses into a reality that only barely impinged on our own. The overwhelming impression was of vastness. Timelessness. I tried to open my eyes, but fortunately I couldn't.

My skin itched and burned. Whatever we were in was desiccating us. Like a horrific allergic reaction. Was Sansu experiencing what I was? Oh, god, Hettie and Alik—

I drooled out the last of my body's moisture, hacking and retching.

But then I sensed something. My eyes and ears still weren't working, but something inside my brain was receiving images. I couldn't tell if they were sound, colour, smell or some other sense humans hadn't evolved.

Surprise. Hesitation.

Not mine. Someone else's. The output of an intelligence, the sudden diversion of a hand that had prepared to swat a bug.

I clutched Sansu in my arms, suspended among the hot, dry waves of time and space. Scared shitless. Trying to protect her was probably useless. We were both going to die.

And then we dropped back into reality.

Sansu and I unrolled from our tight embrace. As we shuddered and dripped, I saw that she must have had her eyes open the whole time. Her corneas were scrubbed into pebbly grey, and the pale exposed skin of her face was flensed blood red. She grinned and panted, her tongue curled, looking like something straight out of hell. Her delicately engineered fingertips were scoured flat and dripping blood. My heart clenched.

I looked around blearily, spitting sand. We weren't where we'd started, but at least we hadn't ended up in the middle of nowhere. I could see the castle silhouetted against the sky perhaps a kilometer away. I took Sansu by the arm and led her toward it. *Step step step.* And there were Alik and Hettie, sunken-eyed and coughing, gulping water but okay. Whatever it was must only have grazed them.

"Water," I croaked. "Sansu first."

Alik said, "What the hell just happened?"

"Water first."

Hettie gave one scared, soulful look at Alik, and began to sluice Sansu's eyes and mouth with water while I fumbled for skinfilm to wrap her hands. I was too burnt-dry and shaky to do it. Alik took over and I sucked in water.

Sansu's lips were moving in a disturbingly repetitive manner. Alik forced her eyelids shut, squirted medigel onto her skin and wrapped a bandage round her head. Her hair stuck out like matted fur. We didn't have time to figure out what she was saying. Maybe she was praying to some God she'd seen. For it was surely a God that had roared though us.

"We'll collect the gear later," I said, when I had enough spit in my throat. "Let's get out of here."

I visited Sansu in the infirmary as soon as I'd recovered a bit. My skin was slathered in ointment, and I had a water bottle permanently clutched in one hand. Night was falling over Town, at last. Through her room's window, the soft, weird blur of the nascent lens showed through a rare clear patch in our hazy atmosphere.

She was sitting up, her head and hands layered in regenerative tissue and foam. Someone had washed her hair, which poked out gleaming ebony above the ruddy, reflective bandages covering her face. Like the flames of hell, I thought, resisting the urge to pat her shoulder.

"Sansu, it's me, Marcus," I said. In case her senses were merely human now.

"Yes."

"How are you?"

She raised her bandaged hands, let them fall. "Blind. Crippled."

I wondered if she thought death would be better. "Hettie and Alik are okay. Get this: they're moving in together." I watched her. "Sansu… why did you expose yourself like that? You might have died."

"I would not have died. I…" She paused. "I want to be alone."

"Sansu—"

"I want to think. Thinking is all I can do, now. Please."

Her voice was small, a far off ringing in my head. No melody, just notes. I put my gnarly old paw gently on her bandaged hand. She didn't notice.

"Please go. I will present my findings to you when they are collected."

"Findings? What have you—" I stood up. "Never mind. Just rest."

I was very frightened. No one here really knew what to do with her. I was still waiting for a response from GalMed like it would do any good. Alik and Hettie had tried to describe what they'd seen from the edge of whatever it was. Apparently Sansu and I had convulsed and blinked out, to reappear immediately like a wavering mirage on the horizon, staggering back to the castle. Meanwhile they had assumed they were caught in a violent dust storm, and had thought only of protecting themselves.

An attendant bot rolled in, inserted a tube into Sansu's mouth and waited as she sucked up some kind of green liquid. It smelled citrusy and fresh. I left her room.

"The things you call castles are not castles."

"Yes, we know. They're just eroded rocks."

She was recovering, sitting in a chair that gently prodded and stroked her. I was there like a lovesick boy, hoping to gain her attention. Or maybe, I realized, more like a parent, hoping for the best.

That sat better on my heart. I had always wanted children, but never found anyone interested in joining me on the project. Maybe I had gained a child? Much better than a lover.

"No," she said, her voice still weak. "A third exists, underground now, forming an equilateral triangle. I... *think* they are the remnants of a foundation, clad with native stone. Possibly the support structure of a photonic laser thruster... possibly the lower terminus of an elevator, though that seems unlikely..." She raised a hand, now bandage-free and pink as a mouse's ear. "I don't know. I only think."

"But—it's part of a, a machine? Just sitting there in plain sight?"

Damn it. *Aliens.* "Can you estimate how old these... structures might be?"

"One hundred and eighty thousand years, with a variance of twelve hundred years."

"For Pete's sake. Wow. How the hell did we not—"

Her body writhed impatiently and I shut up. *Just listen.* Kids, right? I felt a widening in my chest somehow. Like my heart had expanded. She brought her hands together, winced at the touch, and placed the tender, newborn things back in her lap. Bandages still covered her eyes. I wanted nothing more than to take her in my arms and tell her everything would be all right.

"Doctor Kay… Marcus. There is so much here… Layers. Sediments. The dust itself." She pursed her lips, the only part of her face that was visible. "Not sand. Particles. Crystals. Of… of space-time?" She shook her head. "The particles intersected our physical space. I think human activity here caught the attention of something."

"Some*thing*."

"I suspect the activity was the construction of the fold lens."

I sat back, hands on my knees.

I had serious doubts regarding the Recorder's sanity. Was her incredibly complex, engineered brain finding patterns where none existed? Time dust, for God's sake. But the four conspirators had focused on something they believed was real. The beads we'd found were still being investigated. Shaw Sperling and Wendy Kim had brought a lot of hard-to-trace money in with them. Talia Windsong—alternating between sobbing at the loss of Josepha, and snarling with anger—was confined to her home, pending discovery of what she and her co-conspirators knew. Did they have more partners on Thirteen or elsewhere? It wasn't a murder investigation anymore.

What we'd experienced out by the castle was real. I could vouch for that. And Sansu's recklessly magnified senses were real. She probably wasn't crazy, no more than she'd always been.

She continued. "The attention I detected held… sadness. For no reason. A longing for something gone and forgotten. Is this… nostalgia? It is believed that my kind have no feelings. That we are unable to process emotions or even recognize them. But we can. I can."

I heard it in her voice, and wondered if Recorders could cry.

My throat tightened, and I swallowed hard. "Sansu, do you have the sense that this—whatever it is—manipulates time? As well as space? Or merely travels through it?"

Like the folds we humans used, pinches in the vast tracts of space-time. We couldn't make them, only search them out and tune them. We only stumbled upon the first one because it got in the way of a probe that was zipping along minding its own business. We assumed folds were an artifact of QV space, just happening randomly. Compressed quantum vacuum with forced-pair transfer, something I knew of but didn't understand in the slightest. But maybe some*thing* had deliberately constructed them, millennia ago? Some intelligence too vast to see, building ancient gateways through which we scurried like mice, unaware of the trains roaring overhead.

But, *sadness*? Were they just touring the old homestead? Taking the kids on a field trip?

I realized she'd fallen asleep. I sat there, watching her, trying to understand my feelings. After maybe five minutes she started to mumble. "End game... the dust... It's the future, you know. You see? You see? What comes. Logical. The logical. Outcome. End, end."

Could her kind evolve, and if so should humankind be frightened? Sansu could see into the future, perhaps. Mysterious. Magical.

She jerked awake. Her tongue flicked out and in.

Softly, I said, "You and I have determined what killed the victims. They dried up in a time storm. Done in by something vast, insanely weird, and way out of our jurisdiction. It wasn't murder. We need investigate no further."

"Need," she whispered.

I clamped my mouth shut. Need. Want. What did I *need* to do?

Did I need to break my brain sleuthing the mystery of alien contact? No. There were plenty of people already doing that. Alik, Hettie and I had been interviewed, in a very awkward real-time QV blast, by the Assistant Head of Galactic Survey, no less. Sansu's recordings were being unpacked at multiple locations, and Josepha Windsong's little beads were under intense scrutiny. She herself lay in the morgue alongside the first two dried-out husks.

Inquiries came in by the minute, and every available dwelling, office, shed or park bench was fully booked by teams mustering for action.

I'd bet money that Ms. Nalani Kawai and the company she worked for were gnashing their collective teeth over not having had the foresight to nail down leases on the castles. They could have held out for serious compensation.

Sansu had not been contacted directly yet; attempts to enlist her had been going through TunXi, and they pointed out huffily that she had quit. But as soon as efforts ramped up, she would vanish into the Survey's insatiable maw.

Need? I needed to keep Sansu the Recorder by my side. Sansu who had taken over the centre of my life. Not in the way I'd first feared. Not the breathless, reckless lust of a fool. Something better.

I had the sudden belief that she was watching me, right through her medical wrappings, using some sense I didn't have. Some machine trick. Perhaps she could hear the beating of my heart. She put a lot of effort into logic, but she was mostly human. And humans are so rarely logical.

I myself was about to do something completely idiotic.

Leaning close, I said, "Sansu, this planet is about to become a hotbed of scientific investigation. And a Mecca for the mystical." The Divvies were probably booking tickets right now. "You and I experienced the effect directly—and lived through it—which means we will be front and centre. Pulled into the research by our hind legs."

She pried herself up on her elbows and turned her bandaged head toward me. "Before this happened, you asked what my plans were. Do you wish to hear them now?"

"Uh… sure."

"I seek a littermate."

"A what?"

"I have three siblings, separated from me at our release from nursery care sixteen years ago, when we were ten. Two were legally acknowledged and eventually hired by companies similar to TunXi. The other, never officially existing, was sent for augmentation and training."

I felt a chill. "What… what kind of training?"

"It was bought by a shell company." Pause. "Marcus Healy-Kay, I know who you are, and that you understand the training my sibling underwent. When you relocated to Thirteen, I knew what I had to do."

A shell company. Covering for the slave trade. When I relocated… she had been tracking me.

I put my head in my hands. All the guilt I'd managed to ward off came crashing down. That Feroux woman had got away, and Sansu knew I'd helped it happen.

I forced myself to look up and take a breath. "Sixteen years. You've been looking all that time?"

Silence.

"I… I didn't… I never thought…"

She raised a hand to stop me. "I know. When I stumbled and you caught me, I felt the softness within you. I knew you could not have deliberately sent my sibling into slavery."

How was I supposed to take that? "Yeah," I said. "Softness. I've been working on that."

She could see me so clearly, even through pain and loss and bandages. I forgot the eldritch mystery of the aliens and thought about what it meant to be her. A Recorder. An amalgam of everything humans wanted to exploit.

"Sansu, I want to make amends, if that's even possible. What do you need to do? I mean, really *need* to do?"

"I need to seek my enslaved littermate."

"Yes. Anything else?"

"I need to purchase new eyes. Mine are destroyed, and have been obsolete for several years."

"Okay. We're on a roll." Her head cocked to one side. "Keep going."

"I… want to immerse myself in understanding the phenomenon we experienced."

"All right. Me too, actually. A question: is want less than need? And are you prepared to choose?"

She thought about that for quite a while. "Want is less than need. I *need* to find my sibling. I am the only one who will do so."

Okay.

Sansu *needed* to leave Thirteen.

She was out of a job, and couldn't work without eyes.

If she bought eyes, she couldn't afford to go anywhere.

If she left without eyes, she'd be useless wherever she went.

My heart was thumping fast. "And your hands. What about all the… sensory stuff? Will you be able to function as a Recorder?"

"My hands will repair themselves, given approximately ten days. Four if I were in my home crèche. I have new eyes on order and have been paying them off incrementally. I will own them in three years and twenty-seven days."

She'd be blind until then.

She'd get anything she wanted if she joined the Alien Hunt. And the Alien Hunt wanted her badly. But they would never let her go.

Why was it so hard to think? Physically, I felt as if I'd spent the last three days rolling down a hill covered with fire ants. That had crawled into my lungs and nested. I was still hacking out phlegm. Mentally?

I had to grapple with basic themes within my own identity. How selfish was I? What might I be willing to give up, in exchange for something that might not exist?

Though she had good reason to, Sansu was the one being who had never judged me. Never found me wanting. She was, at best, neutral. Could I find a way to tip the scales of her opinion toward the positive?

"That's a long time to wait."

Pause. "Yes."

What with everything going on here, I could sublet my dwelling and medical practice at a tidy profit. Plus I had a few assets, including my accumulated pension fund and some old family heirlooms. Certified Kodachromes of places on Earth that didn't exist anymore, a piece of fossil mammoth tusk; that sort of little thing. So?

I could hoard my assets here on Thirteen, or I could cash everything in and run off with Sansu. Join her in her quest, for it was an honourable one.

If she'd have me.

I stood up. "Well. I'll let you rest now. You need to recuperate as fast as possible, if you plan to get off Thirteen before the shit hits the fan."

She laughed, a muffled and weird sound, clamped down by her bandaged skin. But she managed it.

"As do you, Doctor Kay. My… friend. I have never had a friend."

"Friends stick together," I said.

"I have heard that," she replied.

Publishing credits

"The Doll Ladies"
Originally published in *Amazing Stories*, Vol. 77, Issue 1, Fall 2019

"Her Eyes As Bright As Unsheath'd Swords"
Originally published in *On Spec*, Vol. 1 #1, Spring 1989

"Pick My Bones With Whispers"
Originally published in *Asimov's Science Fiction* Magazine, January 2003

"After the First Death"
Originally published in *Dead of Night* Magazine, #13, Summer 1995, edited by Lin Stein

"The Price of Memory"
Originally published in *The Fantasist*, Fall 2017

"Walk to Bryten"
Originally published in *Matrix* magazine #41, Fall 1993

"Little Feather"
Originally published in *Space & Time* Magazine, Spring/Summer March 2019

"Dance on a Forgotten Shore" (co-written by Alan Dean Foster)
First appeared in *The Magazine of Fantasy and Science Fiction*, April 1988, edited by Edward L. Ferman

"My Mother's Garden"
Originally published in *Food of My People* anthology, Exile
Editions, September 2021

"Doing Drugs"
Originally published in *Northern Frights 5* anthology edited by
Don Hutchison, Mosaic Press, 1999

"Thank Yew Very Much"
Originally published in *On Spec*, Vol. 107, April 2018

"Szabra's Souls"
Originally published in *Descant* magazine, Fall 2003
Reprinted in *Amazing Stories*, Fall 2021

Sally McBride has lived in Toronto, Calgary, Edmonton, Vancouver, Victoria, and (briefly) Florida (her cat didn't like it there). These days she divides her time between life in the mountains of Idaho (with her American husband) and city living in Toronto (close to Canadian family). In all these places, she has found supportive friends and fellow writers who get what it means to stare into the abyss trying to interpret what-ifs, if-this-goes-ons, dreams and wishes, and all the random stimuli that feed a writer's creativity. Sally has two amazing children and some equally amazing grandchildren. She enjoys skiing, reading (of course), and zipping around on her electric bike.